I0642152

the HATE LOVE *duet*

USA *Today* and International Bestselling Author

Lauren Rowe

Copyright © 2020 by Lauren Rowe

Published by SoCoRo Publishing

Cover design © Letitia Hasser, RBA Designs

All rights reserved.

No part of this book may be reproduced in any form or by any electronic or mechanical means, including information storage and retrieval systems, without written permission from the author, except for the use of brief quotations in a book review.

falling out of

HATE

with

YOU

USA Today and International Bestselling Author

Lauren Rowe

ONE

SAVAGE

Hollywood Hills, California

Music is blaring around me as I wade through the packed party, precariously balancing six shot glasses filled to their brims. I come to a stop when I reach my four bandmates—Kendrick, Kai, Ruby, and Titus—plus, our manager, Eli.

"Grab 'em, quick!" I call out over the loud music, and, thankfully, my friends immediately relieve me of the tequila-laden Jenga tower in my palms. Once all glasses have been distributed, I raise mine to our band's drummer and beat-maker, my best friend in the world, Kendrick Cook. "Happy twenty-fifth!" I shout. And, of course, everyone joins me in wishing Kendrick a great one.

According to Reed Rivers' party invitation, we're at his hilltop mansion tonight to celebrate an upcoming issue of *Rock 'n' Roll* magazine—a special issue that's going to feature nothing but the top artists from his record label, an elite group that thankfully includes our band, Fugitive Summer. But since nobody throws a better bash than our label owner—or, as my band has dubbed Reed Rivers, "The Prick"—and since most of the people we would have invited to a separate birthday party for Kendrick are here, anyway—we decided to hijack Reed's fancy shindig to celebrate our boy's birth.

"Do I have drool on my chin?" Kai Cook, our bass player and Kendrick's older brother, shouts above the music, as one of the most head-turning women at the party, a reporter for *Rock 'n' Roll* named Georgina, walks by and waves as she goes.

Our other guitarist, Titus, nudges my shoulder. "The reporter winked at you, Savage! Go get her, Player!"

I roll my eyes. I hate that my bandmates still call me "Player," the same way they've been doing since the beginning, when I was admittedly drunk on all the attention our band—and especially *me* —had started getting. But these days, the nickname isn't nearly as accurate as it once was, not since an "influencer" in Barcelona made my dick the top trending topic on Twitter last year.

Immediately after sex with that spicy little Spaniard, I hopped into the shower in my hotel room, thinking she'd fallen asleep. And that's when she snagged my wallet, snapped some surreptitious photos of me cluelessly washing up, and then promptly posted the shots, along with a detailed play-by-play of our night together. And off she went, into the Spanish night, while I continued singing a happy tune, literally, in the shower. And I swear, I haven't been the same "player," ever since.

It wasn't that I was upset about the wallet. While on tour, I barely ever have anything in it. Condoms, a credit card that was easy to cancel, and my ID. Also, I wasn't all that bent out of shape about the world seeing my naked dong or finding out, through the Spaniard's posted commentary, that I'm a rabid fan of oral sex.

No, as cliché as it sounds, the thing that threw me for a loop was the shocking breach of trust. The realization that nobody out there is trustworthy, no matter how much it feels like they might be, in the moment. It was the realization that anything I might say or do in private, no matter how intimate it might feel in the moment, could end up as a meme on the internet.

In that moment, I knew whatever genuine connection I'd thought the woman and I had shared that night was an illusion. Or worse, if it had been real, she was willing to sacrifice it on the altar of snagging my wallet and her fifteen minutes of fame.

It was the first time I truly understood the downside of this crazy life. The loneliness and eternal separation from normalcy that's inherent in the gig. And it changed me. I've never been a guy who wears his heart on his sleeve, anyway. I don't trust easily and never have. But after that experience, I felt even more closed off and determined to keep myself under wraps.

Kai grabs my arm, like he thinks he's keeping me from chasing after the hot reporter, Georgina. But I'm not even tempted to run after her. Kai yells above the blasting music, "I call dibs on the reporter! And you know I *never* do that, dude! So, you'd better respect The Dibs!"

I'm offended. Why does Kai feel the need to say that to me? I *always* respect The Dibs, more than anyone else in the band, other than Kendrick. Kai should know by now I don't give a fuck which gorgeous woman I wind up with, if any. There are far too many of them in this world, and, certainly, at this party, and I'm far too good at getting whoever I want, to chase after someone who's caught the eye of one of my best friends. Especially when I barely know the woman in question.

I'd call my general mindset in this regard "bros before hoes" or "dicks before chicks," if our bandmate, Ruby, not to mention, my cousin, Sasha, hadn't both made a thing about the words "ho" and "chick" being derogatory. So, maybe "brovaries before ovaries" would be the better bet? The point is that I *always* respect The Dibs. Although, in this instance, Kai probably shouldn't pursue the reporter, anyway. Not because *I* want her. But because I've surmised there are extenuating circumstances.

I reply to Kai, "You never need to 'call dibs' with me. Just tell me you're in hot pursuit and that's that. But I think you're gonna need to set your sights on someone else this time, brother. When I played ping pong with Georgina earlier to talk about my interview,

I got the solid vibe she's already with Reed. Or if not, she's definitely at the top of his To Do List."

"*Reed?*" Kai bellows, like that's a preposterous notion. Like every woman at this party wouldn't give her left tit to get with Reed. The guy with the big house, the fit body, the garage full of sports cars, and a bank account that puts every band member here to shame. But, whatever. My bandmates and I are drinking and having fun tonight, and roasting the bastard who takes way too big a cut of our royalties, thanks to the shitty contract we signed as puppies, before Eli started repping us, is one of our favorite drinking games.

Titus and Kai continue roasting Reed for a bit. And as they banter, I reach for my phone when it buzzes in my pocket. I wouldn't normally check my phone at a party. But only my inner circle has this particular number, and almost all of them are here tonight.

When I check my screen, it's a text from my cousin, Sasha, as suspected, regarding our grandma.

> **Sasha: Are you available to FaceTime, by any chance? Mimi had a nightmare you died in a plane crash. She wants to see your face.**
> **Me: Can't FT. I'm at a noisy party and kinda drunk. How about a quick video?**
> **Sasha: Awesome.**

I shoot a brief selfie video in which I smile, make silly faces, and blow kisses to my grandma amid the noisy throng around me. And after I press send, Sasha quickly replies in all caps.

> **Sasha: IS THAT ISABEL RANDOLPH BEHIND YOU?!?**

. . .

I turn around, and, I'll be damned, one of the most famous movie stars on the planet is standing directly behind me, chatting with a group of suits I don't recognize.

Me: It is, indeed.

Sasha: HOLY SHIT. Do you know her?

Me: Nope.

Sasha: Go meet her and send me a photo for my birffday! Pleeeeease!

Me: Your birthday isn't for two months. But more importantly, doing that for you would require me to speak to a new person, which, as you know, I try to avoid at all costs.

Sasha: Why do you go to so many parties, if you hate talking to new people so much?

Me: Because I like talking to MY people while surrounded by new people I can gawk at but NOT talk to. Especially tonight, when we're celebrating KC's bday.

Sasha: Aw, wish KC happy birthday for me! Have you performed a birthday dare for him yet?

Me: Not yet. He's still deciding what brand of humiliation to inflict upon me.

Sasha: LOL. Don't do anything dangerous.

Me: It's always all in good fun. Give Mimi a hug for me.

Sasha: Already did. She loves the video. Says she loves you and stay safe.

Me: Love her, too, and you. Tell her I'm fine and mostly traveling by bus on the next leg of the tour.

Sasha: Will do. Goodnight. Have a blast.

My cousin is being sincere when she tells me to have fun. But I can't help feeling guilty she's there on a Saturday night, hanging out with our grandma and one of the nighttime caregivers I've bankrolled, while I'm at a star-studded party in LA. Not to mention that Sasha works hard at a real job in Chicago—she's a massage therapist—while I traipse around the world and swoop into town for occasional visits, whenever convenient, like I'm Weekend Daddy after a divorce.

Sasha always says she wouldn't have it any other way. She's ten years my senior and always says she's gotten her partying out of her system. Plus, she always reminds me, she's a homebody by nature, anyway. "I'm happiest when I'm hanging out with Mimi, reading or knitting," she always says. "I like sitting still and watching TV." And so, I bought my beloved homebody her own home last year, where she now takes care of our beloved grandma, along with the caregivers, and mostly believe my cousin when she says she's truly not the least bit angry with me for continuing to play rockstar.

I send a quick goodnight text to my cousin, stuff my phone into my pocket, and tune back into my bandmates' conversation, just in time to hear Titus saying, "I think it's bullshit. I mean, yes, if you'd already gotten to know the reporter, and had done more than spot her across a crowded room, then, okay, calling dibs on her makes sense. But I certainly wouldn't back off a woman, simply because you *spotted* her. And I sure as hell wouldn't back off just because Reed *might* be interested. Would he extend the same courtesy to any of us? Fuck no!"

"Reed's more than 'possibly' interested," I interject. "During my ping pong game with Georgina, I noticed Reed spying on her the whole time from behind a bush."

Everyone laughs at the imagery, except for Titus, who's shaking his head.

"No way," Titus says. "Reed must have been standing near a

bush, looking at his phone or talking to someone you couldn't see. I love roasting The Prick as much as anyone, but there's no way Reed Rivers would hide behind a bush, at his *own* party, while surrounded by some of the world's hottest women, in order to keep tabs on a summer intern at *Rock 'n' Roll*."

My eyebrows shoot up. "Georgina's an *intern* at the magazine?"

Titus gestures to his pink-haired twin sister, Ruby, our keyboardist, who's standing nearby talking to our manager, Eli. "When Ruby and I played cornhole with the reporter, she said she'd just graduated from UCLA and that her 'internship' with *Rock 'n' Roll* is her first professional gig."

"I never would have guessed that," I say.

Titus nods. "Georgina is just a baby. She said she's turning twenty-two next month."

I'm floored. I glance at her across the packed room, where Georgina is presently talking to the bass player of 22 Goats—a sweetheart of a guy named Fish. "I never would have guessed she's that green," I say. "With all that swagger, I would have thought she's large and in charge at *Rock 'n' Roll*." I chuckle. "Well, either way, I know what I saw. Reed was *definitely* spying on Georgina, from behind a bush, like a goddamned stalker."

Titus nudges Kai's shoulder. "Did Reed spy on you when you talked to Georgina?"

"No. Not that I noticed."

"And he didn't spy on Ruby and me playing cornhole with her, either. Huh. I wonder why Reed felt the need to spy on her with *you*, Player."

I wink. "I guess he's only worried about the good lookin' ones, eh?"

Titus flips me off as Kai flags down a cocktail server who's walking by with a slew of margaritas, and we quickly relieve her of her entire burden. His new drink in hand, our trusty manager, Eli, bids the group farewell, saying he's going to "schmooze" for a bit. Ruby joins our conversation, and we continue bantering and people-watching as a full band.

"So, have you decided on Savage's birthday dare yet?" Kai asks his younger brother, Kendrick. Earlier tonight, Kendrick made Kai fanboy all over some blonde actor on a Netflix show I've never heard of. And ever since, Kai has been dying to watch me get equally humiliated.

For the past ten years, on each of our respective birthdays, Kendrick, Kai, and I have played a shitfaced game of "Birthday Truth or Dare." Although calling it that is a misnomer by now, since we've long since taken the "truth" option off the table in our game. Why waste the chance to inflict humiliation in order to ask some stupid question we probably already know the answer to? Kai and Kendrick are brothers, after all, and I've known them both for well over ten years.

"Not yet," Kendrick says, answering his brother's question about my dare. "I'm still weighing my options."

"Oh my gosh!" Ruby blurts. "Savage was right about Reed and the reporter! Look at Reed now, guys! He's totally spying on her from across the room!" We look to where Ruby is indicating and discover Reed covertly staring at Georgina while she chats with the guys from Watch Party. Almost certainly, it's Zach Rosendo—their frontman whom everyone calls Endo—who's attracted Reed's eagle eye this time. That dude's definitely got a reputation as a lady killer.

"I just decided on my dare," Kendrick declares, his mischievous gaze trained on Reed. He looks at me, smiling wickedly and rubbing his palms together. And, instantly, I know what's coming.

"Aw, fuck. *No*," I mutter.

"You're not allowed to say no," Kendrick reminds me.

"I know the rules, motherfucker. Do *you*?" I'm referring to rule number one of our game. Namely, that the birthday boy can't pick a dare that's likely to maim, kill, or send his victim to prison. Rule number two is that the birthday boy is king—a deity whose dare can't be refused, as long as it complies with rule number one. And, finally, rule number three is that the dare has to be something that can be performed on the spot. In other words, birthday dares can't be some elaborate prank or hoax that would require weeks of planning.

Kendrick smiles. "Yeah, I know the rules. And I promise no bodily harm will come to you. The only thing that could possibly happen to you, in theory, is that you'd get onto Reed's shit list. But you're already there. So, really, there's no downside."

He's right. I've been on Reed's shit list for a while now, despite all the money my band makes him—powered in large part by me, personally. All because, years ago, I hit on his little sister, Violet, at my first Reed Rivers party, without having a clue who she was. This was long before Violet met her husband, Dax, the lead singer of 22 Goats. And, frankly, she seemed pretty receptive to my flirting, as I recall. And yet, Reed's held it against me, ever since.

"I don't get it," Ruby interjects. "What's the dare, Kendrick?"

Kendrick motions to me, like he's inviting me to enlighten Ruby.

Rolling my eyes, I say, "I'm assuming he wants me to hit on the hot reporter in front of Reed."

"Bingo," Kendrick says. "Let's test your theory that he's been sleeping with her, or wants to. I want you to hit on her, really obviously in front of him. With enough fuckboy heat you'll lure Reed out of his proverbial bush this time. But not with so much heat he lurches at you like a cheetah and smashes your face against a wall."

I grimace, as everyone else laughs.

"Why on earth would you force me to walk this tightrope?" I say. "You were there when C-Bomb told us that crazy story about what Reed did to the dude who'd fucked his ex."

"What did Reed do?" Ruby asks, her eyebrows shooting up.

But, unfortunately for Ruby, she's asking her question as Kendrick is saying, "Reed would never beat the shit out of you, simply for *flirting* with his woman. Flirting is way less a crime than fucking. Plus, your face makes him way too much money to smash it into a wall, regardless."

"What the hell did Reed do?" Ruby shouts, this time cutting

through the din. She looks at her twin brother, Titus, who's laughing along with Kendrick and Kai. "You know this story?"

Titus nods. "I heard it from C-Bomb." He's referring to the iconic drummer of Red Card Riot—Caleb Baumgarten—who's a good friend to our band.

"Well, he didn't tell *me*," Ruby says.

"You weren't there," Titus replies to his sister.

"Well, tell me the damned story already!" Ruby blurts. "It sounds juicy."

Without further ado, Kendrick launches into telling the tale, which, in summary, is that, in the earliest days of River Records, Reed went batshit crazy after discovering the lead singer of one of his earliest bands had fucked his unnamed ex. Apparently, upon discovering the news, Reed beelined to a party at C-Bomb's house, where the lead singer was hanging out, and promptly smashed the guy's face into a wall. Not content to stop there, however, Reed also dropped the guy's band from his label the next day and permanently shelved their debut album, which, C-Bomb said, was due to release within weeks. "And Reed did all this," Kendrick says, "despite the fact that he'd already invested tens of thousands of dollars into developing the band's music and marketing."

Ruby explodes with shocked comments and questions, which the guys answer with relish. But since I've already heard this story, I let my mind and attention wander. I check out the movie star, Isabel Randolph, for a bit, admittedly feeling star-struck. As a guy with some fame myself, albeit not at Isabel's level, I understand the inner workings of the cult of celebrity and consciously try not to let it seduce me. But, still, I can't deny it's kind of cool to see such a world-famous face, in person.

After a bit, however, when my interest in Isabel flags, I continue surveying the packed, noisy room. I check out several friends as they laugh and chat in nearby groups, noting, in particular, that my buddy, Fish, seems particularly smitten with his cute date. And that she looks absolutely enthralled with him. Good for Fish. Couldn't happen to a nicer guy.

I keep scanning and people-watching. Sipping my drink. But when my gaze lands on Laila Fitzgerald, it stays put.

Laila Fitzgerald.

She's another River Records artist. One I've been dying to meet for some time. And by "meet" I mean "meet, seduce, and, God willing, fuck." When I first saw Laila's most recent scorching-hot music video, that sucker immediately went into my spank bank, where it's been in heavy rotation ever since—and, surprisingly, it hasn't lost a bit of its effectiveness on me over time. In fact, repeat viewings have only made me more appreciative of Laila's sex appeal.

At the moment, Laila is standing in a far corner of Reed's palatial living room, chatting animatedly with two beautiful women. One of them, I know—fellow artist, Aloha Carmichael. The other one, I don't. A Black woman with confidence and high cheekbones. Someone I'd probably consider hitting on, if I hadn't spotted Laila. As it is, though, now that I know Laila is here, there's no other woman in the room.

With her long, sandy hair, light eyes, and peaches-and-cream complexion, Laila isn't my usual type. On paper, she's far more Kendrick's type than mine. Kendrick likes girls who look like they were cheerleaders in high school. Or maybe foreign exchange students from Sweden or Russia.

But, see, the thing about Laila that makes her so uniquely appealing to me, despite her "cheerleader" packaging, is her exquisite and undeniable "fuck you" charisma. Thanks to her full lips, which she wears in a perma-pout, and the persistently naughty look in her gorgeous blue eyes that practically screams "I'm a freak in the sheets!", Laila comes off like a first-class sex kitten. A bombshell. A siren. Which means, when it comes to Laila Fitzgerald, the phrase "not my usual type" isn't in my vocabulary.

As I'm staring at Laila from across the room, admiring every inch of her, she jolts me by glancing over her friend's shoulder and looking straight at me. We're nowhere close to each other in this huge room, so, in theory, she could be looking elsewhere. But I know she's not. I know, without a doubt, she's staring at me with lust in her eyes, the same way I'm staring at her.

When our gazes meet, I feel an instant electricity, coursing all the way down into my balls. And by the look on Laila's face, she feels something similar on her end.

Ruby blurts, "Reed's a psychopath! Are you sure you want to throw Savage to the wolf like that?"

But, still, I stare at Laila, biting my lower lip seductively.

Kendrick says, "Are you kidding? It'll be the best birthday dare, ever." He slides his arm around my shoulders, forcing me to end my staring contest with Laila. He says, "Are you ready to entertain me for my birthday, brother?"

I clear my throat and shift my weight, trying to ease the pressure on the hard-on that's started gaining momentum in my pants. "If you're hell-bent on making me do this, then, yeah, of course, I'm in. Your dare is my command, birthday boy."

Kendrick is giddy. "Where's Reed?" He drops his arm and excitedly peers around the party, like a meerkat on a prairie. "We have to make sure he can see *everything*." Kendrick gasps. "Whoa! Laila Fitzgerald is here!" He flails his arms. "I call dibs! I hereby call dibs on Laila Fitzgerald!"

No.

I follow Kendrick's gaze to Laila, just in time to see Reed walking up to her.

Kendrick sighs. "I've had the biggest crush on Laila Fitzgerald *forever*." He looks at the group. "Do any of you know her? Can you introduce me?"

Please, God, no. This can't be happening. Kendrick and I *never* set our sights on the same woman. Ever. I'd expect to run into this problem with Titus. We're both attracted to women who look like they could commit murder without the slightest crisis of conscience. But not *Kendrick*. He likes his women sweet. He likes women who aren't fucked up and toxic and crazy. Unlike me. I mean, yes, I realize Laila is *exactly* Kendrick's *physical* type. But can't he sniff the crazy, sassy little freak beneath her girl-next-door exterior? Because I sure can. And I'm digging it.

Everyone around me is saying they've never met Laila.

"It doesn't matter," Kendrick says, his resolve written all over his face. "With Reed over there, I can act like I need to talk to him about the tour." He's referring to the fact that we just got back from the eight-month-long international leg of our world tour and will be heading back out onto the road in a few weeks for the three-month-long domestic leg.

"Yeah, I don't think . . ." I begin to say. But I'm saying it to Kendrick's back. He's already on the move. Walking directly toward Laila Fitzgerald. "Hey, KC!" I shout. "Wait up, Kendrick!"

But it's no use. The music is too loud for my best friend to hear me. Or maybe he's hearing me just fine and doesn't give a shit. Something tells me it's Door Number Two—that wild horses couldn't stop Kendrick from heading over to meet Laila right now.

Shit.

For the first time in my life, I don't feel like standing aside when a bandmate has called dibs. For the first time in my life, I feel like running after my friend, tackling him to the ground, and shouting, "I saw her first! I call dibs! *She's mine.*"

But since Kendrick's already halfway there, and it's not my style to seem overeager, and since it *is* his birthday, after all, I force myself to stay put. I tell myself not to panic. Instead, I calmly throw back the rest of my drink and tell myself another gorgeous woman who interests me even more than Laila will cross my path, any minute now. Her friend, for instance. She's hot as hell. The one with the dark skin, lush Afro, and banging body. But, no. Even as I try to talk myself into not giving a shit, I can feel my sights setting on Laila and nobody else.

A cocktail waitress walks by and I grab another drink. Ruby has started telling a story, so I try to focus firmly on that and try my damnedest not to obsess about what might be happening across the room. But it's no use. I can't think of anything else but my sincere desire and hope that my best friend in the world, the guy who'd throw himself in front of a bus for me, is, right at this moment, miserably striking out.

Unable to resist any longer, I sneak a peek across the party, just in time to witness Kendrick getting a huge hug from Laila. Reed is still there, but Aloha and the other woman are gone. And, damn, it looks like Laila is full-blown fangirling over Kendrick. *Whoa.* That's not a normal introductory greeting! That's the sort of hug fans give us during meet and greets. The kind women give their lovers when greeting them at the airport. Jesus Christ. Did I imagine that smoldering, come-hither look Laila flashed me a few minutes ago? Obviously, I did. Was she looking at Kendrick standing next to me the whole time?

I should be happy for my best friend, and I know it. But that's not what I'm feeling. In fact, what I'm feeling is something quite the opposite of that. Something I never feel. *Jealousy.*

When Laila finally breaks free of Kendrick, animated conversation between Laila, Reed, and Kendrick ensues. As the trio talks, Laila's eyes suddenly shift to me. And this time, when our eyes lock, when Laila discovers I'm already staring at her, *again,* she flashes me a wide, beaming smile that simultaneously takes my breath away and kind of pisses me off. She just hugged the crap out of Kendrick and now she's trying to knock me onto my ass with that dazzling smile of hers? For fuck's sake, Kendrick is standing right there, obviously still flirting his ass off with her, and she's ignoring him to smile at me?

My brain feels like it's toggling between primal desire, deep confusion, and downright anger, even as every fiber of my body yearns to return Laila's beaming smile—to let her know I'm interested. Ready to go. *Let's do it, baby.* Ultimately, however, my primary emotions seem to be protectiveness of Kendrick and annoyance at Laila for flirting with both of us. And so, ultimately, I do the thing Kendrick would surely do for me, if the situation were reversed: I clench my jaw, press my lips together, and look away, ceding the runway, free and clear, to my best friend. The birthday boy.

TWO

LAILA

When I enter the party, I'm blasted with blaring music combined with the loud din of laughter and chatter. I take in the grandeur sprawling before me, my lips parted in awe. Reed's house is magnificent—a modern-day palace. Which makes sense, since Reed Rivers is the King of LA—a music mogul known in the industry as "The Man with the Midas Touch."

I scan the expansive room, looking for any sign of my good friend, Aloha. A few minutes ago, she texted she'd find me near Reed's front door when I arrived, but I don't see any sign of her. What I do see, however, is wall-to-wall glamour and hotness. It's silly for me to feel this way, given how much awesomeness has happened in relation to my debut album this past year and a half, but finally getting to attend one of Reed's legendary parties makes me feel like I've really and truly arrived, every bit as much as attending the Grammys earlier this year.

My eyes drift as I await Aloha and stop short when I spot my celebrity crush across the large, crowded room. He's Adrian Savage from Fugitive Summer. If you ask me, Savage is the hottest man alive. Dark hair and eyes. A jawline that could cut glass. A chiseled physique that looks like it was forged in tan marble. And all of it made especially panty melting by his omnipresent "big dick ener-gy." An attitude that apparently isn't false advertising, based on those notoriously mouthwatering photos of him in the shower.

At present, Mr. Donkey Dick is throwing back shots with his bandmates, all of whom I recognize but haven't met. And I must say, he's every bit as gorgeous in person as in his leaked photos and music videos and promo. Even more so, actually. Because, in person, I can physically *feel* Savage's undeniable charisma, even from across a crowded room.

"Laila!"

I wrench my eyes off Mr. Perfect and discover Aloha walking toward me with our mutual agent, Daria Brown. When Aloha and I returned from our tour last year, she generously introduced me to Daria, her hot-shot agent, one of the best in the business—and then proceeded to convince Daria she'd be a fool not to take me on as a client, despite the fact that I'm still a relative newbie in this indus-try. But that's Aloha for you. From day one of our friendship, when I was nothing but an opener with a debut album to promote, she's never once hesitated to help me out and cheer me on and show me the ropes.

After hugging me in greeting, Daria says, "I've got some exciting news for you, Little Miss Laila!" Her smile widens with excitement, revealing white teeth that gleam against her beautiful dark skin. "I sealed the deal! You're going to be a mentor on the eighteenth season of *Sing Your Heart Out!*"

I gasp in disbelief, slapping my palm to my cheek. "I don't believe it!"

"Believe it, girl. It's official."

I launch myself at Daria and wrap her in a grateful hug. "This is a dream come true!"

When we disengage from our hug, Daria tells me the basics of the deal. I'll be assigned to Aloha's team of contestants, thankfully. That's exciting. Also, per usual for mentors, I'll only appear in one episode, but Daria assures me even *one* episode on a juggernaut like *Sing Your Heart Out* will introduce me to *millions* of new fans. I ask a few questions and find out my shooting schedule won't be set for several months yet, since the show is currently shooting the season prior to mine. "The pay is basically nothing," Daria explains. "Union scale. But I *promise* the exposure will be well worth it."

"Oh, I don't care what they pay me," I say. "I'd pay *them* to get to be on the show."

Daria flags down a roving server and the three of us grab flutes of champagne. With a loud whoop, we clink and drink and talk excitedly about the amazing news. But when the topic of conversation shifts, and Aloha and Daria fall into a conversation about a career decision for Aloha, I can't resist sneaking a peek at Mr. Perfect across the party again.

This time, when I peep Savage, I'm shocked and thrilled to discover he's not focused on his friends, like last time. This time, he's looking straight at *me*. My heart stops as Savage's dark eyes fix on mine, but I try to play it off like I'm totally unfazed and only vaguely interested, if at all. I know full well what I'm dealing with here—the kind of guy who can get *any* woman at this party. Actually, in the world. So, of course, on pure instinct, I'm instantly hell-bent on making him think he can't get *me*.

To my surprise, Savage doesn't look away, but continues brazenly staring at me, his dark eyes smoldering and his jaw set. Until . . . Oh, no! Shit! I waited too long to look away and let him do it first. *Stupid Laila.* Talk about a rookie mistake.

Granted, Savage's buddy—the drummer in the band, I think?—put his arm around Savage's shoulders, diverting his attention. So, I don't think Savage looked away from me out of a lack of interest. But, *still*, it was a dumb error by me, all the same. With players like Adrian Savage, a girl should *always* be the first to look away. *Always.* She needs to be the one who couldn't care less. Now that Savage knows he's got me hooked on his line—which is *exactly* the opposite of what I should let him think—who knows if I'll be able to attract his attention again tonight. *Damn.*

"Laila?"

I return to Aloha and Daria to find it's Daria who's spoken my name.

Daria continues, "When does Reed plan to release your second album?"

I'm flustered. Still reeling from the exciting news about the show. Feeling aroused by that sexy smolder Savage flashed me. Also, pissed as hell I've stumbled so stupidly in my effort to ensnare him.

"Oh. Uh." I take a deep breath, collecting myself. "We're not finished recording, but close. We only have a few more minor things to add before sending it off to mixing and mastering. At that point, we'll set the schedule for release, promo, and a tour."

Aloha smirks. "Who were you looking at, babe?"

"Huh? Me? Nobody. When?"

"Just now." Aloha flashes me a side-eye. "Who was it, honey? I know you. Somebody's got you all worked up."

I blush. On tour, Aloha teased me all the time for being attracted to players and fuckboys. The ones who are the most fun to bring to their knees—but the least likely to stay there for long. "Yeah, I was being true to form. Having a staring contest with Savage from Fugitive Summer."

Aloha giggles. "Oh, God, Laila. You're so predictable. Didn't you learn your lesson with Shawn?" She's talking about my last boyfriend—a rookie basketball player for the Clippers I dated about six months ago. Shawn pursued me relentlessly, at first, and said all the right things . . . before turning out to be the world's biggest d-o-g when he finally felt certain he had me.

Aloha looks at Daria. "Poor Laila has the worst taste in men. They're always gorgeous. The hottest guys in the room. But nice boys need not apply."

"Ugh. I can relate," Daria says. She winks at me. "It's a sickness, isn't it? Pure insanity, in the true sense of the word, to think, over and over again, we can be the ones to tame them."

"Exactly," I murmur, rolling my eyes at myself. "The problem is . . . it's so damned fun bringing a cocky bastard to his knees.

Truly, my favorite past-time, though I haven't had the pleasure in a while."

Daria laughs. "Girl, you're my spirit animal. Oh, by the way, honey, don't post about being on the show yet, okay? The deal is done and official. But they're not promoting the next season until this one wraps up. I'm sure they'll want to be the one to announce all new cast members for the next season."

"Is it okay if I tell my mom and sister?"

"Only if you're *positive* they won't blab about it to *anyone,* even unintentionally. The producers are insane about controlling all promo."

"I'll wait, then. Better safe than sorry. My mom would never purposefully let the cat out of the bag, but who knows what she might say, unintentionally, while drinking wine with her best friends." I sigh happily. "My mom will be so excited when she hears the news. We never missed *Sing Your Heart Out* in my house. Every week, my family watched and dreamed of me being on the show one day."

It's a true statement, although, technically, we dreamed of me being the *winner* of the singing competition. Or, better yet, a full-time judge on the show, like Aloha is now. But there's no reason for me to say any of that to Daria, after she's secured such an amazing windfall for me, this early in my career. The singing competition attracts icons to its ranks, even as mentors. The fact that Daria secured a spot for me at all is close to a miracle.

"I truly can't thank you enough, Daria," I say. "This is the chance of a lifetime."

"It's Aloha who deserves most of the credit," Daria replies. "She joined me on the conference call with the producers and convinced them they'd be stupid not to hire you."

I clutch my heart. "Aloha! You did not! *Thank you!*"

Aloha shrugs. "You were a tough sell, dude. They were *convinced* you're a raving bitch who'd be a nightmare to work with, thanks to your face."

I burst out laughing at the inside joke. During our tour

together, Aloha and I teased each other constantly about our resting bitch faces. For both of us, unless we're literally smiling from ear to ear, we look like we're sulking or plotting murder. As a child star on the Disney channel for a decade, Aloha expertly learned to mask her resting bitch face with a perma-smile. But me? Not so much. On a daily basis, *someone* who doesn't know me will undoubtedly ask, "Are you okay, Laila? Is something wrong?" Even when I'm feeling light as a feather and happy as a clam.

Aloha sips her drink. "No, actually, you were an easy sell, Laila. I told them you're the perfect combination of sassy and sweet. The kind of person who'll give the sweetest encouragement to the contestants while doling out unparalleled death glares to Hugh, whenever he acts like a jackass blowhard during the all-cast round table. Which, of course, he will. And, *voila*, the producers were sold."

I giggle and raise my glass. "To aud-sassity!" It's what Aloha and I have coined our special brand of badassery. *Audacious sassiness*. And Aloha and Daria clink my glass and whoop, just as the host of the party, Reed Rivers, walks up.

"Wow, looks like I've found the epicenter of the party," he says. He greets everyone, and we quickly tell him the reason for our toast. Of course, Reed congratulates me on the amazing news and we chat about it for a bit. But when Aloha's darling husband, Zander, the sweetest guy in the world, appears, Aloha excuses herself to meet some friends outside. And just like that, I'm alone with Daria and Reed, two of the biggest power brokers in the music industry, and neither of them is telling me to "scram, kid." Seriously, how did I get here?

Reed says, "When it rains it pours, Laila. I've got some exciting news for you, too." He pauses for effect, his dark eyebrow raised. "The opener for Fugitive Summer's domestic leg had to bow out, unexpectedly, for personal reasons. So, I've decided to push up the release of your album and send *you* in their place."

I gasp. "Are you serious?"

"Very serious," Reed says, just as none other than the drummer of Fugitive Summer approaches the group.

"Hey, Reed," he says. "Oh, Laila Fitzgerald!"

And before he says another word, I throw myself into his muscled arms and thank him, profusely, for the amazing opportunity. "I'm so excited!" I shriek. "I *love* Fugitive Summer!"

"Wow," the drummer says, laughing. "Good to meet you, too."

Reed says, "I just told Laila the exciting news that she's joining your tour. You know, because Alexa Play Music had to bow out?"

"Aaah," the drummer says, returning my hug. "That's awesome. I'm so glad you told her the news, Reed. That's actually what I was coming over to do."

"Oh, I'm sure."

I pull away from the drummer, laughing. "Sorry. Did I hurt you?"

"Not at all." He smiles adorably and puts out his hand. "I'm Kendrick Cook, by the way."

I shake his hand maniacally. "I know! I'm so glad to meet you. Thank you so much for coming over here to welcome me to the tour! That was incredibly sweet of you, Kendrick!"

Kendrick looks at Reed and smiles. "Of course, Laila. We're all *super* excited to have you aboard."

"You *are*? Oh my gosh! What an honor! *Thank you!*" My heart racing, I glance excitedly across the room toward Savage, all prior "I don't give a shit" pretense impossible now. And once again, I'm ecstatic to find him already staring at me. Which makes perfect sense now. Obviously, the band has been sitting on this thrilling news, waiting to see my reaction when Reed finally let the cat out of the bag.

Practically bursting with excitement, I smile broadly at Savage, letting him know, yes, Reed and Kendrick have delivered the amazing, exciting, shocking, thrilling news to me—although, I'm sure Savage has already surmised that fact, given the way I hugged his drummer just now. But to my dismay and acute humiliation, Savage doesn't return my goofy, no-holds-barred smile. Instead, on the contrary, he frowns in the face of my exuberance and immediately looks away like I've greatly offended him. Like he's *pissed* about me joining the tour.

And suddenly, I know the heated staring contest we had a few moments ago wasn't proof of our mutual attraction, like I thought. It was evidence of Savage's disdain for me. His objection to me joining his band on tour. Clearly, Mr. Rockstar doesn't think I'm worthy of the opportunity, but Reed is calling the shots, against his will. I've heard rumors that sometimes happens in the world of River Records—Reed calling the shots against an artist's will. And now I know the rumors are true.

Shit.

I'm going to be stuck on tour with a guy who's not happy I'm there. A guy who's not only gorgeous and brooding and talented and hot . . . but also a flaming fucking *dick*.

THREE

SAVAGE

When Kendrick returns to our group, he's got none other than The Prick in tow. We greet our lord and master, half-heartedly, before Reed says, "I've got some bad news, guys. Cooper went into rehab this morning, so Alexa Play Music won't be able to finish the tour."

Ruby looks distraught, which isn't a surprise. During the international leg of our tour, Ruby became good friends with the talented but tortured lead singer of the opening band. Reed assures everyone Cooper is safe and sound, but definitely out of commission for the foreseeable future, as he confronts his demons, head-on.

"The good news," Reed says, "is that I've already found a new opener who's thrilled to join the tour. Laila Fitzgerald. The timing is perfect. I can push up release of her sophomore album, pretty easily, and make it a win-win."

Everyone but me reacts favorably. They say Laila is incredibly talented and that her debut album was fantastic. They mention the fact that Zeke, our producer, also produced Laila's debut, which is kind of cool. And through it all, I feel like my cells are physically vibrating.

Reed says, "Laila wanted to come over here to meet everyone

and thank you for the opportunity." He rolls his eyes. "But I told her we had a few things to discuss and you'd find her later to say hello."

"I was so relieved you said that," Kendrick chimes in. "I didn't want her coming over here and figuring out the band had no idea."

Everyone laughs at the notion, but I clench my jaw, feeling annoyed. It irks me to no end that Reed has full discretion to slot our tours, without even asking our opinion, thanks to our shitty contract. Yes, Reed's *technically* got full control in these matters, but, still, as a matter of professional courtesy, it's my opinion he should have discussed this with our band before telling Laila. Especially since, if you ask me, Laila's not even a good fit, musically, with our band and brand. Is Laila talented? Absolutely. But that doesn't mean she should be opening for Fugitive Summer. Reed should put her with Aloha. Or maybe 2 Real.

And yet, everyone around me continues reacting enthusiastically, like this is the best idea, ever. My aggravation ratcheting up with each passing second, I look across the room. And this time, when my eyes meet Laila's, she's got no beaming smile for me. No lustful stare. This time, the only thing on Laila's face is a death glare. And I must admit, it's a good look on her.

"She's not a good fit," I declare, turning away from Laila's blue daggers. And everyone stops talking and looks at me like I've yelled the earth is flat. "You should put her with 2 Real," I suggest. "He's going out soon, isn't he?"

Reed's face contorts into an expression of pure disdain, the likes of which I've seen many times from him. "Thanks so much for your opinion, Savage," he says, his tone dripping with sarcasm. "The thing is . . ." He leans forward. "I don't actually give a flying shit what you think about this decision. I wasn't asking for *permission* to put Laila on the tour. I was merely informing you, as a courtesy, that I've already done it, so you won't wonder what the hell she's doing there when she shows up at her first soundcheck." With that, he flashes me a nonverbal "fuck you" before smiling at Kendrick. "I hear it's your birthday, KC?"

"Yep. The big two-five."

"Wow. A quarter century. You can rent a car now." He chuckles. "Feel free to take home any bottle you want from any of the bars. There's some pretty expensive Scotch behind that one . . ." He points across the room, to a bar located near a set of French doors, and names the brand. "Tell the bartender I said you can have the whole bottle."

"Thanks, Reed. I'll take you up on that."

"Please do." He smiles at Ruby, his favorite in our band, by far, and wishes her a good time. And then, with a quick nod to Titus and Kai, he heads off without even a cursory glance at me.

"Fuck you, too," I murmur to Reed's departing frame.

"I'll catch ya later, guys," Kendrick says. "I'm gonna get that bottle of Scotch and ask Laila if she wants to—" He gasps. "No! Fuck my life. Nooo!"

"Well, that was fast," Kai says to his younger brother. And when I follow their mutual gaze, I see Laila in conversation with a good friend of ours—a guy named Cash who plays guitar for another River Records band, Danger Doctor Jones. Cash is in profile to us and standing all the way on the other side of the party, but, even so, it's clear he's currently hitting on Laila with everything he's got.

"Motherfucker," Kendrick declares.

"You snooze, you lose, baby brother," Kai says, whacking Kendrick's broad shoulder.

"It's probably for the best," I say, surprising myself. "Now that Laila is our opener, I think we can all agree she's off-limits." I'm grasping at straws here. Being a manipulative dick. Because, even as the words leave my mouth, I know I'd fuck Laila raw, to within an inch of her life, whether during the tour or at this party tonight in the nearest bathroom, if given half a chance.

"No, I don't agree to that," Kendrick says.

"Come on," I say, forging ahead with my bullshit. With my testosterone-driven gaslighting. "It's a weird dynamic, KC. It's like we're her boss, sort of. Plus, don't forget, you're gonna be stuck with

Laila for *months*. Once things go south between you, which they will, you'll be stuck hanging around with her for however long. Sounds horrible to me."

"I'll risk it."

Shit.

I glance at Laila again. She's still talking to Cash across the room. But after a moment, her gaze flickers to mine, and this time, she flashes me an especially murderous glare that sends tingles shooting straight into my dick. In reply, I flash her a look of total impenetrability, letting her know her daggers have no effect on me. That in fact, they've bounced right off my steel chest, baby. And she reacts by turning to Cash and smiling at him like she wants to suck his dick. The little vixen. I gotta say, I'm digging it.

"Yo, birthday boy!" I shout to Kendrick, over the music in the room, my gaze finally leaving the bombshell who's making my blood simmer inside my veins. "I think I'm ready to do that birthday dare now. Let's do it, brother . . ." I peek at Laila again, making sure she's still looking, before adding, "Let's make *Reed* jealous as shit."

FOUR

SAVAGE

Why hasn't Reed come over here yet? I feel like I've been hitting on Georgina pretty damned aggressively for the past five minutes, mere feet away from him. Giving it my best fuckboy effort. And yet, he's still keeping his distance. Hiding behind his proverbial bush. Is Reed embarrassed to pursue Georgina in front of all these bigwigs, for some reason? Is it because of their age difference? What am I missing? The Reed Rivers I know stops at nothing to get whatever he wants. And there's no doubt in my mind he wants Georgina.

"That's so interesting, Savage," Georgina says. "I'll definitely want to explore that further during our actual interview. Do you find that songwriting is a cathartic process for you?"

I look at her with so much heat, I feel like a parody of my younger self. My eyes smoldering, I lean in and say, "Wow, that's a great question, Georgina." I'm trying to make it sound like I've never heard her question before, despite it being pretty standard fare. "Hmm. Yes. Now that you mention it, I think songwriting *is* a deeply cathartic process for me. I'm not the best at expressing myself, sometimes, in my daily life. Oftentimes, I don't even know what I think or feel about something. But then, I start writing a song, and my true feelings pour out of me like a confession."

Georgina gasps and holds up her arm. "*Goosebumps!*" Her beautiful face aglow, she grabs her phone. "Do you mind if I jot that down? I don't want to risk you forgetting that wording when it's time for your actual interview."

Well, that's adorable. I've said that exact thing at least ten million times in interviews over the past four years. But, obviously, a summer intern for *Rock 'n' Roll* wouldn't know that. I sneak a peek at my buddies over Georgina's shoulder to find them red-faced and holding back laughter. Which means Reed, who was standing behind me the last time I checked, must still be there. And not only that, he must look like a volcano about to blow.

I touch Georgina's hand, signaling she doesn't need her phone. "No need to write that down. I promise, I'll remember it during the actual interview." With the touch of my hand to Georgina's, I sneak a peek at Laila to my right, hoping she's still rooted to her spot next to Cash, shooting me daggers. And to my sizzling delight, she is. In fact, if looks could kill, I'd be splattered all over the walls of Reed's massive living room right now.

Holding back a smile, I return to Georgina, lick my lips like I've just devoured her pussy, and brush a lock of dark hair off her shoulder. "So, hey, Georgina, when do you think we should—"

And that's it. Reed's seen enough.

"I need to speak with you," he barks out, appearing out of nowhere at my shoulder like The Flash.

"Can it wait?" I say. "Georgina and I—"

"*It can't wait,*" Reed snaps. "Follow me."

Without waiting for my reply, Reed grips my sleeve and physically drags me across the room and around a corner into a short hallway, leaving Georgina with her hazel eyes wide and her mouth hanging open.

"Reed, come on, man," I say, smiling broadly at my friends as Reed drags me toward my certain doom. "*You're cock-blocking me.*"

Reed's entire body shudders at my words, but he continues

dragging me until we're away from the party. Once safely outside of Georgina's sightline, Reed whirls around, his dark eyes aflame, and spits out, "Do *not* hit on the *Rock 'n' Roll* reporter!"

I shake my arm free of Reed's vise-like grip. It's a tragedy Kendrick isn't here to witness this moment, but, by God, when I recount the story to him later, I want him to be duly impressed with me. Never let it be said I don't give Birthday Truth or Dare my all.

Leaning my shoulder against the wall, I whine, "But, Reed, she's hot as hell."

Reed's jaw pulses. "*She's hands-off.*"

"Who says?"

Reed pauses, his nostrils flaring and his dark eyes on fire. And against all odds, I feel a tiny pang of compassion for the bastard. I don't know why he's been stalking Georgina from afar tonight. What dynamic, real or imagined, has kept him from making his intentions clear to the world? Whatever the hell is going on, Reed is clearly flustered in a way I've never seen him before.

Reed opens and closes his mouth, searching for his response, before finally blurting—and not convincingly, I might add, "She's here to do a job, not to get hit on." When I raise my eyebrows, conveying my skepticism, Reed adds, "I promised her boss nobody would hit on her."

Well, that's ludicrous. Since when does Reed let anything or anyone get in the way of something, or someone, he wants? Could it be Reed promised Georgina's boss *he* wouldn't hit on her, for some reason? Which I suppose is possible, given her age and inexperience and his position of power and reputation as a womanizer. But even then, I can't imagine Reed would uphold a promise like that for long, if he really wanted Georgina.

I languidly pull a box of cigarettes out of my pocket. I only smoke when I've been drinking. And I couldn't be happier to have a box with me now, given how much Reed notoriously despises cigarettes. Casually, I stick an unlit cigarette between my lips and say, "I think we should let *her* decide if she wants to get hit on or not."

Well, that does it. Reed can't keep it together another minute. His dark eyes blazing, he points toward the end of the hallway, like he's commanding a misbehaving dog into a doghouse. He shouts, "Go find the other writer! Her name is Zasu. She's been assigned to do your interview."

I can't believe my ears. Reed is going to make poor Georgina, a summer intern with stars in her eyes, give up a solo interview with *me*—one of the hottest commodities on the planet right now—solely because, *waah, waah*, Reed doesn't want to risk me seducing her?

I say, "Georgie and I have great chemistry." I heard Fish's date call Georgina that nickname earlier tonight, during our ping pong game, so I'm assuming it'll piss Reed off if I use it, too. I add, "We already have the whole thing figured out."

"You're doing an interview with Zasu," Reed commands vehemently. "*It's not a request.*"

I remove my unlit cigarette from my lips, unable to locate my lighter. "You want Georgina for yourself, don't you?"

Bingo. From Reed's facial expression, it's clear I've hit the nail on the head.

His voice tight, Reed grits out, "My motivations don't matter. The only thing you need to know is the owner of your label is telling you she's off-limits. *Now, go find Zasu.*"

I slip the cigarette back between my lips. "Got a light?"

"No!" Reed booms. He points again, nonverbally ordering me away, and I know I've reached the finish line—the point where there's nothing more I can say or do in this passion play. I pull the unlit cigarette out of my mouth again, wink at Reed, and saunter away, but not before tossing over my shoulder, "You're too old for her, anyway, man. She's only twenty-one."

Ha. That ought to sting.

When I re-enter the main room of the party, I discover my friends buckled over with laughter at my performance. I walk toward them, my arms outstretched like, "Did you expect anything less from the master?" and then, instinctively, glance toward Laila. But, damn, she's not there. As I look around, I don't see her anywhere. Did she storm out, too disgusted by my fuckboy display to stick around? Or, worse, did my aggressive flirting with Georgina prompt her to go into a dark corner . . . with *Cash*?

My heart strumming against my sternum, I look around the large room again, to no avail, suddenly regretting my decision to try to piss her off. Why do I always do shit like this? Why do I always self-sabotage? I thought we were playing a sexy game of "fuck you" with each other. A game of "*I'm* not jealous, *you're* jealous!" You know, lobbing fastballs at each other and daring the other to try to hit it out of the park. But now I'm thinking I miscalculated and totally turned her off.

When I reach my friends, they demand a play-by-play. Which, of course, I give them, eliciting even more raucous laughter, especially from the birthday boy. After a while, Reed comes by and berates me for not following his direct orders and finding Zasu. And so, reluctantly, I leave my friends and take a lap of the massive downstairs area, looking for this Zasu chick—even though I wouldn't put it past Reed to send me on a wild goose chase, solely to get me away from Georgina. But, whatever. Whether Zasu actually exists or not, I'm more than happy to take a lap of the party to pretend to look for her, if only to give me a believable excuse to look high and low for the woman I'm actually interested in finding: *Little Miss Death Daggers Laila Fitzgerald.*

FIVE

SAVAGE

Would it have killed Reed to *describe* this mythical Zasu person to me, if it was so damned important to him that I find her? Fucking prick. As I've rambled around the packed party, I've asked a couple people, half-heartedly, if they know someone named "Zasu," who's supposedly a reporter for *Rock 'n' Roll,* and each and every one of them describes Georgina.

"No, no. Not *her,*" I keep saying.

To which they reply, "Oh. Then . . . I dunno."

Of course, throughout my quest, I've kept my eyes peeled for Laila the whole time. So far, no luck. Not knowing what else to do, I head outside to continue my search in Reed's expansive backyard. If Laila is outside with Cash, or, worse, if she's already left the party with him, I'll be so pissed at myself. It's one thing for me to have refrained from hitting on Laila for my best friend in the world—the guy who's more responsible than anyone else for my current lot in life. But as friendly as I am with Cash, I'd *never* in a million years step aside from hitting on Laila for *him.* No fucking way.

Becoming increasingly frustrated, I wander into the pool area and immediately stop dead in my tracks, and then sigh with relief, when I spot Laila in the far distance, bopping around happily on Reed's basketball court, looking like a kid on a playground during recess. There's a large group on the court along with Laila that includes Aloha Carmichael and the guys from 22 Goats and their dates. *But no Cash.*

I smile to myself. Did Naughty Little Laila ditch Cash's ass the minute he was no longer useful to her—the minute she no longer needed him to make me jealous? I bet she did. Which means I'm still in the hunt, baby. That is, if Kendrick strikes out with her, of course. Obviously. I owe him at least that much.

I watch Laila and her friends for a moment, and quickly discern the group is playing HORSE, based on the way everyone keeps taking the same shots in rotation. And the minute I realize the game, I feel oddly invested in standing here long enough to find out if Laila makes her shot. I make a bet with myself: "If Laila makes her shot, I'll head over there and welcome her to the tour. If she doesn't, I'll head inside and make her come to me."

Fish from 22 Goats takes his shot and makes it and his cute date jumps for joy like he's won a Grammy. Next up, Fish's girlfriend takes her shot and whiffs so badly, I laugh out loud. Immediately, Fish and Laila console her and the girlfriend slinks into Fish's waiting arms.

Finally, after a few other players take their shots, it's Laila's turn. She gets the ball from Aloha's husband, Zander, a buff Black dude I've met here and there, and then heads to the designated spot on the court—a location a few feet behind the three-point line. After taking a ridiculously long time to gather herself, as if the fate of the world depends on her making the shot, Laila bends her knees, exhales, and flings her arms upward, releasing the ball into the air.

And . . . it's a brick. A clunker that thuds to the ground a few feet from the rim.

Confronted with her abject failure, Laila shrieks before peeling off a glorious streak of laughter I can hear all the way over here.

Finally, she drops to the ground, dramatically, and writhes around like she's been shot, making her friends guffaw.

As Laila is writhing on the ground, a couple of tall, muscular guys reach the court. They high-five Aloha's husband, Zander, before standing over Laila and laughing along with everyone else. And that's when I realize one of the guys is the pro basketball player, Malik Wallace of The Knicks. The NBA's Rookie of the Year last year, who led his team, singlehandedly, to win the Eastern Conference Finals. Jesus Christ. Reed's contact list really is the coolest in LA.

As a fan of The Bulls, I should probably hate Malik Wallace, given how much he bitch-slapped my team last season. But it's impossible not to respect such rarified talent and skill.

Heeeey, I think. *Malik would be a perfect cover for me!* I suddenly realize I could walk over there to the court and act like I came to meet Malik, thereby giving Laila the chance to introduce herself to me and thank me for letting her join the tour. Laila doesn't know I had nothing to do with her getting the gig, after all. So why not walk over there to "meet Malik" and let Laila kiss my ass while I'm there, as any grateful opener would do? It's pure genius.

I start walking, feeling pretty damned good about my strategy. It's critical with a woman like Laila Fitzgerald—the kind who can get any man she wants—not to let her know how much I'm drooling over her. I can't let her think she has the upper hand. Otherwise, she'll surely ditch me as fast as she ditched Cash. And maybe Kendrick, too? That remains to be seen.

Fuck.

No.

I stop walking, the hair on the back of my neck standing up.

Of all the people on that court right now, the last one I'd want to be talking to Laila is Malik Wallace. But he's doing just that. And not only talking to her, but brazenly *flirting* with her. She's off the ground now and the pair has drifted off to the side to talk one-on-one.

Crap.

She's laughing now. Swatting flirtatiously at Malik's muscular arm.

Fuck.

Laila calls for the ball from one of her friends, and when she gets it, she hands it to Malik, clearly being sassy with him. She points. And he laughingly steps to the spot where she just airballed her latest attempt. Gracefully, Malik releases the ball and sinks it with nothing but net. And when he's done making his shot—and, presumably, his point—he beelines back to Laila . . . and she gives him an exuberant high-five.

Fuck, fuck, fuck.

They're obviously bonding over there—in record speed.

The pair continues talking as the game continues around them. But, soon, their conversation is interrupted when Dax Morgan, the lead singer of 22 Goats, says something to the group that makes his bandmates—Fish and Colin—huddle up. My guess, based on the way the night has been going, is that Dax just received word that it's 22 Goats' turn to take the large stage in the main room of the party, along with whatever combination of musician-friends they want to invite. My band already played earlier in the night with our selected group of friends, so it makes sense to me that's what I'm seeing.

"Hey, Savage!" a female voice says to my right. And when I turn my head, there's a beautiful Asian woman standing before me. She extends her hand with a bright smile. "I'm Zasu, one of the writers for *Rock 'n' Roll.* Reed sent me to find you to talk about your upcoming interview."

Well, I'll be damned. By now, I'd convinced myself Zasu didn't actually exist.

I shake her hand and say it's good to meet her and she flushes visibly at my touch.

"I'm a *huge* fan," she gushes. "I was elated to find out you'd been assigned to me for the special issue."

"Thanks." I glance at the basketball court again. And fuck my life, Laila is still talking to Malik.

Zasu says something, forcing me to return my attention to her. She's flustered. Blushing. Fanning herself like I've seen many, many fans do over the past few years. And so, I wait, feeling vaguely annoyed. Women react like this upon meeting me all the time. Which is fine, but weird. I mean, I'm the same guy I've always been, yet nobody reacted like this when I worked at a supermarket in Chicago. But, okay. I get it. I'm famous now. And this is part of the gig when I meet fans. But when I meet a *reporter*? Come on.

Zasu laughs at herself and sighs. "Forgive me. This never happens to me. I'm being so unprofessional." She shakes it off, pulls herself together, and starts explaining the general game plan for the one-on-one interviews. Specifically, she says they're going to be different, and more fun, than the typical sit-down.

But since I've already heard this exact spiel from Georgina earlier, I tune her out. By the end of my ping pong game with Georgina, she'd convinced me to go ATVing with her on the day of my interview, since it's something I've never done. Something I've never wanted to do, honestly, but I wasn't going to say no to Georgina. There are worse things than spending the day with a gorgeous woman, watching her ride a fast machine.

As Zasu continues talking, I gaze toward the basketball court again, just in time to see Kendrick and Kai arrive. There are some hugs and handshakes. Some introductions. Kendrick and Kai both visibly recognize Malik Wallace. And, not surprisingly, they stride up to him and Laila and strike up an animated conversation.

Finally, Dax and his bandmates break from their huddle. Dax announces something that wrangles the cats around him, and the entire group begins walking toward the house, with Laila falling into step between Malik and Kendrick.

"So, do you have any ideas about an activity you might like to do?" the reporter, Zasu, asks me. "Maybe something you've never done before?"

The group is even with Zasu and me now, about thirty yards

away behind Zasu's back. Kendrick hasn't noticed me because his head is turned toward Laila. But Laila, who's looking at Kendrick as he speaks sure as hell sees me standing over here in a dark corner with Zasu. How do I know that? Because she's rolling her eyes at me, as if to say, *Again?* And I can't help winking at her in reply. Dude, she's the one who was flirting with Cash earlier, and is now the cream filling between Malik and Kendrick. If Laila's annoyed that I've bounced from one hot woman to the next at this party, then maybe she should look in the mirror and be pissed at herself.

"Savage?" the reporter says.

But my eyes are tracking Laila's movement like a hawk tracking a mouse in a field. With a death glare to me, Laila turns her head and says something to Malik before finally walking far enough forward that I'm now looking at her back. I crane my neck, still watching, as Laila, and everyone she's with, including Malik and Kendrick, disappear through a set of double doors into the house.

"Um. Savage?"

My heart racing, I look at the reporter but say nothing.

"I was asking if you have any ideas for an activity we could do on the day of your interview?"

"No. I have no idea."

"Oh. Okay. Well . . . I can send you a list of ideas, maybe?"

"You know what? I'd rather do the interview by phone. My band will be heading out on tour soon and I'd like to have as few obligations between now and then as possible."

Zasu's shoulders sink with disappointment. "Oh."

A collective roar of excitement blasts from inside the house, followed by the amplified sounds of an electric guitar and Dax Morgan's voice, greeting the crowd.

"*Oooh!*" Zasu shouts. "It's 22 Goats!"

"Go on," I say, gesturing toward the house. "You don't want to miss this."

"That's okay. I can listen from out here, so we can finish our conversation."

"I'm not really up for this right now, actually," I reply, just as the band begins playing one of 22 Goats' biggest hits—a mid-tempo love song called "Fireflies."

"Okay. No worries. Thanks for your time, Savage. I'll be in touch." Zasu pauses, apparently expecting me to respond. And when I don't, she sprints toward the house.

For a long moment, I stand alone in the shadows, trying to decide what to do.

Dax is singing the lyrics to his famous song. But, suddenly, a female voice takes over. It's Aloha. Followed immediately by another female voice taking the next line. *Laila.* The sound of her distinctive voice makes me close my eyes. *Damn, she's good.*

I run my hand through my hair, feeling a rush of adrenaline and yearning. Knowing Laila is in there, dazzling the crowd with her talent and beauty and sultry stage presence is almost too much for me to bear. I want to head in there and watch, more than I want to breathe. But not when I know Kendrick is in there, watching and wanting her. Probably Malik Wallace, too.

Jealousy floods me again. Which makes no sense, given that I've never even spoken to the girl. She's just another hot woman at a party. Another vixen in a music video. A gorgeous artist with astounding talent, yes. But, still, someone I've never even met. So, why should I care if she's off-limits to me, when another woman, just as alluring and desirable, will surely cross my path in a matter of minutes? I need to let Kendrick have her. And that's that.

Several voices launch into singing the famous sing-along chorus of "Fireflies." Yet, the only voice my brain can hear is Laila's. And, suddenly, I feel the urgent need to get the hell out of here. If I don't, I'm going to do something I'll regret. I'll fuck over Kendrick. Or I'll pick a fight with Malik Wallace, of all people. Or, God help me, I'll pick a fight with Laila herself, just to prove to myself I don't want her.

Exhaling loudly, I grab my phone and tap out a message to Kendrick:

. . .

Me: Yo, KC. I'm gonna dip. Not feeling great. Happy 25ᵗʰ. I love you, brother. Have a blast tonight. Good luck with Laila.

After pressing send, I shove my phone into my pocket, grab a cigarette and light it—and then stride with purpose toward a faraway set of French doors. They're a different set than the ones Laila and her group walked through several minutes ago. I don't know where they lead, exactly, but I'm thinking the odds are high they won't take me directly through the main room of the party, where Laila is currently onstage, gracing the world with her insane talent and sex appeal.

Happy Birthday, Kendrick, I think. *For the love of fuck, don't let her leave with Malik Wallace.*

SIX

LAILA

One month later

Well, there's no turning back now.

Not that I'd want to turn back. I'm just saying I couldn't, even if I wanted to. Today is the start of my tour with Fugitive Summer. One of my favorite bands. And the beginning of a whole new, exciting chapter of my career.

I'm sitting in the backseat of a large SUV with tinted windows, alongside my assistant, Katrina, plus the security guy assigned to me for the tour. Which is super fancy. We're driving to Van Nuys Airport outside of LA, rather than LAX, because we're flying private. Also, super fancy. At the airport, I'll board a private jet headed for Philadelphia, where the tour will kick off tomorrow night. After that, we'll spend three months zigzagging the entire country in a fleet of buses before ultimately winding up back in our hometown of LA.

Shortly after that, the new season of *Sing Your Heart Out* will begin shooting, at which point I'll find out when my one-episode stint as Aloha's mentor will begin. And once that happens, all bets will be off. According to Reed and Daria, the one-two-three punch of my second album, this tour, and, ultimately, my stint on the show, will catapult my career to staggering new heights. Fingers crossed, anyway. I've learned that "success" is out of my control. All I can do is work hard, do my very best, remain professional and humble at all times, and let the universe take it from there.

My phone buzzes with an incoming text from Malik. He's wishing me safe travels and says he hopes it'll work out he'll be able to catch my show in New York. I reply and tell him, "Yeah, I hope it works out! Have a great game tonight!" And leave it at that.

Malik's been fairly persistent since Reed's party. But I've been super busy and also wary of his reputation as a manwhore. So, nothing much has happened between us this past month, since he slid into my DMs immediately after Reed's party. At Malik's invitation, I did go to one of his games a few weeks ago—the hometown Lakers vs. Malik's team, The Knicks. I sat courtside at The Staples Center, in the front row, and cheered Malik on. Which meant I was cheering *a lot,* since he was the high scorer in the game.

But afterwards, I only kissed Malik and thanked him for having me, at which point it became clear he'd been assuming we'd go back to his place to bang after the game. I didn't see the point in pursuing something with him, though. Not with me leaving for three months and Malik's schedule being packed with games and events. Not to mention, Malik is based in New York and I'm in LA. Even if Malik does wind up coming to my show in New York, what could really happen between us, after that? The whole thing seems pointless to me.

I shove my phone in my purse as the SUV stops at a security kiosk at the airport entrance. The driver shows his credentials to the guard, along with mine, my assistant's, and the bodyguard's, and then, away we go, toward a private jet parked on the tarmac.

"Are you *so* excited?" my assistant, Katrina, asks, poking my arm.

"*So* excited," I confirm. But that's all I can muster, thanks to the pounding of my heart. I'd never admit this to Katrina, or to anyone. But I'm almost as excited about finally getting to meet Adrian Savage as I am about starting the actual tour.

By now, I've met all the other members of Fugitive Summer. Two of them—brothers Kendrick and Kai—approached me at the party. The other two—twin siblings, Titus and Ruby—were more than gracious and welcoming when I approached *them*. Also, Kendrick and Ruby both gave me their numbers at the party and told me to contact them if I had any questions before the tour. I never did initiate any texting with either of them, however. First off, I wanted to play it cool. But, also, I've been crazy busy this past month, finalizing my album for a rush release in time for the tour and rehearsing with my backing band. But, still, it was incredibly sweet of both of them to make me feel so welcomed and appreciated. Especially Kendrick, who was sweet enough to reach out a couple times to ask about the progress of my album.

And then there's Savage, who didn't speak to me at the party, even once. But, rather, made it abundantly clear, through his glares and body language, he was a) not happy about me joining the tour, and b) way too busy chasing tail to stop and say a single word to me.

During my performance with the Goats and Aloha, I looked for Savage in the audience, but didn't see him. And that pissed me off. Everyone else at the party had the decency to watch our performance, as a show of camaraderie. But Savage couldn't be bothered?

When I got offstage and looked around for Savage, I realized he hadn't seen the performance because he'd already left. My guess? He cut out the nano-second he settled on whichever lucky lady he was going to bang that night. Predictable.

It was in that moment I made a vow to myself: I wouldn't speak a single word to Savage during the tour, unless and until *he* spoke to me *first*. Which means this five-hour flight I'm about to take with him could turn out to be an interesting, and extremely quiet, standoff between us.

The SUV parks on the tarmac. My door flies open. And a

blonde woman greets me with a big smile. "Welcome, Laila!" she says. She introduces herself as Tracy, our tour manager, and says she's thrilled I'm here. I thank her and express my excitement, as someone swiftly attends to my luggage in the trunk.

A moment later, I'm climbing the staircase of the private jet, alongside my assistant and bodyguard, while preparing myself mentally to maintain a poker face when I see Savage for the first time. *Don't stare at him,* I tell myself. *Don't drool. Don't blush. And for God's sake, Laila, look away first.*

I enter the plane, my heart crashing, and I'm immediately greeted by a flight attendant who smells like roses. A staffer whose name I don't catch introduces himself. And then another.

As I speak to everyone, I look around but don't see the members of Fugitive Summer. Which makes sense, now that I think about it. Surely, I was given the first arrival time, to minimize their waiting-around time. Because that's how it works in this business. Everything is geared toward the headliner's comfort and convenience. Aloha never treated me like an underling on our tour. She always treated me like an equal, from day one. But I have to remind myself Aloha is the outlier in this industry. Maybe, one day, I'll be the headliner who'll treat my opener the way Aloha treated me. But in the meantime, I'm happy to be here on Fugitive Summer's tour, and to wait around for them, whenever necessary.

I get settled into a window seat, while my assistant heads to the back to chat with an assistant for Fugitive Summer. I check my phone and find out my band of musicians are already in Philadelphia, since they're based out of New York. I text excitedly with them for a bit, saying I can't wait to see them soon. After that, I text with my mom and sister, with lots of emojis, about how excited I am. And, finally, when there's a commotion at the front of the plane, I look up to find the famous faces of Fugitive Summer boarding the aircraft. There's Kendrick, Kai, Titus, Ruby, and . . . some bodyguards. Some staffers. And that's it. *No Savage?*

Fuck a duck, man. I've been girding my proverbial loins all

morning in anticipation. No, all week. All month! *And he's not here?*

The famous foursome heads into the heart of the aircraft, each one saying hello to everyone they pass. When they get to me, they're gracious, but polite and calm, with nobody mentioning Savage. And that makes me lose my freaking mind. Is *nobody* going to mention the fact that the most famous face in Fugitive Summer isn't here? Because . . . he's kind of important.

"Do you mind if I sit here?" Ruby asks, motioning to the empty seat next to me.

"Please do."

Ruby flops down next to me, her pink hair tied into two adorable buns on top of her head. She says, "I'm so excited to finally have another girl on tour with me!"

"I couldn't be more excited," I reply. And it's the truth.

Ruby begins pulling items out of a backpack, getting herself settled with various devices and chargers. A pillow. Some fluffy socks. And as she does her thing, I admire her adorableness. She's attempted to harden her pixie vibe with piercings and tattoos. But somehow, on Ruby, all of her adornments only accentuate her innate sweetness. The tougher she tries to look, the sweeter she appears.

After shoving her backpack underneath her seat, Ruby leans back and exhales loudly like she's in a Jacuzzi at the spa. Her eyes closed and her head pressing against a pillow, she says, "And so it begins."

I laugh. "And so it does."

She opens her eyes. "During the international leg, Alexa Play Music opened for us. Do you know them?"

"I know of them."

"Four more boys," she says. "So, with our boys and theirs, it was *eight* boys and me. Good God, I'm a saint."

We both laugh.

"What I'm trying to say, Laila, is I'm elated you're here."

"I'm elated I'm here, too. I've never toured with boys. My last tour was with Aloha. So, you'll have to show me the ropes."

"Just don't let them steam-roll you. They don't even realize they're doing it."

"Good advice. But I'm the opener, so I kind of have to let them steam-roll me a bit. It's part of the gig. Or so I've heard. Aloha never hazed me. But I've heard stories about headliners doing that to their openers, as a regular thing."

"Yeah, the guys did some of that to Alexa Play Music. They tend to feel like openers need to know their place in the pecking order, you know? It's stupid, but whatever." She rolls her eyes. "Something tells me that won't happen to you. You've got a knack for making people want to roll out the red carpet for you, Laila."

"I don't expect any special treatment," I say. "I'm just happy to be here."

"I don't think the boys will be able to keep themselves from treating you with kid gloves." She flashes me a snarky look. "Boys are very visual creatures, Laila. And you're a very pretty visual."

I laugh. "Well, thank you. So are you."

She smiles. "It kind of sucks, though, doesn't it? Everyone should be treated with respect, no matter what. Not just pretty girls."

"I agree."

"Good. I'll let the guys know you insist on being treated exactly the same as any other opener."

"Well . . . I don't know if *that's* necessary."

She laughs, and I join her. And just this fast, I know we're going to be great friends.

A noise at the front of the plane attracts my attention and makes my heart lurch. Is Savage here? But, no. The sound is the front door of the plane closing, without Savage appearing. And even though I swore to myself Savage's name wouldn't pass my lips during this entire tour unless he broke the seal and spoke to me *first,* I can't resist asking Ruby what's going on.

"No Savage?" I ask.

Ruby shakes her pink head. "He's been in Chicago this week, visiting family. He's flying to Philadelphia today on his own."

"Ooooh." I smile. "That's good news. This whole time, I was thinking he was pulling a 'rockstar' by making an entire flight of people wait on him."

"Oh, trust me, Savage is perfectly capable of doing that. That boy is many, many things, but *punctual* certainly isn't one of them. It's really annoying, so brace yourself."

"If you're constantly annoyed by his lateness, why don't you ever slap the shit out of him for it? You're not the opener."

"Meh. We pick our battles with him. In the end, it's hard to say which parts of Savage's personality contribute to his mad genius. So, we let him be, in case messing with the shitty stuff will mess with the amazing stuff. We all benefit from Savage being happy and carefree and left alone. That's when he's at his best."

"So, you think if you slap the shit out of him, you might slap some of his genius out of him?"

"Exactly."

I smile and nod. But I'm not sure I could hold my tongue like that with a bandmate. Aloha is a genius in her own right, too. An icon in the music industry. But during my tour with her, she *never* kept anyone waiting. In fact, she was usually early for everything. I remember Aloha telling me, early on, "We're the lucky ones who get to go onstage and experience all the adulation and praise, but never forget it takes a village of crew and staff and musicians to make a tour happen for the thousands of fans who pay their hard-earned money to watch you perform. So, in the end, even if it feels sometimes like it's all about *you,* never forget you're there to create happiness for your fans and hundreds of jobs for your crew and staff. Make art when you make your album, Laila. Make happiness for the fans and *money* for the machine when you're on tour."

I distinctly remember Aloha's words blowing me away. They were a revelation to me. A whole new way of looking at things. And to this day, I've kept them close to my heart at all times. Has nobody ever sat down Adrian Savage to give him a similar speech? Obviously not, based on what Ruby said a moment ago. And that's a shame. I bet Savage would benefit from hearing Aloha's thoughts on the importance of humility and professionalism in our industry.

About twenty minutes after the plane takes off, as drinks and food are served, Ruby and I settle into an easy, interesting conversation.

"Is it weird being the only girl in your band?" I ask.

"Nah," Ruby replies. "You know Titus is my twin brother, right? So, being in a band with him feels totally natural to me. And then, with Kai and Kendrick being brothers, they feel like a single unit, too. So, I don't really feel outnumbered there. And then there's Savage, who feels like an extension of Kai and Kendrick, because he grew up with them. So, I guess I don't often feel like *one* girl in a band with *four* boys. I feel more like part of a duo that's merged with a trio." She makes a cute face. "Does that make sense?"

"It makes perfect sense. Does Savage have any siblings?"

"No, he's an only child." She snorts. "Which, trust me, will make *perfect* sense to you once you get to know him. *If* you get to know him. He's a tough nut to crack."

I bite my lip. I haven't exchanged a single word with the man and I already knew that. Which, unfortunately, is only making him more intriguing to me. Savage is a tough nut to crack? Well, guess what? I just so happen to consider myself an expert at busting balls and cracking nuts.

"Hey, ladies." It's Kendrick. With a huge, handsome grin on his face, he plops himself down across the aisle from Ruby.

I take in his surfer-boy handsomeness, his wavy blonde hair and bright eyes, and, immediately, I'm filled with warmth and happiness at the sight of him. It's the same way I felt when I met Kendrick weeks ago at Reed's party. Warm and safe. The same way I felt when we exchanged texts these past few weeks, regarding the progress on my album.

"I hope you don't mind me hanging out here with you ladies," Kendrick says. "Kai's already annoying the fuck out of me."

"We're happy to have you," I say.

"Speak for yourself," Ruby says. But it's clear she's joking.

"So, Miss Fitzgerald," Kendrick says. "Congrats on the release of your album last night."

"Thank you. Phew! It was a tall order, but we did it."

"I've already listened to it twice and it's a-maaaazing."

I'm floored. "You *bought* it? You didn't need to do that! I have it on my laptop."

"Of course, I bought it. And then, I stayed up late listening to it, twice. And I can honestly say it's a masterpiece. I loved your first album, but this one is next level."

Squealing happily, I get up from my seat and give Kendrick's neck a little hug, making him chuckle. "That means so much to me, coming from you," I say. "*Thank you.*"

He talks into my shoulder. "I'll be shocked if you don't win a bucketful of awards this time. Not just nominations, but *wins.*"

Flushed and smiling, I return to my seat, where I proceed to talk excitedly with Kendrick for the next twenty minutes about the album. And, quickly, it's clear Kendrick is anything but a bull-shitter. Based on his questions and comments, it's obvious he really *did* listen to my musical baby *twice*—and genuinely believes every word of praise he's giving me. As the conversation progresses, however, I begin to realize something I hadn't under-stood before. Specifically, that I think Kendrick is . . . *into me.* Like, totally flirting with me. And not just being welcoming and friendly. Shit.

The thought is flattering to me, of course. Kendrick is a beauti-ful, talented, lovely person. Truly, he's as sweet as can be. But, the thing is . . . if I'm going to sleep with someone in the headliner during this tour—which Aloha has repeatedly advised me against doing, by the way—then it's not going to be Kendrick Cook. Or Kai Cook. Or Titus Connolly. Obviously, I'm not proud to admit this, but if I'm going to sleep with anyone, it's going to be Adrian Savage. *Obviously.* I've had a crush on him forever. As wonderful as Kendrick is, I'd never blow my chances with Savage by sleeping with his bandmate, let alone the one who's apparently his very best friend.

"So, when will the world have *your* next album, guys?" I ask, trying to change the subject and deflect from the flirtatious vibe I'm feeling.

"We'll probably start recording in earnest right after the tour," Kendrick replies. "We've all been on fire writing new songs during the tour. Savage, especially. He's been churning out some amazing stuff—pure gold. So, I'm sure we'll jump straight into the studio when we get back."

"That's so exciting," I say. "If you guys ever give friends 'early listener' copies of your albums, I'd love to be on that list."

"Hell yeah," Kendrick says. "It'd be great to get your feedback. I loved the mix on your new album."

"Thanks so much."

Kendrick smiles broadly, and I return the gesture, simply because that's what Kendrick Cook does to a person. He makes them want to smile. But a little piece of me knows I'm playing with fire here. Is Kendrick interpreting this smile as encouragement of something more than friendship? Because, if so, I've got to figure out a way to tactfully steer him into my friend zone, as soon as possible.

"So, I saw a photo of you at a basketball game recently," Kendrick ventures. "It was a Lakers game in LA, but you were cheering on Malik Wallace?"

And there it is. The look in his eyes that confirms he's interested in me romantically. No doubt about it. "Yeah, Malik invited me to the game. You were there when I met him at Reed's party, right? You met Malik, too?"

Kendrick nods. "Strangely, Malik didn't invite *me* to sit courtside at a Lakers game."

I chuckle, not knowing what else to do. "It was a last minute thing. He slid into my DMs, and asked me, so . . ."

"Are you guys dating, or . . .?" Kendrick asks tentatively.

I don't know why I do it, but I reply, yes, I'm dating Malik. In fact, I use the word "boyfriend." Even though, in reality, that's a massive overstatement. In truth, Malik is nothing to me, really. He's been pursuing me, and I went on a date with him, but we've made no promises, to put it mildly. For all I know, he's screwing someone else right now, and that's perfectly fine with me. But the thing is, I don't want to have to tell Kendrick, point blank, I'm simply not interested in him. I don't want to hurt his feelings or make things weird, especially not on day one of the tour. So, I take the easy way out, when it's offered to me.

"Cool," Kendrick says. "He's a . . ." He sighs. "Cool."

"I barely saw him this past month," I add quickly, not wanting Kendrick to get the impression Malik is the great love of my life or something. "I was so busy expediting the album, and rehearsing for the tour, I barely had time to eat or sleep, let alone see him."

Kendrick tries to smile. "Yeah, well, your hard work really paid off. Seriously, Laila, the album is incredible."

"Thank you so much, Kendrick. You're a great friend."

At that last word, Kendrick looks like he wants to scream. There's an awkward pause as he bites the inside of his cheek before finally puffing out his cheeks in resignation and whispering, "Cool."

I look at Ruby and she's grimacing compassionately, not even trying to hide her awareness of what just happened.

"Hey, asshole," Kai says, appearing out of nowhere and, thankfully, filling the awkward silence. Kai flops into a seat next to his brother and demands Kendrick watch the next episode in some series they've been binge-watching together.

"As long as you ply me with alcohol," Kendrick says.

"You don't need to ask me twice." Kai flags down a flight attendant and we all place orders. As we're doing that, Titus comes over and joins the party. And soon, our whole group is drinking and talking, laughing and swapping stories. Even Kendrick, much to my relief, seems like he's back to himself.

A few times during the conversation, Savage's name comes up, organically, and I feel myself perk up every time his name is mentioned—every time I get a new scrap of insider information about him. I hate that I'm constantly drawn to Savage, considering his obviously oversized ego, but I can't help myself. Not only is he gorgeous and talented, by all accounts he's closed off and prickly, too. Which, unfortunately, I must admit, makes him *exactly* my type.

SEVEN

SAVAGE

Chicago, Illinois

Me: Yo, KC. I decided to fly into Philly tomorrow morning, instead of tonight. Mimi asked me to come to her treatment this afternoon, and I couldn't say no. Don't worry, I'll be there in plenty of time for soundcheck tomorrow.

Kendrick: Does Tracy know?

Me: Yeah. She's pissed. Says I'm cutting it too close. I told her not to stress. It'll work out just fine.

Kendrick: How is Mimi doing?

I look at my grandmother sitting next to me on the couch, looking like a little hummingbird. She's flanked by me on one side and my cousin, Sasha, on the other, as we watch the season finale of Mimi's favorite show, *Sing Your Heart Out.*

Me: She's good. Feisty and funny, as always. Just really tired. Today's treatment kicked her tiny ass pretty hard.

Kendrick: Give her a big hug for me.

Me: Will do. How's tricks on your end?

Kendrick: Good. We're at the hotel, chilling before tomorrow.

Me: Chilling how?

Kendrick: The usual. Watching Netflix with Kai and Titus. Smoking a blunt. Eating way too much pizza. Be jealous.

I sigh with relief. Call me paranoid, but all day long I've been imagining Kendrick and Laila hitting it off on the plane by day, and then fucking like rabbits in Kendrick's hotel room by night. Thanks to Kendrick's response, I'm highly relieved and cautiously optimistic. But, still, I can't help probing a bit more. This time, I get straight to the point.

Me: How'd it go with Laila today?

Kendrick: FUCK MY LIFE, DUDE! SHE'S GOT A BOYFRIEND AND HE'S MALIK FUCKING WALLACE!!!!

No.

My heart is sinking. But not for Kendrick. For *myself.* But why do I even care? I don't know Laila. She's nothing to me but a sexpot in a music video. A pair of blue eyes shooting daggers at me from across a crowded party. A pair of perfect tits. Plush lips I'd do anything to kiss . . .

Fuck!

What's wrong with me? Why do I feel this primal desire to fuck the living hell out of that woman, above all others? It's insane. I know I'm having a classic "celebrity crush," like a teenager with a wall full of posters. Which is so unlike me, it's ridiculous. And yet, I can't help it. From the moment I saw her in that music video, I wanted to fuck her. And not in a fantasy. I wanted to hunt her down, maybe through Reed, or her agent, and meet, seduce, and fuck her. Unfortunately, I was on tour at the time, so it wasn't in the cards . . . and now, she's magically the opener on the rest of our tour, and I'm supposed to hang back and do nothing while Kendrick pines for her and she has FaceTime sex with Malik Wallace, of all people?

Me: *I think I saw Laila with Malik at Reed's party.*
Kendrick: *Yeah, that's where they met. Can you believe it? I missed my chance by minutes. If I'd walked onto that basketball court five minutes earlier and invited Laila to get a drink, she never even would have met Malik.*

And if I'd disregarded Kendrick calling dibs an hour before that, and beelined over to Laila when I first saw her across the party, I'd already have banged her a hundred times by now.

Me: *It's probably for the best, KC. Like I said before, messing with an opener is a bad idea.*

· · ·

Okay, it's now official. I'm going to hell. Because even as I press send on my latest text, I know I'd fuck Laila, whether she's our opener or not, if only Kendrick wouldn't hate me for it. And maybe even if he would.

Kendrick: You're probably right. I've heard horror stories about guys messing around with openers and living to regret it.

Me: Exactly. It would have gone all kinds of bad in the end.

Kendrick: I'm sure the middle part would have made the bad ending well worth it, though.

I exhale a long breath, not knowing what to reply to that. As I ponder my response, my eyes drift to the TV as Hugh Delaney, the crusty old country star who's been a judge on *Sing Your Heart Out* since its inception, tells a wide-eyed contestant what he thought of her second of three performances in the finale show. Shaking his head, Hugh says, "Honestly, Deanna, I was expecting more from you tonight. This is the finale! And yet, I didn't see your usual sparkle. Hopefully, you'll pull a rabbit out of your hat for your final song."

The audience boos, as Aloha leans into her microphone. "I couldn't disagree with you more, Hugh," she says, eliciting rousing applause from the crowd. "Deanna's performance was far more subtle than her prior ones. But that's what made it so moving to me. Sometimes, less is more, Hugh." Aloha looks straight at him. "Try it sometime."

The audience roars its approval of Aloha's assessment—and, even more, her zinger to Hugh. The man everyone loves to hate.

My cousin, Sasha, yells from her end of the couch, "You tell him, Aloha! *Boom!*"

Chuckling, I look at our grandmother between us to see her reaction to Aloha's zinger, as well as Sasha's effusive support of it, and discover our little hummingbird is fast asleep, her tiny body looking peaceful and painless in repose.

"Aw, Mimi," I murmur. "Sweetheart." With a little wink to Sasha, I get up and scoop our grandmother into my arms, bring her into her bedroom, and carefully lay her down. I tuck her in and head to the kitchen, where her regular nighttime caregiver, Stuart, is sitting at the table, eating a bowl of soup. I tell him Mimi is down for the count, and Stuart says he'll take it from here.

I head back into the family room and sit back down next to Sasha, just as my phone buzzes in my pocket. It's another text from Kendrick.

Kendrick: JESUS CHRIST!!!! I just researched Malik Wallace. He's total trash to women, dude. Look him up. Reddit is full of women who say he's a DOG. Which means I'm back in the hunt with Laila, baby! I'm gonna build the friendship during the tour. Become her bestie. Her confidante. Her soulmate. And when her asshole boyfriend fucks it up—which he WILL, mark my words—and she's looking for a broad shoulder to cry on, I'll be the one she turns to. Genius, right?

Seriously? Goddammit. I tap out my reply:

Me: I'd think Ruby would be her shoulder to cry on, don't you? Ruby's great at that.
Kendrick: FUCK RUBY!!!! LOL. Laila's all mine. Ha!

. . .

Well, there's no way out. I can't keep this up. Obviously, Kendrick wants Laila and he's willing to play the long game to get her. It's time for me to step aside and forget this stupid fantasy. Because that's all it is. A stupid fantasy. When I actually meet the woman, I bet she'll quickly bore me to tears.

Me: You're a genius, KC. Go get her, tiger. See you tomorrow.

Kendrick: Try really hard not to be late, okay? Opening shows are always extra crazy. First sound-checks always take twice as long to get everything dialed in.

Me: I'm insulted. When am I not on time? Haha! Gotta go. Sleep tight.

"Who are you rooting for?" Sasha says.

I look up from my phone.

Sasha points to the TV. "Are you rooting for the woman or the man to win tomorrow night?"

"I'm rooting for an asteroid to crash into the studio and kill everyone associated with the show, except Aloha."

"Lovely."

Sasha picks up the remote and turns off the TV. "Well, I'm rooting for Deanna. She's improved, week after week, and she's sweet as can be."

"Good luck to her. I don't care. You wanna smoke a joint on the porch?"

"Hell yeah."

I sit on the porch with my cousin, smoking and shooting the shit. Sasha's a massage therapist, so she tells me a couple stories about her recent interactions with clients at the spa where she works, including a recent story of a guy who wrongly assumed he'd be getting a happy ending from my cousin. We're having a normal, amusing conversation. Nothing earth-shattering. But comfortable and calm. And that's exactly what I want. I know I'm about to re-enter the Twilight Zone for three months, beginning tomorrow—a world where I'm a god among men and nobody but my band ever treats me like a normal human. So, I sit and listen and smoke and enjoy the peaceful moment with someone I trust completely.

After a bit, Sasha does what she always does at times like this. She stands and says, with a gleam in her eye, "Now, let me at that famous body."

It's an inside joke. She's mocking the fact that my body is now a hot commodity around the world. That I've become a product, as much as the music. A piece of meat half the world would die, cheat, or kill to get with. I'm not complaining about it, by the way. This strategy has served me and my band well. But, still, it's a weird thing to think about, and particularly hilarious to Sasha, who still thinks of me as the dorky and angry twelve-year-old who, out of the blue one day about thirteen years ago, showed up on our grandma's doorstep, needing a place to live.

And, of course, as a massage therapist, Sasha is always bizarrely excited to get to work on the ever-present knots clustered stub-bornly in my shoulders and neck. Sasha's weird like that. Her favorite thing in the world, literally, is massaging muscles that are especially knotted and stubborn, and to get to experience the satis-faction of coaxing them into a state of smoothness and relaxation, however temporary. Apparently, from what my cousin has told me, my knotted muscles are among her favorites to knead and coax into serenity, because they're almost always in a state of extreme tightness.

It's funny. The world thinks I'm a rockstar with zero fucks to give at all times. A guy who floats through life, carefree and light as a feather. And I think that way about myself, too, in certain situa-tions. And yet, at least according to Sasha, my muscles tell a very different tale about what's hiding underneath my apparently relaxed exterior.

"Knock yourself out, Sasha," I say. It's the same thing I always say to my cousin when she gets that crazy gleam in her eyes about unleashing her magic hands on me.

Gleefully, Sasha comes around to the back of my chair and gets to work on the mountains of knots and clusters in my shoulders and neck. And as she works miracles on my body, we talk about nothing particularly important for another fifteen minutes or so. But with the weed in my system, that's all the time I can handle of Sasha's magic hands before I'm too relaxed to remain upright in my chair.

"I gotta get to bed," I say. "Big day tomorrow."

"I can give you a full-body massage while you're lying down, if you need some help drifting off to sleep," she offers. "You're pretty tense, Adrian."

"Nah. I'm good. Go finish your book. I'm just gonna knot right back up again on the plane tomorrow, anyway."

I thank my cousin for everything she does for me and Mimi, kiss her on the cheek, and head off to my room. First off, I hop into a hot shower and jack off, thinking, yet again, about Laila. It's the last time I'm going to fantasize about Laila, I decide. Starting tomorrow, she's off-limits to me, even in my mind. Kendrick is obviously *really* into her. And he's the one, unlike me, who actually knows the woman. I've never even said two words to her, for fuck's sake! So, that's it. I'm moving on.

When I'm done with my shower, I slide on a pair of sweats, set my alarm, and reply to a text from my assistant about my travel schedule for tomorrow.

"Back to the grind," I murmur softly, closing my eyes.

But, unfortunately, sleep doesn't come to me, despite the weed in my system.

Finally, I give up. I grab my phone and google "Malik Wallace" and "cheater" and "Reddit," and quickly discern Kendrick was absolutely right. The dude is trash. I guess it's possible some of these stories about his assholery aren't true. There are definitely lots of stories online about me that are pure fiction. But, come on, not *all* of these stories can possibly be fake. Obviously, Malik's not a guy who keeps his word when it comes to women. Which means Laila won't put up with him for long. I don't know the woman, granted. But I know enough to know a firecracker like her, the woman who wanted to murder me for seemingly flirting with Georgina, and then Zasu, at Reed's party, doesn't put up with a guy's shit for very long.

I can't help smiling to myself at the realization that Laila will almost certainly wind up kicking Malik to the curb during the tour. Will she be looking to have a little revenge sex after Malik fucks around on her? Because, if so, I'll be right there to volunteer as tribute.

No.

Stop it, man.

That's Kendrick's plan. You can't steal it.

I take a long, deep breath and exhale slowly.

Actually, I think it's good Laila has a boyfriend. This way, I won't immediately succumb to temptation and betray Kendrick, or otherwise cockblock him. Because a woman having a boyfriend is a boundary I can respect.

Sort of.

Okay, not at all.

But, at least, I can tell myself I respect it. I can tell myself there's double the reason to stay away from Laila. This way, I don't have to resist her, based solely on Kendrick calling dibs. Which, admittedly, is a tall order for me. This way, with Laila dating a guy with as much clout as me, probably even more, I've got double the chances of *not* betraying my very best friend.

EIGHT

LAILA

Philadelphia, Pennsylvania

"They haven't even *started* yet?" I say, feeling flabbergasted. According to today's itinerary, Fugitive Summer should have finished their soundcheck a half hour ago. Which is why I *prematurely* wrapped up an interview in my dressing room to race down here to the stage area, right on time, to begin *my* soundcheck. And now I find out Fugitive Summer hasn't even *begun*? I know the headliner *always* soundchecks first, and takes as long as needed. And delays can happen. But would it have killed our tour manager, Tracy, to let me know the itinerary is no longer accurate, so I didn't miss out on the rest of my interview?

Tracy says, "Savage took a later flight from Chicago than originally planned. But no worries, he's on his way from the airport now and should be here any minute."

She's calm and cool. Which I can't fathom. Savage isn't even in the building yet? Because he didn't fly last night, as planned—as any sane and responsible person would do, when literally *thou-*

sands of people are depending on him? What the ever-loving rock-star cliché is wrong with that man? Who else but him, in his shoes, would travel on the day of any show—let alone the tour opener? It's not like Savage's fans would be perfectly fine to watch a replacement singer tonight, the way audiences accept understudies on Broadway. People pay a lot of money to watch *Savage*, and only Savage, sing, play his guitar, and shake his famous ass! And yet, Savage felt it was a perfectly reasonable thing to risk letting *thousands* of people wait tonight—or maybe even risk letting them down completely? All I can say is that boy had better have a damned good reason for cutting it this close.

I look at my assistant, Katrina, my aggravation probably written all over my face. But I don't care if our tour manager knows I'm pissed. In fact, I want her to know. Now that my soundcheck has been delayed by at least an hour and a half, my assistant will need to reschedule a ton of stuff for me. My hair and makeup. Another interview. Plus, call me crazy, but I was hoping to have a moment to eat and relax before showtime. To call my mom and sister before going onstage. But now, thanks to Savage, I won't be able to do all of it.

"Why don't you take a seat and relax, rather than going back to your dressing room?" Tracy says, emphasizing the word *relax* in a way that tells me she already thinks I'm a raving bitch. She motions toward the front row of seats. "This way, you'll be ready to hop onstage the moment they're done."

"That's a great idea," I say, trying to sound super chill and easygoing. But I don't think I'm fooling her.

Both of us smiling serenely, my assistant and I take our seats . . . and then proceed to quietly gripe about the situation between ourselves for the next several minutes. In the middle of our bitch-fest, however, a male voice behind us takes us by surprise.

"Yeah, I vote we kill him. He's such a dick."

I turn around to find Kendrick sitting behind us, looking highly amused.

"Hello, ladies," he says. "Sorry we're running late. Savage was visiting his family and got delayed."

"Oh no," I say. "I hope everything is okay."

"It's fine. He's on his way now."

"Great," I say brightly, my cheeks turning red. "How long have you been sitting back there, Kendrick?"

His smile broadens. "Long enough to know you've been plotting Savage's murder. But don't worry. You're not the first, and you won't be the last."

My shoulders soften under his warm smile. Clearly, he's not holding whatever he heard against me. But it's a good lesson for me. From now on, I need to keep my nose down and my big mouth shut.

For the next few minutes, Kendrick and I chat breezily as we await Mr. Rockstar's arrival.

And finally it happens. Adrian Savage enters the building. Which I know even before I've seen him, thanks to the sudden shift in the air. The electricity instantly coursing through the building. All at once, crew members who've been working calmly suddenly spaz out. And Kendrick rises from his chair.

"Talk to you later, Laila," he says. "Come eat with us after your soundcheck. We'll be in Greenroom 2 with a full spread. Plenty for you and your band."

"Thanks so much."

Kendrick heads toward a far door, just as Savage's striking face comes into view. He strides into the large venue and toward the stage, and Kendrick greets him warmly and then falls into step with him. At the same time, the rest of the band converges on the stage and gets settled with their instruments in a way that suggests they've all done this before. Many, many times—and on a very tight schedule. When Savage and Kendrick walk onstage to join the rest of their band, everyone waves curtly at Savage. But they don't scold him or otherwise freak out. They just get down to business.

Savage slides the strap of his guitar over his shoulder. "Has this been tuned?"

"Yes," a nearby roadie confirms. "All three are ready to go."

"Thanks." Savage steps up to his mic and taps on it, quickly discerning it's not live. He waves his arm and the soundman at the back of the venue flips a switch. "Hello, Philadelphia," Savage booms when the mic is live. "1-2, 1-2." *Boom.* Savage's eyes land on me. And there it is, again. That same crazy electricity I felt every time my eyes met his at Reed's party. A kind of double-ovarian explosion I've never felt before. "Hello, Laila," Savage says calmly into his microphone, a smirk on his handsome face.

But that's all I get. Without even waiting for me to mouth "hello" in reply, Savage looks down and rips off the opening guitar riff from one of Fugitive Summer's biggest hits—the sexiest song in their catalog, by far—a song filled with double *entendres* about orgasms and oral sex called "Come with Me."

Did Savage just now dedicate this song to me, by saying my name before launching into it? Or am I connecting dots that simply aren't there?

Of course, the full band expertly follows Savage's lead, right on cue, and, soon, he leans into his microphone and begins to sing. And just like that, even during a soundcheck, Savage transforms from a mere mortal into a god before my eyes. Even when there's no audience cheering him on, no collective hysteria to elevate him to superhuman status, Savage nonetheless looks supernatural in this moment. The perfect representation of a man doing what he was divinely created to do. And whether I want to think it or not, despite me actively *not* wanting to think it, as I watch Savage performing onstage, I find myself thinking, on a running loop: *I. Want. That.*

NINE

LAILA

"All I'm saying is it's a lucky thing you've got bodyguards," Kendrick is saying to Savage as I enter the greenroom with my musicians after our soundcheck. "Or else Laila would have murdered you in there."

Crap.

Fugitive Summer is sitting at a large table, eating a meal. And based on what Kendrick just said, it seems Kendrick has been telling his band the story of my earlier bitchfest, the one in which I complained to my assistant about Savage traveling on the day of the opening show.

At the sound of my band entering the room, Fugitive Summer collectively turns their heads toward the door.

"Hey, guys," I say awkwardly, my cheeks blooming. "Have you met my band?"

My heart racing, I introduce everyone—two guys and two women—trying to sound light and bright. And through it all, I steadfastly avoid Savage's gaze.

Kendrick enthusiastically invites us to fill our plates from a buffet at a nearby table. So, we all head over there and begin doing just that, exchanging small talk with Fugitive Summer as we do. We talk about the venue. The acoustics. The amazing sound crew. My musicians compliment Fugitive Summer on their soundcheck, and several of them compliment my band in return, saying they heard our two songs from in here and we sounded great.

As I walk to the dining table with my meal in hand, I feel eyes on me. And when I finally muster the courage to look up, I discover I'm right. But the eyes don't belong to Savage. They belong to Kendrick. He's looking at me apologetically. Like he feels bad he just ratted me out to his friends.

I shoot him a warm smile to let him know I'm not offended in the least. That in fact, I'm well aware I deserved it. Actually, although I'd never admit this to Kendrick or anyone else, I'm kind of glad Savage knows my thoughts about his lateness, albeit not directly from me. Someone needs to tell that boy the truth—that the entire world doesn't revolve around him. It might as well be me.

As conversation at the table between the two bands becomes easier and gains momentum, I muster the courage to peek at Savage, and find him already staring at me. Or, more accurately, *glaring* at me. Glowering, like he wants to beat the hell out of me.

Oh, dear. Is Mister Rockstar pissed about what Kendrick just now revealed? Because, if so, I'm not sorry. The man made me have to reschedule half the stuff on my calendar and cancel the rest. So, I think I'm allowed to be a tiny bit annoyed. Lesson learned, though. Annoyed or not, I'll shut my trap going forward.

Savage slowly slides a bite of food into his gorgeous mouth and chews, not taking his eyes off me.

So, I arch my eyebrow, and do the same.

He subtly mimics my facial expression, like he's mocking me.

So I shoot him a look that says, *Come at me, bro.*

He doesn't hesitate. He makes a face that says, *Oh, I will . . .* and then looks away.

Damn it! When will I learn to look away *first?*

Feeling pissed at myself, I take a big bite of food and tune into the conversation happening around me. It seems Kai and one of my musicians went to the same music school and have several mutual friends.

"I had classes with your older brother, Sebastian!" Kai says to my musician, Tate, connecting the dots.

"No way!" Tate replies.

"Is Sebastian still playing for Alicia Keys?" Kai asks.

"No, not anymore. Right now, he's playing in the house band for *Sing Your Heart Out*. He's been doing that for the past three seasons."

Kai laughs. "Holy shit! Is that a cushy gig?"

"*Super* cushy. No travel. Easy songs and arrangements. Sebastian could do it in his sleep."

"I bet."

Everyone at the table joins in with questions and comments about the show, with Titus rolling his eyes and calling it the most "cringey-ass show ever."

"Yeah, it's cringey as hell," Tate, my musician, agrees. "But a massive gravy train. My brother's salary from the show itself is shit, total shit, but he gets so many side gigs from the contacts he makes on the show, it's turned out to be a goldmine. Now that the show had its season finale last night, he's getting ready to go on tour with Hugh Delaney's band. Who, of course, he met on the show."

"Good for him," Kai says. "Although I'd sooner shoot myself than play Hugh Delaney songs, night after night."

"Hey, it's a steady job," Tate says. "They're not always easy to come by for a musician."

"Oh, of course," Kai says, quickly backtracking. "I know it's tough out there. Any musician would leap at a regular gig on a popular TV show. Good for him."

"I watched the final performances last night," Ruby interjects. "I can't wait to find out who won in the big reveal tonight. I'm hoping Deanna."

"I saw the finale, too," my musician, Tate, says. "Did you see Aloha kick the crap out of Hugh?"

"I saw that!" Ruby says, laughing. "I thought both contestants did such a great job. I think it's so fun to watch people trying to make their dreams come true, any way they can."

"I agree," I say, my heart thumping. As this conversation has worn on, I've felt internal pressure to mention I'm going to be on the next season of the show. The lineup hasn't been announced yet, but that's not why I haven't mentioned it to this group. Obviously, this is a highly trustworthy crowd. I think I've held off because I'm a little embarrassed to admit I'll be appearing on a show half these people think is "cringey-ass." Testing the waters, I say, "In my opinion, the only thing that's really cringey about the show is Hugh Delaney."

"I agree completely," Ruby says. "But even then, watching Hugh *pretend* to be some kind of down to earth everyman, when everyone knows he's secretly the biggest prima donna on the show, is super entertaining to me."

"To me, too!" I say, laughing.

"What does your brother say about Hugh?" Kai asks.

Tate chuckles. "My brother says Hugh is a flaming cunt."

Everyone laughs uproariously while I shift my weight in my chair. If I don't say something now, I feel like it will seem weird later, when my name is announced and everyone realizes I sat here and said nothing.

"Titus and I used to watch the show every week with our mom," Ruby says.

"*You* watched with Mom," Titus says. "I never did."

"Yes, you did. Remember, you were obsessed with that one contestant . . . *Kikuko?*"

Titus grins. "Oh, yeah. *Kikuko.* She was hot."

Everyone laughs, except Savage, who hasn't laughed once during this entire conversation. At this point, I'm not sure if he's even capable of laughing.

I clear my throat, still mustering my courage. "I used to watch with my mom and sister every week," I say, looking at Ruby. "And guess who's always been my mom's favorite?" I snort. "*Hugh.*"

Everyone chuckles. Again, everyone except Savage. And I

suddenly realize this is it. My last chance to mention that I'm going to be appearing as a mentor on the next season. If I don't say it now, the conversation will shift and I'll lose my chance. I take a deep breath. "I'm actually going to be on the show next season. Just one episode, as a mentor for Aloha's team."

The table explodes with congratulations and reactions from everyone except Savage. Most notably, Titus apologizes for calling the show "cringey-ass" earlier.

"No need to apologize," I say. "It *is* cringey-ass."

"But that's its charm," Ruby interjects. "Congrats, Laila. That's *awesome*."

"Thank you. The best part was telling my mom. She shrieked with joy when she found out."

"Yeah, and I bet the paycheck won't suck, either," Titus says.

"Actually, the pay for mentors is almost nothing," I admit. "Only a couple thousand bucks—just enough to meet union minimums."

My musician, Tate, says, "Yeah, my brother says they're cheap-ass bastards to everyone but the judges. The judges make millions per season, while everyone else makes peanuts." He smiles at me. "I'm sure it'll be well worth your while, for reasons other than the salary."

"My label head and agent both think so. Honestly, I'd have said yes for no money at all. Just for the exposure."

Savage scoffs and, for the first time, deigns to enter the conversation. "Never do *anything* for free, unless it's for charity. But definitely not for a cringey-ass TV show that's making money, hand over fist, for everyone but the talent. Always know your worth, Laila. If you don't, nobody else will."

I furrow my brow in surprise. I'm not certain if he was intending to compliment me, or chastise me, with that comment. All I know is it felt like the latter. "There was no way to push back on the money," I insist. "They've got a waiting list a mile long of people wanting to be a mentor. Plus, like I said, Reed and my agent, who's one of the best in the business, *both* said it was worth it to take the gig, so that's what I did. But, regardless, it's one day of work to make my mom extremely happy. And that's enough for me."

Savage rolls his eyes. "Never mix emotion and business, Laila. That's a recipe for disaster."

What the fuck? Who does he think he is? I pull a face that hopefully expresses my extreme annoyance. "I don't know why you think it's your place to offer me unsolicited business advice," I say. "Especially when I've already signed the contract and can't do anything about it now. I had one of the top agents in LA, plus Reed, both *adamantly* advising me to take the deal, so I did."

"I don't know your agent, but I know Reed is always looking out for *Reed*."

"Good, because our interests are perfectly aligned. The show will boost my music sales and profile, so I can make big money down the line, both for Reed and myself. Not everything is about instant gratification, Savage, contrary to what you might think."

He smirks but says nothing . . . but the air between us suddenly feels like it's crackling with electricity.

"Sounds like you made a great decision to me!" Ruby chirps, her eyes telling Savage not to say another word.

Slowly, Savage picks up his water bottle and takes a long, languid sip, his eyes trained on mine and his body language oozing with disdain.

I shouldn't do it. I shouldn't care about his opinion, but I do. My breathing stilted, I say, "So, I take it you agree the show is cringey-ass?"

"I do. My grandmother loves it, so I've seen it a few times. And it gives me hives every time."

I tighten my jaw. "Well, thank goodness, you're not the one they've asked to be on it, then."

"Thank goodness for small mercies." He puts his water bottle down. "Obviously, you're happy about this, so I'm happy for you. Congrats."

I shoot him daggers. Even while saying all the right words, his tone is infuriating. Doesn't he realize my career is at a totally different level than his, and almost certainly will *never* reach the towering heights of his? So excuse me if I've taken a job he considers beneath him. A job I'm honestly really excited about.

Out of nowhere, Savage bites back a smile in reaction to whatever he's seeing on my face. He licks his lips, suggestively, and, suddenly, despite my annoyance with him, I'm feeling highly aroused. Without warning, warmth oozes into my core and between my legs, making me pulse and tingle. And that's how I know there's something *really* wrong with me . . . because being angry with this man only makes me want to fuck him, all the more.

I stand, suddenly feeling the need to get away from him. To save myself. I announce, awkwardly, "I think it's time for me to meet my hair and makeup woman in my dressing room." It's not true. It's not even close to time for that. But that's what came out of my mouth. My gaze still holding Savage's and my cheeks burning, I add, "I'll probably call my mom, too, for a little pre-show pep talk." Why am I saying that? These people don't care about my To Do List. My face blooming, I peel my eyes off Savage's to address the rest of his band. "Have a great show, guys. I'll watch from the wings."

They wish me a great show, too, and I thank them, before turning on my heel and striding out of the greenroom as fast as my legs will carry me, feeling Savage's dark eyes on my backside as I go.

TEN

LAILA

There's music blaring in Titus' hotel suite. Drunk, stoned people are all around me, laughing and playing drinking games. Beer pong and Drunk Jenga, mainly. We're celebrating Titus' and Ruby's joint twenty-fifth birthday tonight at a post-show party. All the musicians from both bands are here, plus, a select group of staffers and crew. And, glory be, I'm the perfect level of drunk. Still totally coherent and in control of myself, but feeling fine as wine and *invincible.*

For what feels like the hundredth time tonight, my eyes drift to Savage across the crowded suite to find him already looking at me like he wants to murder me. Or fuck me. Or fuck my face. With him, I'm never sure which is which.

I should look away, I think. But the second I think it, Savage looks away first. Dammit! The only reason I held Savage's gaze in the first place was so I could look away *first!*

It's par for the course between us. The way it's been since Philadelphia, two weeks ago. We stare and glare and have lengthy nonverbal conversations. But we don't talk. Ever. So, tonight, I've decided to reset the game clock, meaning I'm never going to speak to Adrian Savage again, *ever*, unless *he* speaks to me *first*. Is he *still* pissed about the little bitchfest I had with my assistant about his lateness on day one? Or has he simply decided he doesn't like me because I pushed back on his unsolicited career advice? Either way, he can kiss my ass.

Oh, God. I wish Savage would kiss my ass. And then, the rest of me.

Stop, Laila.

Ha.

I take a long swig from my bottle of whiskey and lean my back against a wall in a corner of the crowded hotel suite. I'm acting like an antisocial weirdo at this party, which is totally unlike me. But I've reached my breaking point with Savage and his constant brooding and glaring. I don't expect him to treat me with the kind of warmth Ruby and Kendrick always do, obviously. Those two are sunshine in human form. But I can't stand this constant tension between us. Something's gotta give. Somehow, I've got to shake things up and force Savage to make the first move. *But how?*

My phone buzzes in my free hand, and when I look at the screen it's a text from Malik, asking me if I'm available to FaceTime.

> **Me: Sorry, no. At a noisy bday party. What's up?**
>
> **Tall_Man: I'm coming to your show in NYC!**
>
> **Me: Which one? Friday night regular show at Radio City or Sat night charity concert with lots of bands at The Garden?**
>
> **Tall_Man: Sat night at The Garden. I'd come to both but I've got a game on Friday. I'll come backstage**

to say hi and take you out for late dinner afterwards. Yes?

Me: Gotta do a dinner thing after the show with Reed and all the other artists on the bill. You can come as my guest, if you want. We're allowed a plus one.

Tall_Man: Hell yeah. See you then, beautiful.

Me: See ya then, dude. Good luck in your game(s)!

I smile wickedly to myself and take a long slug of my whiskey. Well, damn, if I'm looking to shake things up, I think that might very well do the trick.

After putting my phone away, I look across the crowded suite at Savage again. This time, he's looking at something on Kai's phone. So, I scan the party again, this time landing on darling Kendrick, who's already looking at me. When my eyes meet Kendrick's, the smile he beams at me would light up the darkest night.

Aw, Kendrick. I think he's still got a crush on me. In fact, I know he does. If I gave him the green light, he'd throw away our budding friendship in a heartbeat for something more. But, unfortunately, I'm just not feeling that way for him. I wish I were. What sane, functional, self-respecting woman *wouldn't* want a guy like Kendrick Cook? Ergo, I'm a nut job.

I take another long slug from my bottle, just as Savage and Kai approach Kendrick and divert his attention from me. Kendrick says something to Savage that makes him throw his head back and laugh from the depths of his soul. And my jaw practically clanks to the floor. I've never seen that before. Savage can laugh? And like that? Holy shit.

All of a sudden, I'm flooded with a weird cocktail of emotions. A thumping attraction to Savage that physically takes my breath away. And, weirdly, jealousy because I wasn't the one who elicited that laugh from Mr. Pouty Face.

When Savage comes down from laughing, he pulls out a box of

cigarettes and holds it up to his two besties. And then, off he goes, straight out the door of Titus' suite, obviously intending to smoke a cigarette outside.

I don't hesitate. My chest heaving, I march toward the door, eager to seize this unique opportunity to talk to Savage alone. We've never had a private conversation before. Never been in a room alone. And I must admit I'm dying to have his full attention. To get to know him. Maybe even find out what kinds of things make him belly laugh, against all odds. But, mostly, I want to find out why the hell he hates me so much, and has since day one.

When I get outside, the night air is brisk but not uncomfortable. I wander around, briefly, before locating Savage around a corner. He's sitting on the ground in the dark with his back against a building, looking out at the dark ocean below while smoking a cigarette.

As I approach, Savage blows out a long plume of smoke into the night. And I can't help thinking the moment feels like a painting that'd hang in a contemporary art museum: "Moody Demi-God in Contemplation."

"Mind if I join you?" I ask, coming to a stop over him.

Savage pats the ground. "I saved you a seat."

I get settled next to him and he holds up his box of cigarettes, offering me one.

I shake my head. "I don't smoke. I hate the taste, actually." I offer him my bottle of whiskey and he takes a long, greedy sip.

"I don't think I knew you smoked," I say.

He returns the bottle to me. "I only smoke when I'm drunk, which doesn't happen very often." He licks his lips, slowly. Suggestively. "I've got a big-time oral fixation. When I get drunk, it becomes overpowering to me . . ." He licks his lips again. "And I feel like I *have* to put something in my mouth."

Oh, Jesus Christ. The boy just flash-melted my panties.

I clear my throat, pretending I didn't understand the sexual innuendo dripping from his comment. "I noticed you doing shots at Reed's party. I assumed you get drunk regularly, like the Rockstar Manual requires."

"Actually, that was the last time I got shitfaced. It was Kendrick's birthday. In my band, we always get shitfaced on each other's birthdays. It's not optional."

"That was the last time you drank?"

"No. I'll have a beer or whatever. But I won't get *drunk*. I've got a rule I never 'drown my sorrows.' Drinking has to be about having fun for me. Otherwise, if I drink when I'm angry or upset in any way, I wind up being a huge asshole." He shrugs. "Plus, I have to eat and drink fairly clean most of the time to keep myself in shape . . ." He lifts his shirt, haphazardly, momentarily revealing the jaw-dropping grooves in his abs. "Looking like this is a big part of the job. And I can't do it, unless I stay disciplined and committed."

I lift my eyebrows in surprise. "Huh. I think 'Rockstar Cliché Bingo' requires you to drink like a fish, *especially* to drown your sorrows. The last time I checked, there were no bingo squares labeled 'eat clean and stay disciplined and committed to maintain abs of steel.'"

Savage chuckles and takes the bottle from me. "Meh. I already check plenty of boxes in 'Rockstar Cliché Bingo.' No need to check them *all* off, right?"

"You think you're a rockstar cliché?" I ask.

He looks at me, as if to say, *Well, obviously*. But he says, "If I'm not already, then I'm well on my way." He takes a long drag of his cigarette. "Honestly, one of my biggest fears is that I'll become so beholden to the money and fame and all the . . . *expectation*, I'll forget who I am and why I do this. I'll become exactly that—a cliché. A parody of myself." He looks out at the dark ocean. "I mean, come on, I've got to think 'dick pic trending on Twitter' is at the center square on *every* 'Rockstar Cliché Bingo' card, right? So, I'm probably already fucked."

I stare at his exquisite profile for a long moment, overcome by my attraction to him, and finally say, "I heard a rumor you posted that shot yourself—for publicity or whatever. True?"

He scoffs. "Not true." He flicks some ash from his cigarette onto the ground. "I had nothing to do with it, other than I was stupid enough to take a shower after sex with someone I barely knew, without locking the door."

I contemplate that response for a moment, while, again, admiring his gorgeous profile. His lips as he sucks on his cigarette. I hate cigarettes and don't find them sexy. But I must admit the way Savage is sucking on that thing, and licking his lips in between, makes me wonder what it would be like to kiss him. To have him perform oral sex on me. *Sex, sex, sex.* Suddenly, that's all I'm thinking about. Sex with Adrian Savage.

I clear my throat and motion to the cigarette between his lips. "Aren't you worried you're gonna get addicted? Nicotine is supposedly more addictive than cocaine."

Savage shrugs. "Like I said, I only smoke when I'm drunk and feel the overwhelming urge to put something in my mouth." He licks his lips again, this time even more suggestively than before. And, right on cue, I'm feeling the beginning stirrings of arousal again.

I shift my position on the ground, trying to alleviate the faint pulsing between my legs. "My dad was a heavy smoker and my sister and I once stole one of his cigarettes, when we were, like, nine and twelve. And the minute I inhaled, I thought I was going to die. I thought it was the most disgusting thing I'd ever tasted in my life."

"And you've never tried it again?"

I shake my head. "Why would I, when I know how bad it is for me? Plus, I associate smoking with my father, and he's not a good memory."

"Is he dead?"

"No. Just out of my life. And good riddance."

He holds up the bottle. "Cheers to that." He takes a swig and hands it to me.

"Cheers to that," I echo, before taking a long guzzle. "Uh oh," I say. "Does this qualify as me drowning my sorrows, now that I've mentioned my asshole father?"

He chuckles. "Yeah. Probably."

"You seriously *never* drown your sorrows?"

He shrugs. "You associate cigarettes with your asshole father. I associate being an angry, pissed off drunk with mine. Good riddance."

"Cheers to that." I take a swig and hand him the bottle.

"Cheers to that," he echoes, before taking a long sip.

My heart is thundering at this unexpectedly amazing conversation. I don't know how I thought this "confrontation" was going to go when I marched out here . . . but never in a million years did I think it would go like *this*. Savage seems almost normal. Likeable and friendly. And insanely, irresistibly hot.

"So, what do you do whenever you feel like drowning your sorrows, if you don't drink?" I ask.

Savage blows a stream of smoke into the air, but this time, pointedly, away from me. "Various things. I work out. Write a song. Jack off. Or, if convenient, I fuck."

A soft whimper escapes my lips, so I press them together and look out at the ocean to gather myself. Well, that was a fascinating answer.

"You still dating the basketball player?" he asks, out of nowhere. And I'm shocked he knows that false fact about me. Kendrick told him about that? Now, why would he do that?

I pause, not sure how to play this. Should I come clean and admit I lied to Kendrick, because I didn't want to hurt his feelings? Or should I lean into the lie?

Before I've decided, Savage says, "I overheard Tracy putting Malik's name onto the VIP list for the New York charity show."

There's jealousy glinting in his dark eyes, as plain as day. He's trying to hide it, but it's there. The same way it was there when I flirted with Cash in front of him at Reed's party. And, suddenly, I know exactly how to play this. *Lean into the lie.*

"Yeah, he's coming," I reply casually. "He wanted to come to both nights, but he's playing a game on Friday night."

A scornful puff of air escapes Savage's nose. "Have you never googled him, for fuck's sake? Look at the Reddit boards about him, Laila! I wouldn't call him 'boyfriend material.'"

I'm flabbergasted. What an unexpected burst of passion from Mr. I Don't Give a Fuck! "Of course, I've googled him," I retort. "And it ain't pretty. But guess who else I've googled? *You*. And that shit ain't any prettier, Mr. Dick Pic. So, I'd advise you not to throw stones from your glass house."

"The difference is I don't *pretend* to be boyfriend material."

"People change and grow. They learn from their mistakes. Malik swears he's learned from his mistakes, and I believe him."

The first part of my statement is true. Malik has, indeed, sworn up and down he's a changed man who's now looking for a committed relationship. The second part, however—that I'm stupid enough to actually believe what Malik told me—is a bald-face lie. In fact, it's my firm belief Malik only said he's looking for a committed relationship because I told him that's what I'd need to sleep with him. I actually only said that to Malik to torture him. I've certainly had sex outside of a committed relationship in my life. But I won't do that with Malik Wallace. Hell no. There's no way I'm going to be nothing but another notch on that bad boy's belt.

Shaking his head, Savage takes a long slug from the bottle before saying, "Chris Rock once famously said men are only as faithful as their options. Looks like you're going to be putting that theory to the test with your 'boyfriend,' especially in a long distance relationship. Open your eyes, Fitzy. Basketball isn't that guy's only game."

Fitzy? I've never heard that before. It sounds to me like the name of a very tiny dog in a very fluffy tutu. I'm not sure I like it. But I decide, rather than mention this new, surprising nickname he's concocted for me, to call him something I've never called him, in return. "I find it perplexing you've gone to the trouble of googling Malik and his track record with women, *Adrian*. What a strange thing for you to be wasting your time doing."

Savage scowls when I call him Adrian, and then says, "I didn't google him, *Fitzy*. Kendrick did and then wouldn't shut the fuck up about what he'd found."

I feel my shoulders droop with disappointment. But why? I

should have known. Savage had the chance to hit on me at Reed's party, every bit as much as Malik did. And Savage chose to hit on everyone else *but* me, and then leave early with whoever he'd settled on, while I was performing onstage. "Not that it's any of your business," I say, "but Malik and I have had some detailed conversations about his past behavior and I've told him I won't put up with that kind of shit." *True.* "He's assured me he's a new man." Also, true. "I believe in second chances." Again, true, although I'm not sure Malik Wallace is deserving of one. "So, I've decided to believe what Malik has told me, unless and until he proves me wrong." *Lies, lies, lies.* I'm stupid when it comes to men, but I'm not a damned fool.

Savage rolls his eyes, looking remarkably, exquisitely pissed off. "A leopard doesn't change his spots, Laila. Don't be stupid."

"You think maybe you're projecting, *Adrian*? I've googled you, remember? And it looks to me like *you're* the one who's only as faithful as your options."

"That's *false*. I'm one hundred percent faithful, if I've made a commitment." He winks. "Which is why I rarely make one."

I scoff. "You want a medal for that?"

"No. I'm just defending myself. I'm a man of my word, if I've given it."

"So, obviously, you don't give your word regarding *punctuality*, huh?"

Savage's face ignites. "I knew it!" he shouts gleefully. "I knew you've been secretly losing your mind whenever I'm late and biting your tongue about it until it bleeds."

He's right. He's driven me bonkers these past two weeks with his perpetual lateness. Since that first time in Philadelphia, Savage was late for two additional soundchecks, as well as one early-morning departure on the buses. But all three times, I kept my mouth shut and my face neutral, even though I was annoyed as hell to witness him behaving so unprofessionally. I bat my eyelashes at him. "You've been late for something since Philly? I hadn't noticed."

Savage's nostrils flare as he hands the bottle back to me. But he says nothing.

For a long moment, we sit in silence, both of us biting back smiles. Until finally, Savage sighs and says, "Seriously, Fitzy. Dump the basketball player. If your kink is trying to be the one woman a cheater doesn't cheat on, then I've got news for you, baby. You need to find a new kink."

"Oh, yeah? Well, guess what, Adrian? If your kink is doling out unsolicited advice to me, then I've got news for you, baby. You need to shut the fuck up, motherfucker."

He bursts out laughing. I mean, the dude *belly* laughs. And I can't help feeling like I've accomplished something amazing.

His laughter subsiding, Savage brings the bottle to his lips and mutters, "Touché, Fitzy. Too-fucking-shay." I watch him sip and swallow, once again imagining his sensuous lips performing oral sex on me. It's impossible *not* to imagine it. Everything about his song "Come with Me" suggests he's an enthusiastic fan of that particular sex act. And the way he's moving his mouth right now is insanely sexy.

Suddenly, I find myself wondering how the groupie thing works with him. On the one hand, I know his reputation. When I said I've googled him, it was the truth. Not that I needed to google him. Everything about him screams "manwhore." Plus, I saw his reputation in action at Reed's party, firsthand, so I know the dude's got no qualms about hitting on women, one after another, until he gets what he wants.

On the other hand, I haven't actually seen Savage with a single woman during this tour. Do his handlers quietly bring groupies to his room in every new city? I've noticed he doesn't hang out and party nearly as much as his bandmates. Is that because he's typically otherwise engaged in his room?

"Call me *Savage*, by the way," he says, out of nowhere. "Only my family calls me Adrian."

"Only if you agree not to call me 'Fitzy' again."

"You don't like Fitzy?"

"It sounds like the name of a white fluffy dog wearing a tutu."

Savage chuckles. "Well, shit, now I've got no choice. You're Fitzy for life."

"Okay, then you're Adrian."

He pauses like he's weighing his options, and finally says, "Yeah, it's totally worth it."

I roll my eyes. "So, anyway, *Adrian,* the whole reason I came out here was to clear the air with you. I think maybe you've been pissed about me trash-talking you in Philly for being late, and I—"

"I'm not pissed about that."

"No?"

He pulls a face like that's a ridiculous notion. "Why would I give a flying fuck what you think?"

My lips part and my brow furrows. Did this motherfucker just *insult* me while forgiving me for insulting him? But before I've responded, the sound of sharp laughter and familiar voices cuts through the darkness and causes both of us to jolt and lean back like we've been doing something wrong over here.

The voices belong to Ruby, a couple people from my band, and *Kendrick.* And the minute Kendrick's voice becomes identifiable, Savage's entire body stiffens. He hastily stubs out his cigarette, clears his throat, and pops up, looking very much like a kid who's just been caught with his hand in a cookie jar.

"I think I'm gonna crash in my room now," he murmurs. And for a split-second, I think he's inviting me to join him. But, no. He quickly adds, "Do me a favor and tell Ruby and Titus I left the party and said happy birthday, okay?"

"Uh, sure," I reply, feeling vaguely disappointed. But I'm speaking to Savage's back. He's already on the move. High-tailing it out of here like a bank robber on the run. "Don't be late for the buses tomorrow!" I call out. And then add, pointedly, "*Adrian.*"

Just before his frame disappears into the dark night, Savage turns around, so that he's walking backward. Facing me now, he flashes me an impish grin and says, "I'm never late, *Fitzy.* Everyone else is just . . . *early.*"

ELEVEN

SAVAGE

New York, New York

My band and everyone else who played at tonight's charity concert at Madison Square Garden are seated at a long table in a swanky restaurant in Midtown, courtesy of our host, Reed Rivers. *And I'm shitfaced.* Breaking my hard and fast rule about never drinking to drown my sorrows. Because . . . Malik Wallace.

To anyone watching me drinking like a fish tonight, I'm sure I look like I'm merely celebrating tonight's amazing show, along with everyone else at this table. But I'm not. In reality, I'm fixated on that bastard's every movement. His every flirtatious smile, aimed directly at Laila. Basically, I've been drinking while trying to figure out how I can murder that motherfucker and get away with it.

"You called it at Reed's party," Kendrick says next to me, jutting his chin at Reed and his date on the far end of the table. Who's Reed's date tonight? Well, none other than Georgina, the sultry reporter I hit on as Kendrick's birthday present. The fact that Georgina is at Reed's side at all, a full two months later, is shocking enough. But factor in that Reed's brought her as his date to a work event, which isn't Reed's style, *and* that he's been packing on the PDA with her throughout the entire dinner, and I'm thinking this woman has cast a spell on The Prick, the likes of which I never would have believed.

But, whatever. I don't have the bandwidth to focus on Reed and his love life for very long. I'm too fixated on Laila and *hers*. Fucking Malik! When he walked into the greenroom at The Garden earlier tonight, I felt an almost primal desire to pummel his face. And the impulse has only grown as the evening, and my alcohol consumption, has worn on.

Unfortunately, the happy couple—Laila and her handsy MVP —is sitting immediately across from Kendrick and me at this long, crowded table, so I can't avoid constantly staring at them. And guess what? The fucker *never* stops touching Laila with his huge hands. *Ever.* At any given moment, Mr. Basketball's got his arm around Laila's shoulders, or a hand covering hers. Or maybe he's got his hand under the table, doing God knows what to her under there. Or if not any of that, he's touching her hair or leaning in to whisper into her ear—oftentimes, immediately after glowering at *me*.

Actually, I don't know if I'm imagining that last part. The glowering. Is Malik Wallace a mind reader? Or is the booze making my face a whole lot more readable than usual? Either way, the man clearly wants me, and everyone in this restaurant, to know the magnificent, sultry, talented Laila Fitzgerald is *his*.

The crazy thing is I don't get jealous, except when it comes to Laila. Why should I, when there are unlimited fish in the sea? And yet, here I am, contemplating physically attacking a professional athlete, despite my brain knowing, logically, he'd almost certainly beat my ass. Also, logically speaking, I know Malik's got every right to drape himself over his *own* girlfriend. I'm nobody to Laila, after all. If Malik were out of the picture, she'd be in Kendrick's arms. Not mine. And yet, I can't stop staring and plotting Malik's untimely demise.

I think the part that burns me the most is knowing Laila hooked up with Malik after meeting him at Reed's party. If I hadn't left when I did that night, if I'd sucked it up and walked over to her to welcome her to the tour the way my bandmates did, would everything be different now? I thought I was stepping aside for my best friend, which is something I can stomach, though not happily. But it turns out, I was stepping aside for Malik Wallace. And realizing that feels like a special kind of torture.

Kendrick leans into me, just as Malik whispers something to Laila that makes her giggle. "Fuck my life," Kendrick mutters. "Sitting across from them is my personal version of hell."

"Sorry, brother. That sucks. Let's drink another round."

I flag a server—a young woman I'd guess is an aspiring actress or model or dancer, given that this is Manhattan and she's lithe and stunning. And she immediately strides over to me with a big smile on her face.

"Another round," I say, motioning to my empty glass and Kendrick's. "Make 'em both doubles this time."

"Triples," Kendrick says.

"You got it, boys," she says with a wink. She bites her lower lip and leans into me. "If this is inappropriate, I'm sorry. But would you and Kendrick mind taking a selfie with me? I'm a huge fan."

Kendrick agrees, of course, because he's much nicer than me, and she pokes her head between us and snaps the photo. But when that task is done, she doesn't leave. Rather, she turns her attention on me, specifically, in a way I've seen many times, and whispers, "I'm a *huge* fan, Savage."

Well, that's not subtle. If history has taught me anything, she's telling me she's down to sleep with me tonight. If I'm right about that, I'm not interested. However, I couldn't help noticing, as we took that selfie, Laila was watching the interaction with blazing eyes. So, I decide, interested or not, to let Laila think she's not the only one who'll be getting laid tonight.

"Come here," I say to the waitress. I motion to her to lean closer, like I'm going to tell her a secret, and she follows my command with obvious excitement. I lean in, my body language shifting into fuckboy mode, the same way it did when I hit on Georgina at Reed's party. "What's your name, beautiful?"

"Desiree," she replies breathlessly. And I can almost see her heart pounding against her sternum.

"That's a sexy name. What's your favorite Fugitive Summer song?"

She doesn't hesitate. "'Come with Me.'"

It's not a surprise. I don't know if that song is genuinely a top favorite for all the women who've claimed as much. All I know is that song has gotten me laid more times than I can count. Whenever they say they love that one, in particular—my band's most brazenly sexual song—and then look at me the way this waitress is looking at me now—I can pretty much count on the next thing the woman says making it clear she's down to fuck.

The waitress licks her lips and adds, "I listen to that song *a lot,* Savage. *A lot, a lot.*"

It's been a while since I've had this particular conversation, simply because I grew tired of leading women down this predictable path. But I guess it's like riding a bike. You never truly forget how to ride, no matter how long it's been. Especially when you're trying to make a certain pop star with blazing blue eyes and sensual lips feel the same thing you've been feeling all night. *Seething jealousy.*

I glance at Laila to make sure she's still watching the show. She is. So, I decide to turn up the heat. Raising my voice a bit, for Laila's benefit, of course, I ask the waitress, "What are you doing later tonight, Desiree?"

"Nothing at all. I get off at midnight and don't work again until four tomorrow."

"That's convenient," I say. "As luck would have it, we've got a free day tomorrow. No travel. No show. I was planning to chill in my hotel room tomorrow."

Her ample chest heaves with excitement. "If you'd like some company, I could give you my number . . ."

"Sounds good." I glance at Laila again as I pull out my phone, and her face is a forest fire. At my prompting, the waitress tells me her number, and I make a big show of making sure I've entered it correctly.

"Yep, that's it," the waitress says. "I hope you call me tonight."

"I will," I say, although I'm not sure that's true. As long as I get her to sign an NDA, like Eli keeps telling me to do these days, then there's no reason for me *not* to call her. Fucking this waitress for ten hours straight would be a whole lot better than tossing and turning all night, imagining Malik fucking Laila. And yet, for some reason, I don't feel enthusiastic about the idea. In fact, the thought only makes me want to drink some more.

The waitress straightens up. "Crap. My manager is mad at me. I've got to get back to work. I'll get those drinks for you, gentlemen."

"Tequila shots, too!" Kendrick shouts.

"Got it!"

As the waitress strides away, I return my attention to Laila, eager to flash her a smug smile, but to my extreme disappointment, Laila isn't watching me any longer. She's standing and engaged in conversation with Reed.

"Thanks so much, Laila," Reed is saying. "I really appreciate this."

"I'm happy to do it," Laila replies. "Alessandra is adorable, and you know I adore Fish."

Reed says something I don't catch, due to some laughter at the far end of our table, and they wrap up their conversation.

Laila sits back down and immediately fields some seriously angry energy from Malik. I can't hear what he says to her, but, clearly, he's not happy with her.

"*Seriously?*" Laila replies sharply to Malik. She whisper-shouts, "I couldn't say no. Reed's the head of my label! And Alessandra is a brand-new artist who's really sweet. And her boyfriend, Fish, is a good friend of mine. You think, despite all that, I should have said no, so we could 'hang out' tomorrow?"

Malik snaps, "Don't get all pissy with me. You should be happy I wanted you to spend your free day with me."

"Keep your voice down," Laila says, before leaning in and whisper-shouting something I can't make out. Whatever it is, Malik doesn't like it.

"Thank you, Baby Jesus, there's *finally* trouble in paradise," Kendrick whispers to me.

"Sure looks like it," I say. "What did Reed ask Laila to do tomorrow? I couldn't hear."

"You know Fish's girlfriend, Alessandra?"

He motions to the end of the table, but I nod without looking. Everyone here knows Fish's girlfriend, Alessandra, at this point. Not only is she the same girl who looked so smitten with Fish at Reed's party two months ago, not only is she sitting next to Fish at the table now, Fish gave that girl a whopper of a kiss in the middle of the greenroom earlier, in front of *everyone,* and then proceeded to sing to her onstage during the concert. So, yeah, to put it mildly, I know Fish's girlfriend, Alessandra. In fact, so does everyone in the world by now.

Kendrick continues, "Alessandra has a one-song deal with River Records and her music video is shooting tomorrow in Brooklyn. From what I've gathered, it sounds like Reed and the director down there . . . That woman there." He points to a cute brunette who's sitting next to Reed. "Reed and the director came up with some complicated new storyline for the music video, just now, and Reed asked Laila to play a big part in it. Which means she'll be busy shooting all day tomorrow." Kendrick smiles wickedly. "Rather than hanging out with Malik."

I snicker. "What a cry baby."

Kendrick nods. "Hopefully, he'll keep crying until she's pissed enough to dump his ass tonight." He smiles. "And when she needs a shoulder to cry on tomorrow night, I'll be Johnny on the Spot."

Our server, Desiree, arrives with our new drinks and shots—plus, a flirtatious smile for me—and we dig in. We watch Reed making his way around the table, talking to every band, one by one, until, finally, reaching our band. After greeting all five of us, Reed tell us everything Kendrick has already told me about Alessandra's video shoot tomorrow. Except Reed doesn't ask us to come down for the whole day, as he asked Laila to do. He requests we drop by, at any convenient time, to shoot quick cameos. "I know it's your free day tomorrow," Reed says. "But I'll owe you guys a favor if you stop by. The cameos will take no more than fifteen minutes to shoot. You'd sit at a table in a coffeehouse and pretend to watch Alessandra playing her guitar onstage. We'll stitch it all together later in post-production."

Everyone in my band, other than me, says they'll try but can't promise anything. They're not trying to be jerks. It's just that everyone looks forward to those rare days off on the schedule, when we can crash and burn and not have a single obligation.

Reed looks at me, clearly most interested in securing my face, above all others, for the video. "I'd consider it a personal favor to me if you'd come tomorrow, Savage," he says. "It's important to me, for personal reasons, to make this song a huge hit for Alessandra. As big as I can make it." He pauses and it's clear it's going to pain him to say whatever's on his tongue. But he says it, anyway. "Please."

Whoa. That was as close to groveling as I've ever heard from Reed. Even so, I don't care about making Reed happy, or having him owe me a favor. What I *do* care about, however, is that Laila has already committed to being there tomorrow, all day—and, apparently, *without* Malik. Also, that she's looking at me right now, awaiting my response with bated breath.

"Yeah, I'm down," I say. "As long as I don't need to get there until the afternoon." I look at Laila and smirk. "It sounds like I'm gonna be pretty busy tonight and into the first part of the morning."

Laila snarls before looking away and I can't help smiling

broadly at her reaction. God, she's fun. Wind her up and watch her go.

Reed claps my shoulder and thanks me effusively, before moving along to the next band at the table, the guys from Watch Party.

Biting back my smile, I return my attention to Laila across the table and discover she's gotten up and is talking to Fish and Alessandra and Georgina. But guess who's looking straight at me right now? *Malik*. With eyes like laser beams.

I rise, flip him off, and stride to the bathroom on the far side of the restaurant. After taking a piss, I wash my hands and face and stare at myself in the mirror for a moment. "Pull yourself together," I whisper. "If you had her, you wouldn't even want her. You only want what you can't have." Satisfied with my pep talk, I open the door to the bathroom and enter the short hallway, and immediately get slammed, rather forcefully, into a wall.

"Are you fucking her?" Malik whisper-shouts, his large body pinning mine into the wall.

"Fuck off," I say, pushing against his hulking frame. But it's no use. As fit as I am, his body is a brick wall.

He grabs my shirt. "Are you the reason she never answers my calls?"

"Let go of me unless you want to hear from my lawyers, Malik."

He exhales a warm breath on my face and lets me go. Which is a damned good thing because, now that I'm here, I'm realizing my fantasy about strangling him was a pipe dream.

I lean into Malik's angry face. "If I were fucking Laila, trust me, you wouldn't be here tonight to ask me about it. One taste of me, and she'd ditch your ass in a heartbeat."

Without warning, he shoves me again, crashing my back into the wall—although, thankfully, I'm way too drunk to feel it. Immediately, a nearby waiter appears in the hallway and frantically orders Malik to leave the area.

As Malik walks back to the table, I yell to his back, "If you can't keep your woman satisfied, don't blame me!"

"Mr. Savage, please," the waiter says. "Cool off outside. *Please.*"

"Gladly."

My veins flooded with adrenaline and my breathing ragged and hot, I stalk across the restaurant and straight outside into the crisp night, mustering every drop of willpower along the way not to punch a hole in a fucking wall.

TWELVE
SAVAGE

Once outside in front of the restaurant, I bum a cigarette off one of the valet parkers and then pace back and forth, inhaling on it like a lifeline, until, a moment later, Laila bursts outside and marches up to me.

"What the hell is wrong with you?" she shouts. "Malik said you *attacked* him outside the bathrooms?"

I roll my eyes. "Wow, you've got yourself a real gem there, Laila. What are you doing with a psychopath like him?"

Her nostrils flare. "What's it to you?"

My body feels alive with adrenaline and booze—jealousy and lust. "You can get any man you want and you know it. You've got the nicest guy in the world, practically throwing himself at you— which, by the way, he *never* does for *anyone*—and you'd rather be with an asshole like *Malik?*"

She looks at me blankly.

"Kendrick!" I shout, enraged at her lack of comprehension. "Don't pretend you don't know he's totally into you."

Now it's Laila's turn to be enraged. "That's what you want to say to me right now?" she yells. "The most pressing thing you want to tell me in this moment is that you're pissed I haven't given

Kendrick a shot?" She pulls on her hair and screams at the top of her lungs. "God, I hate you! You're so infuriating!"

I blow smoke in her face and she coughs and sputters and waves at the air.

"Put that thing out!" she screams. "Kill yourself, if you must. But leave me out of it!"

I drop the cigarette onto the sidewalk and stub it out angrily with my shoe. "Your boyfriend is the one who attacked me, Laila. Not the other way around. He's convinced you've been sleeping with me."

She looks genuinely concerned. "Are you hurt?"

"Not at all, unless you count the fact that I'm pained you've got such bad taste in men."

Her chest heaves sharply. "Why do you care, Savage? You want me to break up with him, so you can pimp me out to *Kendrick*?" She waits a beat for my reply and when it doesn't come, she turns into a goddamned demon before my eyes. "You'd sleep better at night knowing *Kendrick* was the one fucking me, instead of *Malik*? Huh? Is that what you want? Or is there someone else you'd prefer to do the fucking?"

Oh, God, I want her. I want to pull her to me and press my lips to hers and claim her right here and now. I want to take her back to my hotel room and rip off her clothes and eat her pussy and do every filthy thing imaginable to her. But before I've figured out if I'm willing to betray Kendrick, without first speaking to him about it, a group that includes Kendrick emerges from the restaurant. Besides my best friend, there's Ruby and Kai, Reed and Georgina, the guys from 22 Goats and their dates, and more.

"Come with us, Laila," Kendrick says. "We're going to Times Square to see a billboard of Colin in his underwear." He's talking about Colin Beretta, the drummer of 22 Goats—a tatted badass who hates my guts because I fucked his on-again-off-again girl-friend last year while they were on a break.

"I can't make it," Laila says curtly. "But, thanks."

Kendrick looks at me. "I didn't bother asking you because I

know you've got plans with the waitress. Have fun!" With that, he jogs to catch up to the group, and when I return to Laila, or at least, to the spot where she was standing a minute ago, she's gone—angrily stomping toward the front door of the restaurant.

"Laila!" I shout at the top of my lungs. And she turns around in front of the doorway, breathing hard.

"Break up with him."

She swallows hard. "And then what, Savage? You'd fuck me like one of your groupies? Like that waitress inside? Wow, lucky me! Or would you pimp me out to *Kendrick*? Either way, no thanks." With that, she turns on her heel and marches into the restaurant. And the minute she's gone, some fans who've been standing on the sidelines of our screaming match descend on me, apparently unbothered by my obvious personal turmoil.

The bodyguard assigned to me appears, out of nowhere, and helps me negotiate the onslaught. With his help, I briefly go through the motions, giving a few selfies, until Laila emerges from the restaurant with Malik in tow, both of them looking somber. Quickly, they dip into a dark SUV that's been awaiting them at the curb. And just like that, they're gone. Heading back to the hotel to fight or fuck or both.

And I'm distraught.

I mumble my goodbyes to the remaining fans and quickly take off down the street, with my bodyguard keeping pace behind me. A couple blocks into my journey, I dip into a liquor store and buy a large bottle of vodka, which I drink like Gatorade throughout the remainder of my journey.

Not surprisingly, by the time I arrive at my hotel, I'm not only blitzed out of my mind, I'm also beside myself with rage and regret. By now, I've relived my fight with Laila a hundred times, each time wishing I'd played it differently. Let down my guard. Figured out my feelings in time to say them out loud to her. Whatever those feelings might be. Honestly, I'm still not entirely sure.

I slide the keycard in my door and hurtle myself into my suite and immediately do the thing I've been aching to do all night: I punch a hole in the wall. Because that's what rockstar clichés do, right? They have drunken temper tantrums and trash their hotel rooms.

I can't believe I've been jacking off, alone in my room, every night of this goddamned tour, foregoing every woman who's slipped me her number, all because I've been waiting like a puppy for Laila to be single. For Kendrick to grow tired of waiting for Laila to be single. For Kendrick to do what he always does on every tour —slide into a tour "relationship" with some staffer or crew member —and thereby leave me to finally seduce Laila, boyfriend or not, without worrying that I'm betraying my best friend. The guy who believed in me, when nobody else did, changing my life forever.

My knuckles throbbing from punching the wall, I grab my phone and swipe into my contacts, looking for that waitress' number. But, quickly, I realize I don't want her. If Laila hadn't been sitting there tonight, watching me flirt, I never would have bothered to get that number at all. The waitress was too thirsty for my taste. Just like that model in Barcelona who fucked me and kissed me and said all the right things on a night when I was feeling particularly lonely . . . and then took off with my wallet and made my dick an internet star.

I toss my phone onto the nightstand with a loud grunt, just before a wave of nausea seizes me. I stumble into the bathroom and wash my face with cold water, trying to stave off the inevitable. But it's no use. *Fuck.*

I drop to my knees at the toilet and lose my fancy dinner and drinks into the bowl. When I'm finally empty, I wash my face again, brush my teeth, strip off my clothes, and stagger, naked, into the bedroom. I flop onto the bed, groaning as the room spins around me. As visions of Laila getting fucked by Malik ravage my drunken brain.

Ever since Philly, I've been busting my ass to be on time for Laila—to soundchecks and buses. As much as possible, anyway. Have I been perfect? No. Because, unfortunately, I get easily distracted sometimes. While, other times, I get hyper-fixated. Especially when writing a song, time ceases to exist for me. Which isn't a great thing for time management. Plus, I try to say yes whenever Mimi wants to talk to me, even if the timing is terrible. So, yeah, I admit I'm not going to win any prizes for punctuality. But I have genuinely tried my best, and for only one reason: *to make Laila like me.*

But now, I realize I never should have bothered. No matter what I do, she's always going to hate me and think I'm a selfish rock-star cliché—an asshole who doesn't give a shit about anyone but himself. Well, fuck Laila Fitzgerald. If she thinks she's already got plenty of reasons to hate me, then she ain't seen nothing yet.

THIRTEEN

LAILA

"Cut!" Maddy, the director of the music video, calls out. "That was perfect, ladies! Great job."

I straighten up and let the baseball bat in my hand dangle at my side, as Reed's girlfriend, Georgina, my co-star in this scene, does the same. We're shooting on the street in front of the coffeehouse where we've been shooting throughout the day—a scene featuring Georgina and me bashing the hell out of an old sedan that's supposedly owned by our two-timing boyfriend, played by hunky actor Keane Morgan.

Throughout this particular scene, Keane's been looking on, horrified and helpless, as Georgina and I have smashed his car to smithereens. It's the climactic final scene of our "love triangle" storyline. And I must say, it's been my favorite to shoot. Talk about cathartic! The perfect release after my two fights last night. First, the one I had with Savage in front of the restaurant. And, later, the one I had with Malik in the car, when I soundly told him to fuck right off and never, ever call me again.

As it's turned out, shooting this video was the perfect way to spend the day. The song is fantastic. The artist, Alessandra, sweet and talented. And the video concept is hilarious and adorable. Plus, it's been fun seeing all the River Records artists who've dropped by to shoot their cameos. Surely, with everything this video has going for it, it's going to become a viral sensation.

Not surprisingly, Savage was too busy banging his waitress to keep his word and come down here today. But, luckily for Alessandra, everyone else who gave their word to Reed last night, kept it.

Logically, I know I should have expected Savage to break his promise to Reed. And yet, somehow, my heart stupidly held onto hope he'd finally do something kind and selfless, for once in his life. If only for Fish, who's a great and loyal friend to everyone. But I guess Savage is always gonna be Savage. A narcissist, through and through.

"Okay, guys," our director, Maddy, says. She looks at her watch. "With the remainder of our daylight, I'd like to shoot some close-ups and pickups. Shots of Laila and Georgina standing over the car, raising their bats and looking like badass bitches."

Georgina and I respond enthusiastically, of course. But as Maddy moves us into position, the unthinkable happens. A taxi pulls up a few feet away and Savage emerges, looking like a shit sandwich.

He drags his sorry ass to the stunned group, runs his hand through his dark hair, and says, "Am I too late to shoot my cameo?"

"No, not at all!" Maddy chirps. "We're so glad you made it!" She turns to Georgina and me. "Why don't you ladies take five while we shoot Savage inside for a couple minutes. This will be quick."

"That's okay," Savage says. "Finish what you're shooting here, while you've still got good light. I'm not in any rush."

"Oh, thank you," Maddy says. "Are you sure?"

"Absolutely." Savage walks over to stand with Fish and Reed, who are watching from a distance, while Maddy returns her attention to directing Georgina, Keane, and me.

Maddy says, "Laila, stand over there, holding the baseball bat over your head, like you're going to smash the car."

I comply with Maddy's request, and she looks at a nearby monitor.

"Great. Just move to your left a touch. Perfect. Now, give me your bitchiest face and stick out your chest."

I follow her directions and she hoots with laughter.

"You're so freaking gorgeous, Laila. And *so* photogenic. Okay, we've got what we need from you. Georgina, you're up. Same thing."

As Maddy directs Georgina, I can't help looking at Savage. And what I see there is molten lava. Which, frankly, pisses me off. He has the nerve to look at me with lust in his eyes, after spending the day in a marathon fuck session with that waitress?

I saunter over to Savage and stand next to him, shoulder to shoulder, watching Maddy finish up with Georgina.

"Hello, Adrian," I say.

"Hello, Fitzy."

"You look like shit. You didn't get much sleep last night, huh?"

He says nothing.

I shouldn't do it. I know it. But letting sleeping dogs lie has never been my strong suit. My jaw tight, I say, "I hope you signed the waitress' tits before you sent her on her merry way. That'd be an appropriate souvenir."

The slightest smirk curls Savage's sensuous lips. "I did, actually. Signed her ass and pussy, too."

"Lovely. So glad you two had fun."

"We sure did. How about you and Malik?"

"Oh, we had a blast. I can barely walk today."

"Lovely."

"It was. I'm so impressed you managed to get your ass down here, despite your marathon fuck session."

"What can I say? I'm a saint."

"That's the word I always think of when I think of you. Adrian Savage. He's a *saint*."

"Hey, fun fact. Did you know cheaters are the ones who are

always the most paranoid about their girlfriends cheating on them?"

"Is that so? How interesting."

"It's a proven fact. Cheaters project what *they* do—aka *cheating* —onto their partner. And then, in some cases, attack innocent bystanders outside of restaurant bathrooms, usually because they're insecure about their tiny dicks."

"Well, that's not an issue for Malik."

"Glad to hear it."

"Me, too," I say, my eyes trained on the action in front of Maddy's camera. "In fact, I had the best sex of my life with Malik last night. Wooh! Hot, hot, hot."

"What does the 'best sex of your life' mean to you, Laila? Stamina? Emotional connection?"

"Both."

"Nice. I notice you didn't mention multiple orgasms. Squirting orgasms . . ."

"Oh, well, that, too. *Of course.* In fact, I've never had *two* squirting orgasms in a row the way I did last night. Woo! Man, oh man, Malik really got me going like a geyser."

His features contort with disdain. "You think squirting *twice* is 'coming like a geyser'? Ha! You poor thing." He pats my shoulder. "Thoughts and prayers."

Damn! I wanted my lie to sound believable, so I tried to pick a highly credible number. In truth, I haven't had multiple orgasms before, let alone a squirting one—or *two*—so I thought what I said would sound super impressive. But is having *two* orgasms, in rapid-fire succession, let alone squirting ones—actually unimpressive, or is Savage messing with me?

"We're ready for you, Savage," Maddy says, saving me from myself.

Savage smiles at her. "You only need me to sit at a table and pretend I'm watching Alessandra performing, right?"

"Yep. That's it. Easy peasy."

"Okay, good. If you'd said you need me to walk on-camera, or dance around or something, that'd be a tough one for me. I'm super exhausted from screwing a waitress all night and day and making her squirt, five times, in rapid succession."

"Oh," Maddy says. "Okay. Um. Yeah, no worries there. Just sit and nod your head a little."

"Cool." Savage opens the door to the coffeehouse, cool as a cucumber, and motions for Maddy to pass through. She enters the building, followed by her camera operators and crew. Then, Reed, Georgina, Fish, and Alessandra. Until finally, everyone has entered the building through the door held by Savage, except for me. Smiling politely at me, his dark eyes burning like hot coals, Savage says, "After you, my dear."

"I think I'll stay out here and get some fresh air," I say. "Maybe call my boyfriend and thank him for all the amazing sex last night."

"I'm sure he'll appreciate the call. Where is he, by the way? I would have expected him to come down here to cheer you on. Maybe even shoot a cameo himself. Why not?"

"Oh, he desperately wanted to come, but something came up this morning—some big basketball thing."

"A basketball 'thing'?"

"A meeting."

"A basketball *meeting*?"

"Mm-hmm. So, I told him to go to his thing to talk about basketball things and meet me back in our room tonight for another round of amazing sex."

"Cool. Well, here's hoping Malik watches a few instructional videos on YouTube before tonight, right?" He holds up crossed fingers. "A girl can hope." With that, he strides through the door, leaving me standing alone on the sidewalk, feeling even more homicidal than I did last night when I kicked that bastard Malik out of the SUV—and out of my life—for good.

FOURTEEN

LAILA

Atlanta, Georgia

The crowd cheers as I strike my final note of my final song. And when the music stops, the crowd breaks into a veritable roar. Their applause is mostly for me, I think. But I'm not stupid. I'm well aware they're also thrilled to be that much closer to Fugitive Summer finally taking the stage.

"Thank you, Atlanta!" I shout into my microphone, feeling practically drugged with euphoria. I can't believe I get to do this for a living! And that, in each new city, audiences have increasingly started singing along with *every* word to *every* song. Not just the big hit from my debut album. Not only the lead-off single from my sophomore one. And not just the catchy choruses. They're singing the verses *and* choruses of songs that haven't made a big splash on the charts, as of yet! When this tour began six weeks ago, I never would have dreamed that big.

I know the phrase "this is a dream come true" is frequently overused in this world. But that's the phrase that comes to mind whenever I'm performing. When I'm *offstage,* however? Not so much, thanks to the persistent tension between Savage and me, provoked by his constantly nightmarish behavior. I've said nothing. Held my tongue. But the tension between us could be cut with a knife. It's all worth it, however, because that forty-five minutes onstage every other day makes up for the aggravation he causes me by a long mile.

"Are you ready for Fugitive Summer?" I bellow to the crowd. And, as always, at the mention of the headliner, the crowd's cheering and applause morphs into a tsunami of excitement. Chuckling, I add, "Well, you're in luck, because they're coming out *really* soon—and, trust me, they're gonna blow you awaaaaaay!"

As the crowd continues to go wild, I exit the stage, blowing kisses and waving as I go. Once offstage, I do what I always do in moments like this: I share a group hug with my amazing backing band, accept a large bottle of water from my assistant, and then head down the hallway toward my latest assigned dressing room. Always the smallest one in the building, which is perfectly fine with me.

As usual, my post-show plan is this: I'll immediately remove my makeup and slip into something soft and comfortable. I'll enjoy a light snack and glass of white wine while listening to Fugitive Summer's set from my couch. Sometimes, depending on my mood, I might sneak into the wings to watch the headliner's show, taking care to stand where Savage can't see me. Wouldn't want to give him the satisfaction. But the truth is, no matter how horrible Savage has been offstage these past few weeks—ever since New York, he's turned into a freaking monster!—he's still one of the best performers in the business. To be honest, I not only feel enthralled watching him, every time, along with his fans, I also learn a lot about letting go onstage and leaving it all out there.

Once Fugitive Summer's set is over, I'll head to my hotel room, like I always do, in whatever city, and soak in my bathtub with a second glass of wine. Substitute "hot tub" for "bathtub," if there's one available to me. While soaking, I'll text with my sister or Mom, or Aloha, or read a romance novel, and then head to bed, where I'll watch a show of some sort. Probably pull out my vibrator, if I haven't already gotten myself off in the tub. And then, finally I'll close my eyes and drift off. All of it, to be rinsed and repeated in the next city. And you know what? I love the routine. In fact, I've come to cherish it. Because it keeps me sane to know what comes next in my little corner of the world, amidst Savage's ever-increasing chaos and animus.

Sometimes, I admit I want to break my routine to say yes to Kendrick's frequent invitations to hang out with Fugitive Summer after their show. I adore everyone in that band, other than Savage, and lots of staff and crew members, too. But there's no way I'm going to subject myself to partying with Savage these days. Not when I'm on the bitter cusp of exploding like a bomb and word-vomiting all over him about his horrible behavior throughout this tour, but especially since New York.

"Thanks, Katrina," I say, handing my assistant my empty water bottle. We reach my dressing room and open the door . . . and discover Savage inside the room. Sitting on my couch while flirting intimately with a groupie who's sitting on his lap. *Again.* Jesus! This is the *third* time in two weeks I've stumbled upon this exact vignette in *my* dressing room, immediately after my set! "Get out!" I shriek, the past weeks of aggravation boiling over into an uncontainable flood.

I've been biting my tongue for weeks. But this time, I can't contain myself. I don't care if I'm embarrassing Mr. Rockstar in front of his new fuck buddy. I don't care if nearby staff and crew can overhear me shrieking like a madwoman. I don't care if Savage is the star of the headliner and I'm the peon opener. *I don't care about any of it!* He's turned into a monster these past few weeks—the biggest jerk I've ever met—nothing at all like the surprisingly cool dude I shared a bottle of whiskey with in Providence. And, truly, someone has to put this jackass in his place, once and for all. So, it might as well be me.

I shout, "The much bigger dressing room assigned to the *head-*

liner isn't big enough to contain your massive ego, so you needed to take over both yours *and* mine?"

Savage languidly twirls a lock of the woman's hair around his fingertip, his dark eyes boring holes into my face. "I took a wrong turn, Fitzy. Chill out. These hallways can be confusing."

God, I hate him. Literally growling with frustration, I bolt out of my dressing room, toward his. If Mr. Rockstar is going to hang out in my teeny-tiny dressing room with his latest groupie, then I'm going to hang out in his much larger one, with his band, all of whom I like a million times more than *him*. But before I've reached my destination, as I enter a large backstage area where lots of crew and staffers are busy getting ready for Fugitive Summer's entrance onto the stage, I feel Savage's body heat immediately behind me, sending tingles across my skin, against my will. I hear his footfalls and ragged breath. Sense the shift in the air that always happens in his presence.

He grasps my arm. "Laila. *Stop.*"

I whirl around and face him, breathing hard . . . and immediately lose it. I've been biting my tongue for several weeks now, ever since New York, when we tore into each other on the sidewalk in front of that restaurant—and I can't hold in my contempt for this rude, selfish man-child a second longer. In a torrent of angry words, I let loose on him, ripping him a new asshole for his selfishness, rudeness, and extreme unprofessionalism, especially over the past couple weeks. I rail against him for all the times he's been insanely late for soundchecks and the buses. And then, I scream at him even more passionately about the time, just last week, Savage kept a room full of VIP fans waiting a ridiculously long amount of time.

I wasn't there to see Savage's bad behavior at that VIP event, and it didn't affect me, personally. But I heard about it and it pissed me off! Apparently, when Savage finally arrived, after keeping those poor people waiting far too long for their demi-god, he only half-heartedly rushed through his duties in lightning speed. Totally unacceptable!

Wrapping up my diatribe, I shout, "Remember in Providence,

you told me you feared becoming a rockstar cliché?" I take a step forward and shove my nose into his face, my breathing hot and heavy. "Well, guess what, *Adrian*? Transformation complete!"

Savage's dark eyes drift to my lips for the briefest moment. But then, he takes in the shocked faces of the crew and staffers who've witnessed my tirade. And, suddenly, he transforms into a raging lunatic, before my eyes.

Practically vibrating with rage, Savage grits his teeth and lets me have it for a full five minutes, basically telling me in every conceivable way I need to know my place, mind my business, and shut the fuck up. As the cherry on top, Savage also tells me I'm lucky to be on this tour at all—that, in fact, he didn't want me here, and told Reed as much, from the get-go.

"But since you *are* here, against my will," he spits out, "you should be kissing my goddamned ass, not ripping it a new asshole— and especially not in front of the entire crew." He motions to the flabbergasted crowd of people standing around us, their mouths hanging open—a group that now includes not only staff and crew, but the members of Fugitive Summer, as well. "Know your place, Laila. Or, I assure you, you can and will be replaced." He smiles at whatever panic he's seeing on my face. "You think you're the one who makes every single one of these people's paychecks possible? You think the fans in this stadium paid to see *you*? Think again!"

He steps forward, closing the already small gap between us, and gets right into my face.

"Now, why don't you go to your dressing room and have your little glass of white wine and call your asshole boyfriend to tell him about me being a big, fat meanie to you tonight. Actually, I don't care what you do, as long as you stay the fuck out my way for the rest of the night, so I don't cut your ass from the tour, just to teach you a much-needed lesson in humility." He exhales, and his warm breath releases onto my face. "Now, if you'll excuse me, it's time for me to head onstage to entertain the thousands of people who came out tonight to watch me shake my ass like a motherfucking rockstar cliché."

FIFTEEN

SAVAGE

Phoenix, Arizona

When Kendrick and I step outside the door of his hotel suite, the moonlit air feels unexpectedly warm for this late hour.

"Thanks for the birthday party, brother," I say, gripping Kendrick's sideways palm.

After releasing my hand, Kendrick looks around at the moonlit night and winces. "It's *still* hot as an oven out here, at this hour?"

"Welcome to Phoenix," I quip. As Kendrick knows, I spent my earliest years in this oven of a city, before moving to Chicago at age twelve to live with my grandma in her apartment complex, which was where I met the Cook brothers, whose family lived down the hall.

"You were ruthless in 'Birthday Truth or Dare' tonight," Kendrick says, laughing.

I shake my head. "You were way more ruthless on your birthday. Surely, making the head of our label hate my guts is far worse than me making you *briefly* turn your balls into cucumber slices at the spa."

We laugh together, both of us reliving tonight's silliness. After Kai had passed out on the couch in Kendrick's suite, I dared my best friend to whip out his balls and rest them onto his brother's sleeping eyelids—you know, as if Kai were a customer at a spa and Kendrick's balls were a couple of cucumber slices. And thanks to the rules of our game, Kendrick couldn't refuse. In fact, the dude is such a good sport he even went so far as to remain in that compromised position for a full minute, albeit with his large hands covering his dong, and invited everyone at the party to snap close-up shots of his brother's ball-covered face.

It was priceless. Easily, the highlight of my birthday party. The lowlight, however? Laila not showing up, despite Kendrick extending an invitation to her. I don't blame her, of course. I knew the odds were low she'd come, given that she now hates me passionately. The thing is, as much as I've purposefully *tried* to make Laila hate me for weeks now, for reasons only a clinical psychologist would be able to explain to me, I realized tonight, rather starkly, while looking around at the people at my birthday party, I desperately wanted Laila to be there. I realized, in fact, that I'd very much like a do-over now, please. I'd very much like Laila to stop hating me now, please. The only problem? I have no idea how to dig myself out of this stupid hole I've been expertly digging for weeks. I wanted Laila to hate me with the force of a thousand suns? Well, mission accomplished.

Kendrick yawns. "I'm gonna head inside now, before Tracy falls asleep. Goodnight, brother."

He's talking about our tour manager. For the past week or so, Kendrick has been having a "tour fling" with her, which seems to imply he's finally given up on waiting for Laila to break up with Malik. Surely, it's no coincidence I'm only now regretting my strategy with Laila, after it seems crystal clear my best friend has *finally* taken himself out of the hunt.

To be honest, I would have bet any amount of money Laila

would have ditched Malik's trashy ass by now. And yet, every single time I've walked past her in a hallway, or overheard her as she's stood nearby, she's *always* on her phone, talking with Malik. Giggling with him. Saying stuff like, "Oh, *Malik!* You're so bad, baby!"

It's the main reason I haven't swallowed my pride and extended an olive branch to Laila yet. Simply because I'm so shocked and appalled and downright pissed she's still giving Malik the time of day. What's wrong with her? But suddenly, now that I'm drunk again, for the first time since New York—only this time, thankfully, a happy kind of drunk—a birthday boy kind of drunk—I feel ready to swallow my pride and finally bury the hatchet with Laila. Now that Kendrick is sleeping with Tracy, and he's finally out of my way, I've decided to go for it, in earnest. I don't care if she's still with Malik. Mr. Basketball isn't here. *And I am.*

"Goodnight, brother," I reply to Kendrick, waving to him. "See you at the buses at *nine.*"

Kendrick exhales. "*Eight!*"

"That was a joke."

Kendrick rolls his eyes. "You never know with you. Seriously, don't be late this time, Savage. Everyone is starting to get annoyed with you for being late so much. Not just Laila."

"Yeah, okay. I'll stop being an asshole. I was actually thinking of extending an olive branch to Laila."

"Yeah, that's a good idea. I was actually surprised, now that she's probably single, she didn't stop by the party. But—"

"Laila's *single?*" I blurt, my heart lurching into my mouth.

"Well, I'm *assuming.* I can't imagine she'd stay with Malik after that video of him leaked tonight."

I feel like I'm having a stroke. "*What* video?"

"You didn't see the video of Malik getting blown in a strip club? It's all over the internet! Everyone was passing it around at the party tonight."

Every molecule in my body feels like it's exploding, all at once. "*Nobody showed it to me!*"

"Hang on." Shaking his head, Kendrick reaches into his pocket. "I saw you looking at something with Kai on his phone, laughing your asses off. I assumed—"

"He was showing me Alessandra's funny music video that just released!"

"Okay, calm down." He quickly cues something up on his phone and hands it to me. And a second later I'm watching dark, grainy footage of what looks like Malik Wallace getting head from a woman kneeling between his legs who's wearing nothing but a thong.

My heart is crashing. "Has it been confirmed this is him?"

Kendrick nods. "There's other footage of him walking into the place, in those same clothes. And in that footage, you can clearly see his face." Kendrick takes his phone from me while I walk in tight circles, flailing my arms and breathing hard. After a moment of watching me act like a lunatic, Kendrick lets out a long exhale. "Stop, Savage. It's okay. You've got my blessing."

I stop moving and stare at him. But I don't speak.

"Go get her, man. She's all yours. I know how much you've been wanting her. I've known for a long time. So, go for it."

I can barely breathe. "I'm sorry," I say, a mixture of relief and guilt and excitement flooding me. "I've tried my best not to want her, KC. I've tried to keep my distance and push her away, as best I could, so you could take your shot with her. I swear, I've tried."

"I know you have, brother. Thank you."

I run my palm down my face. "I don't understand my obsession with her. She makes me *crazy*. I haven't even fucked anyone else since I laid eyes on her at Reed's party."

Kendrick's jaw practically drops onto the ground. "But I thought—"

"No."

"The waitress in New York?"

I shake my head. "No. Nobody."

Kendrick processes that for a long moment. "So, you thought making Laila hate your guts would make you want her less?"

"I guess so."

He narrows his eyes. "Or *maybe* you figured her out, even if it was subconsciously. Maybe, you realized making Laila hate your guts would only make her want you more."

"No."

"*Yes.* Don't you see? I've been nothing but nice to that woman since the second I met her. I've been her best friend. And where am I now? Irreversibly in her friend zone. While you've been nothing but an asshole to her from day one. And where are *you*? Firmly in her 'I want to fuck you to death!' zone."

My earlier mixed emotions streamline and converge into nothing but excitement. If that's what Kendrick sees, then it must be true. Because Kendrick Cook is fantastic at reading people, unlike me. I say, "I swear I wasn't trying to cockblock you."

"Not consciously." He exhales. "It doesn't matter. There was no other ending to the story for me. Even if you weren't here, she still wouldn't want me. I realize that now. Clearly, she likes flaming assholes who treat her like shit. Look how long she's hung in there with Malik! I can't compete with that, because I can never *be* that. But you can."

I think maybe he's insulting me. But I feel nothing but complimented. "You think?"

He laughs. "Yeah, I do."

In a flash flood, every drop of desire I've been holding back, denying, and ignoring for so long slams into me. "I'll go to her room now. Would you go inside and ask Tracy to text me Laila's room number?"

"No, Savage. Not now. It's after three and you're shitfaced drunk. Go to *your* room now, get some sleep, wake up and take a shower in the morning and get to the buses on time, and *then* take your shot with Laila in Vegas."

"But—"

"Savage, listen to me. I'm not sabotaging you. I'm *helping* you. You've been smoking like a chimney all night. You know how much Laila hates that. Get cleaned up and talk to her in Vegas, or you'll go there now and wake her up and get into another screaming match with her."

My shoulders slump. He's right, of course. Even if Laila liked me, which she doesn't, she'd shoo me away from her room for smelling like an ashtray. "Okay. I'll get some sleep and talk to her in Vegas. Thanks again for the birthday party." I twist my mouth. "For everything."

Kendrick winks. "Someone's gotta take care of your dumb ass."

"Glad it's you."

"Me, too." He smiles. "See you at the buses at nine."

I crinkle my forehead. "I thought you said eight."

"That was a test."

With a wink, Kendrick heads back into his suite, while I begin walking down a winding path toward my room on the far side of the hotel grounds. But when I reach a slatted fence enclosing the hotel's VIP pool area—an area that's been closed off to the general public for my band's private use during our stay—I suddenly decide a naked, moonlit swim would be the perfect way to cap off my twenty-sixth birthday.

After swiping my keycard and walking through the gate, I look around for an especially dark corner to undress in . . . and that's when I see the universe's birthday gift to me. *Laila Fitzgerald.* She's sitting in a hot tub in a far corner of the space with a large bottle of booze on the ledge, next to her head. Surely, she's drowning her sorrows about that humiliating video of Malik. Which thrills me to no end.

Laila's sandy hair is piled atop her head in a messy bun, making her chiseled cheekbones and plush lips all the more striking. Her alabaster skin, which always sort of glows, looks particularly supernatural in the moonlight.

Without hesitation, I begin walking toward her, whispering to myself as I go, "Happy birthday to me."

SIXTEEN

SAVAGE

I come to a stop on the ledge of the hot tub and look down at Laila . . . and immediately discover that she's naked. *Hallelujah.* And that her body in that water is even more gorgeous than I've fantasized. Man, this birthday just keeps getting better and better.

"You're gorgeous," I whisper, and then press my lips together when I realize I've drunkenly blurted my thoughts aloud.

Laila smirks. "And you're drunk."

I bite back my smile. "A bit."

"Eyes up here, *Adrian.*"

I begrudgingly comply.

She cocks an eyebrow. "I presume you've risked softening your chiseled abs tonight with way too much alcohol, in celebration of your birthday?"

"That's right. Birthdays equal getting shitfaced. No exceptions."

"Happy birthday."

"Thanks. You were invited to the party."

"I was busy."

"Yeah, I bet. I saw the video. You've been drowning your

sorrows tonight, I presume?" I gesture to the big bottle of booze on the ledge.

She takes a long swig from her bottle. "Fuck Malik. I don't want to talk about him."

"Fair enough." I bite my lip. Shift my weight. Stare at her tits. And, finally, address the elephant in the room. "So . . . you're single now?"

"I'm very, *very* single."

Hot damn. My eyes drift to her naked body again. And I swear I have to suck on my teeth, vigorously, not to physically drool down my chin at the sight of her.

"Eyes up here, Adrian," she says. And when I comply this time, she smiles and says, "So, are you finally ready to apologize for being an asshole to me?"

I pull a face. "Which time?"

She snorts. "Let's start with your diatribe in Atlanta and work our way from there."

"Nah. You deserved Atlanta. If anyone needs to apologize for being an asshole in Atlanta, it's *you.*"

"Me?"

"Laila, you read me the Riot Act in front of *everyone* on the tour—and, in case you didn't realize this, honey, you're the *opener.*"

She rolls her eyes. "Okay, I admit I *might* have been a little out of line to—"

"A little? Come on. Nobody's here. Admit you blew it. I had to say what I did. You were way out of line."

She twists her mouth. "I admit I shouldn't have said what I did in front of people. I should have pulled you aside and said it all in private. But I don't regret what I said. All of it was true. Really, all you had to say to me was, 'Hey, let's step outside to talk about this.' Or, better yet, 'No problem, Laila! I'll try to be more punctual and professional from now on, as a courtesy not only to you, but to every hardworking person on the tour, not to mention my fans!' And I would have said, 'I'm sorry I snapped in front of everyone. That was totally unprofessional of me.'"

"It was."

She throws up her hands. "Yes, but I picked a poorly timed fist fight with you, Savage. And in response, you pulled out a freaking Uzi!"

"Whatever, dude. We could go 'round and 'round about what happened in Atlanta, and who was the bigger asshole, until the end of time. It would be you, by the way. But what's the point?"

"I literally *hate* you."

I chuckle. "*Or*, we could stop arguing about this, and agree to disagree, and, instead, move on to you answering a *very* important question for me."

She tilts her head, clearly intrigued. "What's the question?"

I squat down, leveling my eyes with hers. "On the night your boyfriend cheated on you for the entire world to see, do you want to sit here, naked, in a hot tub, arguing with a guy who's got a big ol' dick and knows how to use it . . . *or*, do you want to agree to a temporary cease-fire with said guy, long enough to have the best revenge sex of your life?"

Her blue eyes gleaming, Laila bites back a wicked smile. She runs a fingertip across the rim of her bottle like she's teasing the tip of my cock. And every nerve ending in my body feels it. She says, "If I say yes, nobody can ever know."

I flash her a look like I'm deeply insulted. "You'd be *ashamed* for anyone to know you'd fucked The Great Adrian Savage?"

She replies with a look of her own that says, *Well, duh.* She says, "After the way you treated me in Atlanta, with everyone watching? Hell yes, I'd be ashamed for anyone to know I fucked you. Honestly, I'd be mortified."

"Says the girl who's been dating Malik Wallace for at least two months," I toss out. "But, whatever. *Fine.* Nobody will ever know."

"Promise me."

"I promise."

"It'd be revenge sex—a one-time thing that would never happen again," she declares. "Afterwards, it never happened."

"I get it, dude. No need to say it five different ways. Although I want to be able to tell *one* trusted person."

"Kendrick?" she asks.

I nod. "I tell him everything. Plus, I think it will help him let go of any lingering crush he might have on you."

She juts her lower lip. "Poor Kendrick. He's the sweetest person in the world."

"Don't feel sorry for him. He dodged a bullet. You're a psychopath."

To my surprise, she laughs. "True."

"Too bad for him, you're a psychopath who only likes assholes, eh?"

She doesn't correct me. She merely says, "I get to tell one trusted person, too."

"Naturally. Who?"

"Aloha. She'll scream at me. Tell me I'm a predictable idiot. She doesn't like you very much."

"Why not? I'm amazing."

"She thinks you're a player."

"Pfft. Tell her to get in line, sister. Any other conditions, terms, or stipulations, Fitzy?"

She ponders that for a moment. Or, at least, she pretends to. "No. That's it. I'll probably hate myself in the morning, but I have to know."

"You have to know what?"

Her expression turns wicked. "If those famous shots of you in the shower were real or Photoshopped."

I waggle my eyebrows. "There's only one way to find out."

She pauses. "Do you have a condom?"

"I sure do."

"Okay, then." She pushes out her incredible tits, opens her thighs underneath the water, and purrs, "Then you'd better get your annoying ass in here, before I change my mind."

She doesn't need to ask me twice. With my dick as hard as a stone, I rise to standing and begin peeling off my clothes. When I get down to my briefs, and lodge my thumb underneath the waist-band, the look of molten lust on Laila's face reflects my own desires back to me. Every cell in my body on fire, I slowly pull my under-wear down, freeing my hard shaft and eliciting a sharp intake of breath from Laila.

"No Photoshop there," she purrs with appreciation. "Damn, boy."

I slip into the water across from her and she immediately rises and greets me. Without hesitation, she grips my dick under the water, while I take her stunning face in my hands, beyond excited to finally kiss the lips that have entranced me for so long . . .

But it's not meant to be.

Laila jerks back, saying, "You've been smoking." And when I nod, she adds, "We shouldn't kiss, anyway. That's way too intimate a thing for one-time-only revenge sex."

I'm disappointed, but such is life. I should have known.

I drop my hands to her bare shoulders and guide her to sitting, while she maintains her firm grip on my dick. My heart pounding, I smile and say, "*Kissing* that dirty little mouth of yours isn't what I've been fantasizing about doing to it, anyway."

She returns my smirk. "You admit you've been fantasizing about me?"

"You're not the only one who gets off on the idea of hate sex, Laila." With that, I reach down between her creamy thighs in the warm water, slide two fingers gently inside her and my thumb over her clit, and proceed to massage and finger her, methodically, without variation or mercy, while tracing her gorgeous lips with my free hand.

Soon, Laila's eyelids begin fluttering. A soft, husky groan rises up in her throat. As her eyes roll back, she takes my finger into her mouth and sucks on it, hard, voraciously, like it's giving her life— and a moment later, her body seizes with an insanely sensual orgasm that sends me to the very brink of release myself.

"Time for your penance," I choke out. My breathing ragged, I step up onto the bench, place my feet on either side of her seated frame, and shove my cock at her mouth, nonverbally commanding her to suck it. Thankfully, she follows instruction well, and takes my full length into her mouth without hesitation. Immediately, she begins sucking me off with enthusiasm, like she's auditioning for a managerial position at a brothel.

Muttering profanities, I grip Laila's sandy hair to steady myself. To keep myself from losing it and shattering into a million pieces. Is there anything hotter than getting blown by the same dirty little mouth that, only days ago, told me to fuck off? If so, I can't imagine it. Not in this lifetime, anyway.

But when my pleasure threatens to boil over, I decide it's time to move along. As much as I've fantasized about coming into Laila's mouth, many, many times, I've been dying to split her body in half with my cock, even more.

Shaking with adrenaline and arousal, I pull out of Laila's mouth and moan at the sultry sight of her. Her full lips are slightly swollen from her voracious effort. And the effect is insanely sexy. Her blue eyes are as ravenous and hungry as I've ever seen them. In short, she looks the hottest she ever has to me. And that's saying a lot.

"Come with me," I choke out, taking her hand. I guide her out of the hot tub and lead her to a nearby lounger in a cabana. After grabbing a condom from my pants on the ground and getting myself swiftly covered, I return to her in the dark shadows of the cabana, spread her smooth thighs as wide as they'll go—so wide, her pussy looks like a blooming flower on the cusp of losing its petals—and plunge myself inside her, growling feverishly as her body molds to mine.

I fuck her hard. So hard, I almost fuck her off the lounger. She digs her nails into my shoulders and keens like an animal as I move on top of her, and every sound she makes sends me higher and higher.

"Let me get on top now," she gasps out. "I come when I'm on top."

There's not a doubt in my mind she'd come like this, and any other way I might fuck her, as long as she's fucking me. But now isn't the time to argue. I've got only one shot to convince this woman to do this with me, again and again throughout the rest of the tour, so I'm going to let her have exactly what she wants.

We rearrange ourselves, until Laila is riding my cock while I'm massaging her clit and telling her how insanely gorgeous she is. How good she feels. And in no time at all, she whimpers from the depths of her abdomen, digs her nails into my chest, and comes so hard, the rippling sensation of her muscles gripping my dick snatches every drop of air from my lungs, while threatening to pull the cum from my balls.

Somehow, probably thanks to the booze in my system, I'm able to hang on and keep going. I jolt to sitting and frantically begin devouring her breasts and nipples. I'm a hurricane of lust now. A crazed and rabid animal, and so is she. She pushes me flat onto my back again, and begins fucking me with a kind of fervor I've never experienced before. She's not holding back. And I can't get enough.

As she moves, I grope her ass. Grip her hips and move my body with hers. Sweat is pouring off me, mingling with the water still dripping off me from the hot tub. She's glistening, too, giving it her all.

Finally, when I'm sure enough time has passed and touching her clit will only feel good to her again, I start massaging her the way I've already surmised she likes the best. Little circles in a slow and methodical fashion. And soon, my sexy little freak has an orgasm that's so powerful, so forceful, so *hot*, it's like her body is physically *milking* the cum from my balls.

As I let go and surrender to bliss, stars momentarily blind me. Without a thought in my head, other than "I *want*," I sit up and grip Laila's stunning face in my palms, dying to kiss her. But, once again, same as before, she turns her head and denies me.

Quickly, I drop my palms and lie back, remembering the deal. Trembling, I rest my forearm over my eyes, my body and mind reeling in equal measure. That was the best sex of my life. By far. And that should be enough. I shouldn't want more. But I do. I want to kiss her. I want to taste her pussy, from every angle. And then I want to fuck her, again and again, in every position, in every new city.

But first things first. I'll make her come another ten times, right here in Phoenix.

"Come to my room now, Laila," I gasp out. "We're just getting started. Let me eat your pussy till it's time to board the buses."

She looks amused. "It's been a long day." She pats my cheek. "And the buses leave at eight. Thanks for that great revenge sex, though. I really needed that." With that, she slides off me and pads over to a chair, to a white fluffy robe draped across its back.

I sit up onto my forearms. "Let me make you come again and again, Laila. We're just getting started tonight, baby."

"No, we're done. I told you—one and done."

I scoff. "Come on, Laila. Haven't you heard, revenge sex is a dish best served . . . repeatedly and often, with a guy you can't stand?"

Laila chuckles. "I don't think that's the expression."

I'm encouraged by her smile. "You're *finally* single—and we're stuck together for the rest of the tour—*and you're turning me down?* Who else are you gonna fuck for the next month, if not me? Someone in the crew?"

"Maybe."

"Bullshit. You don't want anyone else and neither do I. We've both wanted this for a long time. So, let's do this." I sit up completely in the lounger as she finishes putting on her robe. "Laila, come on. We'll have smoking-hot hate sex in every position, in every city, for the rest of the tour. And when the tour is over, we will be, too."

Laila flashes the same dismissive look as before. "I told you, quite clearly, honey. This was a one-time thing that will never happen again. I was curious . . . and now I know." With that, she tightens the belt on her robe and begins striding away, tossing over her shoulder as she goes, "Don't be late for the buses, *Adrian.*"

What the fuck? I just offered this woman a no-strings *month* of hate sex with me—with *me*!—a guy half the female population on planet earth would do *anything* to get with—and she's not taking me up on it? Despite the fact that we just had the hottest sex two people can possibly have?

"I'll text you my room number in Vegas!" I call to her. "Come to my room after tonight's show!"

"Not gonna happen!" she yells back.

"It's happening tonight!"

"One and done!"

"Tonight and every night for the rest of the tour!"

There's only silence now. No footfalls. No reply.

"Laila?"

But she's obviously gone.

Exhaling, I get up and grab my clothes off the ground. I dry myself off with my shirt and throw on my pants. And then, I grab Laila's bottle of whiskey, plop into a nearby chair, and stare at the starry night while drinking and replaying what just happened, over and over again, in my head. I knew it'd be hot with her, but *that* hot? Good lord. When we really got going, it was like she was a junkie, chasing a high. A hate sex high.

I freeze with the lip of the bottle against my mouth. *Now, that's a hit song.*

Hate Sex High.

My heart thumping, I grab my phone and record a flurry of voice memos. Some initial lyrics, a melody for the hook, an idea for the dirty, raunchy beat. Finally, when I get enough recorded to keep the song from slipping back into the ethers before I've arrived in my room to nail it down, I throw on my shirt and sprint out of the pool area, all the way to my suite on the far end of the hotel. Once inside the room, I rip off my damp clothes like a madman, grab my guitar, and start writing "Hate Sex High" in earnest, feeling like a man possessed.

When asked about my songwriting process in interviews, I often say it feels even better than sex, when it's going well. But after fucking Laila the Unicorn Freak, the Hate Sex Addict, the woman who just rocked my world like none other, I know my usual comment isn't entirely accurate. Now that I've had hate sex with the one and only Laila, I know the more accurate statement is that songwriting, when it's going well, feels better than regular sex, and *almost* as good as hate sex with the hottest woman who's ever walked planet earth, Laila Fitzgerald.

SEVENTEEN

LAILA

Las Vegas, Nevada

As I speed-walk across the sprawling lobby toward the elevator bank on my way to Savage's suite on the twentieth floor of our Vegas hotel, I chastise myself for giving in to temptation. I shouldn't be heading to Savage's room. Not right now. And not at all. The plan, as of mere *hours* ago in Phoenix, was for me to resist Savage and his insanely delicious fingers and cock, that incredible body, those soulful, burning eyes and cut jawline, for the rest of the tour. On principle. To teach that rockstar cliché a lesson about the way he reamed me in Atlanta in front of everyone. To let him know his abundant charms have absolutely zero effect on me.

Ha.

I'm so mad at myself right now. And yet, powerless to change course. At least, if I was going to give in to temptation, which I swore to myself I wouldn't do, then self-respect *demands* I wait at *least* a full week to do it. *At a bare minimum.* Not mere hours. And yet, here I am, speed-walking like a middle-aged mom with a Walkman across this expansive lobby, on my way to Savage's room for Round Two, feeling like a hungry dog who's just heard the dinner bell.

Walking away from Savage on that lounger this morning, and not taking him up on his offer to head to his room, was one of the hardest things I've ever done in my life. But I did it! And I was so damned proud of myself! And now, here I am, not even waiting until after tonight's show to admit I'm hopeless.

I tried to resist Savage when I got his text a half hour ago, telling me his room number and begging me, literally, to let him eat me "from every angle" after tonight's show. Upon receiving that text, I put my phone down on the nightstand in my hotel room and muttered, "Nope. You have zero effect on me, Savage." But when I felt my resolve quickly crumbling like a beachside cliff, I stuffed my phone into my pocket and marched downstairs to the lobby, intending to spend the next few hours before soundcheck in the casino. What better way to distract myself?

But, unfortunately, I ran into our tour manager, Tracy, in the lobby, before making it to the casino. And that's when she mentioned Fugitive Summer had just finished an interview and that all the members of the band were heading to their respective rooms to chill for a bit before soundcheck. In that moment, I felt possessed by a demon. Incapable of waiting a second longer to let Savage make good on his offer to eat me from every angle. I knew, whether I liked it or not, I was a goner.

And now, here I am. Pounding on the call button at the elevator bank in the lobby like my very life depends on it. After only one time with Savage, I feel physically addicted to him. Like I don't care what pride I need to swallow to have him.

When one of the elevators opens, I lope over to it, lurch inside, and punch the button for the twentieth floor. But just before the doors close, two young women enter the small space, and immediately gasp.

"You're Laila Fitzgerald!" one of them says.

"I am. Hello."

"We love you!"

I thank them, and they ask for, and receive, a selfie.

"Are you going to the show tonight?" I ask, intending to offer them tickets if they say they're not already going.

But it's a moot point when they reply, "Hell yes, we're going! Fugitive Summer is our favorite. And you, too!" They look at each other and at the same time, scream, *"Savage!"* And then quickly burst into gleeful, giddy laughter at their silliness.

"He's definitely one of a kind," I say.

One of them says, "Everyone says he's your boyfriend?"

"No!" I bark, involuntarily, unable to keep the panic out of my voice. I clear my throat and try again, this time more calmly. *"No."*

But the damage is done. I've obviously come off as a lunatic. The woman who doth protest *way* too quickly and loudly. The girls pause, apparently sensing, accurately, that I'm off my rocker. "Sorry if we assumed," one of them says, slowly, like she's talking a jumper off a bridge. "We saw that video of you and Savage shouting at each other and—"

"That was a misunderstanding," I reply, my heart thumping. "But there's nothing going on between us, I assure you." They're referring to a video of Savage and me in New York, taken while we screamed at each other on the sidewalk in front of that restaurant. Thankfully, the street noise and other ambient sounds were too loud to capture our words with any clarity. But our body language was clear enough—fierce enough to instantly spark rampant rumors Savage and I were having a passionate lover's spat.

"Well, good, that just leaves him for *us*, then," one of the young women says, making her friend giggle.

The elevator stops on their floor, but one of them holds it open while asking me if I can get them backstage tonight. But now that I've revealed myself to be a total nut job, I'm too embarrassed to see them again.

"No, I'm sorry," I say. "I'm not allowed to do that."

"Oh well. It was worth a try. Say hi to Fugitive Summer for us, okay? Especially Savage!"

"I will!"

After the doors close between us, I begin pounding on the button for Savage's floor, despite it already being lit up. Now that I'm this close to Savage, I can feel his magnetic pull on me. Indeed, my mouth feels like it's physically watering at the thought of what I'm going to do to that man, the minute I have him alone. Hopefully, he'll be smart enough not to speak when I arrive. Or else, quite possibly, he'll talk himself right out of the best blowjob he's ever gotten.

As the elevator glides the rest of the way to the twentieth floor, the horrible thought occurs to me that Savage might not even be in his room, despite what Tracy said about the members of the band heading to their rooms. Savage gets easily distracted, after all. It's one of his defining characteristics. The thing is, if I don't go to his room now, and throw myself at his mercy, if I wait until *after* the show tonight, as his text mentioned, I'm quite certain I'll physically explode.

The elevator pings and stops moving and the doors glide open. As I walk into the hallway on the twentieth floor, I glance at Savage's text to remind myself of his room number, and quickly realize, based on the room numbers nearby, I've unwittingly used the least convenient elevator bank in this sprawling hotel to get here—one that put me all the way down on the farthest end of this long hallway from Savage's suite. As I begin making the trek down the hallway, I feel electrified with anticipation. I hate giving Savage the satisfaction of showing up at his room, especially this quickly, but I can't wait another—

I stop walking abruptly.

Savage has emerged from an elevator bank ahead of me in the hallway and is now walking toward his room at the far end of the hallway, with his back facing me. *And he's not alone.* Besides his two usual bodyguards, one walking ahead of him, and one behind,

Savage is accompanied by an attractive brunette. Savage's left arm is draped casually over her slender shoulders while his right hand holds a large bottle of booze. Much to my dismay, the brunette is practically squealing with joy, the same way every one of those groupies sounded each and every time I walked in on Savage in my dressing room.

I try to catch my breath, but I feel like I'm hyperventilating. I'm instantly sick to my stomach. *Stupid, Laila.* A half hour ago, Savage sent me a text, begging me to come to his room tonight. And now, he's bringing some random woman to his room for a quickie before soundcheck?

My desperate brain decides to give the guy the benefit of the doubt. *You're misreading the situation,* I think, before speed-walking a few yards in order to get close enough to overhear Savage's conversation.

"I can't believe I'm here!" the woman is gushing, pressing herself into Savage's side.

Savage pulls her into him, making her squeal again. "You're my birthday present to myself."

My blood runs cold. When I was on top of Savage and fucking him passionately this morning, he looked at my body moving on top of his, grabbed my tits, and whispered, "Happy birthday to me." And now he's saying basically those same words to this woman? I feel so gullible. So *played.*

"I feel a little tipsy," she declares. "How'd you convince me to have a drink this early? I never day-drink!"

"Hey, it's five o'clock somewhere," Savage says, laughing.

The woman squeezes Savage with enthusiasm. "Happy birthday, Adrian. Now, let me get my hands on that famous body!" She laughs. "*That's* your birthday present! I'm gonna make it extra good!"

"Knock yourself out, Sasha."

Okay, that's it. I've heard enough. Making an "eeww!" face, I turn around and start sprinting down the hallway, feeling physically ill. Where did he meet this one? At the interview he just finished? Was she the interviewer or maybe someone he spotted in the casino on his way to his room—and he simply couldn't resist inviting her back to his room for a quickie before soundcheck, the same way he so deftly invited that waitress to spend the night with him in New York?

I realize Savage never explicitly said his invitation to have sex with me for the rest of the tour would be an exclusive arrangement. But I don't think it's crazy that I assumed as much, given that he texted me his room number and *begged* me to come to him, mere *hours* after having sex with me. At the very least, I think it was fair for me to assume Savage wouldn't have sex with someone else before we possibly reconvened for Round Two in his room in only a few hours.

I pound the call button for the elevator, trembling with adrenaline. How did I let myself think I'd rocked Savage's world on that lounge chair, the way he'd rocked mine? After this morning's tryst with him, I couldn't even sleep, despite my drunk exhaustion. I was too wound up. Already enslaved by what he'd done to my body. And I assumed, like a fool, he was lying awake in his room, too, also reliving the deliciousness in his head.

Well, there's only one conclusion to draw now. The dude is a stone-cold sex addict. A megalomaniac narcissist who literally *needs* fawning validation every single minute of his life.

Rejection.

Humiliation.

Hate.

All of it is coursing through me, all at once.

But, mostly, *hate.*

An elevator going down finally opens and I step inside, physically shaking with rage.

You know what? I don't even care. Screw Savage. Screw Malik, too. And screw my cheating ex-boyfriend, Shawn, while I'm at it. I don't need a man. Especially not one who's going to make me forfeit my self-respect to be with him. *Never again.* Savage once told me to know my worth. Well, guess what? I'm going to follow his advice, from now on.

As the elevator descends, I tap out a text to the personal trainer assigned to the tour—a buff guy named Charlie. He's not on the tour for me, of course. He's a perk for the headliner. But Tracy, our tour manager, told me I'm welcome to use Charlie's services, whenever he's not otherwise engaged. Up until now, I've met with Charlie only here and there, out of respect for my place in the hierarchy. But now, screw it. I'm going to throw myself, and all these negative emotions, into a whole new obsession. A *positive* one. Namely, getting healthy, once and for all, in my mind, body, and spirit.

Me: Hey Charlie! By any chance, are you free to meet me in the hotel gym in fifteen for a session?

Luckily, Charlie replies immediately:

Charlie: I sure am. See you in 15.

The elevator doors open on my floor and I march toward my room to change into my workout clothes. Fuck Savage. And fuck every man like him. I'm officially done with bad boys, for good. Before now, the history of my romantic entanglements could be summarized as follows:

Laila: Is that a red flag? Nah. Couldn't be, despite its red color and uncanny "flag" shape.

Narrator: *And then she fucked him. Only to find out later, yes, it was, indeed, a red flag.*

Well, no more. Starting now, and for the foreseeable future, but especially for the remaining month of the tour, I'm sending myself to bad boy rehab. I'm going cold turkey, bitches! Thanks for the unsolicited advice about knowing my self-worth, Savage. I promise I'm not going to forget it, ever again.

EIGHTEEN

LAILA

Six weeks later
Los Angeles, California

"You clean up nice, yourself!" the woman onstage says brightly to her co-presenter. She's a longtime country star who won this same award last year, and he's a young buck with his first hit this year—an up-and-comer in tight jeans and a cowboy hat whose ass should be in a shadow box. And as the pair continues their scripted banter, aided by the teleprompter, I can't help craning my neck around a nearby production assistant, searching the backstage area in vain for any sign of my co-presenter, Adrian Savage—who, true to form, is ridiculously late. This time, cutting it so close, I feel like I'm going to have a heart attack.

It's the Video Music Awards and I'm standing in the wings, as instructed, right on time, awaiting my turn to present the next award with my assigned co-presenter. After the current duo finishes their thing, there will be a commercial break, thank God, which gives us a tiny margin of error. But then, whether Savage has arrived or not, I'll have to walk out there and present this damned award, one way or another. If he doesn't show up, I'll have to disregard all the scripted banter on the teleprompter, everything I practiced earlier today at the rehearsal Savage didn't attend, and I'll have to wing it. Which is something I hate doing, ever. But especially on live TV.

I haven't seen Savage since the tour ended two weeks ago, and barely saw him throughout the entire last month of the tour. I certainly didn't ask to be paired with him today. Apparently, the producers, like the rest of the world, saw that viral video of Savage and me screaming at each other in front of that restaurant and decided we'd bring in the ratings as co-presenters. It's fine, though. I got good at ignoring Savage for the final month of the tour, after seeing him for exactly who he is in Las Vegas. So, I can certainly summon my superpowers, once again, and ignore him while reading off a teleprompter.

I'm told Savage didn't make it to the quickie rehearsal earlier today, thanks to a flight delay out of Chicago. But now that he's not here, and the seconds are ticking down, I'm wondering if his supposed "travel delay" earlier was a flat-out lie. Is he standing me up, on purpose, to get back at me for ignoring him for the last month of the tour?

I look down at myself—at the dress I decided to wear tonight. If Savage doesn't show up and see this gorgeous work of art on me, I'll be so pissed. It's basically form-fitting netting with well-placed swirls that artfully, but barely, hide my most scandalous lady bits. I wouldn't have worn *such* a naughty dress for an awards show, typically. Even one as raucous as the Video Music Awards. But knowing I was going to see Savage for the first time since the tour ended spurred me on and made me want to remind him what he missed out on.

That nearby PA suddenly exhales with relief, the same way I've seen so many others do before her while awaiting Savage. And that's how I know Mr. Rockstar has arrived, approximately three minutes before we're set to walk onstage on live TV.

The air shifts and electrifies. And then, there he is. Rounding a corner.

Casually, he sidles up to me, like he's got all the time in the world. His eyes wide, he looks me up and down and says, "Damn, Fitzy. That's quite a dress. *Fuck.*"

"Hello, Adrian," I say curtly, pretending not to notice the way his eyes are popping out of his head. His cologne and charisma, the intensity of his gaze . . . all of it is hitting me like a ton of bricks. But I ignore it all.

The superstar onstage says, "And the award goes to . . ." She opens the envelope and immediately stiffens at whatever she's seeing inside. She looks out at the crowd and smiles thinly. "*Hugh Delaney.*"

Savage, the production assistant, and I simultaneously snicker, as the audience in the theatre collectively does the same. There's some scattered, half-hearted applause before the woman onstage finally chokes out, "I'm told Hugh can't make it tonight, so Taggert and I accept this award on his behalf!"

Savage leans into my ear, making my skin tingle at his proximity. I feel his warm breath as he says, "Yeah, no shit Hugh couldn't make it tonight. Ha."

I can't help snorting with him, totally contrary to my strategy of ignoring him. "Yeah, Hugh's a little busy tonight . . . *imploding spectacularly.*"

It's an understatement. Four days ago, the world found out the fifty-three-year-old, iconic country star who's been the elder statesman on *Sing Your Heart Out* since the beginning, has been cheating on his world-famous actress-wife with their kids' Brazilian nanny—a twenty-year-old who claimed, once the sex tape of them leaked, she'd been "coerced" into having a long-running affair with Hugh.

In response to the shocking allegations, Hugh went on an epic bender, drove his Range Rover into a tree, and promptly got arrested for DUI. Right after that, Hugh's wife filed for divorce, while the nanny filed a civil lawsuit and sold her story to a gossip rag. The day after that, as in, two days ago, *Sing Your Heart Out* announced Hugh's termination, two weeks before shooting on the new season is set to start, saying he'd breached his contract's strict morality clause. And now, here we are, celebrating Hugh's win for Best Country Music Video.

The scandal has been catastrophic news for old Hugh, obviously, but fantastic news for whoever his last-minute replacement on the show will turn out to be. It's a long shot, but my agent, Daria, is already hard at work, trying to make Hugh's replacement *me*. I don't expect her efforts to bear fruit. I'm barely famous enough to have snagged a spot as a mentor this season. But my profile has expanded significantly since the success of my second album. Not to mention, since that video of me fighting with Savage in New York caused Google searches of my name to spike by one thousand percent. So, my agent figured it was worth a shot.

Daria's pitch to the show's producers has been: "You've already publicized Laila as a mentor this season and the response has been fantastic. So why not make a surprise announcement that you've expanded her role because you've realized she'll bring a fresh energy to the judges' table? Who better to replace Hugh at the last minute than his polar opposite—a young, enthusiastic woman?"

Yeah, we don't have high hopes that pitch will work. Almost certainly, they'll replace Hugh with another big star, another man, who'll appeal to Hugh's same demographic. They've *always* had *one* woman and *two* men at the judges' table, since the beginning—and Aloha is still under contract for the next four years of the show.

The PA hands Savage the short script for our banter. "This is all cued up on the teleprompter," she assures him. "But you'll probably want to read this before walking out there, so you don't stumble on anything."

"I'll do that. Could you give us some space to rehearse in private?"

"Sure. Let me know if you need me. I'll come back and cue you, right before the announcer introduces you both."

As she walks away, Savage tosses the script onto a nearby speaker. "You're stubborn as shit," he says to me.

"Excuse me?"

"I kept my word and told no one. For a full month, I pretended nothing happened between us, whenever anyone was around. I kept my word to you and showed you I'm trustworthy. So why didn't you come to my room, even *once*? Why not answer a single one of my texts—either during the tour, or over the past two weeks? At the very least, you could have replied to *one* of my texts! But you just can't help yourself, huh? You're so used to being a bitch to me, it's now your default mode."

I grit my teeth. "Yeah, interesting to note I'm only a bitch with you. I'm actually really nice with everyone else. And if you must know, I never received any of your texts, except the ones you sent in Vegas, because I blocked your number."

Savage rubs his face, closes his eyes, and lets out a long and tortured exhale.

"If you actually got to know me," I say, "beyond the little sex kitten bitch nut job you think I am, you'd find out there's a whole lot more to me than all that."

He whisper-shouts, "How am I supposed to get to know you when you block my fucking number!"

"Look, there's no point to this. I told you it was a one-time thing. I said it would never happen again, so it shouldn't have surprised you in the least when it *didn't*."

He looks fit to be tied. "Yes, I know what your mouth said that night, Laila, but your body told me something *very* different."

I scoff. "Obviously, not. Or else I would have come to your room, wouldn't I?"

It's a dagger to his heart, obviously. "How did you resist me, though? That's the part I can't wrap my head around."

"Oh, jeez."

"No, seriously. Not because I'm 'Savage from Fugitive

Summer.' Not like that. Because . . ." He shifts his weight, betraying his utter torment. "Laila, I've been losing sleep over this. How did you resist coming to my room, night after night, for a full month, after what happened between us in Phoenix? *How the hell was that even possible?*"

In this moment, I'm dying to tell Savage what I witnessed in Vegas—the sucker punch of him bringing a groupie to his room, the same way he'd brought those groupies into my dressing room. Although, in Las Vegas, unlike the times before, Savage couldn't have known I'd see him. And that fact laid to rest a certain theory of mine, once and for all. Before Vegas, I'd stupidly entertained the crazy, magical thought that *maybe* Savage had brought those groupies into my dressing room *only* to mess with me, but not to *actually* screw around with them. But when I saw him with that woman in Vegas, I knew I'd been deluding myself.

For so long now, I've wanted to tell Savage what I saw and how much it hurt me. I've wanted to scream at him, "How could you?" But, always, I decide, like I'm doing now, that small moment of vindication, that momentary "gotcha!" wouldn't be worth admitting I practically sprinted to Savage's room mere minutes after receiving his text.

In the face of my silence, Savage leans in, looking like a madman on meth. "You started fucking Charlie right after me, didn't you?"

"What?"

"Don't deny it. It's the only thing that makes sense. I saw you two together, all the time, after Phoenix. Always laughing and eating meals together. Always looking so damned cozy together."

I bite my lip to keep from laughing out loud. Savage thinks I had a torrid love affair during the tour . . . with *Charlie?* A man who recently married the great love of his life . . . a former Marine named *Dave?* I know for a fact Savage had numerous sessions with Charlie during the tour. Did he not ask the man a single personal question, in all that time? Did he not try to get to know Charlie, the tiniest bit? That's so Savage, I hate him even more for it.

"Oh no," I whisper. "You figured me out. Did Charlie tell you? Shoot. I made him swear he wouldn't tell a soul about us." I lean forward. "Just like I made *you* promise the same thing after I fucked *you*."

Savage's nostrils flare. "Cut the bullshit, Laila. Did you fuck Charlie or not? I *need* to know."

"It's none of your business. But, yes."

"Are you messing with me or telling me the truth?"

"Wouldn't you like to know."

"I *deserve* to know, after everything you've put me through."

"After what I've put *you* through? Ha! Why do you even care who I've been with, when there's an endless supply of groupies, all of them *dying* to 'get their hands on you'?"

Savage's dark eyes are a scorching pyre of jealousy and fury. "Stop it. What happened the night of the hot tub was off the charts for both of us, and you know it. Let's press the restart button and give this a try. Laila, I can't get that night off my mind."

"Well, that's your misfortune, then. I've certainly been able to get it off mine, thanks, in part, to the masterful way Charlie fucked me, every single night of the tour after Phoenix . . . and *continues* doing to this day."

It's all a lie, of course, even besides the Charlie part. In truth, I've thought about that mind-blowing night with Savage in Phoenix on a running loop. Every single day since it happened. And even more so every night, when I'm all alone and lonely in bed. Hell, I've even started dreaming about Savage! But there's no way I'd admit that to him now. If he's feeling tortured and confused by my supposed immunity to his charms, then *good*. Serves him right.

Savage opens his mouth to reply, looking absolutely furious, just as the PA appears. "Here we go," she says brightly. She presses on her headphones, briefly, before nodding and holding up three fingers. 3-2-1.

An announcer bellows, "Please welcome Savage from Fugitive Summer . . . and Laila Fitzgerald!"

The audience applauds. The PA tells us to go. And Savage and

I begin striding onstage, shoulder to shoulder, our eyes locked and our jaws clenched, with an energy I'd caption "homicidal lust" coursing between us.

NINETEEN

LAILA

I toss my hair behind my shoulder, like I'm getting ready to throw down in a wrestling ring, and belt out the last powerful note of my latest single—the third one off my sophomore album that's been taking off like a rocket. And when my song ends, Sylvia Lennox, the beloved host of this long-running daytime talk show, leaps up and applauds with her studio audience, before beckoning me to join her in a cozy sitting area.

As I walk toward my glamorous host, I wave and smile at the boisterous crowd, even though I feel like collapsing onto the floor in relief. I've felt extreme nerves during other high-stakes performances in my young career, especially lately, but nothing compares to *this*. I couldn't sleep last night, worrying I'd somehow screw this up. But, thank God, I think I just nailed it.

"That was *fantastic!*" Sylvia shouts above the din, before giving me a warm hug. "I *love* that song, Laila! So catchy!"

"Thank you so much, Sylvia."

We take our seats and make brief small talk about the album, and then about my weird hobby of making pottery on a wheel. Or, more accurately, *trying* to make pottery on a wheel. Until, finally, Sylvia crosses her legs, leans forward, and says "So, let's talk about your upcoming appearance on *Sing Your Heart Out*." She turns to her audience. "Have y'all heard Laila is going to be Aloha's mentor this season?" The audience claps, confirming, yes, they've heard the exciting news, before Sylvia returns to me. "Has shooting on the show started yet?"

"Not yet. Very soon."

"I've heard Aloha helped you get the job. True?"

"True." I tell the story, briefly, and sing Aloha's praises, and the audience claps.

"Who do you think will replace Hugh at the judges' table?" Sylvia asks. "It's a hot topic. They haven't made an announcement yet."

"I have no idea." Unfortunately, it's the truth. All I know is, it's not going to be me. I add, "I'm as excited as everyone else to find out who they pick."

Sylvia flashes me a suspicious side-eye. "Is it *you*, by any chance, Miss Laila, and you're being remarkably coy with me?"

I giggle. "No. And by the way, I'm perfectly happy being a mentor."

It's true, even though I'm slightly bummed the producers didn't bite. Apparently, the producers said they're not interested in a relative newbie like me as a judge. I'm way too green, they said. Plus, as predicted, they also claimed their "tried and true formula" is having two men and a woman at the judges' table. So, that was that.

Daria thinks there's still a slim possibility she could convince them to reconsider their position, if I do exceptionally well today on *Sylvia*. Or, if not, she said a particularly buzz-worthy interview today will almost certainly open *other* doors for me. So, either way, she encouraged me, strongly, to say or do *something* to make this interview go viral. So, that's what I plan to do.

"Well, if you ask me," Sylvia says, "they should give you Hugh's spot. I think it's high time they had *two* women at the judges' table. Don't you?"

The audience claps energetically.

I chuckle. "Did my mother pay you to say that, Sylvia?"

Everyone giggles and claps again. "In all honesty," I say on an exhale, "I'm thrilled to be on the show, in any capacity. Growing up, my mom, sister, and I had two shows we watched religiously. Yours and *Sing Your Heart Out*. So, I'm a lucky girl to have two of my biggest dreams come true."

"Aw, you're so sweet, Laila. Isn't she sweet?" The audience confirms my sweetness. "I hope you don't mind me saying your darling personality kind of surprises me."

I feign offense, making Sylvia chuckle.

"It's a compliment," Sylvia insists. "Your songs are so fierce and sassy, and you're such a confident performer, I assumed that's how you'd be offstage, too. Who would have thought the woman who belts out those sassy songs like a ferocious little tiger is actually a sweet little pussycat?"

I chuckle. "Well, I'm not *always* a sweet little pussycat. My tiger's teeth and claws come out, when appropriate. But, yes, I admit I'm a softie, in real life. It's the push and pull of being a strong woman, don't you think? My mom always taught my sister and me that nobody is better than us, and we're no better than anyone else. So, we try to live up to that, as best we can."

Sylvia claps with the audience. "Words of wisdom! Don't you just love this strong and talented woman? I adore her!"

The audience claps their agreement, and I sigh with relief. So far, so good. I don't think I've said anything to make this clip go viral yet, however, unless maybe my mother's mantra resonates with the internet?

Sylvia shifts her position in her armchair. "Speaking of your tiger's teeth and claws . . . let's talk about some of the lyrics on the album. More specifically, some of the *inspirations* for the lyrics." She flashes me a side-eye. "Girl, *someone* did you dirty."

I join her in chuckling. "I should say, in my defense, I try to get all my murderous impulses out in my songwriting. My mother would be so disappointed if I went to prison for murder."

Sylvia laughs. "How much are your songs inspired by real people and events?"

"Quite a bit. That's how I write. Autobiographically."

"That's what I thought." She cocks an eyebrow. "Care to name names?"

What the hell is she doing? Sylvia has to know I *never* confirm my romantic entanglements, including the inspirations for my songs. In fact, it's become a "thing" for my fans to decode my lyrics, with the help of internet sleuthing, to try to discern which songs are about which potential exes.

As if reading my mind, Sylvia adds, "I know you don't usually confirm who or what inspired your songs . . ."

I nod. "I prefer to let the songs speak for themselves."

"You don't even confirm your *relationships*."

"Correct."

"No making it 'Instagram official' for Laila, huh? Even when there are paparazzi photos basically doing it for you."

I shrug. "The world can think what it wants. I like keeping my private life private, as best I can. Otherwise, I worry I'll start to feel like I'm *performing* in my relationship, rather than being genuinely present in it."

"That makes sense. I do think that could be a double-edged sword, however. Since you've never confirmed or denied anything, rumors become perceived fact, until the whole world is certain they know the full list of your exes, when that might not be the case."

"Oh, I can confirm that *isn't* the case." I chuckle. "If the internet is to be believed, my list of exes is so long, I'd have a revolving door in my condo."

"Ooooh," Sylvia says, wiggling her fingertips. "I like this line of conversation."

Uh oh.

Sylvia leans forward. "Tell us someone you've been linked to, *falsely*. I respect your privacy, darling, but telling us someone you *haven't* dated couldn't *possibly* violate it."

Clever woman.

I normally wouldn't play this game. But Daria *did* tell me to make this interview go viral. And what better way to do that than giving Sylvia an "exclusive scoop" about my love life?

"Okay, Sylvia," I say. "I'll give you a little something-something. But only because it's you."

She squeals. "How exciting!"

I lean forward, like I'm Deep Throat in a parking garage, about to spill a state secret. "Colin Berretta. The drummer for 22 Goats? All the rumors about us having a torrid fling are *false*. We're nothing but friends."

Shoot. The look on Sylvia's face tells me Colin's name wasn't the one she was hoping for. In fact, if this conversation were a game of basketball, I'm pretty sure I just airballed a free throw. It surprises me, to be honest, considering Colin's high profile since his Calvin Klein underwear campaign. He's a hot commodity lately. So why isn't his name doing the trick?

"What a pity," Sylvia says, apparently trying to salvage my airball. "Colin is gorgeous. Have you seen his Calvin Klein ads?"

"I have. And, yes, he's a gorgeous man. But we're just friends."

"Friends can become more."

"Not in this case. He's a really nice guy. And that's a big problem for me, Sylvia."

She laughs, along with the audience, and I know I'm onto something here.

I nod solemnly. "Unfortunately, I've got a fatal weakness for bad boys, Sylvia." I lean forward. "I'm that friend you want to slap silly for her horrible choices in men."

The audience bursts into laughter and applause, and Sylvia visibly perks up.

"Oh, we've all been there, sweetie, especially in our twenties." Sylvia turns to her audience. "Haven't we *all* had a 'bad boy' phase, against our better judgment?"

Everyone claps and hoots, confirming that, yes, we've *all* had a bad boy phase.

Sylvia winks. "It's okay, sugar. Take it from me, this is the perfect time in your life to get burned by the deliciously toxic flame of a scorching-hot bad boy."

"Or two or three," I mutter, again making Sylvia laugh.

She pats my arm. "It's okay. How else will you learn to recognize Mr. Right when he finally comes along and treats you *right*?"

"That's a lovely spin on an unhealthy addiction. Thank you."

"It's not a spin," Sylvia insists. "The only way to rid yourself of the bad boy addiction is to overdose, go to rehab, and vow to yourself to never relapse."

"I'm actually in the rehab phase now. At least, I'm trying to be."

"Is that so?" She snickers, signaling she's not convinced. "We all saw that photo of you sitting courtside at a Lakers-Knicks game earlier this year . . ."

I shake my head. "No comment."

"Mm-hmm. And what about the video we've all seen of you arguing with a certain bad boy rockstar? Someone with whom the entire world is certain you've had a torrid love affair . . .?"

And there it is. How did I not see this coming? Shoot. The last thing I want to do is give Savage the satisfaction of hearing me say his name on national TV. Especially on a show as popular as *Sylvia*. But I can already see where this is headed, and that my fate is sealed. Sylvia is a salivating dog before me. And there's no way she's going to release this bone without me giving her something spicy.

"Aw, come on, Sylvia," I say in a last-ditch effort to stave off the inevitable. "Have mercy on me."

Sylvia giggles. "What fun would that be, when you and Savage have so much chemistry?" She addresses a guy in a headset behind a camera. "Tom, can we put up a photo of Savage, please? Any ol' photo of him will do."

Poof.

In a flash, a photo of Mr. Pouty Pants magically appears behind us on a large screen. And, no, it's not just "any" photo. It's from a smoking-hot photo shoot he recently did for the cover of *Gentleman's World* magazine—a cover that caused quite a stir when it came out a few days ago. In the shot, Savage is particularly drool-inducing. His jaw looks like it was forged in steel. His dark eyes look particularly penetrating and soulful. And, of course, his famously chiseled abs are on full display, peeking out of an unbuttoned shirt.

"Isn't he *gorgeous*?" Sylvia coos, her eyes trained on the screen behind us. She turns to the audience. "For anyone who's been living under a rock, this is Savage of the rock band, Fugitive Summer." She fans herself. "How is someone *so* talented, also *so* gorgeous? Those abs could grate cheese! That jawline could sharpen my knives! And those *lips*." She touches my forearm again. "Please, Laila, tell me you've at least had the pleasure of kissing those lips, if only for a chaste little peck!"

Well, that's a lucky break. The way Sylvia has worded her question, I don't even have to lie. "I'm sorry to disappoint you," I begin. "But, no, I swear on my life my lips have never touched Savage's. Not even for a chaste little peck." I mean, yeah, my lips have been wrapped around his thick, juicy cock. In fact, I've sucked that man's dick like I was sucking an orange through a watering hose. But that wasn't the question, now was it?

Sylvia grips her chest dramatically, like I've shot her with an arrow. "Noooo!"

I nod. "It's sad but true. All those rumors about Savage and me having a secret romance are categorically . . . *false*." It's yet another true statement, if you ask me. Nobody in their right mind would characterize one drunken, meaningless tryst as an actual "romance."

"Well, I'm heartbroken," Sylvia declares. "Is there any hope of you two getting together in the future?"

"No."

"No?"

"No."

"Well, that seems awfully final."

"Because it is."

"Again, you surprise me. If I were you, I'd take a big ol' bite of that apple, if given half the chance." She arches an eyebrow. "Weren't you two on tour together pretty recently—for several months?"

Cheese on a cracker. The woman is relentless. "Yes, we were—for three months. But, to be honest, our personalities didn't really mesh."

Sylvia's face ignites. "Oooooh. Now, we're really getting some exclusive dirt!"

I shrug. "Not really. You've all seen the video. It certainly wasn't a secret during the tour that we didn't get along. If Savage were here, I'm sure he'd say I was as infuriating to him as he was to me."

Sylvia's face is positively on fire now. "*Infuriating?* My, my. Such a *passionate* word."

"*Annoying*," I correct, quickly, feeling my cheeks redden. "I'm just saying we got under each other's skin."

"*Under each other's skin.* Oh, Laila. Freud would have a field day with you."

Fuck! How did I lose my grip on this tiger's tail so quickly?

Sylvia smirks. "Speaking of that video . . . Hey, Tom, can we put that up now? Thanks."

And there it is. The famous video of Savage and me that's been making the rounds—the one where we're screaming at each other in front of that restaurant in New York.

"You've seen this, right?" Sylvia asks.

"I have."

"It's impossible to hear what you two are saying, unfortunately. Can you fill us in?"

"I don't remember. It wasn't anything important. We constantly annoyed each other, so . . ."

"*Constantly?* Does that mean you two had more fights than this one during the tour?"

Crap. Does she have a spy who's already told her about our knock-down, drag-out screaming match backstage in Atlanta? Or is she simply fishing? "No, that argument was the only one," I say, trying to sound casual. "Adrian and I mostly stayed out of each other's way during the tour."

"Adrian? You're on a first-name basis with him, huh? I don't think I realized that's his first name. What a sexy name."

"I . . . I used to call him that to annoy him, while he called me Fitzy to annoy me. See? There were no fireworks between us. More like grade-school teasing, combined with total and complete *indifference.*"

"*Huh,*" Sylvia says, conveying an ocean of disbelief with that one syllable. She addresses the guy with the headset again. "Can we bring up the meme now? Thanks."

Holy hell. The meme, too? I feel like I'm being waterboarded.

Poof.

Like magic, the meme that's been flooding social media this past week, ever since the Video Music Awards, appears on the screen behind us. It's a photo of Savage and me, taken as we walked onstage together, our eyes locked in fiery anger. In the shot, Savage is smoldering at me like a volcano about to blow, while I'm glaring at him like I'm plotting his slow and painful dismemberment, starting with the piecemeal removal of his cock and balls. And, of course, since this is a meme, there's a caption across the top and bottom that reads: "I hate you so much . . . *I want to fuck you to death.*" Although for Sylvia's daytime audience, the f-bomb in the caption has been blurred out.

"Have you seen this one?" Sylvia asks innocently.

"I have."

Sylvia addresses her audience. "Have y'all seen this one?"

The audience applauds, confirming they've seen it, too.

"I don't know, Laila," Sylvia says. "Looking at this photo, I can see why those pesky rumors about you and Savage simply won't die. I mean, look at the chemistry between you two! Those are some serious sparks!"

The audience expresses its agreement, while I find myself wondering how the heck I managed to walk straight into this land-mine. Did Daria set this up with Sylvia, to make sure this clip went viral? I bet she did.

"Those aren't *sparks*," I say. "They're *daggers*. Right before Savage and I walked onstage, we had a little disagreement. Surprise, surprise. So, what you're seeing there isn't me wanting to jump his bones, as the meme would have you believe. It's me wanting to murder him."

Sylvia smirks. "I think you're missing the whole point of the meme, darling. The point is that—and this is something I think we can all relate to—a woman can *simultaneously* want to murder a man *and* jump his bones. It's called hate sex, honey. And from my experience, it can be awfully fun."

The audience roars with laughter. Oh, Sylvia. She's a gem.

Sylvia continues, "I'd think that'd be especially true when you're having hate sex with a specimen who looks like *that*." She motions to the screen behind us while I gape like a fish on a line, fruitlessly racking my brain for a witty retort. Finally, before I've managed to find adequate words, Sylvia looks directly into one of the cameras and says, "Big thanks to the lovely and talented Laila Fitzgerald for joining us today! Buy her album and watch her on *Sing Your Heart Out* this season! When we come back, we'll be joined by Chef Claude, who's going to teach us how to make the perfect French *croissant!*"

The audience applauds. The red lights on the various cameras turn off. A producer announces, "We're clear." And Sylvia throws her head back and lets loose with a belly laugh.

When she straightens up, she grips my forearm. "That was solid gold, Laila. Absolute *perfection!*"

I exhale what feels like my entire lung capacity. "It was?"

"It was brilliant." She mimes a chef's kiss. "I don't know if you just lied to my face about Savage, little girl. Or if you're silly enough *not* to have taken a big ol' bite of that apple during your tour. But, God help you, if you were stupid enough to resist him when you had the chance, then take some advice from a woman twice your age." She leans forward. "Fuck that man, Laila. Call him

now and tell him to meet you in a hotel, and fuck . . . that . . . man."
She guffaws at my flabbergasted expression. "Honey, when you get
to be my age, you'll realize the only regrets in life are the things you
didn't do. The mistakes you *didn't* make." She smirks. "Trust me,
honey, having hate sex with a man who looks like that delicious
specimen is one mistake you'll *never* regret."

TWENTY

SAVAGE

The air is electric. The stage, flooded with lights. The packed audience in this massive arena is singing along with me to "Hate Sex High" . . . which makes no sense, now that I think about it, since the album with that song on it is currently being mixed and mastered. Did someone at the label leak the rough cut of the album?

A warm breeze wafts over my body, caressing every inch of my skin . . . including my dick and balls. And when I look down, perplexed, I realize I've been prancing around onstage . . . completely in the nude.

I look behind me, at the gigantic Jumbotron projecting my every movement, and, yup, there's my naked dick, blasting out into the arena, as big as a barn. My eyes drift to Kendrick behind me at the drum kit and he guffaws at my stupidity, while not missing a beat in the song.

I turn around again, toward the audience, and discover everyone is holding up their phones, trained on me. Or, rather, trained, with sniper-like precision, on my dick. Which means, here we go again—my dong is once again about to become an internet star.

I suddenly hear Eli's voice, screaming my name. Shit. My manager already knows about this latest fuck-up? Panicking, I look toward the wing of the stage, assuming that's where I'll find Eli. But the person I behold in the wings is a whole lot hotter than Eli. *It's Little Miss Laila.*

Well, well, well. I knew she'd finally come crawling back to me, eventually, begging me for another ride on my pony. She's standing in the wings, wearing that eye-popping dress from the awards show —the one that left only the tiniest sliver of flesh to the imagination. Not that I need my imagination to fill in the gaps when it comes to Laila's gorgeous body, since I've already seen every glorious inch of it on the best night of my life. Every inch, that is, except her glorious pussy, up close and personal.

What did Kendrick say last week while showing me Laila's interview on *Sylvia*? He said, "I think you've got a fish on your line, brother." And now, *hallelujah*, it turns out Kendrick was *right*.

Laila's blue eyes burning with sexual desire, she begins banging her fist against a nearby wall, commanding me to stop gawking at her and get my ass over to her in the wings.

"Patience," I coo, enjoying her little tantrum. After everything Laila has put me through, I must admit I'm enjoying her obvious desperation. Taking my sweet time, I stroll languidly toward her, like I've got all the time in the world, like I haven't been dying for this moment to arrive for half my life. And when I finally come to a stop mere inches from Laila, when the tip of my naked cock brushes against the sheer fabric on her belly, I physically spasm with pent-up arousal and anticipation.

I lick my lips, poised to say, "I knew you wouldn't be able to resist me forever."

But she shuts me up by gripping my cock, the same way she did the night of the hot tub.

"Don't speak," she cautions. "And don't kiss me, either. Just fuck me. Fuck me, hard, like you did in Phoenix."

Exhaling a stilted breath, I wordlessly unzip her dress and peel it off her, until it's in a crumpled heap at her feet. With my cock dripping, I pick her up by her glorious ass, push her back against the wall, press my aching tip against her wet entrance, and—

"Savage!"

No.

It's my manager, Eli, again.

"Savage!" he shouts. "Open up. It's an emergency!"

No, no, no!

All of a sudden, Laila disappears from my arms in a puff of sensuous smoke. There's another banging sound. And then Eli's voice rips me from my dream and into stark consciousness. I open my eyes and discover I'm not backstage in an arena, on the cusp of finally fucking Laila again. I'm in a hotel room. Naked and alone in bed, in the late morning light. Also, damn, I'm nursing one hell of a hangover.

Groaning, I rub my pained forehead—and as I do, Eli's yelling and banging on the door persists and becomes even louder. I glance at my phone on the nightstand and curse at the time: 10:18. That's way too early for anyone to wake me when I'm not on tour, especially the morning after Kai's birthday party. Whatever brought Eli here, it'd better be damned important.

At the thought, goosebumps erupt on my skin. And not the good kind.

Mimi.

Quickly, I swipe into my texts, making sure I don't have something from Sasha. And, thank God, I don't. Exhaling with relief, I throw on a pair of underwear and shuffle to the door. And the minute I see my manager's facial expression, I know whatever "emergency" he's come to tell me about this morning, he's not here to tell me the worst possible news. The news I've been dreading since Mimi took a turn for the worse. Which means, whatever it is, I really don't give a fuck.

Scratching my belly, I lean against the doorjamb and yawn so wide, I'm sure Eli can glimpse the inside-bottoms of my ball sacs through my mouth. "Whatever this 'emergency' is," I drawl, "it'd better be damned important. I was in the middle of an amazing dream."

Eli motions to the hard-on bulging from behind my briefs. "So I've gathered. Put that thing away before you poke someone's eye out." He barges past me into the room and scowls at my briefs again. "Jesus, Savage. Seriously. Think about drowning puppies or something." He strides toward the bathroom. "Are you alone in here, Player?"

"Yeah."

Ignoring my reply, he peeks into the bathroom to see for himself.

"Why ask me, then?" I mutter, flopping into an armchair. I'm not surprised Eli wants independent corroboration of my answer. As Eli has said many times, he doesn't consider me a "reliable narrator" on my best day, let alone after a night of hard partying with my best friends.

When he returns to me from the bathroom, he looks furious with me.

"What's wrong with you?" he yells. "You signed the contract on Thursday morning and turned around and breached it on Friday *night*?"

"I didn't *breach* it," I assure him. "All I did last night was—"

"I know exactly what you did! And so do the producers! Savage, you know how paranoid they are about avoiding scandals with their judges this season, big or small, thanks to The Hugh Debacle. They told you, repeatedly, in writing and verbally, they want you to be a Boy Scout for the entire season."

"And I will be. Shooting begins on Monday. Don't worry. I didn't do anything bad. It was all in good fun."

"I know everything you did!" he shouts. "And you wanna know how? Because you stupidly threw Kai's birthday party in the pool area of a busy hotel—where *any* guest of the party, and any guest of the hotel, or any *employee* of the hotel, could see your antics—and by that I mean your naked swan dive into the swimming pool!—and snap as many photos and videos of you in action as they pleased. *Which is exactly what a whole lot of them did!*"

I chuckle. "It's fine. It's nothing the world hasn't already seen. I've told you about 'Birthday Truth or Dare,' right? It's harmless fun."

"Not harmless!" he shouts, practically pulling out his dark hair with frustration. "You signed a multi-million-dollar contract that included a strict morality clause. And a day and a half later, a screen shot of your dick is, yet *again,* trending on Twitter!"

I put my palms together in prayer. "At number one?"

"Fucking hell, Savage!" he shouts, his dark eyes bugging out. "This isn't funny! The producers called me an hour ago, wanting to terminate your contract."

Well, that gets my attention. "Because of a little full-frontal nudity?"

"That, and the fact that they don't trust you as far as they can throw you. You made promises that you've totally disregarded. It's a family show! And Hugh has sullied their brand. They need to know they can trust you—that they can *control* you. What was one of the most important rules they impressed upon you at the meeting? *No more going viral for all the wrong reasons!*"

My pulse is racing now. "Shit. I didn't think they'd care if I added a couple more shots to my internet dick pic collection. It's part of my branding by now, don't you think? Might even help the show, I'd think."

He shakes his head, looking like he wants to slap me. "I hate you right now. You made a promise—a four-million-dollar promise —and now they think you've broken it. It's as simple as that."

I take a deep breath and rub my forehead. "Okay. I get where they're coming from, I guess. How about we give them a call and I apologize? I'll tell them I'm sorry and it won't happen again."

"Oh, we're way past that now, fuckwit. You have no idea how much shucking and jiving I had to do this morning to keep them from *immediately* announcing your termination." He takes a deep breath. "Thankfully, I think I've got them sold on an idea to make lemonade out of last night's lemons. They've given me until five today to deliver on my idea, or else you're toast."

My chest suddenly feels tight. "Whatever you have to do, you need to fix this for me, Eli."

"I'm trying, Savage. But you're gonna need to work with me."

"I will. I *promise*."

"Don't you dare use that word with me. It's meaningless."

"No, it's not. Yes, I was stupid last night. But I totally get it now. I'll do whatever it takes."

"I don't believe you."

"Well, you should." I sigh. "I didn't want to tell you this yet, but . . . I signed a contract to buy that house yesterday."

Eli looks flabbergasted. "The house for Mimi?"

I nod.

"Savage, *no*. I told you *no!*"

"I know. But I had to do it. Who knows when or if it'll ever come on the market again? I wanted Mimi to have it. You know we're running out of time."

Eli looks sympathetic. "Please, tell me you haven't told Mimi about the house yet, so you can back out, if I can't fix things with the show."

"I've told her. She cried tears of joy."

Eli flops into a chair. "*Savage.*"

"I had to get it for her. You know the story of that house."

"How much did you agree to pay? Please, tell me you at least got a smoking good deal?"

I pause. It seemed like a no-brainer at the time when I knocked on the door of that house last week and made them an offer they couldn't refuse. The house wasn't even on the market, actually. And they insisted it wasn't for sale, at any price. So, I offered to pay them a king's ransom to change their mind. I figured, *Why not?* The tour was massively successful, which means I can afford to burn my entire salary, and then some, from *Sing Your Heart Out* on a gift for Mimi. But now, I'm thinking maybe it was a wee bit extravagant to blow every penny of my salary, and more, on that one purchase.

"Okay, actually, I told you a little white lie," I admit. "The house wasn't actually on the market . . ."

"Oh, God. No. How much, Savage?"

I grimace. "Five million."

"No!"

"I had to offer that much, or else—"

"Savage, no!"

"It's okay. For what it's worth, the house is going to be in my name, so, one day . . ." I trail off, not wanting to think of the ending to that sentence—the obvious implication that Mimi won't be around to enjoy her fancy new house on a hill forever.

"Your salary from the show won't cover that," Eli says, like I don't know basic math. "Not to mention, you won't even get paid, all at once, by the show—assuming I can fix this for you. Plus, even if you do wind up staying on the show, *if* I can save your stupid ass today, then half your salary will go to taxes and commissions."

"*Half?*" I blurt. "Well, shit."

Eli looks genuinely distraught on my behalf. He fidgets in his armchair for a moment. "Savage, even if I can get the show to keep you on, that was the most irresponsible purchase, ever. You already bought Sasha a house last year—and you don't even have one for yourself!"

My stomach flip-flops. "Look, I'm not gonna apologize. I had to do this for Mimi. She's the first person in the world who ever truly believed in me, even when I didn't believe in myself. The first person who told me I actually mattered." I swallow hard, keeping my emotions at bay. "There's no way to know how much time she has left, Eli. But things aren't looking good. So, whatever time she's got, I want her to get to lie in a huge bed fit for a queen in the master bedroom of *that* particular house, while watching me sit at the judges' table—in Hugh Delaney's fucking chair—on her all-time favorite show."

Eli runs his palm down his face. "Aw, Savage. You're such a fucking . . . *softie.*"

I press my lips together. That's not how I thought Eli was going to end that sentence. I was expecting him to say idiot. Or maybe asshole. And I can't deny his word choice has moved me.

"I'm sorry I messed up last night," I murmur. "I considered last night a last hurrah before I turn into a pumpkin, you know? I truly didn't think they'd care if I added to my dick pic collection."

"You were already a pumpkin. That's my whole point. The contract was effective the minute you signed it. And the infuriating part is that I told you that."

"The good news is that, besides that *one* naked swan dive, I truly was a Boy Scout last night. A popular Instagram model practically *begged* me to take her upstairs to my room, but I said no." I gasp. "Hey, let's call the producers and tell them about *that*!"

"They already know, dumbass. *Everyone* already knows because that highly popular Instagrammer posted a video about her interaction with you this morning, which is now making the rounds on the internet, right alongside screenshots and videos of your gigantic dong, mid-flight."

TWENTY-ONE

SAVAGE

I furrow my brow at my manager. "What do you mean the Instagrammer made a video about her interaction with me last night? There was nothing to say because I turned her down."

"That's exactly what she said," Eli replies. "It's the supposed *reason* you turned her down that's making her video take off. And thank God it is, because that video is the only reason I've got a snowball's chance in hell of fixing this mess for you."

I blink in confusion. "What'd the Instagrammer say in her video?"

"Tell me your version of your conversation with her, first. Word for word, if you can."

I release a puff of scornful air. "I can't remember what I said to her, word for word. I was drunk. Plus, the party was noisy, so I couldn't hear everything she said."

Eli rolls his eyes. "Okay, I'll get you started. She approached you at the party and said she's a huge fan. Sound about right?"

"Yeah. But that's what always happens. And then, she suggested we head upstairs to my hotel room for sex. Or to fuck. Something like that. And, like I said, I turned her down."

"But what reason did you give for turning her down?"

I pause to recollect. "Honestly, I wasn't interested in her. But I didn't want to hurt her feelings. So, I think I said something like, 'I can't because of the morality clause in my contract with the show.' Now, show me her video. I'm freaking out."

Eli hands me his phone, all cued up. "Fair warning, this is going to piss you off. But keep in mind this video is your saving grace."

My stomach churning, I look down at the screen in my palm, and there she is. The Instagrammer from Kai's birthday party last night. Long, sandy hair, blue eyes, full lips. She's gorgeous, obviously. But not my type. Apparently, besides being gorgeous, she's also a greedy little bitch who didn't hesitate to spew lies about me for her fifteen minutes of fame. So, good on me for sensing her character and immediately turning her down.

With a deep sigh of resignation, I press play on the video and the frozen woman on my screen instantly springs to life. "Hey, guys!" she says brightly. "You won't believe what happened!" And off she goes, telling the story of last night's "star-studded" birthday party. First off, she admits she basically sneaked in, thanks to a friend of a friend with a connection. Next, she talks about the famous people she saw. And, finally, she gets to the part I've been waiting for—the part about me. "He's even hotter in person, guys," she gushes. "He's *godlike* in person."

"I like her," I declare, making Eli chuckle.

"And when I told him I'm a model," she says, "Savage goes, 'Well, I'm not surprised about that. You're *stunning*. Actually, you know who you remind of . . .?'" She pauses for effect, her blue eyes dancing, before finishing with, "'*Laila*.'"

"Oh, Jesus," I mumble.

"Pause it," Eli commands. And when I comply, he asks, "Did you say that?"

"I . . . I don't know," I stammer. "Would it be bad if I did?"

"There's no good or bad answer here. Only the truth."

I shrug. "I guess it's possible. Like I said, I was drunk. And she definitely looks a bit like Laila."

"She's her doppelganger."

"No way. Laila is way hotter." Eli furrows his brow with surprise, so I quickly bark out, "Can I press play again, please?"

"Sure."

My heart pounding, I cue the video. And once again, the woman springs to life.

"So, after some flirting," she says, "I decided to make my move. I suggested we head to Savage's room upstairs—"

"See?" I mutter.

"So he could make my fantasies come true. And guess what Savage said to me in reply to that? You won't believe it. Brace your-selves. He said, 'Sorry, I can't . . . because of . . . *Laila.*'"

"Bullshit!" I blurt.

The woman clutches her heart, just above her ample breasts. "I was like, 'I knew it!' And Savage just laughed and winked."

"I did not. She's a *liar.*"

The Instagrammer continues, "And then, *I* said, 'You're the sweetest boyfriend, *ever.*'"

"Fuck!"

"And he goes, 'I'm not being *sweet.* I made a *promise* to her, and I'm going to keep it.'"

"What the fuck?" I yell. I pause the video and practically hurl the phone at Eli. "I said none of that! Zippo. Zero! Either she's lying, or she misheard me. I think she said something like, 'Thanks for being so sweet about this.' And I said, 'I'm not being sweet. I made a promise.' But I was talking about my contract! The morality clause! I didn't say I couldn't fuck her because of *Laila.* Why would I say that? I'd never say that! Laila never even crosses my mind!"

Eli chuckles. "Calm down, Player. I know she's full of shit. And so do the producers. If you ask me, the most logical explanation is that you said she *looks* like *Laila,* which she does, and then, when you said the next thing, she made the mental leap that you'd said the word 'Laila' *again.* My bet? You told her you needed to 'lay low' because of your contract."

Oh, thank God. I feel like he's just thrown me a lifeline. "Yes!"

I shout. "That's exactly what I said! *Lay low!* Not *Laila!* That's obviously what I said!"

"You use that phrase a lot."

"I do! I totally do!" I exhale with relief. "I remember everything now. I said I had to 'lay low' because of the show. And when she said thanks for being sweet, I said, 'I'm not being sweet, I made a promise to the show.' *Boom.*" Oh, God, I'm so relieved. I sit quietly for a beat, rubbing my forehead, feeling like I've dodged a bullet. Until, suddenly, a horrifying thought strikes me—one that makes my blood turn cold. "Oh, fuck. Laila can't see this video, Eli! Hand me my phone. I've got to post a rebuttal video, explaining what I *really* said, so Laila doesn't see this bullshit and think—"

"Like hell you will. That video, and the fact that the whole world believes every word of it, is the only thing keeping your job on life support right now."

"How?"

Eli gestures to the phone in my hand. "Watch the rest."

With a loud groan, I press play again, and this time, the woman says, "So, guys, I can confidently report the exclusive scoop that Savage and Laila Fitzgerald are, indeed, secretly together, despite their denials."

"I've never denied anything," I mutter.

She continues, "Am I disappointed about Savage being off the market? Absolutely. But, at least, I'm thrilled to know he's so happy and devoted to his girlfriend." She leans into the camera. "Now, don't you dare break our Savage's heart, Laila. Or I'm coming for you, bitch." She snarls comically and the video ends.

I hand Eli his phone, my heart thudding in my ears. "I don't see how this isn't a horrific disaster for me. The thought of Laila seeing that and thinking I actually said any of that stuff makes me want to throw myself off a bridge."

Eli laughs. "Forget Laila's reaction. That's a casualty of war. All that matters is what the world thinks. And thanks to that, the producers have given me until five today to pull a rabbit out of my hat."

"What rabbit? Stop speaking in code and tell me what's going on."

Eli grins. "A rabbit called *Laila*. If we can convince her to be *your* team's mentor this season, rather than Aloha's—and for *three* episodes, rather than one, and if—"

"Kendrick's going to be my mentor this season!"

"Not if we can get Laila."

"She won't do it. She hates me. Even for a three-episode stint, she'd never agree to it."

"You didn't let me finish. There's something else she'd have to do besides being your mentor for three episodes." He smiles. "She'd also have to pretend to be your girlfriend."

My jaw hangs open. My manager has rendered me speechless.

Eli smiles. "Just like the Instagrammer said."

"That's . . . the stupidest thing I've ever heard."

"Maybe so," Eli says with a shrug. "But it's the only way for you to stay on the show. The producers don't believe the Instagrammer's version of the story, any more than I do. But guess who *does* believe her? Your fans and Laila's. You should see the comments online. People are losing their minds. They're obsessed. And that's got the producers' attention. After the debacle with Hugh, they're desperate to lock in some huge ratings this season. And they think this storyline—a romance between you and Laila, unfolding before the audience's eyes for three whole weeks—will be a ratings bonanza."

My mind is racing. "Did they tell Laila about this idea yet?"

Eli nods. "They called her this morning. I'm told her answer was, 'Hell to the fucking no.'"

I throw up my hands in exasperation. "Then why are we even talking about this?"

"Because it's your only option, Savage! Because I have to believe Laila's agent is smart enough to tell Laila that her knee-jerk reaction, if, indeed, that's truly what it was, was stupid. I have to believe Daria, Laila's very smart agent, has only conveyed her client's alleged knee-jerk reaction, if that's what it was, as a negotiation tactic. Daria is one of the best in the business. She knows this is a massive opportunity for Laila—the kind of exposure that will make her a household name. I have full faith Daria will eventually help us talk some sense into Laila."

"Good luck with that. Nobody can talk sense into Laila Fitzgerald."

"Well, we have to do it. And by five o'clock today."

"So, you're saying you think Laila's agent only said Laila flatly refused, to get her more money?"

"*Exactly*. She's playing hardball."

"Okay, then. Cool. Call the producers and tell them to sweeten the pot. What does that have to do with me?"

Eli shakes his head. "I already tried. They were adamant they won't negotiate against themselves. It's *our* job to get Laila to agree to the deal—or, at least, to come to the table to negotiate more money—by five o'clock today. The producers didn't say this, but I have to believe, if Laila says she's *open* to being your mentor and fake girlfriend for the right *price,* they won't let this ratings magnet slip through their fingers. They know this would be a win-win-win."

"The problem still remains, Eli. I can't convince Laila Fitzgerald to do a damned thing. Trust me on that."

"Well, you've got four million reasons to try. If you want to keep your job—and the fat salary that comes with it—then you'd better do or say whatever it takes to make her say yes."

I scoff. "If I knew how to make Laila say yes, trust me, I would have done it a long time ago. Plus, this isn't going to work, regardless. Now that Laila knows I *need* her to keep my job, she'll say no, just to spite me."

"Do you think I'm stupid?" He leans back in his armchair. "Laila doesn't know you need her. I made sure the producers won't tell her that."

I flap my lips together. "*Fine.* I'll do my best. But I'll need to call Laila from your phone, because the little psychopath blocked my number during the tour."

Eli scoffs. "You're not gonna *call* Laila, dumbass. You're gonna do this in person."

"What?"

He stands. "Come on. Get showered and dressed, Player, while I call room service for some coffee and breakfast for you. And make sure you put on some cologne and make yourself look extra irresistible. Your future fake girlfriend and her agent are expecting us at noon."

TWENTY-TWO

LAILA

"Look, I get that you think Savage is an arrogant jerk," my agent, Daria, says, although she doesn't know the half of it. "But I think you should put your emotions aside and think about this as a business decision, Laila. I really think this could be a game changer for you."

I'm sitting across from Daria in her Beverly Hills office. I'm in jeans and a T-shirt. She's dressed like the goddess she is in a Gucci pantsuit and large gold hoops. And, honestly, I don't know why I'm here, seeing as how we've already talked about this on the phone and I've told her the offer is a non-starter. If it were anyone else, I would have refused to race down here to talk about the producers' crazy offer, yet again, only this time in person. But I suppose, at the end of the day, I respect my agent's opinion far too much to ignore an "urgent" request from her.

"I'm sorry," I say. "Like I said on the phone, I couldn't pull off a fake romance, even if I wanted to. My dislike of Savage runs too deep. After one episode, let alone three, the whole world would know I'm a liar."

"Aw, I have faith in your performance skills," Daria coaxes. "All you'd have to do is focus on nothing but Savage's physical beauty, and ignore everything else about him, and, *voila*, you'd convince yourself he's the great love of your life." She leans forward across her sleek desk. "In other words, I'm telling you to think like a man."

We both giggle at the joke.

Daria leans back in her high-back chair again, steepling her fingers. "Do you think you'd be able to fall in 'fake love' with Savage for the right price?"

I shake my head. "You know they reserve the real money in their budget for the judges. They'd never offer me anything even close to what I'd need to feel tempted."

Daria lifts an eyebrow. "Ah, so you admit there *is* a number, at least, theoretically, that could make you say yes."

"Hypothetically, sure. But whatever that number is—and, honestly, I don't know what it would be—the show would never offer it to me, so it's a moot point."

Daria looks like the gears in her head are turning. "I'm not so sure about that. When I spoke to the executive producer, Nadine, this morning, she played it cool, but I could tell she was *dying* to make this happen. Thanks to that video of you and Savage arguing on the sidewalk in New York, and your interview on *Sylvia*, and, the meme from the awards show, and now, this Instagrammer's viral video, I don't think it's an understatement to say you and Savage are a powerhouse. A shoo-in to grab massive ratings. Surely, Nadine knows that."

None of this is new information. Daria said all of this, essentially, during our conversation on the phone.

When I shrug and say nothing, simply because I don't believe for a minute the show would pay me what it would take, Daria puts her elbows onto her desk and smiles.

"What do you make of that Instagram video?" she asks. "Do you think she was telling the truth about what Savage said?"

I snort. "Heck no. If a beautiful woman suggested going upstairs, I guarantee I didn't even cross Savage's mind. Obviously, that Instagrammer came up with a story she knew would make her video go viral."

Daria looks unconvinced. "Well, for God's sake, don't let on you don't believe the video when you see Savage. Let him think you believe every single word."

"I don't plan to see him. Even when I'm on-set in a few weeks, I'm going to avoid him like the plague."

Daria smirks. "Actually, you'll be seeing Savage sooner than you think." She looks at her watch. "He was supposed to be here five minutes ago, actually."

"Daria!"

She shrugs. "His agent called and begged me for a meeting and I felt it would be in your best interests to hear him out."

I cross my arms over my chest. "I don't want to see him."

"Come on. At the very least, won't it be fun to torture him by pretending you believe every word that woman said? That has to be his worst nightmare."

I twist my mouth. She's got a point. "Still," I say, "the fun in that wouldn't outweigh the discomfort I'd feel at seeing him."

"Why do you hate him so much?" Daria narrows her eyes. "You two really did get together, didn't you? You fell for him, and he cheated on you?"

"Oh, God, no. Daria, listen. I sincerely appreciate you looking out for me and fighting so hard for my career, but there's no point in having this meeting with Savage and his agent. The show won't offer me enough to tempt me. And you said yourself three episodes as a mentor won't make that much more of an impact than one."

"You're misconstruing what I said."

"Regardless, it's not like they're offering me a seat at the judges' table with a paycheck to match. So, let's just—"

"Well, now we're getting somewhere," Daria interrupts. "Are you saying, if I *could* get you that—a seat at the judges' table with a paycheck to match—you'd say yes?"

My lips part in surprise that she's even saying that out loud. "They already said they don't want me as a judge. Hence, the reason they hired Savage to replace Hugh, rather than me."

"True, but that happened before today—before that woman's

video went off like an atomic bomb on the internet." She leans back and swivels in her chair. "I could be wrong, but I've got a hunch the landscape dramatically shifted underneath Savage's feet this morning. Don't you think it's a bit weird his agent called me, asking for this meeting? He made it sound like Savage was willing to do *you* a favor by saying yes to this . . . but would Savage *really* do a favor for you?"

"Absolutely not." I pause. "So . . . what, then?"

"I'd bet money Savage's job is on the line this morning, thanks to his shenanigans last night. My hunch is that Savage's head is on the chopping block, and thanks to that woman's video, and everything that's come before, the producers have made *you* a condition of Savage's continued employment."

My mouth hangs open as my eyes widen with glee.

"Now you understand why I begged you to come down here for this meeting. If I'm right about Savage's job depending on *you*, and if I'm right about the show practically drooling over this idea, then I think I can leverage both sides against the other to get you an offer you simply can't refuse."

I clutch my heart, feeling like it's beating a mile a minute. "Okay, this might be a stupid question, but if you're right about Savage's job being on the line, then why wouldn't I say *no* to being his fake girlfriend, thereby getting Savage shit-canned, and then swoop in and take his job?"

Daria shakes her head. "I'm sorry, honey. If they fire Savage, I'm sure they'll replace him with some other heartthrob. On your own, your platform simply isn't big enough yet. But with Savage, you're in the cat's seat. So let's agree to help Savage keep his seat at the judges' table . . . as long as he agrees to help you get a seat right next to his."

I gasp. "At the judges' table? Not as his mentor?"

"Correct. For the entire season. With a salary to match."

I'm reeling. Losing my mind. "You really think that's possible?"

"It's a long shot, so don't get too excited. But it's worth a try. My gut tells me Savage is desperate, and the producers are frothing at the mouth. So, let's see if we can exploit all of it to your advantage."

I look out the floor-to-ceiling window of Daria's office at the glamorous hustle-bustle of Beverly Hills for a moment, trying to collect myself. And when I finally return to my agent, I can't hide it. I'm excited. "Okay," I say on an exhale. "Let's give it a try."

As Daria whoops, a buzzing noise rises up from the intercom on her desk, followed by a male voice announcing, "Ms. Brown, Eli McKenzie and his client are here to see you."

A demonic smirk lifts one half of Daria's mouth. "Keep a poker face at all times. If I say something blatantly false, nod your head subtly and roll with it."

"Got it."

Daria presses a button on the intercom with her long fingernail and says sweetly, "Thank you, Hunter. Please, escort my guests to my office." She winks at me. "We're ready for them."

TWENTY-THREE

SAVAGE

The office door opens and a striking Black woman I vaguely recognize is standing before Eli and me. She says hello to Eli, whom she clearly already knows, and introduces herself to me as Daria Brown, before leading us into her elegant office.

We follow Daria into the spacious room and find Laila sitting in a corner, her body language in her armchair like she owns the place.

When Eli and I reach Laila, she doesn't stand. Eli greets Laila with a handshake, but I don't bother extending my hand. She won't take it, anyway.

"Hello, Fitzy," I say, as I take a seat next to Eli on a small couch.

"Hello, Adrian," she replies stiffly.

"You're looking well," I say, leaning back and spreading my legs slightly. It's an understatement. Every time I see this woman, she hits me like a ton of bricks. I add, "As always."

"Thank you. So are you." She smirks. "As *always*."

I don't know how Laila does it. Her words were complimentary, like mine, but her tone somehow transformed them into a dig. But that's Laila for you. A master at throwing shade that gives you whiplash.

"Sorry we're a bit late," Eli says, eliciting a barely audible scoff from Laila—one that conveys she's not the least bit surprised. Eli pauses, briefly, at Laila's interruption, before adding, "A couple paparazzi were waiting for Savage as we left his hotel. So, we took the long way around, to be on the safe side."

Laila's blue eyes are fixed on mine now, so I flash her a look regarding Eli's explanation that says, *See? This time, it wasn't my fault.*

In reply, Laila shoots me a look that says, *I don't believe it for a second.*

And in reply to that, I roll my eyes and look away.

Daria, the agent, says, "It was the right call to play it safe. If we're successful in putting together a deal, we wouldn't want anyone knowing about this backdoor meeting."

"Exactly my thoughts," Eli says.

"There's no need to apologize for being late," Laila says sweetly. But when she shifts her gaze back to me, her expression turns snarky. "I was on tour with Savage for three months, remember? I never expected him to be on time for this meeting, in the first place."

Eli chuckles at Laila's dig, while I exhale and shake my head.

"Well, this is gonna be fun," I mutter.

Daria clears her throat. "Why don't we get down to business, fellas." She leans back in her armchair and crosses her legs. "You gentlemen requested this meeting, so go ahead and make your pitch to Laila as to why she should do this huge favor for Savage."

"Oh, it wouldn't be a favor for *Savage*," Eli insists. "Like I said on the phone, this would be Savage doing a huge favor for *Laila*. He knows how much this would help her career, and—"

"Cut the bullshit," Daria snaps, jerking forward. "Nadine told me everything, on the down low, so let's skip ahead to the part where you try to convince Laila to save Savage's ass from getting shit-canned."

I can't believe my ears. Eli swore Laila would never know I need her to save my job! My jaw hanging open and my eyes bugging out, I look at Eli, as if to say, *Can you believe Nadine ratted me out?* And, instantly, I know I've screwed up when Laila's agent across from me blurts, "I knew it!" while pointing at my face.

"Goddammit, Savage," Eli says, shooting me a murderous glare. "I told you to maintain a poker face at all times."

I look down. Shit. He totally did.

Laila chuckles. But I'm too pissed to look up at her. Fuck.

Daria says, "It's time to put your cards on the table, Eli. Savage messed up last night and, now, his ass is in a sling. The question is: what is Savage willing to do for Laila to save himself?"

Eli leans back. "Savage doesn't need to do a goddamned thing for Laila. This opportunity is way too big for her to pass up. Savage could walk away from this show and still have a monster career that's ten times bigger than Laila's. I'm sorry, Laila, but it's true. This opportunity would be a game-changer for you. You need to be smart."

"Don't address my client directly, please," Daria says. "Especially not to condescendingly tell her to 'be smart.' I represent her in this negotiation, and I'll tell her what I think is 'smart.' And then she'll use her big ol' brain to make the final decision."

Eli bristles. "I apologize, Laila. No disrespect intended."

"It's fine."

Eli returns to Daria. "I'll say this to you, then. You're doing your client a *huge* disservice, if you're letting her think, even for a minute, she should turn this opportunity down."

Daria sniffs. "I disagree. The per-episode fee for mentors is an insult, especially when they want Laila to take on the added duty of fawning all over your client like he's the great love of her life."

"Fair enough," Eli says. "Then do your job. Rather than sitting here busting my balls about the money, call the producers and demand a sweeter deal."

Daria looks fit to be tied. "Oh, is that how negotiations work, Eli? Thanks for mansplaining it to me." She narrows her eyes.

"Believe me, I know exactly what I'm doing. Before I'd even *think* about calling the producers to 'demand a sweeter deal' for my client, we'll first need to reach an understanding between ourselves about our joint demands."

Eli pulls a face. "Our joint demands? We have none. Whatever 'demands' you might have, they're between Laila and the producers."

"Jesus, Eli. Either you're full of shit, or genuinely terrible at this. I'll assume it's the latter, and break it down for you. If you want to lure *my* client to the negotiating table with the producers, then *your* client will need to promise to present a united front with her, during those negotiations, on all her key demands."

Eli sighs and drapes his arm over the back of the love seat. "Which are?"

"Thank you for asking." Daria smiles. "Laila would consider taking part in the proposed fake romance, *if* she's doing so as a full-fledged *judge* for the entire season."

"Ha!" Eli blurts, as I sit forward gaping like a fish.

Daria calmly says, "We want a seat at the judges' table for Laila, and we want Savage to help her get it, or this whole deal will be dead and Savage can kiss his job goodbye."

I look at Laila, trying to gauge if she's onboard with this attempted extortion, but her face is impassive. A perfect poker face, unlike mine.

"It's impossible," Eli says.

"Nothing's *impossible*," Daria insists. "They hired *Savage* as a judge, in the first place, despite his reputation for being a woman-izing man-child who can't keep his donkey dick off Twitter." She smiles at me. "No offense, Mr. Savage."

I can't help returning her smile. "None taken. I actually thought you were complimenting me."

Daria bursts out laughing. "And there's that famous charm. By the way, I thoroughly enjoyed Twitter this morning. That was a top-notch swan dive."

"Why, thank you. I was simply doing my part to spread joy in an otherwise bleak world."

"You're a saint."

"Would you tell Laila that, please? She seems to think I'm the devil." I glance at Laila and smile when I discover her poker face has been replaced by a grin. A reluctant one, but it's there. I explain to Laila, "It was Kai's birthday last night. He dared me, so I had no choice."

"Ah. Birthday Truth or Dare," Laila says, having heard stories about our long-running game from Kendrick. She adds, "Well, then, screw the morality clause in your contract. You had no choice but to strip down and take that naked flying leap."

"See? I knew you'd get it. Why can't the producers?"

Her reluctant grin widens, and for the first time in a long time, we share an easy smile. One that feels genuine and not laced with arsenic. And I can't help thinking that's probably a good sign for my chances here.

Daria says, "The producers know The Savage and Laila Show would bring in record ratings. And that's all they care about, really. *Ratings.* So, let's work together to convince them that's exactly what they'd get."

Eli chuckles. "I admire your tenacity. But you're aiming too high. They haven't budgeted for a fourth judge and the season starts shooting in two days. Please, Daria, let's talk more realistically and find a middle ground we can—"

"There's no middle ground," Daria says flatly. "Laila needs to be offered a full-fledged judgeship this season, with a salary to match, or she'll stick with her current contract and appear for one episode as *Aloha's* mentor. Agree to present a united front with us on a phone call, or this meeting is over."

I flash Laila a look that says, *Damn, maybe I need another agent.* And she flashes me a return look that says, *Right? She kind of scares me a little bit.*

I smile.

So does Laila.

Again.

And, suddenly, I feel tingles skating across my skin.

"For the record," Eli says, "I think you're trying to climb Mount Everest in stilettos. But we're willing to stand united with you, while you try. Right, Savage?"

I nod. "Honestly, I think Laila would make a great judge. I'm all for it."

In truth, I'm deeply skeptical Daria can make this happen for Laila, but why not let her try? It'd be no skin off my nose, if Laila became a judge. In fact, I'd kind of like having her around. First off, to amuse and distract me while I try to stave off the inevitable hives that will surely come from my presence on such a stupid show. But, more importantly, the more weeks Laila appears on the show, the more time that will give me to try to get her into my bed—to finally convince that stubborn woman to let me eat her pussy while she eats her words. The ones that have been torturing me for two months. *This will never happen again.* If Daria's pitch isn't successful, I'm sure she'll cave and negotiate some middle ground for Laila —which, in the end, will keep me on the show, either way.

"Thank you, Adrian," Laila says, looking genuinely touched. And I feel a sudden jolt of optimism that maybe Laila could find her way to falling out of hate with me, at the end of all this.

I wink. "Sure thing, Fitzy. I truly meant that. I think you'd be great." Laila beams a huge smile at me and I feel myself blush. My heart racing, I look at Daria. "All right, then. Let's make the call and convince the producers to make Laila's little girl dreams come true."

TWENTY-FOUR

LAILA

"I can't emphasize this enough," Nadine, the executive producer of *Sing Your Heart Out,* says to our foursome— Daria, me, Savage, and his agent—on speaker phone. "*If* we were to bring Laila on as a fourth judge this season, we'd require Savage and Laila to really sell the romance, both on and off camera, for the *entire* season—plus, a one-month grace period after the finale airs, so nobody thinks the romance was a set-up."

We've been talking to Nadine and some other producers on her end of the call for the past twenty minutes. And much to my shock, Nadine and her people *still* haven't hung up the call and/or told us to pound sand. On the contrary, without committing to anything, Nadine and her team keep artfully testing the waters, lobbing out different concerns and hypothetical non-negotiables they'd require "if" they were to agree to Daria's "unthinkable" proposal. And through it all, true to his word, Savage has maintained a united front with me, casually saying "not a problem" to literally every-thing the producers have demanded.

Which, by the way, included the shocking demand that Savage and I would cohabitate this season in a location supplied by the show. When I freaked out, Nadine explained it would make the relationship more believable. Plus, it would make it easier for us to post daily on social media, like a real couple, which would be another requirement. And, finally, Nadine assured us the chosen place would be large enough for Savage and me to cohabitate without murdering each other, and full of enough amenities we'd feel like we're on vacation. And what did Savage say to that particular bit of craziness? To my surprise, all he said was, "Just as long as our place has a hot tub. Laila and I would *definitely* need a hot tub."

Savage was equally unfazed when the producers made it clear they'd require him to quit drinking for the duration of the season, *if* they were to agree to Daria's proposal. All Savage said that time was his usual, "Not a problem."

Currently, Nadine is saying, "We'd also expect Laila to help keep Savage in line. You know, make sure he gets to the set on time and keeps his dick off Twitter."

Everyone on the call, and in Daria's office, laughs, while Savage pushes back for the first time.

"I don't need a babysitter," he says.

"Shut the fuck up," Eli says.

And Savage presses his lips together and looks out the window.

"So, is everything doable, then?" Nadine asks on speaker phone.

"Savage?" Eli says.

"Fine," Savage replies.

"Laila?" Nadine asks.

"Fine for me, too," I say. I look at Savage. "But if I'm going to babysit you, you'd better not give me any trouble."

Savage flashes me a look that says, *Hey, I make no promises.* And without meaning to do it, I smile in reply.

Nadine says, "We're a bit concerned about the relationship being outed as fake. The last thing we'd want is for a flurry of your recent hookups to come out of the woodwork and create a 'cheating scandal' for us. How far back can we safely say this relationship started?"

Savage and I look at each other, neither of us wanting to speak first. On my end, I haven't been with anyone since Savage. And before him, I hadn't been with anyone since my ex-boyfriend, Shawn. So, I'm a clean slate for the past six months. But I certainly don't want to tell Savage that, especially not after our tiff backstage at the Video Music Awards, when I demonically fanned the flames of Savage's ridiculous jealousy about Charlie.

"What if we were to say you two have been living together for the past . . . month?" Nadine ventures. "Would that work?"

Everyone in the room, including me, looks at Savage, since we all know his reputation with women. Indeed, from what I saw first-hand on tour, I can't imagine Savage hasn't been with a virtual army of women over the past month.

Nadine continues, "In theory, we could track down a *few* people and ask them to sign an NDA to make this work. But if we're talking about too many people, then the risks of a leak are probably too high."

Again, the room stares at Savage, prompting him to blurt, "Why is everyone looking at *me*? Laila's the one who jumps from relationship to relationship, from basketball player to fitness trainer, without pausing to catch her breath."

I glower at him. "Hello, pot. Meet kettle."

"Actually, I've been a monk this past month. Since we got back from the tour, I've been keeping crazy hours in the studio, recording our new album."

"Well, that's a lucky break," Nadine says. "Talk about dancing through raindrops! Laila? How about you?"

I can't find my voice. Savage hasn't been with *anyone* since we got back from touring a full month ago? I shouldn't do it. But I have to know. I ask, "You mean everyone you've been with this past month has already signed an NDA, so you're all set?"

"No, I mean I haven't been with anyone. I've practically been living in the studio, except for when I flew home to Chicago for a short visit. I've barely had time to work out this past month, let alone screw around."

I make a face that says, *Color me shocked.*

"Laila?" Nadine repeats. "Can you make that timeline work on your end?"

Crap. I've *so* enjoyed letting Savage think I had a torrid fling with Charlie the Personal Trainer during the tour—and that, maybe, said fling has continued since then, right up until last night. But, oh well. I've got no choice. On the bright side, Nadine only asked about this past month. If I had to admit the full truth, that I haven't had sex with anyone, other than Savage, over the past six months, I'm certain I'd die of humiliation.

I clear my throat. "I'm all clear for the past month, too. I've been really busy myself."

Savage's face is lit up like the Fourth of July. "You've been busy doing *what*?" he asks. Surely, he knows I haven't been hard at work on my next album. Not this soon, when my current album is still spitting out singles. Luckily, though, I've got a fairly credible answer at the ready. One rooted in truth, even if it's not entirely true.

"I've been working a ton on a couple of side projects," I reply. "A collaboration with 22 Goats and a duet with Alessandra Tennison—the one from the video shoot? Her single is doing so well, she got a full-album deal."

"Good for her," Savage says, apparently believing my every word.

I sigh with relief. The projects I've mentioned are real. But while I've laid down vocals for both tracks this past month, the time commitment for both projects combined amounted to only two sessions in the vocal booth. Hardly enough time to claim I've been "working a ton" this past month. In reality, I've been decompressing from the tour. Hanging out with my family, binge-watching shows, working out, and making weird butter dishes, bowls, and vases on my pottery wheel for friends and family who'll never use them. But there's no way I'm letting Savage know I've been a lazy bum this past month, with ample time, but zero interest, in dating.

"So, have we heard all your terms, Nadine?" Daria asks.

"Yes," Nadine confirms. "Are Savage and Laila prepared to agree to all of them?"

Looks are exchanged on our end of the call. Nonverbal confirmations given.

Daria announces, "Yes. Savage and Laila agree to everything."

A cheer erupts on Nadine's end of the call.

"Wonderful!" Nadine says. "We'll email the contracts to you within the hour and—"

"*Whoa*," Daria interjects, holding up her palm, despite Nadine not being here to witness the hand gesture. "Let's not get ahead of ourselves. We still need to deal with the small matter of Laila's *salary* before—"

"Laila's *salary*?" Nadine booms, sounding genuinely flabbergasted.

Daria furrows her brow. "Of course. Now that Savage and Laila have agreed to *your* terms, the next item on the agenda is negotiating—"

"Fucking hell, it is!" Nadine shouts, going from zero to sixty in a heartbeat. "This whole conversation, we've been assuming Savage and Laila had already worked out Laila's additional compensation on *their* end!"

"What?" Eli shouts. "Of course, not!"

Nadine counters, "*Of course!* We assumed you called us to offer *two* judges for the price of *one!*"

Well, that's it. Eli loses his mind, going off on a diatribe that makes Daria sit back in her chair, calmly steeple her fingers, and smile. And that's how I know this isn't a glitch. This isn't a sign that everything is falling apart. That, in fact, as far as my brilliant and conniving agent is concerned, everything is going exactly according to plan.

Savage leans into me. "Sorry it didn't work out for you, Fitzy. Honestly, I was pulling for you."

"Thanks for trying," I say. And it's all I can do not to smile wickedly as I say it. I don't know what Daria is up to, exactly. But whatever it is, I'm here for it.

After much shouting on the phone call, Nadine says to Eli, "I told you, quite clearly this morning, we don't have another cent in the budget to add to Laila's salary. We offered her a deal where she'd be Savage's mentor for *three* episodes, and that's all the money we've got at our disposal. Any compensation Laila requires in order to be promoted to a full-fledged judge this season—which, by the way, would give her the kind of publicity money simply can't buy— would need to come out of *Savage's* pocket, not ours."

Well, that gets Savage's attention. He jolts to standing and barks, "There's no way I'm paying Laila a dime of my salary. I was willing to support her crazy idea, as a *favor* to her, as long as it didn't affect *me,* but—"

I jump up, matching Savage's angry body language. "As a favor to *me,* my ass. You did it to save yourself! If anyone is doing a favor here, it's *me* doing one for *you!*"

"Bullshit," he grits out. "You know you've got me between a rock and a hard place, and you're shamelessly exploiting me."

"*Exploiting* you?" I retort. "*You're* the one who breached his morality clause, not me. *You're* the one who needs a fake girlfriend to 'redeem' your stupid fuckboy ass this season. You'd already be fired right now, if it weren't for me and the world's bizarre obsession with us being a couple."

Savage scoffs. "Gee, Laila. I wonder how the world got obsessed with that idea? Could it be you purposely fanned the flames of that rumor on *Sylvia,* for your own benefit?"

"I did not!" I shout. "I tried to put the fire *out* on *Sylvia!* I literally denied we're a couple!"

His tone dripping with sarcasm, Savage says, "Yeah, and you did it *sooo* convincingly." He rolls his eyes. "Ninety percent of all human communication is *nonverbal,* Laila. And guess what *your* nonverbal communication screamed on *Sylvia?* 'Hell, yes, we're totally fucking!'"

I gasp like this is news to me, even though countless friends texted me after that interview to razz me about that very thing. But good friends can tease me about that—not assholes I hate! Assholes who texted me their room number, begging me to show up so they could finally taste me, so they could "eat me from every angle," and then, minutes later, brought yet another groupie to their room.

"People were already obsessed with us being a couple before my interview," I insist. "That's why Sylvia brought up your name. And you should be grateful she did, because that interview going viral is what convinced Nadine to hire you as Hugh's replacement in the first place. Right, Nadine?"

"No comment."

"So let me get this straight," Savage says. "You shamelessly used me as click-bait on *Sylvia* to further your own career, and you want me to *thank* you for doing it?"

"Oh, you mean, kinda like how you used *my* name as click-bait last night, with that Instagrammer?"

Savage pulls a face like I've just barfed straight into his mouth. "I didn't even mention your name to that Instagrammer last night! I said I needed to 'lay low' because of the *show*."

"Sure, Jan," I say, invoking a famous meme from *The Brady Bunch*.

Savage says, "If you think a single word of what that Instagrammer said was true, then you're either crazy or projecting, or both."

"Projecting *what?*"

"*Your* obsession with *me* onto *me!*"

I roll my entire head, not only my eyes. "Oh, please. I haven't given you a moment's thought since the tour ended."

"Sure, Jan," he says, throwing my comment back to me.

"Was last night some kind of a staged set-up?" I ask.

Savage's features contort with disdain. "You're asking if I conspired with a random Instagrammer I'd just met at a party to post a crazy story about you and me . . . for publicity?"

It sounds even crazier when he says it back to me. But I persist. "Maybe. You had to know she's got a *huge* following."

"I didn't, actually."

"And you also had to know she *constantly* posts about her infatuation with *you*. She's practically president of your fan club! So, I don't think it's crazy to assume you knew she'd post about her interaction with you, however insignificant—see exhibits one through a million on Twitter—and you decided to give her something to post about. Something you knew would go viral."

Savage shakes his head. "You know you sound like a deranged lunatic right now, right?"

He's right. I do. I'm a stone-cold nutter. But I don't care. I'm a runaway train. "It's not any crazier than believing you told her you had to 'lay low' and she heard 'Laila.' Come on, Savage. We both know you said my name. And you *knew*, with all the publicity we've had lately—we're a freaking meme, dude!—that mentioning my name would be like throwing a lit match onto a puddle of gasoline!"

"I didn't say your name, for the love of fuck!" he roars, absolutely beside himself with frustration. "Thanks to your stupid interview on *Sylvia*, she *assumed* we must be fucking—just like everyone else assumes it! Do you have any idea how many friends texted me after seeing that interview? They were like, 'Dude, if you two aren't already having sex, then buy yourself a huge box of condoms, pronto, because Laila's gonna show up on your doorstep any day now, demanding to fuck you for a solid week straight!'?"

I gasp loudly.

"Don't even bother fake gasping with me, Laila Fitzgerald," Savage says. "I spent three months on the road with you. I know nothing fazes you."

He's right. That gasp was totally fake. And, unfortunately, a little over the top. But I don't care. I gasp again and say, "Nobody sent you a text about me after *Sylvia*. You're a liar."

"*Everybody* did," he replies.

"And by 'everybody,' you mean Kendrick and Kai?"

"Kendrick and Kai and lots more. C-Bomb . . ."

"And . . . ?"

"Lots of people."

"Bullshit."

"Swear to God.

"Prove it."

"I can." He pulls out his phone and starts swiping angrily. "I saved *all* their texts, in case I'd ever have the opportunity to rub them in your smug little face."

I snort. "Ha! That was a trap, Einstein, and you walked right into it. If your goal is to convince me you're *not* totally obsessed with me, then admitting you saved a bunch of texts about us being secret fuck buddies isn't helping your cause."

"I didn't *save* the texts," Savage insists. "I never *deleted* them, because I didn't get around to it."

"Wow, shocker. Yet another thing I can't stand about you. All your unread texts! Look at your inbox right now and tell me how many you have. I bet it's more than a thousand."

He looks down and makes a face that tells me I've guessed right. "They're not *all* unread. Just because I haven't clicked on them doesn't mean I haven't seen them in the preview pane or—"

"Hey, guys," Nadine interjects on speaker phone, and we both freeze. She continues, "This is highly entertaining. Truly, it is. But I've gotta stop you now." As Savage and I exchange a look I'd call, *Well, that's embarrassing,* Nadine chuckles and says, "Damn, I wish I had a big bowl of popcorn right now. Or maybe a vibrator."

Everyone on Nadine's end of the call explodes with laughter, as Savage and I return to our seats and exchange angry looks that say, *This is all your fault!*

"You two really would be ratings gold," Nadine says wistfully. "Great job, guys. If this 'fight' was your clever way of coaxing us to throw some more money into the pot for Laila, consider your tactic a success. We really don't have another dime in the budget to offer, but in an effort to close the deal, we're willing to offer Laila a performance slot in the finale."

Whoa.

That's the brass ring. The kind of publicity that catapults any song straight into the Top Ten, if not to Number One.

I look at Daria and she winks, yet again confirming everything is going exactly according to plan.

Eli interjects, "Savage would require a performance slot, as well."

Nadine exhales with annoyance. "Hold, please." She places the call on hold for an eternal moment, during which Savage and I exchange dirty looks to the beat of the elevator version of "Fuck You" by CeeLo Green. Finally, Nadine returns to the call and declares, "Okay. We'll give Savage and Laila a *shared* performance slot in the finale. They can do a mash-up of their respective singles, or anything else they come up with. But we only have *one* performance slot to offer the happy couple, collectively. So they'll have to learn to *share*."

Savage and I look at each other, conciliation slowly passing between us. It's not ideal, granted. But we could make it work. We might both have been posturing like peacocks with splayed tails for the past few minutes, but there's no denying a performance slot in the finale, even a shared one, is too big a perk to pass up.

"I could make that work," Savage murmurs.

I nod and look away, letting him know I agree, but only *barely*.

"Laila is on board, too," Daria says. "Unhappy about it but on board."

"Wonderful," Nadine says. "So, can I *finally* send over the contracts, then?"

"Not quite yet," Daria replies. "We have a deal, as far as *you're* concerned. But we still need to reach an agreement on our end about Laila's compensation."

"Jesus Christ, Daria," Eli snaps. "Savage isn't going to pay Laila a dime out of his pocket!"

Daria shrugs nonchalantly. "Then I'm sorry to say the deal is dead." She smiles ruefully at the phone on her desk. "Thank you for your time, everyone. We're sorry we couldn't make this work, but Laila is still thrilled to be Aloha's mentor for one episode this season."

"Eli!" Nadine barks. "Don't be a fool! Negotiate with Laila

about her compensation. For the love of all things holy, Savage is the one who screwed everything up here—so, if someone has to lose an ass cheek to make this work, it's going to be *him!*"

Savage and his agent exchange a look, and I know, in my bones, Savage realizes the truth of what Nadine said. It's a surprising development, to say the least, to witness Savage being so willing to make this work. Especially given what I know he thinks of this show. He said himself, in Philadelphia, he thinks it's cringey-ass. So, why did he say yes to being Hugh's replacement in the first place? And why is he fighting so hard to keep his job now? All I can think is the show must have offered Savage an arm, a leg, and two huge butt cheeks to do the show—some amount of money that made Savage willing to endure the "hives" he's sure to contract every time he steps on-set.

I look at Daria and it's instantly clear she's thinking what I'm thinking. *How much money did the show offer Savage to get him to say yes?*

"Hey, Nadine," Daria says, leaning over the phone on her desk. "What's Savage's salary this season?"

"Don't answer that," Savage's agent barks. "That's none of her business."

"I can't divulge that," Nadine confirms.

Daria places her palms on her desk, on either side of her phone. "I know what Aloha is making this season. Ten mill." She looks up at Savage, apparently trying to gauge his reaction. "I'm guessing, all things considered, Savage's deal would be *significantly* less than that. Maybe . . . a third of that?"

"Say nothing, Nadine," Eli shouts.

"I can't confirm or deny," Nadine replies. But something in her tone feels a whole lot like she's screaming, "Confirm, confirm, confirm!" Daria turns her dark, sultry eyes on Eli. "Come on, Mr. McKenzie," she coos. "Let's get this deal done. Both of our clients stand to make a shit-ton of money from endorsements and increased music sales after the season."

The adults in the room begin sparring, and while they do that,

Savage sidles up to me at the proverbial kiddie table, his body language cocky and decidedly sexual. He takes an empty armchair next to me.

"Hey, Fitzy," he says, like we're back in Providence, sharing a bottle of booze outside the twins' birthday party in the moonlight.

"You can't charm me into taking less money," I say flatly.

Savage bites his lower lip, well aware he looks irresistible when he does that. "I'm not trying to charm you into doing anything. I'm merely pointing out that, if we do this, we'll be stuck together in a kickass house—with a hot tub—for three months." He licks his lips in a way I've seen him do many, many times. Like he's thinking about performing oral sex. "I'm saying all the orgasms I could give you during our fake romance should be factored into your calculations. I'd think they'd be worth *something*."

I roll my eyes, even as every inch of my skin erupts in lustful goosebumps. "Not gonna happen. I told you that was a one-time thing that will never happen again."

Savage straightens up, all hint of seduction gone. "I'm not paying you a dime, Laila. Everything Daria's already negotiated for you is well beyond anything you dreamed was possible when you woke up this morning. So, stop being greedy."

I clench my jaw. "I'm not being greedy. This is business, and I'm letting my agent get me the best deal possible, which is exactly what your agent initially did for *you,* and what he's also doing now. Don't think, even for a minute, your donkey dick is some kind of dangling carrot for me."

"Sure, bunny. You're not any more believable now than you were on *Sylvia.*"

"If anyone is being greedy, it's you. You're the one who messed up, not me. So, you should be the one to have to sacrifice to fix your mess."

Sexual heat washes over him. He leans forward sharply, sending his sexy cologne into my nostrils. "You wanna see me being greedy, sweetheart? Then let me eat your pussy. I'll show you a kind of greed that'll take your breath away."

I inhale sharply, taken aback by the hungry look in his eyes.

"Laila!" Daria barks from across the room. "Stop talking to him right now!"

I lean back sharply, feeling like a kid who's been caught saying a curse word. "He wasn't convincing me of anything," I blurt. But even I can hear the lie in my tone.

"Oh, jeez," Daria mutters, throwing up her hands. "Seriously? The world is full of big dicks, Laila. He's got nothing to offer that can't be found elsewhere." She leans into the speaker phone. "Nadine, we're gonna have to call you back. Savage is trying to charm the pants off my client, literally."

Nadine replies she'll give our side fifteen minutes to reach a deal. "We're running out of time here, folks," she says sternly. "If you don't call us back within fifteen minutes, saying you've reached a deal on your end, we're going to cut bait and move forward with our Plan B—someone else we've already lined up to replace Savage, if needed."

Well, that gets everyone's attention, especially Savage's.

Daria ends the call and rests half her bottom on the edge of her desk. "Okay, gentlemen. You heard Nadine. She's already got someone else lined up. So, the question Savage needs to ask himself is this: 'Do I want one hundred percent of *nothing* . . . or *fifty* percent of *something?*'"

"He'll give her *ten* percent," Eli says.

And Daria replies by launching into a long speech about why I'm not going to take anything less than half Savage's salary, whatever it is. "This would have to be an equal partnership in all ways," Daria says. "Because Savage needs Laila as much as she needs him."

Eli protests. Daria gives as good as she gets. And through it all, I bite my lip to prevent myself from caving. Honestly, if left to my own devices, I'd take the offered ten percent and be done with this. At this point, if push came to shove, I'd do the damned show for free, for nothing but the exposure and that invaluable performance slot in the finale.

"Laaaailaaaaa," Savage coos softly, like he's camped between my legs and has just raised his head. "Sweetheart, call off your pit bull. Let's do this. Ten percent."

"Mr. Savage," Daria says, "Laila hired me precisely *because* I'm a pit bull. Fifty-fifty, or she walks. Tick tock." Daria glares at me, her dark eyes commanding me to keep my mouth shut. But I can't help myself. The pressure is getting to me. Maybe I am being greedy here, like Savage said.

"Savage, I have family members I want to help out with—"

"No, Laila!" Daria commands, putting up her index finger. "You don't need to justify getting yourself paid. Men negotiate *massive* paydays for themselves in every industry, and *nobody* ever holds it against them or wonders if they have family members to support."

I look at Savage, suddenly remembering our conversation in that green room in Philadelphia, when I admitted I'd been hired as a mentor on *Sing Your Heart Out.* "Actually, that's an excellent point, Daria. In the past, I've made the mistake of mixing business and emotion and not realizing what I'm worth. A really savvy businessman once told me not to do either. So, this time, I think I'll follow his brilliant advice."

Savage narrows his eyes and practically snarls.

"So, what's it gonna be, gentlemen?" Daria says. "We've got four minutes before Nadine hires Savage's replacement. We want fifty percent of Savage's take, whatever that is. Final offer."

Eli throws a Hail Mary. He says Savage has four bandmates, and a shitty deal with River Records, which means he nets far less from his music royalties than we probably think.

"Cry me a river," Daria replies. "Fifty percent. Yes or no?"

The guys huddle up. And as they do, I clutch my sides and rock in place, feeling like I'm going to explode from anxiety. But, finally, Eli and Savage break free of their conversation and confirm we've got a deal.

"Hallelujah!" Daria shouts, springing out of her chair. She shakes Eli's hand, and then Savage's, before wrapping me in a warm hug. And when I nuzzle my face into my agent's neck, a dam breaks inside me. As I cry into Daria's neck, she whispers into my ear, "This is gonna change your life forever."

After thanking her profusely, I disengage from Daria, expecting to find Savage awaiting me, the same way his agent is doing. But to my surprise, as I shake Eli's hand, Savage is sulking in a corner of Daria's office, gazing out the window.

"I'll call Nadine and tell her the good news!" Daria chirps, ignoring the thick anger wafting off the rockstar in the corner. She picks up her phone, but pauses. "Real quick. Now that we've shaken on it, what's Laila's fifty percent worth?"

Eli addresses his sulking client. "You wanna tell her?"

Savage turns his burning eyes from the window to me, leveling me with a glower that takes my breath away. "Congratulations, Miss Fitzgerald," he says, his jaw tight. "You just extorted me for two . . . *million* . . . bucks."

TWENTY-FIVE

SAVAGE

With jackets draped over our heads, Laila and I are guided into the backseat of an SUV in Daria's underground parking garage—the chariot sent by the show's producers to whisk us off, discreetly, to whatever overnight "hideaway" they've arranged until our permanent digs can been finalized. I hear the click of the back door as I settle into the backseat next to Laila's body heat. Then, the sound of the car's front doors opening and closing, followed by the voice of one of our two handlers—a bodyguard and driver sent by the producers—announcing, "All clear. You can uncover your heads now."

I remove the jacket from my head to find Laila, her sandy hair mussed and her face aglow, sitting next to me in the large SUV. Without delay, the driver starts the engine, prompting Daria and Eli to wave goodbye to us through the windshield like proud parents, and off we go, under cover of dark tinted windows, out the garage and into the midday sun on Wilshire Boulevard.

"This is wild," Laila says, sounding giddy. "I feel like 'the package' in a spy thriller!" She touches her ear, like she's talking into an earpiece. "The Package . . . is on . . . *its way*."

She giggles, but I'm still too pissed about the money to join her.

I was more than happy to help Laila secure a seat at the judges' table, if doing so didn't impact *me* and my bottom line. But I never would have lifted a finger to help her if I'd thought, even for a minute, it would pave the way for her to fleece me out of half my salary. I need every dime of that salary, and then some, to comfortably pay for my grandmother's house. I'm sure I can make the deal work somehow, probably with a loan. But a loan wasn't part of my plan when I decided to buy that house.

The giddy expression on Laila's face evaporates when she sees my sour one. "Oh, come on," she says, shoving my shoulder. "You're *still* grouchy about the money? Let it go!"

"Yes, I'm *still* grouchy. It's been less than an hour since we signed our contracts, through which you extorted me for two million bucks."

"Extorted," she mutters, rolling her eyes. "You made a willing and informed decision, based on expert guidance from your agent. Now, get up, dust off your knees, and get over it."

"*Get over it?* Laila, I'm rightfully going to be pissed about two *million* bucks until the day I die."

She holds up her water bottle, like she's toasting me. "Well, here's hoping that day comes sooner, rather than later, for both our sakes."

"I never even wanted to do the stupid show!" I blurt. "When they first offered it to me, I said *no*. They offered me two mill, and then three, before I finally, begrudgingly, said yes for four. I never would have done it for two mill!"

"Well, lesson learned," she says. "Maybe next time you won't take a two-million-dollar naked swan dive into a swimming pool where anyone could see you, huh?"

"It was a *dare*."

"No," she says. "It was Drunk Savage's way of self-sabotaging— of getting himself out of a contract he wishes he'd never signed in the first place."

I open and close my mouth. Is she right about that? It rings true. I've definitely had a problem with self-sabotage throughout my life.

Case in point, the way I pushed Laila away, so vigorously, during the tour. I lean toward her. "Tell the truth, Laila. Now that the contracts are signed and your agent isn't here to get you all fired up about the gender pay gap, you *know* you let Daria commit highway robbery on your behalf today, right?"

She scoffs. "Absolutely not. Am I elated about the way things worked out? Hell yes, I am! *Whoop!* This is one of the best days of my life." She narrows her eyes. "But I don't feel sorry for you. You're already making more money in a year than most people make in a lifetime. Way more than me, I'm sure, despite what your agent said about you having four bandmates and a shitty deal at the label."

"I'm not nearly as flush as you probably think. I've made some big purchases recently."

"Oh, *waah, waah.* You're blessed to be doing the thing you love most as your actual job, for some amount of money that would make anyone else feel like they won the lottery. So, suck it up. Your agent advised you to give me half your already-inflated 'salary' so you wouldn't get fired, due to your own screw-up. If you want to be mad at someone, be mad at yourself for being a self-sabotaging idiot."

Well, damn. I look out the window, so she won't see me smile. I don't like getting bitch-slapped by most people in this world. But when Laila does it, I can't deny that it turns me on.

Laila continues speaking to the back of my head. "Now, if you don't mind, I need you to stop complaining about the money, so I can try to get into character, which I can't do when you're acting like a whiny little bitch."

I return my gaze to hers. "Get into character?"

She nods. "Somehow, against all odds, I need to convince myself I'm not in deep *hate* with you, but in deep and abiding *love.*" At that last word, she sticks out her tongue, like a cat getting rid of a fur ball. And, once again, I look out the window to hide my grin. A lot of things suck about this situation. But being stuck with Laila for the next three months ain't one of them.

For the millionth time, I find myself wondering how she resisted coming to my room in Vegas and beyond. I would have bet *anything* she'd have caved at some point. In fact, I was so positive she'd relent and come to me in Vegas, I stayed up all night after that show, alone in my bed, waiting for her. Thinking every sound outside my door was her. I must have opened my hotel room door or peeked out my peephole ten times that night. Each time, feeling more and more deflated when she wasn't there.

"So, that's it?" Laila says, filling the silence. "You're going to look out your window and sulk and not speak to me?"

I take a deep breath and return my gaze to hers. "I'm not *not* speaking to you. I'm processing everything that's happened. It's been a crazy day and I've still got a hangover."

"Speaking of which, you think you'll be able to handle not drinking for the next three months?"

"Starting tomorrow, mind you. And yes, I'll be fine."

"I'll do it with you, if you'd like."

"They didn't require that of you."

"True, but what self-respecting fake girlfriend would make her fake boyfriend resist temptation for three months, all by himself?"

"Thanks. I'd appreciate that."

"Sure thing," she says. "You want to get shitfaced with me tonight, as a last hurrah?"

"I'm down."

"Fair warning: I'll probably be a lightweight tonight," she says. "I haven't been drunk for a while. I've been on a health kick lately. Eating clean."

"Yeah, you look *really* good."

"Thanks. So do you."

Heat passes between us. Or, at least, I feel it. And, again, I find myself wondering how the hell she resisted me for a full month— after *knowing*, for a fact, we're a five-alarm fire together. Was Charlie *that* amazing in bed?

My phone buzzes in my lap and I look down to find a text from Kendrick, asking me what happened at today's meeting with Laila.

I motion to my phone. "Kendrick is wondering what happened at the meeting today. Do you think it'd be a breach of my contract to tell him the truth about the situation? You know, about you and me?" As Laila knows, the producers were adamant that the truth about our fake relationship is "top secret." To be divulged only on a "need to know" basis.

Laila purses her lips and shifts her position on the car seat. "I think it's fine. The producers said not to tell anyone not directly related to the show, remember? But Kendrick *is* directly related to the show, since he's going to be your mentor this season. Even if you didn't trust him like a brother, I'm sure his contract contains a confidentiality clause, the same as ours."

"Excellent point, counselor."

"But don't worry, if I'm technically wrong and you aren't allowed to tell him, I promise on our fake love not to rat you out to the producers for spilling the beans."

Warmth pools in my chest at the adorable look on her face. "Thanks. If you want to text your mom and sister and tell them the situation, I also promise on our fake love not to rat you out. I know how close you are with them."

Laila's eyebrows shoot up in surprise. "How do you know that?"

My chest tightens. "You talked about them during the tour."

"Not to you. I'm sure I never told you anything about my mom and sister."

I feel my cheeks turning red. "You told Ruby or Kendrick when I was sitting nearby, I think . . ."

She looks floored but says nothing.

My cheeks burning hot, I say, "You mentioned your mom a couple times during your hideously exploitative *Sylvia* interview. You know, the one where you used me as click-bait? So, maybe that's what I'm remembering."

Laila rolls her eyes.

"So, are you going to tell your family or not?" I ask, desperate to deflect.

"No. I think I'll keep things to myself for a while. My sister is trustworthy, but give my mom some wine and a few of her best friends, and she'd likely babble the whole damned story, without meaning to do it."

I chuckle. "Yeah, it's probably best to keep things tight as a drum for now, and stick with only telling people directly involved with the show."

"Agreed. Better safe than sorry."

"So, are you gonna tell Aloha, then?" I ask.

"Yeah. She's going to laugh her ass off." Chuckling, she grabs her phone while I grab mine.

"Tell Aloha I say hi," I say.

"The same to Kendrick. Oh, hey . . ." She pushes on my thigh, and her touch sends a blast of arousal streaking through me. "Ask Kendrick to send me the scoop on babysitting Adrian Savage, since keeping you from self-destructing is apparently my actual *job* now."

"I can already tell you what he's going to say: 'You're fucked. There's no owner's manual. Every day with every one of Savage's many personalities is a new adventure.'"

She snorts. "More like a *nude* adventure."

I can't help laughing. "Are you complaining about that? Because if so, you're the only one."

"Oh, God. I've got to endure three months of this?" With that, she looks down and starts tapping away. I watch her for a moment, admiring her profile. And, finally, grab my phone and tap out a reply to Kendrick.

Me: Crisis averted. The meeting was IN-FUCKING-SANE, but, in the end, I'm still a judge, by the skin of my teeth, and you're still my team's mentor. But in a shocking twist, Laila is now the show's first-ever fourth judge and my live-in fake girlfriend for the entire season.

Kendrick: WHAAAAT?!?!?!

Me: It's reality TV, baby! LOL. They think a "romance storyline" will bring in record ratings. They're getting us a cool pad with lots of amenities so we can do tons of behind the scenes social media stuff. You know, like a real couple.

Kendrick: I'm shook. I got a text from the producers a few minutes ago, telling me to pack an overnight bag, clear my schedule for the rest of today and tomorrow, and stay tuned for further info. What's that about?

Me: They're pulling together a last minute promo shoot with the full cast this afternoon. They want to have everything ready to go right after tomorrow's press conference.

Kendrick: Where are you right now?

Me: In a car with Laila, being driven to some secret hideout for tonight.

Kendrick: I'm surprised you agreed to go along with this. But I'm SHOCKED she agreed.

Me: It took half my salary to get her to do it. And by that, I mean I'm literally paying her half my salary out of my own pocket.

Kendrick: WHAT?!?!?!?! WHY?!?!?!?!

Me: Long story. I'll tell you in person. Trust me, I'm not happy about it. But, in the end, it'll be worth it.

Kendrick: Yeah, regardless, you're still getting paid a shit-ton of EASY money, dude. And the show will sell a lot of records for us.

Me: Exactly.

Kendrick: Yo! I just got a text from the show. They're sending a car for me in an hour.

Me: Then I guess I'll be seeing you soon.
Kendrick: Be nice to Laila in the meantime.
Me: Now, why would I do that, when she likes assholes so much?
Kendrick: LOL. Okay, Player. You do you.

And then, hopefully, Laila, I think. But, of course, I don't say that to Kendrick. He's been cool about me getting with her in Phoenix, but there's no need for me to rub salt in my best friend's wound.

"Did Kendrick have any good babysitting tips for me?" Laila asks, when I put my phone in my lap.

"I forgot to ask him. But, like I said, there's no point. His reply would be, basically, 'You're fucked.'"

"You never know. Ask him, anyway. I've never babysat a full-grown man-child before, and I need all the help I can get."

I tap out the message and read Kendrick's immediate reply. "Kendrick says, 'Babysitting Savage is all about giving him positive reinforcement when he's a good boy, redirecting or gently scolding when he's a bad boy (but only if you catch him in the act). And, most importantly, always give him lots of chew toys so he doesn't destroy your couch or slippers because he's got a major oral fixation.'"

Laila giggles. "Tell him thanks. That's actually very helpful."

Damn. The look she just shot me was pure fire.

She motions to my phone. "Aren't you gonna tell him thanks?"

My eyes drift to her lips, briefly. "Uh. Yeah." I tap out the message and then plop my phone onto the car seat between us. I ask, "So, you want to start hashing out the backstory of our 'romance' before tomorrow's press conference?" It's what the producers told us to do, so our answers sound credible and consistent.

"There's no time like the present," she says. "What's the story of how we first got together, my darling? Let's start there."

"Hmm," I say. But before I've said more, our SUV hangs a right onto a quiet residential street, and, suddenly, I know exactly where we are—and where we're headed. I gesture toward the distinctive iron gate coming into view at the end of the long street—the one I recognize as the gate in front of Reed Rivers' hilltop mansion. "Looks like we're staying at Reed's tonight."

"Oh, wow . . ." she says, peering through the windshield. "That's his gate?"

"It sure is," I mumble. "Shit."

"You don't like Reed?"

"I like him fine," I lie. But, really, me not liking Reed isn't the problem. The truth is, I was looking forward to spending the evening alone with Laila. She already mentioned she's down to get shitfaced with me. And the last time we were both shitfaced, I practically fucked her off a lounge chair. But it's fine. Whether we're alone or staying at Reed's tonight, the plan is the same. It's now my mission from God to eat this woman while making her eat those fateful words that have plagued me since the night of the hot tub: *This will never happen again.*

TWENTY-SIX

SAVAGE

After our SUV passes through Reed's iron gate and comes to a stop in his large, circular driveway, there's a flurry of activity already in progress in front of the large house. Several vans and cars are parked there, and an army of workers are coming in and out. One of our bodyguards advises Laila and me to stay put in the backseat for a moment while he "inspects" the area for paparazzi, and when he's satisfied we're all clear, he swiftly escorts us from the SUV into Reed's house, as Laila giggles and makes another crack about the imaginary "spy thriller" we're starring in.

Upon entering the mansion, we're greeted by the executive producer of *Sing Your Heart Out*, Nadine Collins, who explains the workers are busy creating a studio in Reed's game room, where Laila and I, and the entire cast—all four judges and their assigned mentors—will shoot some promo videos and photos to be released after tomorrow's press conference—which, Nadine explains, will also take place at Reed's house, to minimize the potential for leaks.

"I've sent production assistants to collect some personal items for your stay tonight, as well as at the permanent location," Nadine says. "We should have the new place lined up by tomorrow night."

We thank her and she asks if we have any questions.

"Have you been able to confirm my mentor yet?" Laila asks. As was discussed today during one of our phone calls with the producers, now that Laila has been unexpectedly promoted to judge, both Laila and Aloha will need mentors, both of which will be selected by the producers with an eye toward maximizing ratings.

"We've got several mentor candidates we're in talks with," Nadine replies. "I've got a scheduled call to finalize our decision in . . . " She looks at her watch. "Damn. I'm late for my call. Reed is out back having a get-together with some friends. He said for you to come outside and join him." She calls to an elegant older woman who looks to be Latina, and when she arrives, the woman introduces herself as Reed's longtime housekeeper, Amalia. Nadine tasks Amalia with escorting us outside and getting us fed before scurrying off for her call like a chicken with her head cut off.

"Would you prefer to see your rooms before joining Reed outside?" Amalia asks. "Or *room*, if that's what you prefer?"

"We'll definitely need separate rooms," Laila replies. "Is there food outside?"

"Yes, lots of it."

"Then I'd prefer to go outside now and see our rooms later, please. If that's okay. I'm starving."

"Of course, dear. As you wish. I'll be here all night."

We follow the elegant housekeeper toward a set of double doors. And I can't help feeling an illogical pang of disappointment Laila said we'll need separate rooms.

Outside, we find Reed partying with a small group of friends. We're introduced to the only people we haven't met before—a couple Reed introduces as Henn and Hannah. From there, we greet the rest, all of whom we know. When Laila greets everyone, she gives them hugs like they're her lifelong besties, while I dispense a series of simple hellos. I'm especially standoffish with the wife of Dax Morgan, the lead singer of 22 Goats. Dax's wife, Violet, is also Reed's little sister. The one I flirted with a few years ago at a party, long before Violet had met Dax, without me realizing her connection to Reed. I don't know if Dax knows the story, but I wouldn't put it past Reed to tell him, and I feel a bit awkward about it.

Besides Dax and Violet, I'm relieved to see Fish, the bass player of 22 Goats, and his cute girlfriend, Alessandra, the artist from the music video in New York, are also here. Those two are as nice as humans come from the factory. So, at least, until Kendrick gets here, I won't feel like the entire party hates me.

As conversation continues, I hang back and watch my fake girl-friend flit around Reed's patio like the social butterfly she is, easily engaging with everyone, the same way she did during our tour. Staff, crew, musicians. It didn't matter during our tour. There was nobody Laila Fitzgerald couldn't charm and easily befriend. Unlike me. I mean, I can charm people. That's easy. But genuinely befriending them comes a whole lot harder for me.

As Laila and I are talking to Fish and Alessandra, Reed point-edly brings his date over to say hello to Laila and me. And, once again, like in New York, his date is none other than Georgina. The sultry reporter for *Rock 'n' Roll*. How Reed still hasn't gotten bored with her and moved along to the next yet, or, conversely, hasn't royally messed things up with her, I have no idea. But, plainly, by the couple's body language, they're still going strong.

As Laila hugs Georgina in greeting, Reed trains his steely gaze on me. "You remember my fiancée, Georgina, don't you, Savage?"

Reflexively, my eyes dart to Georgina's left hand. And, I'll be damned, she's wearing a glittering golf ball on her ring finger.

Laila expresses effusive congratulations to her friend—appar-ently the women bonded quite a bit during the music video shoot—while I say, "Yeah, of course, I remember Georgina. Congratula-tions, Reed. You're a lucky man."

"Yes, I am," Reed replies. And there's no doubt in my mind he means it. Also, that he's still holding a grudge from months ago, when I had the audacity to hit on Georgina when she appeared to be a single reporter at a party. It's so on-brand for Reed to be holding a grudge for something so stupid, I can't help chuckling to myself.

"What's funny?" Reed asks.

"Nothing. I'm so happy for you, I'm bursting with joy."

Reed glares at me like he wants to punch the smile off my face. So, I smile even more broadly at him. Why does Reed always have to make it so damned hard to like him? For the love of fuck, I didn't know Violet was his little sister when I hit on her a thousand years ago! And I didn't know Georgina was destined to become his future wife when I hit on *her*! Which, by the way, I only did for Kendrick's birthday amusement, in the first place.

Feeling thoroughly annoyed, not to mention kind of peopled out, I wander away from the group to fill a plate at a nearby food table. Once I've got my meal in hand, I wander to a quiet corner and gratefully take a load off.

After a while, Laila appears, holding her own plate and a glass of wine. "Is this seat taken, fake boyfriend?" she asks.

"I was saving it especially for you, fake girlfriend."

She sits. "Crazy day, huh?"

"It definitely took an unexpected turn."

"Are you still mad about the money?"

"Nah. I'm over it. It's only money. I can always make more."

"Now, that's the spirit." She peers at me. "You still look grumpy."

I shrug. "That's just my face."

She laughs. "I'm the same way. Unless I'm smiling, everyone thinks I'm pissed or angry. The irony is, when I'm smiling, it's far more likely I'm plotting murder. So never judge my emotions by my face."

"I think you've plotted my murder a time or two."

"Or a thousand."

"At least."

We eat in silence for a bit, until Laila says, "You don't like parties very much, huh?"

I pick up a chicken wing. "I like parties, as long as I'm not required to speak to anyone I don't know."

"Yeah, I picked up on that during the tour. You never once came to a single game night with the crew and staff."

"They had game nights?"

"Every Thursday night. It was fun."

"Nobody ever invited me."

"Would you have come, if they did?"

"No. But it would have been nice to be invited."

We're silent again for a while, eating and drinking. Looking at the spectacular view.

After a while, I say, "I don't think it's weird to prefer hanging out with my best friends, rather than strangers. Doesn't everyone prefer that?"

"Yes and no. Sometimes, it's nice to meet new people. Get to know them. Hear their stories."

I shudder and she laughs.

"You really hate to mingle, don't you?"

"I *hate* it. We have to do it so much in our line of work, so when I'm not 'on,' I'd much rather be totally 'off.'"

"I get that."

"But it's not the way you're wired."

"Not really. I love being alone to recharge, for sure. But I also love being around people, too." She takes a long sip of her wine, and I watch the movement of her lips as the fluid passes them, suddenly feeling overwhelmed with the desire to taste them. I remember them wrapped around my cock. The way they were swollen and red when I pulled myself out of her mouth.

"What about Fish?" she asks, pulling me from my reverie.

"What about him?"

"He's a friend of yours, right?"

"He's a friend of everyone's. He's like Kendrick. Why?"

"I was surprised you seemed kind of standoffish around him, earlier."

"I wasn't being standoffish. I was just . . . standing."

"It seemed like you were upset."

"Laila, that's just my face."

Laila laughs. "Okay."

"Honestly, I'd probably hang out with Fish a lot more, if he wasn't always hanging out with his bandmates."

She furrows her brow. "You don't like Dax and Colin? How is that possible?"

"I like them. They don't like *me*."

Laila scoffs. "That's impossible. Dax and Colin like everyone."

"C-Bomb is a good buddy of mine." I don't need to say anything further. Everyone at River Records, and probably in the world, knows the 22 Goats' smash hit, "Judas," penned by Dax, is about Dax's beef with the drummer of Red Card Riot.

Laila nods, apparently buying my explanation. I don't think it's the whole truth, though. But there's no way I'm going to mention I once hit on Dax's wife and also had a fling with Colin's ex-girl-friend to the woman I'm hell-bent on sleeping with.

"So, should we talk about our backstory now?" she asks.

Reflexively, my eyes drift to her mouth again. "Yeah."

"If we go by Nadine's suggested timeline," she says, "we got together around the end of the tour."

"Mm-hmm." My eyes are on her tits now. I haven't spent this much time in Laila's presence in a long time. I'd forgotten how intoxicating her simple presence is to me.

She takes a bite of food before saying, "The only bummer about that timeline is that it makes me out to be a bald-faced liar on *Sylvia*. Two weeks ago, I swore on national TV there was no truth to the rumors about us. And now, suddenly, it turns out we're in love and *living* together? So embarrassing."

"It serves you right," I say. "You *were* a bald-faced liar on *Sylvia*."

"No, I wasn't."

"Laila, I made you come three times, and during your last orgasm, you saw God. So, saying there was *no* truth to the rumors was, to put it mildly, not a true statement."

She pushes a lock of her sandy hair off her face. "Having meaningless sex with you *once* doesn't equate to me having an actual *relationship* with you—which is what Sylvia asked me about."

"You implied we'd never so much as kissed," I say. "Which was a lie."

She drops a chicken wing onto her plate in protest. "Sylvia specifically asked me if I'd ever had the pleasure of kissing your lips, and I *truthfully* said no."

When she mentions my lips, my eyes flicker to hers, ever so briefly, and when my gaze returns to her ice-blue eyes, she's smirking.

"So, what are you suggesting we do?" I say. "If you're suggesting we should say we got together *after* your interview on *Sylvia,* just so you can avoid looking like a liar, then no dice. I'd need way more time than that to fall in love with you. More than a month, actually. But I'm willing to say that to avoid the mess of our relationship overlapping with the tour."

"You'd need longer than a whole month to know you want me?"

"No. I'd need half a second to know that. I'm saying I'd need longer than a month to know I *loved* you. To want to live with you. Or, so I'd imagine. I've never fallen in love or lived with anyone before. But I think a month would be lightning quick for me to do either."

"Well, it's not like we *met* only a month ago. We've known each other for a long time now. Oh! I know! We could say you were secretly in love with me throughout the tour. That'd give you plenty of time to develop feelings of love, wouldn't it?"

For some reason, my breathing has become a bit difficult. "I'm not gonna be the simp who sat around, pining for you, while you fucked Malik, and then Charlie, during the tour. Fuck that."

She pauses. Opens and closes her mouth. And finally says, "It was only an idea."

"Yeah, and a terrible one. I'm not gonna be your puppy, Laila, even in a fake romance. You're gonna have to suck it up and admit you lied on *Sylvia*. We'll say we wanted our privacy and people will understand."

"Fine. But in exchange for me being outed as a liar, then you have to admit you were the one who caught feelings first. *You're* the one who pursued *me*."

"Well, of course, I pursued you. Look at you."

She giggles. "How did you finally make your move?"

I pause to consider. "When the tour was over, I realized I missed seeing your face every day. Your bitchy, evil little face."

She laughs again.

"So, I called you—from Kendrick's phone, of course, since you'd blocked my number—and I asked you to come over to my hotel room for pizza and fucking, minus the pizza."

She snorts. "Wow, how romantic."

"How would you prefer I did it?"

She twists her sultry lips. "You invited me to your house for dinner. But not *pizza*. Wine and dine me, dude!"

"I'd have to come to your place if that's the story. I've been living in a hotel since we got back from the tour."

She gasps. "Why?"

"Because I don't own a place."

"You mean you rent?"

"I mean I don't have a permanent residence. There's no point. I'm on the road so much."

"Ugh. I'd hate that. I love my condo."

I shrug.

"Okay, so you called me and apologized profusely. So, I suggested—"

"Apologized for what?"

"You know for what. Let's not go down this road again."

I pause. "Okay, fine. I apologized. But only after you did, for reaming me in front of everyone on the tour."

"Hell no! You apologized first."

"That's not believable," I say. "Anyone who knows me knows I *never* apologize first."

"Well, neither do I."

We stare at each other for a long moment, at an impasse.

She exhales with frustration. "Why would you call me after the tour to take your shot and *not* apologize first? That makes no sense. The way it went down is you called me and apologized for being a dick during the tour, and then *I* apologized, too, and invited you to my condo for pizza. And you said, 'Pizza? Hell no! Let me cook for you, baby.' And then, you came to my house and made me an amazing meal that melted my panties and made me invite you to stay the night. And you never left. Which makes perfect sense, since you don't have anywhere else to live."

I purse my lips for a beat. "I can live with that."

"Fabulous. So can I. What did you make me for dinner when you came to my place?"

I flash her a flirtatious smile. "Do you like seafood?"

"I *love* it."

"Then I made you my specialty. My grandma's recipe for *cioppino*."

"Oooh. That's sounds fancy. What's that?"

"Italian fish stew in a spicy tomato broth. Growing up, my grandma made it for me on my birthday every year. It was a big deal because money was tight and the ingredients are expensive."

"Is your grandma Italian?"

I nod. "Her parents came here from Sicily."

Her eyes darken with heat. "I should have known you've got Italian blood in you. Italian men are always the most gorgeous—and *passionate*."

My body jolts with arousal at her sexual tone. "My family's name in Italy was *Salvaggio*, but my great-grandparents changed it to Savage after coming here to sound more American."

"Ha! This whole time I thought Savage was a stage name."

I wink. "Nope. I was born Savage, baby."

She giggles.

"So, it's settled," I say. "I made you my specialty. And the look on your face while you ate it was so hot, I didn't let you finish your meal. Midway through, I pulled you out of your chair, laid your back on the table, and ate your pussy like I'd been dying to do since the tour." I smile wickedly. "I ate your sweet pussy, *greedily*, like it was a goddamned bowl of *cioppino*."

A long, involuntary exhale escapes her. "Okay. I can get behind that."

"After that," I say, "I dragged you off the table, bent you over it, and fucked you from behind while fingering your clit, until you came so hard, you squirted all over my cock and balls."

Her chest heaves. "Whoa. That sounds . . . good."

I'm on the cusp of leaning in and kissing her, but before I do, a commotion on the other side of the patio draws our attention. A big group has entered Reed's patio—this season's cast of *Sing Your Heart Out*: our fellow judges, Aloha and legendary rocker, Jon Stapleton. Kendrick and another mentor, the one assigned to Jon. And last but not least, there's the drummer of 22 Goats, Colin Beretta. The guy who hates me for having a short fling with his ex when they were on a break. Damn. When I saw Dax and Fish here, and not Colin, I thought I'd magically dodged a bullet tonight and wouldn't have to feel the discomfort of Colin shooting me death glares. I guess not. Is Colin here to party with his two bandmates . . . or is he a cast member?

"Look, it's Colin!" Laila chirps, getting up excitedly. "I wonder if he's here to hang out, or if he's a mentor this season." She gasps. "If he's a mentor, I wonder if he's assigned to Aloha . . . or *me*?"

I bristle at the hopeful way she says *me*. But I shrug and say nothing.

"Come on, Savage!" she says brightly. "Let's go say hi to everyone." She squeals. "This is gonna be so much *fun*!" And off she goes, traipsing across Reed's patio like a happy gazelle.

"Fuck," I mutter, shuffling behind her, suddenly consumed by a sense of dread.

Laila swore on *Sylvia* that she and Colin have never hooked up, right before swearing the same about me. And I can't help thinking, If she lied about *me* in that interview, did she lie about Colin, too?

Which then leads logically to my very next thought: Did the clever producers of *Sing Your Heart Out* hire Colin to be Laila's mentor this season, specifically hoping his presence would stir up a little trouble in paradise for the happy couple? My gut tells me the answer to that one is almost certainly going to be . . . *yes.*

TWENTY-SEVEN

SAVAGE

The promo shoot is done. We got a whole bunch of stuff—video spots and still photos—with the four judges and each of their assigned mentors. Also, with each judge/mentor pair. As it turns out, my hunch about Colin was spot-on. He's Laila's mentor this season, fuck my life, while Fish is Aloha's. And now, we're back out on Reed's patio, having a legit party with the entire cast and their dates, some producers and crew, and some of Reed's friends. We're all letting it rip in recognition that tomorrow the grind will officially begin. Kicking off with tomorrow's press conference, followed the next day, on Monday, by our first official day of shooting.

At present, I'm sitting on one end of the patio with Kendrick, who's been talking me off the ledge about Laila and Colin, while Laila is sitting in a group by a large fire feature on the other end of the patio—a group that naturally includes Colin, since he's close friends with all *Laila's* closest friends. *And I'm slowly losing my mind.*

"Did you see the way Colin flirted with Laila during the entire photo shoot?" I say to Kendrick. It's a running theme. I've been obsessing about Laila's chemistry with Colin for the past hour. Ever since they looked at each other during their judge/mentor photo shoot like they wanted to rip each other's clothes off.

"He wasn't *flirting* with her," Kendrick says, his annoyance with me plainly escalating. "He and Laila did what the photographer asked him to do. The guy said, 'Smile at each other.' And that's what they did. It was the same thing *we* did in our photo shoot. Were you flirting with *me,* big boy?" He walks his fingertips up my arm, like a cartoon character would do when flirting, making me laugh, despite my foul mood.

I wink at him flirtatiously. "Maybe a little bit."

Kendrick chuckles and drops his flirty flingers.

"Seriously, KC. I'm not imagining this. They have insane amounts of chemistry."

"So what? All that proves is he's not blind and neither is she. You've seen his underwear campaign, right? He's a good looking dude."

I take a sip of my drink. "That's my point. He's a good-looking dude and she mentioned him on *Sylvia,* right before mentioning me. So, I can't help thinking this must be a set-up. Did the show hire Colin to set the stage for a love triangle plot twist midway through the season? Are they gonna pay him a little bonus if he breaks up the happy couple? Because I'm not doing that shit, Kendrick. Laila's supposed to be *my* faithful girlfriend who's totally in love with *me.* I'm not gonna look like the fool who turned down that Instagrammer, so she could drool over Colin Beretta on national TV."

"Calm down, Tiger. She's not gonna do that to you."

"She's already doing it to me, right this very second! Not to mention, she did it to me, repeatedly, during the tour!"

He looks at me like I'm crazy. "Laila didn't do *anything* to *you* during the tour. Malik was her *boyfriend* during the tour, Savage. *You* weren't. Have you forgotten what a prick you were to her?"

I exhale and guzzle my drink. He's right, of course. But I can't help the way I feel, even if it's irrational. Throughout the tour, I felt the same way I do right now. Jealous. Like Malik, and then Charlie, were horning in on *my* woman. I realize I acted like a prick to her, unfortunately, but only because . . . I'm a flaming idiot. Why'd I do that again? Shit. I run my hand through my hair. "I can't keep watching her do this to me, Kendrick. Every time I turn around, I've got to compete for her attention. It's driving me fucking insane."

"You're your own worst enemy. Get out of your own way, man. Stop lashing out and *chill*."

I take another sip of my drink. "The thing I'm worried about is Colin setting his sights on Laila, not because he genuinely likes her, but to get back at *me* for having that fling with his ex."

Kendrick pulls a face that says, *Quite possibly*. But what he says is, "Laila's not stupid. And she's totally into you."

"First off, Laila *is* stupid—she dated Malik Wallace for how long? Also, she's emphatically *not* into me. She thinks I'm Satan's spawn."

"Yeah, and lucky you, her celebrity crush is Satan."

I can't help chuckling at that, despite how tightly wound I'm feeling in this moment.

Kendrick says, "Whatever you do tonight, do *not* let Laila know you're jealous of Colin. Trust me on that, Savage. You let her know she's got that power over you, then she'll use it against you."

"I'm not stupid," I say.

"Oh, yes, you are."

"Yeah, but not that kind of stupid."

"Oh, yes, you are."

"Hey, boys," a woman says. And when we look up, it's that British pop star, Penelope something, who's going to be Jon's mentor this season. She holds up an unlit cigarette and smiles flirtatiously at me. "A little birdie told me you might have a light?"

"Sorry, no," I reply. "My girlfriend hates cigarettes, so I quit."

Kendrick looks at me funny, probably thinking, *I saw you smoking like a chimney last night at my brother's birthday party.*

I add, "I quit tonight, actually. For Laila."

Penelope flashes a snarky look. "She's your *girlfriend*, eh?"

"Mm-hmm. Yep."

Penelope snickers, leans forward, and whispers, "The cameras aren't rolling yet, love. That same little birdie told me your 'relationship' is starting *tomorrow*." With a wink, she throws her unlit cigarette into a nearby bush. "I don't smoke, anyway. I was looking for a reason to come over here." She giggles, but I don't join her. She's blocking my view of Laila and Colin, which is causing me distress. If Colin is hitting on Laila, and I can't see it and sprint over there to stop it, I'll make this British chick rue the day.

Penelope makes a few more attempts at small talk, mostly directed at me, as I crane my neck to spy on Laila. Finally, Kendrick throws himself on his sword and enters into a full-blown conversation with her. Which is Kendrick for you, in a nutshell. The guy's the best friend in the world.

Gratefully, I get up, muttering something about the bathroom, and then start walking toward Laila and Colin, who've drifted away from the group and are talking one-on-one. But on my way to my destination, I get stopped by Aloha, who's tickled pink by today's unexpected events. She's with her husband, Zander, a cool dude I've met a couple times. We chat for a moment while my gaze continually drifts over Zander's extremely broad shoulder at Laila and Colin. But when I notice Laila's body language seems particularly flirty, particularly animated, I disengage from my conversation and barrel over to my fake girlfriend.

When I get close enough to overhear Laila and Colin's conversation, Laila is in the middle of saying, "No, I swear! Savage told her he had to 'lay low.' He didn't say *Laila*. But the producers ran with it. It's all about ratings, baby."

"Hilarious," Colin says.

"*Laila*," I bark out, lurching forward and invading their personal space. "I need to speak with you, my *love*. Right now."

"Is something wrong?"

"Yes, something is very, very wrong." I pull her up, avoiding Colin's glare, and yank her across the patio and into Reed's house, down a hallway, and through a random door, which empties into a laundry room.

"What the hell?" Laila blurts, as I whirl around from shutting the door.

"What do you think you're doing?" I demand, my heart racing.

"What? When?"

"Your conversation with Colin!" I shout. "I heard every word, Laila."

She wrinkles her forehead, apparently not understanding. "Every word about *what*?"

"You told him the truth about our 'relationship'!"

"So?"

"You're not supposed to tell *anyone*! It's top secret!"

She's flabbergasted. "But Colin's my mentor. He's part of the show! We agreed on the way over here we could tell anyone from the show, remember?"

"No, that's not at all what we agreed. Not *anyone*. We agreed I could tell *Kendrick* because he's my best friend and is *also* on the show. And you could tell Aloha for the same reason. We didn't decide we could run around telling every single person in the entire cast and crew!"

"But Colin is my friend and assigned *mentor*. I trust him. Besides, he signed a contract today that surely contained a confidentiality—"

"We're not telling anyone but Kendrick and Aloha!" I shout, sounding like a maniac, even to myself. "That's what we agreed. As far as Colin or anyone else needs to know, we're an actual couple, Laila. You're *my* girlfriend. You're in love with me. Head over heels and totally addicted." Suddenly, I stop short, as the upside of what Laila said to Colin suddenly hits me like a ton of bricks. "Wait. You admit I didn't say *Laila* to that Instagrammer? You've been fucking with me this whole time, pretending you believed I said your name?"

"No. Of course not. I'm one hundred percent positive you said my name to her. I just told Colin your stupid fake story because he was needling me about the whole thing and I wanted to be nice and save you from embarrassment."

"Bullshit."

"It's true."

"Well, if it's true, which I don't believe, then you didn't do it to be *nice* to me. You did it because you want Colin to think you're available."

"Absolutely not."

I throw up my hands. "You can't do that, Laila! I just got finished telling that Penelope chick you're my girlfriend! And that's how I expect you to play this, too—to remain in character at all times, with everyone, including Colin."

"You don't get to decide that."

"I sure as hell do. I paid two million bucks to get to decide that and anything else having to do with this ridiculous arrangement."

Uh oh. She's no longer amused. She's downright pissed now. "And '*anything* else'?" she parrots. "What am I—a mail order bride? A blowup doll?" She scoffs. "News flash, Savage. You paid two million bucks to save your own ass. *Not to purchase me.*"

"You know what I meant."

"Yeah, I do," she says. "And that's the problem. Regardless, even if I were going to agree that you're my lord and master and omnipotent in all ways, we still can't put the genie back in the bottle regarding Colin. He knows we're not really a couple, and that's that, unless you want me to run out there and scream, 'Just kidding! I'm actually desperately in love with Savage!'"

"Sounds like a plan to me. Go on now, baby. Chop chop."

She rolls her eyes.

"At a bare minimum," I say, "I demand you to stop flirting your ass off with Colin."

She gasps. "I wasn't flirting with Colin!"

"Well, he was sure as hell flirting with *you.*"

"We're *friends.*"

"Have you ever fucked him?"

"No, not that it's any of your business."

"Kissed him?"

She shakes her head. *"We're friends."*

I narrow my eyes. *"Friends* don't smile at each other like that, Laila. And they don't lean in like that." I scoff. "Oh, don't look at me like that. I know what I saw."

"You're insane."

"Not everyone here is associated with the show. The photographer is still here. Same with the caterer. And what about Reed's friends and housekeeper? What's to keep any of them from hearing the news about our 'relationship' at tomorrow's press conference and then realizing, 'Huh. That's weird. I saw Laila flirting with some other guy all night long. Hey, I think I got some video of her flirting with him in the background. Why don't I post that now on Twitter!'"

"You belong in an insane asylum."

"No, I'd be insane if I didn't learn from my past experiences. I'm once bitten, twice shy." I take a few steps to my right, lean against the washing machine, and sigh. "You've never experienced my level of fame before, Laila. I'm not saying that to be a jerk. I'm trying to explain you can never be too careful. You *never* know who might leap at the chance to get their fifteen minutes, on your back. I'm saying we can't take *any* chances. I don't want this job to get fucked up, because you forgot this isn't actually a romcom we're starring in together, it's a spy thriller."

Well, she can't help grinning at that, no matter how annoyed she's felt up to this point. Her shoulders visibly soften. Her eyes sparkle. "I understand. I'll be much more careful, going forward."

"Thank you."

"And don't worry. If Colin seemed to be flirting with me a tiny bit, I promise it was harmless. He and his girlfriend recently broke up, and this is the first time we've both been single at the same time, so I think—"

I throw up my hands again. *"You're not single, Laila!"*

She jolts at my sudden shift in tone.

I can't help myself. I shout, *"You're in a relationship with me.*

What have we been talking about this whole time? Jesus Christ, Laila!" When she looks at me like I'm crazy again, I see myself through her eyes and realize I might really and truly be devolving into madness. Quickly, I add, "That's what you need to be thinking. That's what I mean. Like you said in the car, we need to stay in character. Like, you know, method actors."

"When we're in front of the *cameras*."

"No, at all times, or nobody will buy our performance. Haven't you heard about method actors who won't let anyone call them by their real name on-set? Ever seen *Fast Times at Ridgemont High*?"

"No."

"Oh. Well, we gotta watch that one together. Sean Penn played this stoner surfer dude. And he stayed in character throughout the entire shoot of the movie, both on and off camera. Wouldn't let anyone call him by his real name. Only the character's name— Spicoli. Because that's the kind of commitment it takes to make a performance truly *believable*."

She pauses for a very long moment. "Which actor is Sean Penn? What else has he been in?"

"Sean Penn's illustrious career doesn't matter! All I'm saying is that from this point on, unless you're *sure* we're alone, behind closed doors, and nobody else is around, then we need to agree we're always going to remain in character."

She twists her mouth adorably, no longer looking pissed. But she says nothing.

And, suddenly, thanks to the way she's contorting her sensuous lips, I'm flooded with the urge to kiss her. I clear my throat. "I know you're pissed when I bring up the money, Laila, but have mercy on me. I'm paying you two *million* bucks. The least you can do is deliver an Academy-award-worthy performance."

She licks her lips, drawing my gaze to her mouth again. And when my eyes return to hers, I feel a shift between us. Heat crackling in the gap between our bodies.

"Okay," she says softly, her gaze drifting to my lips. "I promise I'll do my very best."

My chest is tight. My skin hot. "Thank you. That's all we can both do."

"Better safe than sorry," she says, her gaze drifting, yet again, to my lips.

I step forward, deciding this is it. The moment, at last. I'm going to kiss Laila and then bend her over that washing machine and fuck the living hell out of her. But when I step forward again, she steps back. So, I freeze. She takes a deep breath, clears her throat, and says, "I'm really glad we talked. Thanks for setting me straight." And then, after licking her lips and taking a shuddering breath, she turns on her heel and literally sprints out of the small room.

TWENTY-EIGHT

SAVAGE

After my conversation with Laila in the laundry room, she played a few rounds of Beer Pong with her friends, while I sat at the fire feature, watching her while pretending to listen to Jon Stapleton, my co-judge, give me advice about being on the show. But when Laila left her post at Beer Pong to play Team Jenga—during which she was paired with Alessandra, thankfully, while Fish was paired with Colin—I excused myself from Jon, grabbed a bottle of whiskey from behind Reed's bar, and slithered my shitfaced ass into a dark corner to watch her.

The good news? As promised in the laundry room, Laila's been noticeably ignoring Colin's flirtations during their entire game. The bad news? Based on Colin's body language, it seems clear he's the sort of sick fuck, like me, who gets off when a hot woman ignores him.

A large whoop rises up from the game as Aloha's husband, Zander, makes a move for his two-person team—Aloha and himself. And in response, everyone but Zander and his popstar wife throws back another shot, at which point Colin leans into Laila and says something that makes her throw her head back and laugh.

It's worst-case scenario, actually, because I can tell Laila wasn't *trying* to flirt with Colin. She didn't laugh to mess with me. He *genuinely* made her involuntarily guffaw. I've got to think that's a very bad sign for me.

My inebriated blood flash-boiling, I jerk to standing, every fiber of my body telling me to march over there and mark my territory. To kiss her in front of Colin. And then throw Colin into the fire.

"No, Savage," a voice says sharply. And when I look, it's my boy, Kendrick, standing before me and physically blocking my movement with his muscular body. "Sit down, brother," he says. "Don't do it."

The devil on my shoulder is whispering, "Do it." But, somehow, I manage to reply casually to my friend, "Don't do *what?*"

"Whatever you drunkenly decided to do to Colin." He points at my chair. "Sit back down and listen to me for a minute."

Reluctantly, I sit. Kendrick rarely orders me around. So, when he does, I listen. "I wasn't gonna do anything bad," I murmur. "I was just . . ." I trail off. There's no point. Kendrick's staring at me like he can read my mind. Which he probably can. He's known me for almost half my life now. He, better than anyone, knows how my mind works.

Kendrick takes the chair next to me and leans his forearms on his knees. "It's time for you to put that bottle down, walk inside the house, and go to bed."

"I'm not ready for bed yet."

"Nothing good will come of you sitting here, alone in a dark corner, drinking whiskey from a bottle, watching Laila get hit on by Colin."

"Aha! So, you admit he's been hitting on her! I told you so."

Kendrick leans back. "I think he's doing it to piss you off, more than anything else. So, don't give him the satisfaction. Play it cool, brother."

I take another long sip of whiskey and mutter, "Tonight was supposed to be a fun last hurrah before I'm not allowed to drink anymore. I thought Laila and I would party together. I never intended to sit here, alone, marinating in whiskey and jealousy."

"Then get up and join the party. You always do this, Savage."

"I don't want to join the party. I want to sit here, alone."

"Then, that's your problem."

"But when I pulled Laila into the laundry room, she said she'd stay in character, from now on. And yet, she's been playing games with her friends, and Colin, ever since."

Kendrick blinks slowly. "*When you pulled Laila into the laundry room . . .?*"

I immediately realize my mistake. "To talk to her . . . about the importance of keeping up the charade at all times. So the truth doesn't get out."

He's onto me. "You told her you're jealous of Colin."

"Of course not. I simply told her she can't flirt with Colin, or anyone else, because someone could see that and post about it."

"You dragged Laila into a laundry room and chewed her out about Colin, didn't you? And now you're sitting here, drinking from a bottle in a dark corner, watching her with him like a stalker. Like Reed behind that bush, however many months ago. Does that summarize the situation accurately?"

I pause, weighing my options. And quickly decide lying to Kendrick isn't in my DNA. I speak on an exhale, "Yeah. That's pretty much it. I've become Reed fucking Rivers, standing behind a bush."

Kendrick leans back and rubs his face. "When will you learn?" He takes a second to collect himself before letting out a long exhale and sitting forward again. "Okay, buddy. Listen to me. I know this chick better than you do. Do you want her?"

I groan. "So much."

"Then, it's simple. You have to remember she's exactly like *you*. I love you both, okay, so this is said with love. But you're both the same kind of sick fuck. You both always want what you can't have. The truth is, if you knew Laila like I do, I don't even think you'd even want her. Not the *real* her. She's actually super nice. A sweetheart."

"*Yeccch.*"

"Exactly. You'd hate her, if you knew her."

"She sounds awful."

"She is. Awfully sweet and cool and funny and surprisingly goofy. None of which you know about her, I'm sure, because you're always on the outside, looking in. Provoking her. Savage, I'm not trying to piss you off here. I'm saying I think you want her because you can't have her. Because she's the one woman who doesn't fall at your feet. So maybe recognize that's what's happening and try to get some perspective here."

I say nothing.

Concede nothing.

But, instead, take a long pull from my bottle and watch the Jenga game for a long moment, where Laila is just now throwing back yet another shot with her partner, Fish. After a moment, the tower collapses, and it's clear the current game has ended. In short order, the game gets rebuilt and the teams reshuffled . . . and this time, Laila gets assigned to her new partner, *Colin*, through no fault of her own.

"Oh, hell no," I mutter, standing. "I don't care *why* I want her. The end result is that I *do*."

Kendrick rises and grabs my shoulder. "*Sit down*. I'm not finished talking to you."

"No, Kendrick. I need to pull her away and—"

"*No*. That's the last thing you should do. Not when you're drunk and jealous and the press conference is tomorrow. *No*." He points at the chair. "Sit down."

I pause, breathing hard. But sit.

With a sigh, Kendrick resumes his seat. "If you want to sit her down and tell her how obsessed you've been since the tour, then do it. But not tonight. Not now. Do it after you get to know her a bit and figure out if she's who you really want. Because, I swear to God, if you give her that speech and then turn around and dump her, I'll fucking kill you for hurting her."

I swallow hard.

"Plus, I doubt your speech would move the needle with her

right now, anyway. Because she doesn't know you any better than you know her. Not really. She still thinks you're this asshole fuckboy who doesn't give a shit about anyone else. Because that's all you've ever shown her because you're scared to death to show her anything else."

Again, I say nothing. I can't remember the last time Kendrick bitch-slapped me like this. It's blowing me away.

He exhales a big breath. "You really want her?"

I nod.

"Then don't let her know how much you want her. Not yet. And, for fuck's sake, don't let her know her attempts at pushing your buttons are working. I know her *way* better than you do. Like I said, she's the sweetest girl you'll ever meet. But when it comes to men she actually wants to sleep with—a group that *clearly* doesn't include me—she craves a challenge, the same way you do. You can get any woman you want. Well, Laila can get *any* man she wants. And she knows it. She's you, in female form." He sighs. "It's actually crazy how much you two are similar. So, think, dumbass. If she's exactly like you, then what will make her want you?"

I pause. "Me not wanting her."

He touches his nose. "I once overheard Laila talking to Ruby about her exes. And, dude, I'm telling you, she gets off on bringing a player to his knees. But guess what happens when she gets him there? Can you guess, Savage?"

"She . . . loses interest?"

He touches his nose again. "She gets bored and moves on. It's all about the thrill of the chase for her. Sound familiar?"

"So, what's your point? Laila and I are gonna be living together for the next three months. You want me to *ignore* her, while living under the same roof with her?"

"No, but you need to keep your cards close to your vest for a bit. Keep her guessing. For instance, she doesn't need to know you're jealous of Colin. Why give her that? Play it cool. Let her chase you a bit. Let her get frustrated that her usual tactics aren't working. And in the meantime, get to know her over the next few months. Figure out if the attraction you think you've been feeling has more to do with *Laila*, as she really is, or conquering some fantasy girl who doesn't fall at your feet."

I take a long chug from my bottle but say nothing.

"Now, go to bed. The longer you stay down here, watching her and drinking from that bottle, the higher the chance some kind of shit will hit the fan. And you don't want that. Nadine is still here. She's inside, talking to Reed. Do you want her to hear some drunken screaming match between you and Laila, after you go over there and pick a fight with Colin? Because if you stay down here, that's where this is headed."

He's right. As usual. I look across the patio, where Laila is happily doing yet another round of shots with her friends. "Thanks, brother."

"I've got your back, Savage. I'll always have your back."

"I know. I have yours, too. For what it's worth."

"I know you do."

"Will you make sure Laila gets to her room tonight—*alone*?"

"I will. Now, go on. Walk into the house without so much as a glance at her. I promise, it'll drive her crazy."

I resist the urge to look at Laila. "Okay. Goodnight." I stand. "Thanks again."

"Don't you dare go knocking on Laila's door tonight, looking for a booty call."

I scoff. "I'm not stupid."

"Yes, you are."

"True. But I don't know which room is hers."

He laughs. "Goodnight."

"Goodnight, brother." With that, I fist-bump Kendrick and do as I'm told: I head toward the house, without even a passing glance at my fake girlfriend.

TWENTY-NINE

SAVAGE

When I enter Reed's house, I glimpse his housekeeper, Amalia, slipping into the kitchen, so I follow her in there, like a drunk driver following tail lights. When I enter the kitchen, I find her dressed in a sleek robe and slippers, quietly filling a kettle with water.

"Oh, hello there," she says when she notices me filling the doorway.

"Hi. Amalia, right?"

"That's right, Mr. Savage. I'm making myself tea. Would you like a cup?"

"Sure. Thanks."

I take a seat at the large kitchen table and watch her putter for a long moment. As she approaches with two steaming mugs, I say, "You remind me of my grandma. She loves tea."

Amalia takes a seat after placing a steaming mug in front of me. "Are you close with your grandma?"

I nod. "She's the one who raised me."

"And look at you now. She did a fine job." She blows on her steaming tea. "Is your grandmother still alive?"

I nod. "She's really sick, though."

"I'm sorry to hear that. I hope she recovers."

"The chances are low. But she's a fighter. We still have hope."

Amalia puts a hand on mine. "I'll pray for her. What's your grandmother's name?"

"Maria. But I've always called her Mimi, rather than grandma."

"I'll keep Mimi in my prayers, Mr. Savage."

"Thank you. Call me Adrian."

She smiles warmly. "Are you able to see your grandmother very often?"

"As much as I can. She lives in Chicago. I visit about once a month, whenever I'm not on tour. But I FaceTime her almost every day. I sing to her or tell her a story. She likes seeing my face. The medicine she takes gives her weird nightmares."

She touches her chest. "Oh, bless her heart."

I bring my mug to my lips, but the tea is too hot to drink. "I offered to take the year off to hang out with Mimi while she's in treatment," I say, "but she was adamant she didn't want that. She insisted on getting to watch me 'being a rockstar.' She loves that I've been touring the world. Performing for huge audiences. She collects every interview and magazine cover."

"She must be so very proud of you."

"It's all because of her. She bought me my first guitar when I was twelve. Our first Christmas together. She thought making music would help calm me down. Help me work out my anger issues. I was a handful back then."

"All the more reason for her to be proud of you now."

"Honestly, she'd trade all my success with the band to watch me settle down, get married, and give her a great-grandkid." I chuckle. "I told her, 'Sorry, Mimi, that's not gonna happen. At least, not any time soon. A kid can't raise a kid.'"

"How old are you?"

"Twenty-six. But, see, when you're in a band, that's like being eighteen or nineteen."

"Like dog years, only in reverse?"

"Exactly. Dog years make a dog older than their chronological age, and 'musician years' make a guy younger, in terms of emotional maturity. Especially if he's the lead singer or guitarist. Double points if he's both, like me."

She chuckles. "Why is that, you think?"

I shrug. "Lead singers, at least the ones like me, always get the most attention. Everyone tells us we're gods among men, so we start believing the hype. In my case, it's especially hardcore because my face and body are a big part of our branding. We shamelessly sell me as much as we sell the music."

"That sounds exhausting to me."

"It's fine. I was born with this face, so might as well make money off it. And I'd work out, anyway, because I like being fit. I'm sure I'd drink more and eat more crap if I didn't feel like my looks were a big part of the job. I'm actually glad I have good reason to stay healthy and take care of myself." I lean in. "I've got some self-destructive tendencies, Amalia."

"Oh, dear. Well, I'm glad you know that."

I blow on my tea. "Honestly, I'm always one tick shy of becoming a train wreck."

"Why is that, Adrian?"

"I don't know."

"If things are happy, you don't trust them?"

"I think that's a fair statement."

"If things are happy, you start testing them? Poking at them, trying to test your theory they're not as happy as you think. And then, by poking at them, you ruin them?"

I waggle my finger at her. "Hey now. Get outta my head, woman."

She laughs.

"That's probably why I don't even have a permanent place to live. I feel like I can't sit still. Whenever I'm not touring, I live in a hotel or in my best friend's spare room."

"Oh, dear. I'd go crazy if I didn't have a place to call home. I love staying in hotels for vacation, but in my real life, I need security and consistency."

"I don't care where I live. When I was little, I slept in a closet, literally. And when I moved in with Mimi, we lived in her tiny, shitty apartment in Chicago. The place was the size of a shoebox! Want to hear something amazing? When I moved in with Mimi, she didn't even know I existed before then. My 'father,' her son, hadn't even told her about me because he was too ashamed he'd gotten some random chick, my mother, knocked up. But Mimi took me in, anyway, even though she barely had two nickels to rub together and certainly wasn't planning on raising a wild little asshole at that point in her life."

"Ah. Interesting. So now, you don't let yourself get too settled, huh?"

I shrug. "I just don't like the feeling of being tied down too much. I like being able to live out of a duffel bag, and not need much. I like feeling like a hotel room is more than enough."

Amalia sips her tea, looking like her mind is turning. "You never dream of living in a house like this one?"

I scoff. "No way. I'd get lost. Literally."

She chuckles. "Reed throws a lot of parties here. The house serves him well. Although, I admit, now that Georgina lives here, it feels much less like a 'venue' and more like an actual home."

"I didn't realize Georgina lives here. Wow. That was fast."

Amalia nods. "It was. But I have no doubt it's a wonderful thing for them both."

"How fast did she move in?"

"That's personal, I think, Adrian."

"Sorry."

"That's okay, dear." She pats my hand and smiles.

"Just tell me one thing. Was it faster than a month?"

Amalia's dark eyes sparkle. "Yes, it was."

"*Whoa.*"

Amalia lifts a brow and sips her tea, almost like she's acknowledging she just "spilled the tea" about Reed and Georgina. Or maybe my drunken brain is imagining that little sass in Amalia's expression.

I ask, "Do you live here with Reed and Georgina?"

"During the week, yes, unless there's a big party or event on the weekend, like today. I have a place of my own, where my children and grandchildren come for dinner on Sundays."

"I bet you're an amazing grandma. What do your grandchildren call you?"

"*Abuelita*. Or Abu, for short."

"I love Abu. It's like the monkey in *Aladdin*. Can I call you that, too?"

She flashes me a smile that makes me blush. "I would love that, Adrian."

"Cool." I sip my tea again. "Hey, Abu. If you ever get sick of Reed—because, come on, there's a lot to get sick of there—then will you come work for me? Don't let anyone else hire you away from me, okay? Once you kick Reed to the curb, you're mine."

She flashes me a chastising look. "Don't speak ill of my Reed, Adrian. I love him from the depths of my soul."

"Yeah, but you have to know he's a prickly motherfucker."

"*Adrian*."

I flash my most charming smile and by the look on her face, I know she can't resist me.

"Where would I work for you, anyway? I'm a housekeeper, remember? And you just got finished telling me you don't even have a house."

"I'd buy one, so you could keep it for me, my beautiful Abu."

"Oh, my. What an honor. But, like I said, I love Reed with all my heart. He's like a son to me and I'll never work for anyone else."

"Aw, come on, dude. Never say never. Even if you love Reed, you never know what might happen in life. And I've got lots to offer you."

"Like what?"

"Well, like I said, I have the maturity of an eighteen-year-old. What grandma could resist taking care of someone like *that*?"

She giggles. "You're quite the salesman."

"Also, I'm *amazing* at singing grandmas to sleep. Has Reed ever done *that* for you?"

"No, I can't say he has."

"Ha! Also, I'll happily play gin rummy with you, or any other boring card game. *And* I'll even suffer through watching *Sing Your Heart Out* with you, if that's your jam."

"No wonder Mimi adores you, with all that to offer. And no wonder *Sing Your Heart Out* hired you to replace Hugh. I can tell you're quite the charmer, my dear."

"Yeah, I can turn it on like a light switch when I want to impress someone." I wink.

"Clearly. Do the powers that be at *Sing Your Heart Out* know they've hired a judge who has to 'suffer through' watching their show?"

"They sure do. It's why they wanted me so badly. 'Cause I'm too cool for school."

"I see."

"A little secret, Abu? Everyone wants what they can't have."

"Ah. Well, aren't you smart."

I tap my temple.

"Is your grandmother excited about you being on the show?"

"She's *ecstatic*. It's her all-time favorite show. She even watches reruns, for reasons that escape me."

"I watch them, too. They're on every night after *Jeopardy*."

I laugh. "But why watch reruns of a singing competition, when you already know who won that season?"

"I like already knowing the outcome and seeing how my favorite contestants blossomed throughout the season. And in later seasons, I absolutely love watching Aloha being her sassy little self. She's my all-time favorite judge."

"You mean besides *me*."

"You haven't been on the show yet. Once you've appeared on the show, then, yes, you'll become my new favorite."

"Thanks, Abu. Unless, of course, my girlfriend edges me out.

Something tells me Laila's gonna give me a run for my money this season. She has a way of making people fall hard for her."

Amalia puts down her mug, her face contorting with affection for me. "You two make a beautiful couple. In a way, you remind me of Reed and Georgina. You're both so attractive together. Two obviously strong-willed individuals who seem so sweet together."

"Well, *I'm* sweet. But make no mistake about it: Laila's a holy terror."

Amalia giggles.

"Lucky for me, I don't like my girlfriends to be sweet."

"No?"

"Well, I mean, I like 'em sweet, down deep, as long as it takes a whole lot of effort to get to the sweet stuff. Like going on a treasure hunt or getting to the tootsie roll inside a Tootsie Pop."

"That sounds like a lot of work to me, Adrian."

"Nah. I like a good challenge or else I get bored. Ever seen the movie *Mean Girls*?"

"It doesn't ring a bell."

"It's a comedy, set in high school. The lead girl is the 'new girl' in school. That's the one we're supposed to be rooting for. But I don't even remember her name. The villain, on the other hand, that's Regina George. She's the leader of the popular girls known as The Plastics. We're not supposed to like Regina. We're supposed to hate her because she's so 'mean.' But guess who I've always wanted to bang, Abu?"

"*Adrian.*"

"Have sex with."

Her nostrils flare. She truly can't resist me. "Regina?"

I nod. "*Reginaaaaa.* My biggest childhood crush."

Amalia giggles. "Do you talk this way with Mimi?"

"Of course. She loves it. She says I'm a . . ." I scratch my head and mutter, "What does Mimi always call me? A hoe? No . . . a 'rake'!"

Amalia loses it. She laughs and laughs, so I join her, enjoying my best laugh of the night. When we quiet down, we take long sips of our tea, now that it's finally at a perfect temperature.

Amalia asks, "Why do you think you prefer the mean villain over the nice new girl?"

"I have no idea."

"Hmm." She sips her tea again, and her body language suggests she's holding her tongue.

"Well, spit it out, woman. If I'm going to be completely myself around you, then you've got to return the favor."

"I don't want to overstep."

"You couldn't possibly. Come on. Spit some knowledge at me, Abu."

She replaces her mug on the table. "Well . . . you said your grandmother raised you?"

I nod. "From age twelve."

"If you don't mind me asking, is that because your mother passed away, or because your mother needed to work long hours, or . . .?"

"It was because my mom didn't give a shit about me and didn't have a maternal bone in her body."

Amalia nods. "I'm sorry to hear that."

"It worked out for the best. Mimi was the shit. Why did you ask the question?"

"Well, this is nothing but amateur pop psychology, of course, but I think you prefer Regina in the movie, and also in your love life, because you feel abandoned by your mother. You prefer women who present a challenge to you, women who are hard to win over, because that way, when you finally *do* win them over, you experience the pleasure you never got to experience as a child. Namely, the joy of winning over a woman the same way you always wished you could have won over your mother."

I'm speechless for a long moment. But, finally, I whisper, "And they call *me* Savage."

Amalia winces. "Did I overstep?"

"Not at all. You just blew my mind! Tell me more, Abu Dabu.

What else do you see in your magic crystal ball? Can you see my future?"

Amalia winks. "The only thing I see in your future, my dearest Adrian, is that you've got a big day tomorrow and you're very drunk and you should probably get some sleep now." She motions to my mug. "Finish your tea, dear, and let's get you to bed."

I do as I'm told, drinking the rest of my tepid tea down in one long gulp, and stand. "It's been amazing talking to you, Amalia. Thanks for the psychoanalysis."

"You're very welcome. Goodnight, dear. Best of luck to you."

I stop walking. "Does that mean you're not planning to see me again?"

She chuckles. "No, not at all. I'll see you in the morning at breakfast."

I exhale with relief. "Cool."

I resume shuffling toward the exit of the kitchen, feeling worlds lighter than when I entered the room, but stop and turn around in the doorway. "Amalia? Sorry, but I just remembered why I came in here." I grimace. "I have no idea which room is mine."

Amalia bites back a smile. "No worries. It's a big house. I'll show you again."

She leads me out of the kitchen toward a dramatic staircase with wrought iron railings, saying, "Do you get drunk like this often, dear?"

"No, not at all. The last time I was drunk was . . . Oh. Last night. But before that, it'd been well over a month."

"Good. Let's keep it that way."

"Don't worry about me. I have a rule I don't drink to drown my sorrows. I wasn't intending to break my rule tonight. Tonight was supposed to be a happy occasion. A 'last hurrah' before I'm not allowed to drink for the whole season."

"Oh?"

"The producers made it part of my contract. They think I make 'bad choices' when I 'drink to excess.'"

"Are they right about that?"

I snicker. "I'll put it this way. My dick is *still* trending on Twitter, a full twenty-four hours after I got drunk at a birthday party last night."

She can't resist giggling. "Oh dear."

"I wouldn't normally drink two nights in a row, either. But, like I said, tonight was supposed to be my last hurrah, so . . . Fuck it."

"Well, I'm glad you had fun tonight."

"I didn't. I hated tonight, actually. Except for talking to you. You're the best part of my night."

"Thank you. I enjoyed talking to you, too." She stops in front of a doorway at the end of a long hallway and motions. "Here we are. Nighty night."

I enter the room—a guest room decorated in elegant hues of white—and Amalia follows me inside, telling me where I can find additional blankets and towels. She points out this and that amenity, and, lastly, asks if I need anything further or have any questions.

"I have one question," I reply.

Kendrick would tell me I'm an idiot for what I'm about to ask. But I don't care. I can't lie in bed under the same roof as Laila Fitzgerald and not at least *try* to finally get to eat that woman's pussy.

I smile at Amalia. "Could you tell me which room is Laila's? I think I'll shower and get ready for bed, and then check in on her to make sure she got to her room, safe and sound."

THIRTY

LAILA

I tiptoe out of my bedroom, wearing nothing but a midriff-baring T-shirt and undies, and creep down the dark, quiet hallway, headed to parts unknown. And that's where the "brilliant strategy" portion of my quest ends and the "winging it" portion begins.

Crap! Why didn't I ask Amalia which room Savage is staying in tonight? Stupid Laila! This house is as big as the hotel in *The Shining*, and I literally have no idea which door is hiding Mr. Smoldering Pouty Pants.

Unfortunately, I was stupid and/or naïve enough to think I could resist him. Not only tonight. But for the entire season of the show. What I didn't count on, however, is how horny I get when I drink. And how freaking hot Savage is when he's jealous. Good lord, put the two together, and the boy is like crack to me.

As Savage sat in that dark corner of Reed's patio earlier tonight, watching me getting hit on by Colin, I felt so turned on, I could barely keep myself from sprinting over to Savage and launching myself at him like a missile. Despite all the reasons not to do it, I decided, right then and there, I'd invite Savage to my room whenever he *finally* approached me again. I imagined myself leaning in and whispering to him, "Come to my room later, so you can finally eat my pussy 'from every angle.'" I imagined myself saying it to him in a sultry, breathy kind of whisper—the kind that would have made Savage pop a boner, right on the spot.

But then, the jerk never approached me again at the party! On the contrary, he got up and marched into Reed's house, without even *glancing* at me! Which royally pissed me off, I must say. Savage is the one who screamed at me in that laundry room that we needed to remain in character at all times, whenever anyone else is around. And then, what did that hypocrite do? He sat in a dark corner, all night long, looking like a crazy person, not interacting with his supposed girlfriend, at all, and then waltzed out of the party, without even saying goodnight to me—the supposed love of his life! What kind of dickheaded boyfriend would leave a party without even saying goodbye to his girlfriend? Not mine, that's for sure. Or if he did, he wouldn't be my boyfriend for long. So now, I've decided to find Savage, wherever he is in this massive house, and give him a piece of my mind.

I stop in the middle of the hallway and look around. Which of these doors is hiding Mr. Sexy Pants Crazy Man? None of them look on the cusp of singeing, due to Savage's proximity. For all I know, Savage's room is in an entirely different hallway. Or maybe even on the first floor.

Not knowing what else to do, I pick a random door and press my ear against it, hoping that, miraculously, I'll hear Savage's voice behind it, or maybe detect some kind of supernatural Savage-infused vibration humming from inside the room. But, no, the room is silent and the air doesn't feel super-charged with rockstar electrons in the slightest.

"Savage?" I whisper, ever so softly, my lips brushing the wood of the door, my voice as soft as flapping butterfly wings. But, sadly, perfect silence answers me.

I tiptoe to the next door in the hallway and repeat the same exercise. But again, I'm met with the same result. When I move away from the door this time, however, I notice a frozen figure at the far end of the long hallway, watching me.

I inhale sharply. *It's Savage.* Wearing nothing but dark briefs. His chiseled, gorgeous chest is heaving visibly. His nipples are two perfect dimes. His abs cut and taut. And, hot damn, his dark eyes are two lustful laser beams taking in the sight of my barely clothed body.

For a half second, we both stand, silently drinking each other in from opposite ends of the long hallway, our chests rising and falling in synchronicity. Finally, Savage wordlessly points toward a doorway to his right, nonverbally inviting me to enter. Or was that a command? Either way, I don't hesitate. My pulse thumping and my skin hot and alive with tingles, I glide down the length of the endless hallway, and finally walk straight past him into the room with both my head and chest held high.

Savage follows me into the room—a bedroom decorated in hues of white—and quietly shuts the door with a soft click. After turning from the door, he glides up to me, slides a palm to my cheek, leans in, and, without hesitation, presses his mouth to mine—instantly provoking a long and shuddering exhale of excitement from us both.

Savage kisses me tenderly at first. Like he's savoring a first mouthful of expensive wine. But after initial entreaties, when I realize he doesn't taste the least bit like cigarettes, but, instead, like toothpaste and lust and the remnants of whiskey, when I open my mouth and enthusiastically invite him to take me in earnest, Savage's warm tongue breaches my lips and begins leading mine in swirling, sensuous strokes, an increasingly voracious dance of our tongues and lips that quickly sets off a breathtaking barrage of fireworks inside my core.

As a torrent of arousal slams into me, I slide my arms around Savage's neck and begin devouring him enthusiastically. In response, he slides his arms around my torso and deepens his kiss, until, soon, I'm jerking and jolting in his arms, gasping for air as shockwaves of pleasure and arousal throttle my every nerve ending, but especially that pulsing bundle of nerves between my legs. If there were surveillance footage of this white-hot kiss, I'm positive there'd be visible sparks flying off our bodies in this moment.

As our kiss deepens and intensifies, I inhale him, savoring the taste and scent of him. In addition to the delicious scents I've previously detected, I smell soap and shampoo now, too. And, still, not even a trace of cigarettes. Savage smells nothing but clean and delicious and sexy. *Perfect.*

"You didn't smoke tonight," I gasp out into his lips.

Savage nuzzles his nose against mine and smiles wickedly, brushing his bulge against me down below. "I knew my fake girlfriend wouldn't kiss me if I did—and I was going to get this kiss tonight, if it killed me."

I inhale sharply at the implication—that Savage consciously decided, hours ago, to forego smoking a cigarette, solely to kiss me later in the night. And at my obvious excitement, Savage kisses me, even more passionately than before, this time grabbing my ass cheeks firmly in both palms and pushing me into his hard bulge. When I moan with pleasure, he leans his body away from mine, slightly, enough to be able to slide his hand into my underwear. He reaches between my legs and moans when he discovers how wet I am, how swollen and aroused, and immediately begins fingering me in a way that elicits a loud growl.

As he massages my hard, swollen clit while finger-fucking me, I'm absolutely at his mercy. I begin buckling and growling like I've put my finger into a light socket, immediately hurtling toward an orgasm that's sure to make my knees give out.

"I have to lie down," I gasp out. "I can't . . . keep going standing up."

Without hesitation, Savage drags me to the bed, lays me down on my back, yanks down my underwear like they're gravely insulting to him, and dives right in with a loud and shuddering exhale of excitement. As he licks me, he groans and moans, and then pushes open my thighs as wide as they'll go. He licks and laps at me, at first, with a wide and greedy tongue. But, in short order, he zeroes in on his meticulous work, devouring my clit with precision.

I clutch the bed covering and writhe as Savage decimates me in the most delicious way imaginable. And when he adds his fingers to the mix, it only takes a couple swipes at my G-spot before my body explodes with an orgasm that sends me groaning loudly with deep relief and pleasure.

I sit up, eager to return the favor, but Savage stops me. His breathing ragged, he pulls off my shirt, and then his briefs, letting his big, thick cock spring to freedom. And just when I'm about to ask him if he's got a condom, he flips me over, rather forcefully, pulls me onto all fours, and starts eating me from behind.

"Condom," I choke out.

"Don't need it," he murmurs. "I'm only gonna eat you."

I'm shocked to hear it. But not disappointed. I relax into it, now that I know he's not planning to plow into me, uncovered. And quickly, my body ramps up, again. Savage is voracious back there. Fucking me with his fingers while licking and eating and biting and sucking every inch of me with his mouth. And by that, I mean, really and truly, *every* damned inch of me.

It takes me a little while to get there again, simply because it seems like he keeps pulling back, right when I'm about to release. Over and over again, he gets me right to the edge of orgasm, and pulls back. Is he doing that intentionally? Teasing me? Torturing me? Finally, thank God, he brings me right to the edge, yet again, but this time, exuberantly pushes my pleasure overboard. And when I finally come, something unexpected happens to me. Something that's never happened before. Fluid squirts out of me during my orgasm. As intense pleasure grips me, I scream, unable to contain the rapture I'm feeling and way too drunk to care if someone in this big house might overhear me.

When my body-quaking, squirting orgasm subsides, Savage turns me over onto my back again, looking positively feral. Breathing hard, he lies next me on his back and pulls at my arm.

"Sit on my face," he commands breathlessly.

"Savage," I gasp out. "Get a condom. I want you to fuck me."

"Sit on my face, Laila. *Now*."

Trembling, I do as I'm told, and when I lower myself onto his mouth, the pleasure feels supernatural. I lean forward as I ride his face, stroking his gorgeous, hard cock with my hand, and he moans his appreciation underneath me in reply. I look down and see his chin as it moves. My eyes drift to his chest and abs, and then to the tip of his cock peeking out of my hand. It's dripping with arousal now. So, I lean forward, slowly, allowing his mouth to keep up. And then, as he continues eating me from behind, I take his hard, dripping cock into my mouth and get to work, causing him to jolt and jerk and groan with pleasure.

We're absolutely going for it. Both of us. Losing our minds. Not holding back. And when I finally have an orgasm against Savage's mouth, he growls and has one, too—gushing his release into my mouth in a shockingly warm and salty torrent that fills my mouth to the brim.

My brain understands it's time to swallow him down, of course. But, as it turns out, commanding my throat to swallow while having an orgasm isn't in the cards. At least, not when the volume of Savage's release is this big.

As my eyes roll back into my head and my body warps with violent waves of pleasure, Savage's cum dribbles out my mouth and down my chin, and then, partially, onto his stomach. When I'm finally released from my rapture, I lower myself down and lick up my mess from his stomach, like a kitten licking up spilled milk off the floor. And when I'm done, and all traces of Savage's orgasm are gone, I continue licking and sucking on every inch of him, simply because he tastes so damned good.

Midway through kissing his abs, I freeze, suddenly feeling a dramatic shift in my body's equilibrium. When the room tilts sharply, I get up and stand at the edge of the bed, trying to right the ship. But it's no use. I think I'm gonna be sick.

"Come here, Fitzy," he coos. "I'm not even close to done with your pussy yet."

Murmuring something incoherent, I turn and bolt to the bathroom, drop to my knees before the toilet, and lose the entire contents of my stomach into the bowl: however many tequila shots and beers, a lovely meal of chicken, rice, and grilled vegetables . . . and a shocking deluge of salty cum I sucked out of the famous donkey dick attached to the sexiest man alive, Mr. Adrian Fucking Savage.

THIRTY-ONE

SAVAGE

"Oh, honey," Aloha says as Laila shuffles into Reed's expansive kitchen in the late morning light, looking like dogshit that's been stepped in twice. And it's not hard to surmise what's elicited the reaction. Laila's sandy hair is a mess on top of her head. Her normally glowing skin is pale and lifeless. She's got dark circles under her eyes and her sultry lips, usually dewy and sumptuous, are dry and pinched with her misery.

Yet, still, even like this, the woman does crazy things to my body. Involuntary things. Indeed, at the mere sight of Laila's raggedy ass shuffling into the kitchen, my entire body instantly perks up. My heart rate elevates. My skin tingles. Even the memory of Laila barfing at the end of our tryst doesn't dampen my body's attraction to her. Apparently, I'm an addict now. Addicted to a drug called Laila. And there's no turning back.

Weirdly, I didn't really mind the barfing part. Not that I have some kind of weird barfing kink. Obviously, I would have preferred that part didn't happen and thought it was totally gross. But I can't deny when it happened, and I held back her hair, so it wouldn't dip into the toilet bowl, when she whimpered pathetically in gratitude at my gentle touch, my heart kind of skipped a beat. I already knew

I was attracted to Sassy Laila. To Bitchy Laila. And, of course, to Sexy, Squirting, Screaming From Ecstasy Laila. But in that moment, I discovered I kinda dig Broken, Pathetic, Needs Me to Hold Her Hair While She Barfs and Act Like Her Knight in Shining Armor Laila, too. I mean, not too often, please. But now and again, sure. It turns out, I'm down to volunteer as tribute for that job, occasionally.

When Laila was done being sick, I helped her wash up, led her to the bed, tucked her in, and held her close while she whimpered and groaned. When she swore she was going to die, I stroked her hair and kissed her cheek and assured her she wouldn't. And, to my surprise, in between telling me to fuck off and to stop correcting her, she actually snuggled me, thanked me for taking care of her, and whispered my name like it was a little prayer. And the best part? She didn't steal my wallet or take a single surreptitious photo of me and post it on Twitter.

But that was then, and this is now. When I woke up this morning, Laila wasn't there. And when I went to her room and peeked inside, there she was. Fast asleep. Looking like road kill. And, instantly, I knew why she'd left my bedroom and staggered back to hers. Because a drunken tryst in the middle of the night with an asshole like me is one thing, according to Laila's Rulebook. But waking up in the morning, and seeing me lying next to her in the light of day, is something else entirely. Right then, I knew we might as well have been back on tour. That she'd drunkenly fucked me in the middle of the night, the same way she'd done on the night of the hot tub. And that now, she was going to pretend it had never happened, the same way she did back then.

Laila croaks out a pathetic "good morning" to the small group at Reed's kitchen table as she enters the room. Along with Aloha and me, the "second wave" of people eating breakfast this morning is comprised of Aloha's husband, Zander, Fish and Alessandra, and Reed's fiancée, Georgina. And of course, as the group eats, Amalia is puttering away adorably on the other side of the kitchen.

Moving like molasses, Laila grabs some coffee and a muffin

from a breakfast spread on the counter and then takes a seat next to me at the table.

"You look pretty," I say sarcastically. "Like a Picasso."

"Shut up," she murmurs before laying her forehead onto the table.

"And they were stupid enough to hire *you* to be *my* babysitter?" I say to her lowered head. "Pfft. I want a discount."

Laila flips me off without lifting her head.

"Thank God there's a professional hair and makeup person here today, eh?" I say. "Hopefully, she's a good one. She's got her work cut out for her with you."

"*Please, shut up,*" she murmurs into the table. "I'm trying to die over here. Which is okay, I've decided. I've had a good run. Tell my mother and sister I love them."

Aloha addresses her husband. "Babe, will you make Laila one of your hangover miracle smoothies?"

"You bet."

Georgina offers to assist Zander, saying she was a bartender in college, and he cheerily accepts her help.

As Zander and Georgina begin whipping up the concoction, Aloha's phone rings, and she heads off to take her call, which prompts Fish and Alessandra to head out of the kitchen, too, hand in hand. And, suddenly, Laila and I are sitting alone at the table, side by side.

"I'm gonna die," she murmurs.

I rub her back. "You're not gonna die."

"Don't tell me what to do."

I laugh.

"Have you taken some Ibuprofen, Laila?" Amalia asks from across the kitchen.

"No, ma'am. I couldn't find any."

"Poor baby. I'll get you some."

"Thank you, Amalia," Laila croaks out.

"You're the best, Abu Dabu," I call to Amalia as she leaves, prompting Laila to turn her head, placing her cheek flush onto the table with her eyebrows furrowed, and say, "*Abu Dabu?*"

I smile. "Abu is a cute name for grandma. Abu Dabu is my spin on it, because Amalia's like a fortune teller with a crystal ball. Crazy smart, that one."

Laila pulls an adorable face that practically screams, *What the fuck?*

I shrug. "Amalia and I bonded last night. The woman just gets me."

Laila chuckles and then groans with pain. "Don't make me laugh."

"Aw, you feel like a shit stain, huh—not even good enough to feel like the actual shit?"

She grimaces. "Exactly."

I brush my fingertips against her high cheekbone. And then, against her lower lip, reliving our first kiss last night in my mind. Damn, that was an amazing kiss. The best of my life. I didn't even know a kiss could be that exciting. I'd put a lot of stock into finally kissing those mesmerizing lips of Laila's, and yet our kiss exceeded my most enthralling fantasy.

She whimpers. "Last night was supposed to be a last hurrah. Not *suicide*."

It serves you right for ditching my ass last night and trying to make me jealous, I think. But what I say is, "Poor baby," while rubbing her back.

"That feels nice. Thank you."

"Even shit stains deserve a little mercy."

She sticks out her lower lip. "That's the sweetest thing anyone's ever said to me."

Zander appears and places a hideous green smoothie on the table in front of Laila, as Georgina takes the seat on the other side of her.

"Oh my God," Laila says, beholding the monstrous-looking concoction in front of her.

Zander says, "Drink the whole thing down within five minutes, and I promise you'll be magically back to normal within an hour."

Laila makes a face I'd expect to see on a person who's been dropped into a snake pit. She says, "Is this a *prank*?"

Zander chuckles. "I know it looks heinous, but, trust me, it works like a charm."

Georgina encourages Laila to drink it, so Laila finally picks up the glass, takes a tiny sip, and then winces comically, making everyone laugh.

Amalia returns with pills for Laila, and then heads out to work in another part of the house.

Zander leaves after a bit to find his wife, which prompts Georgina to say she's going to find Reed. And, suddenly, I'm alone at the table with Laila and her nasty-looking smoothie.

"What's in that thing?" I ask, as Laila takes another recalcitrant gulp.

"I have no idea," she replies, wiping her mouth. "Whatever it is, it tastes like *ass*."

"Well, if it tastes like *your* delicious ass, then sign me up."

She flashes me a snarky look. "I knew you'd bring that up, the first chance you got."

"You want me to pretend last night never happened, like on tour?"

"I do, actually. Thanks."

"I'm not doing that again, Laila. Especially not when we're going to be living together for the next three months. Last night happened, baby. Deal with it. Especially since it's going to happen again and again and again, every night for the next three months."

"Don't confuse my desire for a drunken booty call with my desire to jump into some kind of three-month-long arrangement with you."

"Why *wouldn't* we jump into an arrangement while living together? It's not like we can mess around with anyone else while we're pretending to be in love. So, let's have some fun."

She sniffs. "You smoke when you drink, and I fuck Adrian Savage when I drink."

I roll my eyes. "So, are you planning to be celibate for the next three months? Because I'm sure as hell not." I lean forward. "Especially when I already know how good you taste."

"Has it escaped your notice that *both* times we've fooled around, we've *both* been shitfaced drunk?"

"That's not why we fooled around, and you know it."

"I don't know that. When I'm sober, I'm not stupid enough to find you irresistible."

"Booze doesn't make you stupid, Laila. It makes you *honest*. And booze certainly isn't what makes me irresistible to you."

She snorts.

"Why would you even want to resist me, when I'm so damned delicious?"

"Candy is delicious, too, Savage. But too much candy isn't good for me."

"But you don't *expect* candy to be good for you, so there's no false advertising. You eat candy for instant gratification. Because it's delicious and *fun*." I smile. "Come, Laila. Let's have some delicious fun together."

She twists her mouth like she's genuinely considering it. But rather than speak, she brings her hideous smoothie to her lips.

I'm a shark smelling blood. A bloodhound on the scent. She's losing her resolve. I can *feel* it. "Come on," I coo. "When you know, going in, you're bingeing on candy, then nobody can get hurt." She purses her lips, but doesn't say no, so I forge ahead. "Whatever made you want to hunt me down for a booty call last night is still there now, even without a drop of alcohol in your system."

"I didn't hunt you down for a booty call last night. You hunted *me* down for a booty call."

"Oh, *really*? What were you doing creeping around in the hallway in the middle of the night in your underwear, if not hunting me down for a booty call?"

She bats her eyelashes. "I got hungry and wanted a snack."

I snort. "Laila, I saw you pressing your ear against a door. Obviously, you were trying to figure out which room was mine."

"Maybe. But not for a booty call. I wanted to chew you out for leaving the party without saying goodnight to me."

"In your underwear?"

"I didn't think about what I was wearing. I was too drunk and annoyed. You're the one who said we should always stay in character, whenever we're not alone. And then, you left the party without so much as a wave goodbye to me? Ha! Would a real boyfriend leave a party without saying goodnight to his girlfriend who supposedly rocks his world? No way!"

I can't help smiling. I should have known Kendrick would never steer me wrong. The guy is a king. I say, "I left without saying goodnight because I didn't want to bother you while you were obviously having so much fun with your friends. Plus, the only people left at the party at that point were good friends who were associated with the show, so I knew you were in good hands."

"You're such a hypocrite! That's exactly what I said about Colin!"

I bite back a smile. Pushing her buttons is so damned fun. "Let's not rehash the Colin thing, okay? The bottom line is you flirted with him last night to make me jealous, because you're evil, and it worked because I'm stupid and predictable. Can we agree we're both idiot-assholes and move on, please?"

She looks extremely pleased with that response. "Yes. As long as we agree you're *more* of an idiot-asshole than me, then I'm prepared to move on."

"No. We're tied."

She pauses for a beat before exhaling and saying, "Fine."

"Thank you. Now, admit you were creeping around the hallway in your underwear last night because you were looking for a booty call."

"What about you? What were *you* doing in the hallway in your underwear?"

I grin wickedly. "Like you said, I was hungry and looking for a snack." I lean forward. "And, lucky for me, the snack I found was even tastier than I'd fantasized it'd be. So damned tasty, I can't wait to eat it again and again, starting tonight."

She bites her lip but says nothing. And I know she's on the bitter cusp of agreeing to fuck my brains out every night for the next three months.

"Aw, come on, Laila," I coo in my most seductive voice. "Why fight it? Let's have some fun."

She exhales. "I don't want it to get confusing."

I furrow my brow. "In what way?"

She shrugs. "Won't it be weird if we're working together, living together, pretending to be head over heels for each other . . . *and* having sex every night? Doesn't that seem like a recipe for disaster?"

"For who? Are you saying you're worried you're going to catch feelings, Fitzy?"

"Of course not. I'm saying I'm worried *you're* going to catch feelings."

I scoff. "I'm not the one we need to worry about, sweetheart. I'm not the one who went on *Sylvia* and couldn't stop talking about me."

"And I'm not the one who couldn't stop talking about me to that Instagrammer."

"Oh, come on. You don't believe her stupid story. Not for a second."

"I believe every word of it."

"No way. You're messing with me. You know I said I needed to 'lay low' because of the show."

"No. I believe, with all my heart, you said you didn't want her because of Laila."

"Why would I turn her down because of *you*?"

"Exactly. Why would you do that, Savage? Tell me."

I pause, my heart racing. "I *didn't*. You didn't even cross my mind in that moment. When you're not physically in front of me, I literally forget you exist. Hell, I barely remember you exist when you're right in front of my face."

She rolls her eyes.

"Seriously, Laila. If you're worried I'll 'catch feelings' from having sex with you while I'm stuck with you anyway, then don't. I'm perfectly capable of separating fact from fiction. The real question is can *you*?"

"Of course I can."

"Even if you're living with, and sleeping with, and working with, your fake boyfriend who's an irresistible god-among-men rockstar who's hung like a jury?"

She scoffs. "I won't catch feelings, Savage. Under any circumstances. Honestly, I don't even like you."

"Perfect, because I don't like you. We're a match made in heaven, if you ask me."

She bites her lip and I know I've got her. *Finally*.

"So, we're doing this then?" I say.

Laila pauses. "We'd be fuck buddies only. No strings. And nobody catches feelings."

"Of course. It'll be nothing but fun and a whole lot of orgasms."

She puts out her hand. "Deal."

I feel like jumping for joy but manage to maintain a neutral face while shaking her hand. "Now give me our first *sober* kiss to seal the deal." With that, I pull her toward me. And when our lips meet, the kiss hits totally differently than our drunken, animalistic kisses from last night. This time, as my lips open hers, and my tongue slides into her mouth and begins slowly tangling with hers, I feel every nuanced sensation. Every shudder of arousal. Every inhale and exhale that tells me her temperature is slowly rising, the same as mine.

As our sensuous kiss deepens, I pull her out of her chair and guide her to straddle me in my chair, and, soon, she's grinding against me as her tongue goads me on. I begin caressing her breasts over her tank top, pinching her stiff nipples, and burying my hands into her thick hair, every fiber of my body aching and yearning to get inside her.

"We've got time," I murmur into her lips. "Come to my room. Let me fuck you."

"Yes," she breathes.

But she's no sooner said the word than a voice in the doorway says her name. When we break apart, breathing hard, there's a production assistant in the doorframe.

The PA says, "I'm sorry to interrupt." She clears her throat. "Nadine sent me to fetch Laila and bring her to hair and makeup. She said we're on a tight schedule."

Laila smiles and kisses my cheek. "Rain check?" She slides off my lap and points at the noticeable bulge behind my sweatpants. "I'll see *you* later tonight."

I slap her ass as she turns to go. "Count on it, *girlfriend.*"

"Don't miss me while I'm gone, boyfriend."

"I can't miss someone who ceases to exist when she's not in my presence."

"Sure, Jan."

With that, she swishes her hips with extra flair, and disappears through the doorway with the PA. When she's gone, and I know she can't possibly hear me, I sit back in my chair, smiling from ear to ear, my hard cock throbbing and my heart racing, and whisper to myself, "*Hallelujah.*"

THIRTY-TWO

LAILA

I follow the staffer outside and across Reed's patio, heading toward Reed's guest house in the back of Reed's huge estate. Apparently, the hair and makeup woman has set up camp there. As we walk, we come upon Kendrick. He's sitting on a patio chair with a laptop on his lap and headphones over his ears.

When he sees me, Kendrick pulls down one side of his headphones and greets me. "I just got the final mixes for our album!" he says effusively.

"Ooooh!" I say. "When can I listen? I seem to recall someone saying, on day one of our tour, I'd get to be one of your early listeners."

"Absolutely. We'd love to get your feedback on the mixes. Give it a listen as soon as you can and let me know if you hear *anything* that sounds wonky to you—anything at all you think is too low or high in the mix."

"It'd be my honor. I can't wait."

Kendrick clicks on his keyboard for a moment. "I just sent you a download link."

I look at my phone. "Got it! Woohoo! I'll listen now, while I'm getting my hair and makeup done!"

"Awesome. Thanks."

"No, thank *you*."

I say my goodbyes to Kendrick and resume following the PA to Reed's casita, where I'm immediately greeted by the hair and makeup woman. After the woman gets me settled in her chair, we talk briefly about the look we're going for today—sexpot, of course—and once we're both on the same page, I settle back, put a pair of earbuds in, and press play on the first song of Fugitive Summer's highly anticipated album.

Right away, it's obvious the first song is going to be a massive hit, although I'd personally make the bass line a touch louder in the mix. Next up, the second song begins and I quickly fall equally in love with it. How does this band do it, album after album? Every song of theirs is like crack to me. And Savage's voice and delivery is always mesmerizing. From what I understand, he writes the lion's share of the band's lyrics, which is probably why he always delivers them so believably. Say what you will about Savage, the man, being deeply flawed and mercurial, but as an artist, that boy is a true genius.

The third song begins as the makeup artist finishes applying foundation and moves on to my eyes. And, once again, even before Savage begins singing, based on nothing but the sexual, dirty beat and groove and flashes of Savage's phallic electric guitar, I already know I'm going to love this one. It's got a vibe that's reminiscent of "Come with Me," the band's most sexual song, without it feeling like a copycat or redux. Indeed, the sexual vibe of the song is reinforced, even before the first verse begins, as Savage growls out a few sensual "yeahs" to kick things off, his strained voice sounding remarkably like he's getting a blowjob in the recording booth.

Finally, as the bass-heavy beat gains momentum, Savage counts off—"One, two, three, let's go!"—and away he goes, launching into the lyrics of the first verse.

Almost immediately, as Savage sings, I open my eyes, recognizing myself in the song. Is this a coincidence . . . or is Savage singing this song about *me*?

No way.

Why would Savage write a song about *me?*

"Close, please," the makeup artist says, referring to my eyes.

"Hold on a second," I say. I quickly look down at my phone, curious about the title of this one. And when I see it, I gasp. *Hate Sex High.* That's what the song is called. Which definitely makes me think I'm not crazy to think the song could be about me. Maybe? But I've no sooner had that last thought than the song barrels into its chorus . . . and the lyrics there make my jaw practically clank to the floor.

THIRTY-THREE

SAVAGE

I wander out of the house with a cup of coffee and take in the view for a moment, scratching my bare belly. I feel light as a feather right now. Like everything is clicking into place. I gotta hand it to Kendrick. The man is a genius. Speaking of Kendrick, I notice him sitting in a chair with his laptop and decide to head over there to tell him he's the man—that, thanks to his advice, I've now got Laila eating out the palm of my hand.

When I reach Kendrick, he's got headphones on, and he's nodding his head to a beat only he can hear.

When he notices me, he pulls off one side of his headphones and blurts excitedly, "Did you see Zeke sent the final mixes?"

My heart lurches. "No. When? I left my phone in my room."

"Twenty minutes ago. I'm listening now and everything sounds *amazing!*"

"Oh, my God. Let me hear something!"

Kendrick hands me his headphones and I slip them on, while Kendrick presses play on the first song—"Shockwave"—a banger that's one of my favorites on the album.

"Oh my God. 'Shockwave' sounds *so* good," I say excitedly.

"Although I'd add a touch more bass to the mix. Ask Kai what he thinks, obviously, but that's my opinion."

"Yeah, okay. I'll ask him."

I listen for a long moment again, before saying, "Zeke sent the link to Reed, too?"

"Yeah. I saw Reed a few minutes ago. He was super stoked. He headed straight to his office to listen now."

"Cool. So excited."

"Same. Reed said he'll send it to some people with really good ears."

"Awesome. Is he sending it to Dax Morgan and Dean Masterson, you think?"

"Yeah, he mentioned both. Fish, too."

"Perfect. Fish's ears are impeccable."

"I know. If Reed didn't send it to him already, I would have done it myself. I sent it to C-Bomb, too. He said he'll take a listen today. Oh, and Laila, too. Just now. She's got amazing ears."

My heart stops. "Laila? You *already* sent it to her or you're *planning* to send it to her?"

"I already did. She said she'd listen right away, while she gets her hair and makeup done."

"Kendrick, no." I can barely breathe. "How long ago was that?"

"What's wrong?"

"When was that?"

"Just now. Like, ten minutes ago. Fifteen, tops. Why?"

"Where is she? Did she say where she was going?"

"Hair and makeup."

"Yes, but *where*?" I'm shouting now, as panic rises sharply inside me. "Where is hair and makeup, Kendrick?"

"I don't know. She went that way." He points. "What's wrong? Laila is totally trustworthy."

My heart is crashing. My breathing shallow. I point maniacally at Kendrick's laptop. "Quick, look to see if she's already downloaded it! If not, cancel her access. Now, Kendrick!"

"*Why?*"

"Just do it!"

"I'm doing it. Calm down." He starts clicking on his keyboard, looking frantic. "What's the problem?"

"'Hate Sex High,' Kendrick! I don't want Laila listening to that one right now. Not *yet*."

"*Oooh*." He taps on some keys before looking up from his screen, his features contorted in apology. And even before he's said a word, I know what he's going to say. But he says it, anyway. "She already downloaded it, dude. It's too late."

I take a deep breath. "Maybe not. It's only been a few minutes. Maybe Laila isn't listening to the album yet. Or if she is, maybe she hasn't gotten to that song. Where is it in the order?"

Kendrick checks the screen and grimaces again. "Third, like you requested."

"*Fuck!* She went that way?"

"Yeah. I think there's a guest house over there. Maybe that's—"

But I'm not listening. Without further ado, I sprint away in the direction Kendrick indicated, cursing a blue streak as I go . . . feeling uncannily like I'm running *toward* a ticking time bomb.

THIRTY-FOUR

LAILA

As the third song on the album—"Hate Sex High"—reaches the end of its first chorus and barrels into a sort of sing-along post-chorus section that causes my head to explode, there's a commotion at the door. A sudden movement attracts my attention, and when I look toward the doorframe, none other than Savage is standing there, his chest heaving and his eyes bugged out.

I look at him, rendered speechless, as Savage's voice continues singing in my ears . . . about *me*. And whatever Savage sees on my face in this moment prompts him to say, quite obviously, the word "Fuck." I can't hear him saying the word, but I can sure as hell read his lips, as Savage's voice launches into the second chorus of "Hate Sex High" in my earbuds:

You're falling, falling, falling, falling, falling in hate with me
I'm feeling, feeling, feeling, feeling something I don't want to feel . . .

. . .

Savage begins walking toward me, and when he mouths the word "Laila" before me, it's coincidentally at the exact same time he sings my name in the song, in the post-chorus section where Savage sings, repeatedly: "La la la la la la la la la *Laila Laila.*"

I rip out my earbuds, just in time to hear Savage asking the hair and makeup artist to leave. As the woman scurries out the front door of the casita, the song continues wafting from the earbuds in my hand, now sounding compressed and tinny, but otherwise clear as a bell.

Savage's voice in the earbuds sings: "And I'm feeling, feeling, feeling, feeling . . . *something I don't want to feel.*" And Savage before me inhales sharply and jolts in response.

"It's not about you!" Savage blurts, his face flushed. "I know how it must seem, but it's, you know, creative license. Pure fiction. Not about you."

Pure fiction? That seems highly unlikely. Partial fiction, maybe. But there's just too much obvious truth, too much coincidence in the verses, for the entire song to be *pure* fiction.

I say, "*Pure* fiction?"

"I mean, there might be kernels of truth in the verses," he acknowledges. "Here and there. Tiny kernels, which I then spun into popcorn lies in the chorus."

"I get it," I say, my heart crashing in my chest. But I'm not sure I get it. It's interesting he felt the need to single out the chorus, without me mentioning it. The part where someone is *falling* into hate with Savage and he's *feeling* something he doesn't want to feel for someone.

"When I wrote the chorus," Savage says, his features tight, "I chose words that went together well. I liked the way 'falling' and 'feeling' sound together, that's all."

"Yeah, that was a cool word choice. When I write, I like putting words together that sound good, too. I'm often motivated by the sounds of words more than their meanings."

"*Exactly,*" he says. "The meaning is secondary. Not even important."

There's a long, awkward pause between us, during which he looks remarkably flustered.

Savage shifts his weight. "*Maybe*, subliminally, the night of the hot tub played a small part in inspiring the song. I think I remember writing that song shortly after we got together. So, I'm sure it'd be fair to say that night gave me the initial spark of an idea for the song, but then I ran with it and it became something totally fictitious."

Totally fictitious? That's what I'm thinking. But what I say is, "I totally get it."

"By the time I got done writing it, it was almost pure fiction."

"I write the same way sometimes. Something real gives me an idea, and I run with it."

"I know you get it. You're a fantastic songwriter, by the way."

"Thanks. So are you." My heart feels like a jackhammer. "I love the songs I've heard so far. I've only heard the first three, but they're all amazing." I swallow hard. My mouth is dry. "I hope you don't mind me saying this, but I'd personally make the bassline a bit higher in the mix on the first song. Just the tiniest bit."

"I thought the same thing. Great feedback. Thanks."

"Sure. I'll keep listening carefully to the rest, if—"

"Yeah, please do. Thanks."

"Sure."

He shifts his weight again. "Cool."

The song ends in my earbuds and a new one begins. So I grab my phone and press pause. "I'm honored to get to hear the album early, by the way. Thanks for that."

"We like having trusted people—people with good ears . . . " He trails off and takes a deep breath. "I only ran down here to talk to you because I didn't want you thinking—"

"I don't. I understand the writing process."

"The song isn't some kind of . . . confessional or anything. Don't read too much into it."

"I don't. I get it." But, still, I'm not sure I get it.

Savage breathes a huge sigh of relief and his shoulders soften. "Cool."

I bite the tip of my finger. "I mean, why on earth would I think you were 'feeling' something you 'didn't want to feel' . . . for *me?*"

His shoulders stiffen again.

"Especially back then," I add. "I know you've discovered I'm a tasty treat nowadays, and kind of fun to hang out with, if you've got no other option, but back then, we hated each other's guts. *Right?*"

"We still do, as far as I'm concerned," he says.

"Good. Me, too."

"Good."

My eyes are locked with his as I try to discern if this feeling in my belly is delusional or not. "I mean, back then, you were *way* too busy mowing through groupies in every city of the tour to be feeling 'something' you 'didn't want to feel' about *me. Right?*"

He pauses, briefly, before saying, "Right. Absolutely."

We stare at each other for a long beat, the only sound the crashing of my heart in my ears.

"Okay, well . . ." Savage finally says. "I'm glad we talked about this. It's a good thing you're so familiar with songwriting and the creative process, or this could have created a huge misunderstanding. Especially going into our . . . arrangement."

I press my lips together. "It's a good thing, indeed."

He motions toward the door. "So . . . should I tell the makeup artist to—"

"Yes, please. We're running tight on time, apparently, and she's got quite a bit more to do to make this shit stain look halfway decent."

"Actually, I would have thought she's already done. You look great."

"Thanks. Zander's hangover cure worked, exactly as promised. I feel . . ." Weird. Confused. Shocked. Skittish. Suspicious. Freaked out. "Remarkably good, actually."

"Glad to hear it. Okay, well, I'll go get the makeup artist for you. See you at the press conference."

"See you then."

He turns to leave.

"Actually, one quick question."

Savage turns around slowly, his facial expression saying, *And I was so close to escaping, too.*

I smile. "In the second half of the chorus, that sort of post-chorus sing-along part . . . Are you singing, 'La la la . . . *Laila*' there?"

He flushes. "No."

"No?"

"Nope. I'm singing 'la la.'"

"Yeah, I know, but at the tail end there. After the string of 'la la's,' you didn't cap it off with 'Laila'?"

"No. I sang, 'La la' the whole way through."

"Huh. That's so weird. I was positive I heard you singing my name."

"That's what being a narcissist will do to you, I guess. You think everyone is singing your name."

I smile sweetly. "Takes one to know one, honey."

We chuckle awkwardly. But, seriously. I swear I heard that part as Laila.

His face is red. His Adam's apple bobs. "I was definitely singing 'la la' there. But if you think it sounds too much like *Laila*, then I can re-record that part, very easily, to make it crystal clear what I'm actually singing—which absolutely isn't 'Laila.'"

"No need. I'm sure I was just imagining it. Thinking the world revolves around me, like you said. I'm sure when I listen again, I'll laugh that I ever thought you sang my name on that part."

Savage chuckles with me. "Yeah, that's funny." He claps his hands together and exhales. "Okay, well, I'll let you get to it. Like you said, time is tight."

"Great. Thanks."

Looking a bit out of sorts, Savage practically stumbles out the door, and a moment later, the makeup artist returns. After she's picked up her eyeshadow palette, and I've settled back into my chair, I shove my earbuds back in, restart "Hate Sex High" from the beginning, and listen to every single word, this time extra carefully:

Hate Sex High

Yeah, yeah, yeah, yeah
One, two, three, let's go

You're falling, falling, falling, falling, falling in hate with me
I'm feeling, feeling, feeling, feeling something I don't want to feel

Saw you with him at the show
I didn't like it
I played it cold to your face
But I was on fire
He said you were his all along
And I didn't like it
Turns out I imagined it all
Went back and punched a hole in the wall

You're falling, falling, falling, falling, falling in hate with me
I'm feeling, feeling, feeling, feeling something I don't want to feel
You're falling, falling, falling, falling, falling in hate with me
I'm feeling, feeling, feeling, feeling something I don't want to feel

Lalalalalala la la
Lalalalalala la la

. . .

I shouldn't-a said what I did
  Not tryna deny it
  The harder I pushed you away
  You wanted to ride it
  I fucked with your body, baby
  You fucked with my mind
  You said it meant nothing to ya
  But you came three times

  You're falling, falling, falling, falling, falling in hate with me
    I'm feeling, feeling, feeling, feeling something I don't want
to feel
    You're falling, falling, falling, falling, falling in hate with me
    I'm feeling, feeling, feeling, feeling something I don't want
to feel

  Lalalalalala la la
    Lalalalalala la la

  I fucked with your body, baby
    You fucked with my mind
    You said it meant nothing to ya
    But you came three times
    Girl, you came three times
    You came three times
    You're chasing a
    Hate sex high

. . .

The song cycles through a few more choruses, until, finally, in an outro at the very end, Savage speaks conversationally over the music, his voice purring sexually above the sex-laden beat: "Did *he* make you come *three* times? Yeah, didn't think so." And I know, without a doubt, that's absolutely one of the "kernels of truth" Savage admitted were buried in the song. Unless, of course, he was making every groupie he screwed come three times, the same way he did to me on the night of the hot tub, and was also totally obsessed with his achievement in regards to them, as well.

I listen again, from the very beginning, and, once again, I can't help hearing my name at the end of the "la la la" section. Granted, Savage didn't pronounce it like he normally would, almost as if he was pronouncing my name in a purposefully vague sort of way, like he was trying to reserve himself some deniability. Like he was *pretending* to sing "la la" in that part, while *secretly* singing "Laila" with a smug little smirk on his handsome face. In fact, I can almost picture Savage in the vocal booth, smirking wickedly while recording that part, as if he thought he was getting away with a fast one.

I feel a tap on my shoulder and open my eyes.

"All done," the makeup artist mouths, and I pull out my earbuds and look in the mirror.

"Beautiful," I say. "Thank you."

"You're an easy canvas."

She begins cleaning up her station, getting ready for whoever is coming next. But I'm too lost in thought to move a muscle. Savage admitted he wrote "Hate Sex High" based on "kernels of truth" which he then spun into "popcorn lies." Like I told him, that's a concept I can fully understand, in general, since I've done the same thing in my own songwriting, too.

However, in reference to *this* specific song, a song called "Hate Sex High," in which my name sure seems to be buried artfully among a string of "la la la's"—a song about a woman chasing a "hate sex high" while Savage makes her come "*three* times"—a song about a woman falling into hate with Savage while he feels "something" he doesn't "want to feel"—I can't help wondering, in regards to this specific song: which parts are the admitted "kernels of *truth*" . . . and which are the supposed "popcorn lies"?

To find out how to stream or download "HATE SEX HIGH", go to www.laurenrowebooks.com/music-from-the-hatelove-duet
And while you're there, check out tons of spoiler-free BONUS MATERIAL about Savage, Laila, and many River Records artists.

falling into LOVE with YOU

USA Today and International Bestselling Author
Lauren Rowe

THIRTY-FIVE

LAILA

As Savage leaves Reed's guest house after our stilted, awkward conversation about "Hate Sex High," I shove my earbuds back in, press play on the song, close my eyes, and listen carefully. A moment later, the makeup artist taps my arm, letting me know she's returned from outside, so I nod to her and close my eyes again, finding it hard to give my attention, even fleetingly, to anything but Savage's voice in my ears.

Presently, Savage's sexy voice is singing, *"You're falling in hate with me/I'm feeling something I don't want to feel . . ."* And I can't help wondering . . . what is the *something* Savage was feeling when he wrote this song—the *something* he didn't want to feel? A few minutes ago, Savage swore, up and down, that the entire song was "pure fiction." But then, he immediately backtracked and said the chorus was a "popcorn lie" he'd spun from various "kernels of truth" in the verses. The thing is, though, I hadn't even mentioned the chorus when Savage felt the need to vehemently deny its truth. So now, I can't help thinking the dude doth protest too much.

The song continues to the second half of the chorus, the part where Savage sings a string of *"la la's."* And, once again, I hear *my* name at the ends of those lines. *Repeatedly.* Yep, that's definitely my name! Granted, Savage's voice is buried in the mix, artfully interwoven with his bandmates' voices singing "*la la.*" Most likely to preserve deniability for Savage. But, nonetheless, anyone with the ability to hear would be able to discern *my* name at the end of those *la la's.*

A flash of energy courses through my veins. Does Savage singing my name in the song *enthrall* or *anger* me? I can't decide. All I know for certain is that hearing Savage belting out *my* name, for the entire world to hear—knowing he's explicitly identifying *me* as the muse for this raunchy song—is making my blood simmer and every hair on my body stand at full attention.

The song continues, with Savage making a big thing about his muse coming three times. "Girl, you came three times," he sings, *twice*, before speaking the line in a smug, matter-of-fact tone. Finally, Savage concludes in the bridge, "You're chasing . . . a . . . hate sex high"—and as Savage sings the titular lyrics of the song, a shiver skates across my skin. As freaked out as I am in this moment, I can't help reliving the night of the hot tub as I listen. The night I did, in fact, chase a hate sex high with Savage, all the way to three glorious orgasms that felt far more intense and electrifying than anything I'd experienced before.

I feel a tap on my shoulder and open my eyes to find the makeup artist smiling at me. She holds up a makeup brush as if to say "all done!" So, I stop the song, which is currently barreling into its final chorus, and check myself out in the mirror.

"Looks great," I say. "Thank you."

"You're welcome."

"Who's sitting in your chair next?" I ask, hoping she'll say Aloha, and when she does, I tap out a text to my darling friend, asking her to please get her ass down to Reed's guest house as soon as possible—earlier than scheduled—because I need to talk to her about something urgent.

Three minutes later, Aloha appears, her famous emerald-green eyes practically glowing. After greeting the makeup artist, Aloha asks me, "Is everything okay?"

I jut my chin toward the makeup artist, who's presently preparing her station, to let Aloha know the urgent thing I need to talk to her about is confidential, and Aloha instantly gets the message.

"Hey, Susanna," Aloha says. "Would you mind taking a quick break before we get started? I came early to chat with Laila."

"Of course," the makeup artist replies. "How's fifteen minutes?"

Aloha looks at me, her eyebrows raised. And when she sees the expression of pure panic on my face, she says, "Let's make it twenty."

The door closes behind the makeup artist, and before I've said a word, Aloha lurches at me and yells, "What did Savage do to you last night, you little freak? My room was across the hallway from Savage's and I heard every scream and moan!" She takes the chair next to mine, smiling wickedly. "And don't tell me all those noises were you barfing, and not the sounds of pure ecstasy. I know barfing when I hear it, and that wasn't it."

I roll my eyes, even as I'm blushing. "The second half of what you heard was me barfing."

"And the first half?"

I can't help smiling. "The sounds of pure ecstasy."

Aloha squeals. "Tell me *everything*."

"There's not much to tell. Savage ate me from every angle and I was too drunk to care if anyone in the house heard my reaction."

Aloha fans herself. "Girl, you never disappoint. How did you even wind up in Savage's room?"

"I was horny and drunk and didn't know which room was his, so I crept down the hallway on my tiptoes, in my undies, and went looking for him."

Aloha hoots. "Laila Fitzgerald! You little horndog!"

I snort. "I pressed my ear against a couple doors, hoping to feel some kind of 'Savage vibration' emanating from the other side. And then, lo and behold, there Savage was in *his* underwear on the far end of the hallway, on his way to find *me*."

Aloha reacts gleefully.

"But that's not the urgent thing I needed to talk to you about. I need you to listen to something that's making my head explode. Talk me off the ledge, Aloha. I'm freaking out." I grab my phone, anxiety coursing through me, and get "Hate Sex High" cued up. My heart thumping, I explain, "This morning, Kendrick gave me an early copy of Fugitive Summer's new album, so I could listen to the mixes." I hand my phone to Aloha. "Listen to the third track. 'Hate Sex High.' It's about *me*—about the night I told you about, when I screwed Savage's brains out during the tour."

"Holy crap," Aloha whispers, taking my phone and earbuds.

As she begins listening, I get up and pace back and forth in the small guest house, unable to keep my body, or mind, from spazzing out.

"Love the beat," Aloha murmurs. "Cool baseline." She pauses. "Ha! That's so Savage. It sounds like he's getting a blowjob."

"Keep listening," I say. Clearly, she's only gotten as far as the introductory "yeahs."

Suddenly, Aloha's eyebrows lift. Her eyes widen. She begins muttering things like "Whoa" and "Wow." Finally, she shouts, "He's singing *Laila*! What the fuck!" She presses pause. "He's called you out by *name*?"

"*Right*?"

"*Dude*." She presses play again and a moment later shrieks, "You came *three* times with him that night?"

I blush and nod. "More last night."

Aloha flashes me a snarky look. "Well, damn. No wonder you don't care if he's an asshole." She snickers to herself before quieting down to listen again. And then, "Wow, he's proud of those three orgasms, huh?" She pauses. "Okay, Savage, we get it. She came *three* times." She snorts. "What a smug little shit to put this song as the *third* track on the album, as yet another nod to those three Os. That's so Savage."

My pulse lurches. I hadn't thought of that, but she's right.

Aloha continues listening for a moment before snorting and

saying, "He just had to gloat, one more time, at the end. Such a cheeky bastard." She presses pause and takes out the earbuds. "So, Laila. I have a question not answered by the lyrics. Something that wasn't clear." Aloha furrows her brow, like she's trying to solve the secrets of the universe. "Did Savage, by any chance . . . make you come *three* times?"

We both break into raucous laughter. Even in my present state of total freak-out, I can't help giggling with my good friend.

I resume my chair next to Aloha. "So, you agree he's singing my name in those 'la la' parts, right? Because Savage denied it."

"You've already talked to Savage about the song?"

I nod furiously. "He burst in here, while I was midway through listening to it. Apparently, Kendrick gave me an early copy of the album without consulting Savage first, and when Savage found out, he hightailed it straight down here to find me."

"Interesting."

"And then, when Savage realized I was already listening to 'Hate Sex High,' he had the nerve to *deny* he sang my name in the song! He *insisted* he was singing 'la la' all the way through."

Aloha scoffs, her expression making it clear she doesn't buy Savage's explanation for a minute.

I continue, "Savage insisted I was only hearing my name because I'm a 'megalomaniac' who thinks the world revolves around me."

Aloha laughs in a way that would have resulted in a spit-take if she'd taken a sip of a beverage immediately beforehand.

"Preposterous, right?" I ask.

"Utterly and totally preposterous. Not to mention, insulting to your intelligence. He's singing 'Laila,' over and over again. Plus, come on, the verses track what happened between you and Savage during the tour—the stuff with Malik in New York and your hookup later on. So, there's no doubt, even if he didn't call you out by name, which he *did,* that the song is one thousand percent about *you.* But, yes, there's no question he *also* says your name, repeatedly, to emphasize his point."

"*But what's his point?*" I ask breathlessly. "Is his point what he sings in the chorus? The part where he says he's feeling 'something' he doesn't want to feel for his muse—for 'Laila' who's falling into hate with him?"

"You mean, Laila who's coming *three* times while chasing a hate sex high?"

I exhale loudly. "Honestly, it's the chorus that's freaking me out the most, even more than all the sex stuff. I don't know if it would be hitting me so hard if Savage hadn't raced down here with bulging eyes the minute he found out I had an early copy. But, Aloha, when Savage burst through that door, he looked like he was going to have a heart attack at the thought of me listening to *that* particular song. And then *he* brought up the chorus first, to *deny* it was true, before I'd said a word about it. So, I don't think his main worry was the sex stuff."

Aloha bites her lip, processing. "How'd you leave it with him?"

"He conceded the song was 'inspired' by me. That there were 'kernels of truth' in the verses. But he said he took those 'kernels of truth' and spun them into 'popcorn lies' in the chorus. But why would Savage feel the need to *sprint* down here, like a bat out of hell, unless he *knew* that chorus admits he caught feelings for me during the tour?" I let my mouth hang open, wide, as if to say, *Can you believe it?*

But Aloha's face reflects skepticism. "Well, I mean, he could have been worried you'd be livid to be called out, by *name*, as someone he'd screwed." Aloha pauses, waiting for a reaction from me, and whatever wilted expression she's seeing on my face makes her sigh with compassion. "Okay, let's look at this objectively, honey. Savage is the guy who had sex with you on the night of the hot tub, and then, mere hours later, turned around and screwed someone else. So, even if he *is* singing in the chorus about 'catching feelings' for you, then how much stock do you really think you should put into those supposed feelings?"

I look down at my lap, feeling embarrassed about my show of excitement.

"Aw, I'm sorry," Aloha says quickly. "Maybe you're right. I'm certainly not trying to rain on your parade here . . ."

I take a deep breath and look up, making a concerted effort to wipe all traces of disappointment off my face. Aloha is right. I'm assigning *way* too much depth and importance to that chorus, when the obvious truth is that Savage proved himself a diehard woman-izer in Las Vegas. A man who'd felt nothing but lust toward me, the same thing he'd felt toward countless other women across the globe. Truly, it was the height of self-delusion for me to think the song is about Savage catching feelings for me, when the truth is that I was never anything special to him. Nothing but another conquest.

Aloha apologizes again and tries to backtrack, but I wave her off, saying, "No, no, don't apologize. I asked for your honest opin-ion, and you gave it to me. I'm glad you never pull any punches with me."

"But, honey, I never want to 'punch' you in any way. I just wanted—"

"No, no, stop. Like you said, even if Savage *did* catch feelings for me after the night of the hot tub, which is unlikely, his 'feelings' wouldn't be something I should rely on, based on his subsequent behavior. I need to remember the timeline of events here. There's no other conclusion to be drawn when I look at Savage's *actions*, rather than projecting some fairytale fantasy onto a few stupid lyrics in a song."

Aloha looks sympathetic. "Oh, Laila, I'd *love* for you to be the woman who brought Mr. Fuckboy to his knees. I'd *love* that for you. I just don't want you to get hurt. In the past, I've seen Savage in action, from afar, and let's just say his reputation as a lady killer is well-earned."

I nod. "Yeah, I know. I always want you to be nothing but totally honest with me. Even if the truth hurts, that's what I want to hear."

Aloha puffs out her cheeks. "Okay, well, if I'm being *totally* honest with you, it seems to me the song is a 'gloating song' about Savage having sex with you. A song written to taunt Malik, far more than to express any secret feelings he was having for you. I mean, Savage literally asks, at the end, if 'he'—meaning Malik—made you come three times, the same way Savage did. If that's not a pissing contest between two dudes—if that's not Savage running a victory lap—then I don't know what is."

My heart feels like it's lodged in my toes. Aloha is right, yet again. After his tussle with Malik in that restaurant, Savage wanted his adversary to know he'd won the game and claimed the prize. Also, that he'd done all of it exceedingly well. Savage sat down and wrote "Hate Sex High" to deride Malik, not because he felt tortured by his blossoming feelings for me. In the end, the song had very little to do with me, actually, and everything to do with his desire to flip the bird at Malik.

Suddenly, I feel like I'm standing in that hallway in Las Vegas, all over again. An acute sensation of rejection washes over me. I feel pathetic. Foolish. *Embarrassed.* Why do I *still* want Savage to want me, more than anyone else—but especially more than some random groupie he just met? Why does he *still* have this ridiculous hold over me?

Aloha says, "Aw, Laila. I could be wrong. After the night of the hot tub, was there *any* indication Savage was feeling 'something' he didn't want to feel toward you? Think back."

Images flood me. Savage's arm slung over that groupie's shoulders. A booze bottle dangling in his free hand. The woman's obvious excitement that Savage had deigned to choose *her.* I hear her voice saying, "Let me at that famous body!" And every molecule in my body recoils and shudders at the memory. "No," I reply, my spirit heavy. "On the contrary, the only indication was that Savage felt the same thing men always feel for me: nothing but lust." I take a deep breath to regulate the pang of embarrassment twisting my core. How on earth did I hear "Hate Sex High" and turn it into a confessional about Savage catching feelings for me, when the truth is so damned obvious?

Aloha juts her lower lip in sympathy. "Aw, honey. Who cares what I think? I wasn't there, and you were. Trust your gut."

"I do. And my gut is telling me you're right. It's telling me I heard what I wanted to hear in the song, not what was actually there."

Sighing, Aloha gets up from her chair and hugs me. "Oh, sweet Laila. You and your horrible taste in men." She kisses my hair. "Why can't you ever fall for guys who aren't players and heart-breakers, girlie?"

I nuzzle into Aloha's dark hair and exhale. "It's my fatal flaw. I see a guy with multiple red flags sticking out of his hair and ears and asshole, and I run *towards* him, at full speed, rather than away."

Aloha chuckles, while I groan in misery.

"I don't even like Savage, as a person," I say softly. "He's an arrogant jerk. It's like he's cast a spell on me. Like I'm a drug addict and he's my drug. I know he's bad for me, but I can't stop wanting him."

Aloha pulls back from our embrace to level me with her green eyes. "Do you really want him—or do you want *him* to want *you?*"

"I want *him* to want *me!*" I shout, without hesitation. "*Why doesn't he want me, Aloha?*"

Aloha chuckles. "Well, it seems pretty clear, from what I heard coming out of Savage's room last night, you both want each other—physically, anyway." She smooths my hair, presses a kiss to my forehead, and resumes her chair. "Buckle up, Buttercup. It sounds like the next three months are going to be a wild ride for you. You're going to be living and working with Savage, and probably having amazing sex with him every night, too, if those sounds I heard last night were any indication. So, do yourself a favor and make sure you're not projecting feelings onto him that might not be there. Or else, the next three months could really mess with your heart."

I sigh. "Don't worry. I've got my head on straight now. Savage has no idea Malik was nothing to me. I made him think I was with Malik for weeks after I'd already kicked him to the curb in New York. Obviously, it drove Savage crazy to think there was one woman on planet earth who was resistant to his charms. That's what the song is about."

The makeup artist sticks her head inside the door. "Ready for me?"

Aloha raises her eyebrows, asking me if I'm good.

"Yeah, come in," I reply, flashing a wistful smile at Aloha. "We're done here."

"I'm always here for you," Aloha says softly.

"Thank you. I'm good. If you don't mind, I think I'll hide out here for a bit. I promised Kendrick I'd listen to the whole album, and I don't want to go out there and bump into You Know Who while I'm doing that."

"Stay as long as you like—provided you let me know if there's another song about you."

"God help me," I mutter, before leaning back and shoving my earbuds in again. But, thankfully, as I listen to the rest of the album, I don't hear another song that contains my name buried in the mix or a single lyric that feels even remotely like it was inspired by me.

THIRTY-SIX

SAVAGE

As I exit Reed's guest house following my conversation with Laila about "Hate Sex High," the makeup artist I'd asked to step outside on my way in is standing outside the door, looking stressed. Clearly, the poor woman has a tight schedule before the press conference and the last thing she needed was some asshole rock star showing up and asking her to step outside.

"Sorry about that," I mutter. "You can go back in now."

"No worries. Have a good one."

"You, too."

As the woman heads inside to return to Laila, I begin traipsing up the pathway toward Reed's gigantic main house, physically shaking with adrenaline. I *think* I persuaded Laila, pretty convincingly, not to put too much stock in my lyrics. In fact, by the time I left the guest house, I *think* I had Laila pretty well convinced "Hate Sex High" is mostly fiction, other than the obvious references in the verses. Obviously, there's no getting around the fact that Laila was the one who chased a hate sex high with me, all the way to three orgasms. But, thankfully, I think I persuaded Laila not to freak out about the chorus—specifically, the one lyric I didn't want her to hear the most.

If I'd had the balls to tell Laila the truth about that particular lyric a moment ago, the one in which I confessed I was feeling something I didn't want to feel for her, I would have had to tell her I was flat-out obsessed with her by the time I stumbled upon her in that hot tub. I would have had to tell her I became even more obsessed with her after finding out sex with her was hotter than my hottest fantasy. I would have had to tell her my obsession with her morphed into downright madness, once she'd started ignoring me and all my texts, in city after city, beginning in Las Vegas. And that my madness only amplified when she started showing up *everywhere* with motherfucking Charlie the Fitness Trainer, looking like she'd just finished sucking his dick. But I couldn't tell Laila any of that. Not yet, anyway. Not now.

After rounding a corner, I come upon Kendrick, sitting in the same spot on Reed's patio where I left him earlier, his MacBook open and his headphones on.

When my best friend sees me approaching, he rips off his headphones. "Well?"

I come to a stop in front of Kendrick and exhale. "When I walked in, Laila was in the middle of listening to 'Hate Sex High'— a fact I knew, instantly, because of the look on her face." I mimic Laila's expression, making the same sort of look people make during a jump-scare in a horror movie.

Kendrick grimaces. "What'd she say about the song?"

I take a chair and tell Kendrick the whole story, in great detail, concluding with, "Thankfully, by the time I left, I think I had her pretty well convinced the song is just, you know, *inspired* by her, but with *lots* of artistic license taken, especially in relation to the chorus. The part that matters the most."

Kendrick sighs. "Well, it's a relief you were able to talk to her right away, so the situation didn't spiral out of control on you."

"Mm-hmm," I say, simply because, the minute Kendrick says the word *relief*, I realize that's not the predominant emotion I'm feeling. That, in fact, I'm feeling mostly *disappointment* that Laila believed my bullshit about the song not being completely true. Did I secretly hope Laila would see right through my lies and force me to come clean and confess everything to her? No. That's a ludicrous thought, especially since I don't even know what "coming clean" and "confessing everything" would mean in this situation. What do I honestly feel for Laila? I know Laila blasted her way into my sexual fantasies when I saw her music video during the international leg of our tour, and that she cast one hell of a spell on me when I laid eyes on her at Reed's party. But like Kendrick's said to me in the past, I think it's highly possible I've only wanted what I can't have. Is Laila nothing but a sex kitten fantasy for me, and the real Laila, if I got to know her, wouldn't interest me at all? Honestly, I don't know. And until I do, I'm sticking to my story that "Hate Sex High" is only *based* on the truth.

"*No*, Savage," Kendrick says, out of nowhere, apparently, reacting to my facial expression. "We talked about this last night."

"What?"

Kendrick's jaw tightens. "Feel free to mind fuck anyone else, if that's what gets you off. Make anyone else fall for you, right before you toss them aside because they've become 'boring' to you when the chase is over. But don't you dare pull any of your usual shit with Laila, or I swear, I'll take it personally, like you've pulled that shit on *me*. You understand?"

I exhale. "You already said all this to me last night."

"But not when you were sober. I'm just making sure we're clear."

All of a sudden, it hits me like a ton of bricks: Kendrick is *in love* with Laila. Or, at least, he thinks he is. Surely, his head knows by now he can't have her, but his heart still hasn't gotten the memo. "We're clear," I reply softly. "I promise I won't pull my usual bullshit with her."

Kendrick's Adam's apple bobs. He nods, but before he's said a word, a female voice sings out, "Hey, boys!" And when we turn to look, it's Aloha, coming up the path from Reed's guest house along-side Laila, both women looking made-up and camera-ready.

"Hey, girls," Kendrick replies brightly, while I look down at my toes, feeling awkward about my earlier conversation with Laila.

The women reach Kendrick and me and Laila announces she's listened to our entire album and loves it. Kendrick thanks her, so I look up and thank her, too. But the minute our eyes meet, Laila quickly looks away.

"I had a couple notes on the mixes," Laila says to Kendrick. She itemizes them and I'm impressed by her observations.

"Awesome notes, Laila," Kendrick says, giving voice to my thoughts. "I'll send your thoughts along to Zeke and the band. I'm sure we'll make a few adjustments."

Laila responds to Kendrick, and as she talks, I can't stop staring at her, willing her look at me. But no dice. She only has eyes for Kendrick. My gaze drifts to Aloha's green eyes to find her staring at me. And the second our eyes meet, Aloha flashes me a look that reinforces everything Kendrick said to me a moment ago: *Don't fuck with my friend.*

I look away from Aloha's scowl, feeling exposed. Embarrassed. And, mostly, annoyed. It's one thing for my best friend to bitch-slap me. He has that right. But I'm not going to cower to anyone else. Least of all a Disney princess who's obviously passed judgment on me, based on something she knows nothing about. Aloha is good friends with both Colin's ex and Dax's wife. So I'm sure she's heard plenty of stories from both women about me being a player. Come to think of it, I think I might have ghosted Colin's ex after we hooked up. Maybe? So, I guess Aloha has good reason to dislike me. But, still, there's no reason for Aloha to send me that big a nonverbal "fuck you." I didn't kill anyone, for fuck's sake. I just didn't return a few texts!

I look at the ground, since that's the only safe place for me to look right now, and a moment later, a production assistant arrives to let us know we're minutes away from the press conference. "We need the full cast to get dressed and head into Reed's game room," she says.

Aloha and Kendrick head to their respective rooms to get dressed, but I touch Laila's arm and ask her if we can talk alone for a second.

"We don't have a lot of time," Laila says.

"This will only take a minute." I clear my throat. "I just want to make sure we're good."

Laila crosses her arms. "Why wouldn't we be?"

"Because of what we talked about in the guest house. The song?"

"Oh, *that*," Laila says. But it's horseshit—yet another over-the-top performance by Miss Fitzgerald. She shrugs nonchalantly. "Honestly, I'd already forgotten all about that."

My stomach flip-flops. This should be great news. I should be feeling relieved Laila is ready to move on. But that's not how I'm feeling. "I just want to be sure you're not mad or maybe confused about some of the lyrics . . .?" I clear my throat again. "I mean, coming on the heels of that Instagrammer's video, I have to think you're pretty confused about what the hell I'm—"

"I'm not confused at all," she says flatly. "I don't believe a word that Instagrammer said, Adrian. I only said I believed her to torture you." She pats my arm. "Don't worry. I'm well aware 'Hate Sex High' was about you taunting Malik—letting him know you'd fucked me, and done it well—rather than you confessing you'd caught feelings for me." She scoffs. "I know you were pissed Malik physically attacked you in New York, and you wanted to mess with him. That's *all* that song is about. Only a fool would think otherwise."

Shit. That's what I'm thinking, even though I should be thinking, "Thank God."

"Hey, you know what?" Laila says, her blue eyes blazing. "I know I said earlier it wouldn't be necessary to rerecord those 'la la' parts, but I've changed my mind. On second thought, I don't want the whole world to know, for a fact, *I'm* the woman who came three times."

"Okay. No problem. Should be an easy fix."

"Sorry to ask you to change your art, but—"

"I'm the one who offered, remember? I think maybe I'll replace those last 'la las' with 'whoa-ohs,' so there won't be any chance of confusion."

"Perfect," she says. She stares at me for a long moment, like she's expecting me to say more. And when I don't, she says, "Well, if that's all you wanted to talk to me about, then I think we'd better get dressed and head to Reed's game room."

"Yeah."

"Don't be late, Adrian," she warns, her index finger wagging. "I'm your babysitter now. If you're late, that's on me."

"I won't be late."

"I know you had a great ol' time messing with me during the tour," she continues. "But I'm begging you not to pull that shit on me again. Being on this show is a dream come true for me and I want to do a good job."

I feel a pang of guilt for all the times I messed with Laila during the tour. Why'd I do that, again? "I promise I'll be a good boy for you, Laila," I say. And when her face plainly says, *I'll believe it when I see it,* I add, "Laila, when I give my word about something, you can take it to the bank." I shift my weight under her scornful stare. "Okay, maybe you can't take it to the bank, *every* time. But you can count on my promise *this* time."

Again, she looks unconvinced.

"Also, as a rule of thumb going forward," I continue, "I'd say you can count on my word being my bond . . ." I smile. "A solid *eight* times out of ten."

THIRTY-SEVEN

LAILA

E xactly nine minutes after my conversation with Savage on Reed's patio, I walk into Reed's game room to await Savage's imminent arrival. Or, rather, Savage's imminent *non*-arrival, so I can ask a PA to march up to his room and drag his infuriating ass down here. But to my surprise, when I enter the spacious room, Savage is already here, chatting with Kendrick. In fact, I'm the last cast member to arrive.

I head over to Savage and Kendrick, noting that Savage looks especially gorgeous. Savage often rocks edgy designer duds onstage, also when he's on-camera for an interview or awards show, so I'm used to seeing him looking like a runway model. But Savage looks especially yummy right now, like he leaped off the pages of *Gentlemen's World*.

"Hey, Fitzy," Savage says when I reach him.

"Hey, Fitzy," Kendrick echoes.

"*No*. Just *me*," Savage says sharply to Kendrick, wagging his finger to emphasize his point. Savage pauses, making sure Kendrick got the message, and then returns to me with a smile. "What took you so long, *Fitzy*? I've been waiting on you for five minutes."

I roll my eyes. "Sure, Jan."

"It's true," Savage says. "Ask Kendrick."

Kendrick nods. "It's true."

Savage looks me up and down, taking in my minidress and thigh-high boots. "I have to say, you were worth the wait. Damn, girl."

"Yeah, you look great, Laila," Kendrick concurs, his tone pointedly platonic, unlike the one used by Savage.

"Thank you. You both look very handsome, too." I address Savage. "Thank you for not making me hunt you down on Day One of my babysitting gig." I look at Kendrick. "I assume I have you to thank for that."

"Nope. Savage was already here when I arrived."

My eyebrows ride up in surprise.

Savage says, "I promised I'd be on time, so I was. Remember when I promised Reed I'd show up for Alessandra's music video shoot? My word is my bond, baby. Mostly. Sometimes. On occasion."

I can't help chuckling, along with Kendrick and Savage. Even when he's annoying, Adrian Savage is incredibly charming. There's no denying that.

"Yeah, so I guess that VIP meet and greet you barely made it to was one of the two in ten times your promise is worth nothing, huh?" I say. "If you ask me, being an *hour* late for a professional obligation is the same thing as breaking a promise."

I've intended to razz Savage, lightheartedly, with my comment. But Savage looks like I've slapped him across his chiseled face. And that's all it takes for me to realize there's been a shift between us, without me realizing it until now—a shift that's made me seem like a petty bitch for bringing up that VIP event, yet again. Did the shift between us happen last night, when we shared our electrifying first kiss? Or did it happen while I was sitting on Savage's face, screaming in ecstasy? Did it happen when Savage held my hair to keep it from falling into the toilet? Or when Savage said yes to every stupid, ridiculous thing the producers asked of him yesterday, and then agreed to pay two million bucks out of his own pocket to seal the deal?

Whenever the shift between us happened, it's now clear that stupid VIP meet and greet is off-limits for me to bitch about, along with all the other petty stuff that pissed me off during the tour. I already reamed the guy about all of it in Atlanta, after all, in front of *everyone*. And the man is obviously trying to get off on the right foot in our new adventure by arriving here early. So, perhaps I should shut my mouth and turn the freaking page and try to get along.

"I shouldn't have said that," I blurt quickly, before Savage can reply to my barb. "That was petty of me. You've bent over back-wards to get me this job, and I'm grateful to you." I bite my lip. "I think it's going to take some conscious effort to rewire my brain not to immediately switch into 'bitch mode' as my default around you. But I promise I'll try my best, starting now."

Savage swallows hard. "I don't blame you for constantly putting up your dukes around me, Laila. I was a royal prick to you, over and over again, during the tour."

My lips part in surprise. That sounded awfully close to an apology. "Well, it takes two to tango," I murmur, my heart thumping. "I reacted to you. You reacted to me. And around and around we went."

"Yeah, but I think we both know who was leading our tango."

Holy fuck. I'm floored. I stare at him in disbelief for a long moment, as palpable conciliation passes between us. Or maybe that's nothing but our usual white-hot lust. Whatever it is, it's enough to make Kendrick clear his throat and excuse himself, mumbling something about needing to talk to Fish, who's chatting with Aloha nearby in the game room.

When Kendrick is gone, Savage says, "Listen, Laila. I can't explain away all the times I was late during the tour. Sometimes, I lost track of time, which happens to me a lot. Other times, I showed up late on purpose to piss you off. But regarding that VIP meet and greet, specifically, I had good reason to be late. As I was leaving to head over there, my cousin called with some bad news about our grandmother. Mimi—that's my grandmother—had been in treatment for cancer for a while at that point, and my cousin called to say she'd taken a turn for the worse."

"Oh no."

"So, after hanging up with my cousin, it took me a while to pull myself together enough to head over to the meet and greet, where I knew I'd be expected to take selfies and smile. I'm not great at interacting with strangers, in the best of times, but—"

"Oh, Savage," I interject. My heart feels like it's exploding with sympathy, along with remorse for the way I tore into him about his lateness for that particular event. "I get it. How is your grandma doing now?"

The man shakes his head woefully, looking devastated. "Not well, unfortunately. She's decided to quit treatments altogether and let nature take its course."

I look around the large room at the other cast members and staff milling around, and feel an overwhelming tidal wave of regret flooding me. I can't believe I screamed at Savage in Atlanta about his tardiness for *that* particular event, and he never once defended himself by telling me the situation. I ask, "Is your grandma here in LA?"

Savage shakes his head, his devastation palpable. "No, she lives in Chicago with my cousin. I visit as much as I can. Usually, about once a month."

Chicago.

At the mention of that city, I feel even more regretful. That's the city Kendrick mentioned the day our tour kicked off, when I was all bent out of shape that Savage had flown into Philadelphia the same day as our opening show, thereby messing up *my* schedule with his lateness. *My* interviews and hair and makeup. As if any of those things mattered more than Savage maximizing his time with his ailing grandmother.

"I had no idea you were carrying such a heavy burden all this time," I say. "Why didn't you tell me about your grandmother when I was ripping you a new asshole in Atlanta?"

Savage screws up his face, looking confused. "Why would I tell you about my grandmother being sick?"

"To defend yourself! I went on and on about you being a selfish and unprofessional prick for being late for that event, and then going through the motions, halfheartedly, once you got there. But in reality, you showing up *at all* to that event was the epitome of self-lessness and professionalism! Savage, you were a saint to show up to that event at all, given what you were going through that day. But you didn't tell me any of that."

Savage shrugs. "I didn't say anything about my grandmother because you were right about everything else you accused me of doing. Why defend myself about the *one* time I hadn't done anything wrong, when my rap sheet was long and embarrassing, regardless? Plus, I was in a particularly foul mood in Atlanta and it felt good to unload on you. That was the day my cousin called to say my grandmother had decided to stop treatments, so—"

"Oh, for the love of fuck!" I yell, palming my forehead. "No wonder you tore into me that day, after I tore into you, so cluelessly —and in front of *everyone*."

"I wasn't in my right mind in Atlanta," he says. "I was scared to death for my grandmother. Angry at God for making humans mortal creatures. So, when you read me the Riot Act in front of everyone, I just sort of used it as an excuse to get all my anger out. I mean, don't get me wrong, I was pissed at you for tearing into me in front of everyone. That was lame of you to do that, Laila. But I wasn't nearly as pissed at you, specifically, as it seemed. I was mostly just taking a whole lot of shit out on you."

I rub my forehead, feeling physically dizzy and disoriented by Savage's words. After months of casting Savage as the villain in my narrative, I suddenly feel like I was equally villainous, if not more so. At least, in relation to what happened in Atlanta. But before I've figured out what to say in response, a PA approaches and tells us it's time to line up on the far side of the game room, in order to await our cue to enter the press conference.

As the PA escorts Savage and me across the room, she tells us Sunshine Vaughn, the longtime host of *Sing Your Heart Out,* has already started making some opening remarks. The PA explains, "After Sunshine finishes her opening speech, the judges will be trotted out to answer questions for about thirty minutes, and then, at the very end, we'll invite the mentors to join the panel, too."

I feel a squeeze to my hand and realize Savage must have taken it as we walked across the room. Or did I take *his?* I don't even remember how it happened that our hands came to be joined. It happened so naturally, so easily, I don't know who made the first move.

When we reach our destination—a spot behind Aloha and Jon across Reed's large game room—Savage and I make whispered small talk with our fellow judges for a few minutes. And through it all, Savage and I never let go of each other's hands. Not only that, I can't stop sneaking peeks at Savage's striking profile, my heart squeezing and my stomach flip-flopping. Clearly, I misjudged this man during our tour. Not about *everything,* obviously. But about a lot. I turned Savage into a caricature by the end of the tour. A one-dimensional villain. A man without a shred of decency or conscience.

Well, enough of that. I wasn't faultless during the tour, either. I don't think I can forgive Savage for everything he did during the tour—at least, not for that groupie in Vegas—but I decide to wipe the slate clean, as best I can, and give our fake relationship a genuine shot.

THIRTY-EIGHT

LAILA

As we await our cue to enter the press conference in the next room, we hear the voice of the show's longtime host, Sunshine Vaughn, as she cheerily welcomes the assembled press—the reporters and influencers who've come here today on a Sunday afternoon to interview the show's judges, and especially to hear the "shocking announcement" they've been promised is going to "rock their worlds." Although I'm sure every last one of them would have flocked here, regardless, if only to tour the legendary mansion of Reed Rivers and get to interview Hugh Delaney's buzzworthy replacement—the savagely sexy rock star whose face and abs have become as much of a permanent fixture on magazine covers lately as his dick has become one on Twitter. And, oh yeah, the dude also sings and plays his guitar pretty well, too.

I take a deep breath to calm my racing heart, and in reaction to my body language, Savage squeezes my hand, leans in, and whispers, "You're gonna be great. The world is going to fall head over heels for you."

Aloha, who's standing in front of us, turns around and says, "Amen, sister. The world is going to *love* you, Laila, every bit as much as I do."

"Thank you for everything you've done for me," I say to Aloha. "You've been my guardian angel." I look at Savage. "And thank you, too. Being on this show is a dream come true for me. I wouldn't be here if you hadn't said yes to every ridiculous demand by the producers and my agent. I'm grateful to you."

Savage shakes his head. "You saved my ass, Laila. This show is my grandma's all-time favorite, and I'd already told her I was going to be a judge when the shit hit the fan for me yesterday. You did me a huge favor by saving me from having to tell her I'd gotten myself fired."

I press my lips together. The hits just keep on coming. *Savage agreed to do the show for his ailing grandma.* How did I not know about this man's diehard devotion to his grandmother before now?

In the other room, the show's host bellows, "And now, let's welcome our panel of judges!" Excited applause rises up as Sunshine says, "First off, it's our resident Teddy Bear . . . Jon Stapleton!" A production assistant cues Jon, prompting him to head into the adjacent room. Sunshine continues, "And now, it's our beloved queen . . . *Aloha Carmichael!*" The PA waves Aloha into the room, and her entrance elicits even louder applause than Jon's. "And nooooow . . ." Sunshine teases, prompting a hushed anticipation to fall over the press conference. "Please, welcome our *two* new judges! That's right, we've got not *one*, but *two* new judges this season: Savage from Fugitive Summer *and* his gorgeous and talented *girlfriend*, a superstar on the rise . . . Miss Laila Fitzgerald!"

A collective gasp rises up as Savage and I appear, our hands clasped and happy smiles plastered on our faces—and by the time we're taking our assigned seats between Jon and Aloha at a table facing the assembled press, the room is pure pandemonium.

Once we're seated, there's a photo shoot for a long moment, as Savage and I, along with our two fellow judges, oscillate our smiling faces like sprinklers on a lawn, allowing every camera in the room to get a perfect shot of this season's judges. Although, based on the number of reporters shouting at Savage and me, specifically, it seems the lion's share of photos being snapped are of the happy couple.

"Let's get to your questions!" Sunshine calls out, before pointing at one of the reporters.

The reporter stands. "Savage and Laila, are you *really* a couple or is this a publicity stunt?"

Well, that was fast.

"We're a couple," Savage answers smoothly, sliding his arm around me, and I instinctively rest my cheek on his broad shoulder.

"In fact," I say, "we've recently moved in together."

The room titters in response to that little nugget.

A reporter shouts, "So, Laila, did you lie about Savage during your interview on *Sylvia?*"

I lift my head from Savage's shoulder and grimace at my fake boyfriend.

"Time to 'fess up, babe," he says, smirking.

Sighing dramatically, I address the room. "Yeah, I lied through my teeth!" Everyone chuckles, along with Savage. "I wanted to keep our relationship under wraps for a bit longer, so we could make sure it was rock solid before we subjected ourselves to worldwide attention."

Savage nods. "I respected where Laila was coming from on that, even though I was ready to shout about my feelings for Laila from the rooftops. Laila said she didn't want to feel pressure to 'perform' our relationship for the world, and I understood that."

Clever boy. He just paraphrased something I said to Sylvia about why I don't like making my relationships "Instagram official."

Savage continues, "But then, when that Instagrammer made her video, broadcasting to the world everything I'd drunkenly babbled to her in private, I told Laila, 'There's no turning back now, babe. Let's make it official!' But before we'd decided how or when to do that, the producers called to say they'd decided to promote Laila from mentor to judge this season." He smiles at me. "And now, here we are."

"Ah, so this *is* a publicity stunt," a reporter yells.

"No, not at all," Savage insists. "The powers that be at the show determined Laila sitting at the judges' table would make things especially fun and interesting this season. But that doesn't make our relationship any less real. All that means is Laila and I will get to spend a whole lot more time together over the next few months." He looks at me and smiles. "Which is a great thing, as far as we're concerned. Who wouldn't leap at the chance to work with the person they're head over heels in love with?"

Whoa. The man is *good.*

"How long have you two been together?" that same reporter asks, all prior skepticism gone from his tone.

"It happened little by little during our tour," Savage explains. "But we've been glued at the hip for about the past month."

"To be clear," I interject, my finger raised, "I wasn't lying to Sylvia when I said Savage and I didn't get along during most of the tour. As a matter of fact, we couldn't stand each other for a large portion of it."

"No, *you* couldn't stand *me*," Savage corrects, making everyone chuckle. "And rightly so. I was like a kid pulling her pigtails on the playground, guys. But after we got back from the tour, I called Laila and charmed her pants off . . . *literally.*" Everyone guffaws, while I bat Savage's shoulder playfully. "And then, everything took off from there, on a rocket." Savage leans forward. "That 'rocket' being the one in my pants."

As the room explodes at Savage's raunchy comment, Sunshine chokes out, "It's a family show, Savage." But by the expression on Nadine Collins' face at the back of the room, it's clear our executive producer isn't upset in the least about Savage's sexual innuendo. In fact, her expression makes it clear the head honcho is pleased as punch.

"How'd you convince Laila to board your *rocket*, Savage?" someone shouts.

"*Have you seen me?*" he says cheekily. And, again, everyone in the room rolls with laughter. Savage waves the air in front of him. "No, no. Actually, it required some good old- fashioned groveling to get things going with Laila. I called her after the tour and apologized for my bad behavior, and, thankfully, things took off from there." He looks at me. "I'm not the best at apologizing, usually. At least, not first. But, somehow, my desire to win Laila over outweighed my ego and pride." He kisses the top of my hand that's still clasped in his. "It was the best decision I've ever made."

Awwww, everyone in the room says in unison. And I must admit, I'm swooning along with them. I know, intellectually, this is all fake. A pitch-perfect performance from one of the world's best performers. But my heart and body can't resist reacting to this moment as if what Savage is saying is very, *very* real.

"What'd you think when Savage called and groveled, Laila?" someone yells.

I look at my fake boyfriend adoringly. "I thought 'Is this a prank?'"

Everyone chuckles.

"But then, Savage shocked me by letting down his guard. He told me some personal things that made me realize I'd misjudged him during the tour. And that's when he *really* turned on the charm." I grin at Savage. "He told me that, ever since we'd been home from tour, he'd been desperately missing my 'beautiful face,' and—"

"No," Savage interrupts. "I said I'd been missing your beautiful *smug* face. And I didn't use the word 'desperately.'"

"Yes, you did."

"That word isn't in my vocabulary."

"Well, it was that day." I address the crowd, rolling my eyes, and it's clear they're eating up this interaction with a spoon. "Savage told me he'd been 'desperately' missing my 'beautiful *smug* face'—I admit he used the word 'smug.' And then, he said he was sorry for being such a 'jerk' to me during the tour. He explained he'd had some personal stuff going on during that time that had been difficult for him, and my heart cracked wide open." I look into Savage's dark eyes. "After that, this man crawled right into the crack in my heart he created that day, during that first phone call, and he's never crawled back out."

Savage is blushing, which I find surprising. Humans can't fake blushing, can they?

"I feel like I should mention," Savage says, "Laila apologized to me, too, during that first phone call. Don't leave me hanging out here, looking like too big a softie, Laila."

"Yes, it's true. I apologized to him, too. Profusely. If Savage had been a kid pulling my pigtails on the playground, then I'd been the annoying girl who'd purposely tried to provoke that exact reaction. Lucky for me, Savage accepted my apology, and we both agreed to press the reset button. And we haven't looked back, ever since."

A collective swoon rises up in the room and Savage and I look away from each other again. And this time, Savage isn't the only one blushing.

"Thank you for sharing that beautiful story," Sunshine says reverently. She looks at the crowd. "I don't know about you, but I'm all aflutter here. *Wow*." She returns to Savage and me. "Tell us about your first date."

Savage says, "At the end of our first phone call, Laila invited me to her place for pizza. And I was like, '*Pizza?* No, I'll cook for you!'"

I interject, "So, he came over to my place that night and made me a *phenomenal* meal, and"—I smirk suggestively at Savage—"we've been inseparable ever since."

The crowd applauds.

"Wonderful!" Sunshine bellows. "And now, are there any questions for Jon and Aloha?"

Nadine at the back of the room shakes her head sharply, telling our host it's not yet time to shift focus to the other judges. And Sunshine, pro that she is, instantly changes course. "Actually, the floor still belongs to Savage and Laila! Any other questions for our happy couple?"

A reporter yells, "Laila, what did you think when you found out Savage had let the cat out of the bag about your relationship to Sheree Dawson—the influencer who then made that viral video?

Were you mad? Sheree's got a huge following and notoriously loves Savage and Fugitive Summer, so he must have known she'd post something."

"To be clear," Savage interjects, before I've replied, "I had no idea who she was. But I do admit I was drunk and bursting at the seams to tell the world about Laila and me by then. So, you do the math. I'm not known for making sound decisions on my best day— but particularly not when I've been drinking."

The entire room chuckles. Surely, all of them thinking of Savage's naked swan dive into that hotel pool.

"What exactly did you say to Sheree, Savage?" the reporter asks.

"I said she reminded me of Laila, which she did," Savage replies. "And I guess, once I said Laila's name to her, it was like I'd broken the seal or something—and, suddenly, I couldn't stop myself from babbling everything about us."

"Adrian's always got loose lips when he drinks," I say, pinching Savage's chiseled cheek. "But I wasn't mad at him when I saw the video. In fact, I thought it was sweet he couldn't keep our secret any longer. I mean, my boyfriend spilled the beans while turning down a woman who was flirting with him. What girlfriend could be mad about that, at the end of the day?"

After a few more questions, Sunshine steers the conversation away from Savage and me toward Aloha and Jon for a bit— although, in keeping with today's apparent theme, the first reporter called upon asks Aloha and Jon what they think of the addition of Savage and me to the show.

As Aloha and Jon talk, my mind wanders. It seemed preposterous to think Savage might have mentioned my name, at all, to that Instagrammer when I first saw the video. I assumed she was chasing her fifteen minutes of fame. But after hearing Savage's smooth explanation of what supposedly went down—it seems logical that he might have at least commented on how much she looks like me. Could the story he told just now be based on a kernel of truth? Surely, she misheard Savage when he went on to say he had to "lay low" because of the show. But is it possible Savage thought of me when he saw that woman, and then actually said my name to her?

"Hey, Savage," a reporter says, jerking me from my thoughts. "Are there any songs about Laila on your band's upcoming album?"

"No," Savage says, and I sigh with relief. "The album was written before Laila and I got together."

Another reporter asks, "Are you two planning to release any music together, now that the world knows about you?"

To my surprise, Reed Rivers, who's been standing at the back of the room next to Nadine Collins, answers before Savage or me. "They are!" Reed calls out. "Stay tuned for details."

"They're going to premiere a song during the finale!" Nadine shouts.

And that's that. I look at Savage, as if to say, *Well, that took a turn,* and he smiles mischievously, letting me know he's on board for this brazen money grab. I don't blame him, really. If someone swooped in and unexpectedly snaked two million bucks out of my pocket, I'd be down to make some of it back with a hit song, too. Especially one advertised and performed on national TV.

A reporter stands and introduces herself to Savage and me as a writer for a popular women's magazine. She says, "I know my readers would *love* to know what you two love about each other, if you wouldn't mind speaking to that."

"Savage?" I say, feeling my heart rate spike. How can I possibly answer that question, even for pretend?

But Savage is the portrait of ease and charm. He says, "Actually, this is an easy one. Obviously, Laila is physically gorgeous. I love that she looks like she could murder me in my sleep, right after coming home from cheerleading practice."

Everyone in the room, including me, chuckles at that description.

"Also, she's incredibly talented," he continues. "I can't tell you how many times she's given me goosebumps with her voice. But, at the end of the day, it's Laila's personality that attracts me the most.

I love that she's tough and fierce, but also a softie. In fact, Laila can be downright goofy, once you get to know her. Like, when she misses a shot in a game of HORSE, for example, she'll fall to the ground and writhe around like she's been shot."

My eyebrows shoot up to my hairline. *How'd Savage know about that?* He was nowhere near the basketball court when I did that at Reed's party. Or, at least, not that I saw. Wasn't he hitting on that pretty Asian woman by the pool around that time?

Savage's dark eyes locked with mine, he says, "I also love how close Laila is with her family—her mom, sister, and baby niece. How easily she makes friends. During our tour, *everyone* loved Laila. Musicians, makeup artists, roadies, caterers, bus drivers. *Everyone.* Laila even went to weekly game nights with the crew. But did they invite me, even once? *Nope.*"

"You're a huge star," I say. "It was nothing personal."

"That's not why, Laila. They invited *you* because you make every person you meet feel special. Like they're your friend. That's a rare gift—and one I certainly don't possess."

Heat is wafting between us. Without thinking about it, I lean in and give Savage a peck on the lips. Even if that speech was a load of complete crap, it's making my heart flutter and sending butterflies into my belly. Without hesitation, Savage grabs my face and turns my peck into a whopper of a kiss—a deep and passionate one that sends electricity scorching into every nerve ending of my body while setting off fireworks in my abdomen.

The assembled press in the room variously titters and whoops. Cameras begin clicking furiously, capturing every moment of our kiss.

"Wow, guys," Sunshine Vaughn says, when Savage finally releases me from his hungry lips. "I'm swooning here, right along with Laila."

I look down at the table, breathing hard, realizing Sunshine is right: I'm physically *swooning*. Literally, dizzy with adrenaline and excitement. And not only because of the passionate kiss Savage bestowed upon me, in front of the world, but also because of the speech he gave right before it. Were any parts of Savage's speech based in truth—or was *all* of it for show?

Sunshine says, "Your turn, Laila. What do you love about Savage?"

I force my blushing face to address Savage. His cheeks are flushed. His dark eyes sparkling. I take a deep breath and say, "Well, he's obviously physically gorgeous, as you can see, and incredibly talented and charismatic and charming. The whole world is in love with this man, for all of those reasons, so it shouldn't be hard to understand why I feel the same way."

There. I did it.

Sunshine says, "But what's something we don't know about him, that you do? Something you find endearing about your boyfriend, behind closed doors?"

Fuck.

Seriously?

I look into Savage's dark eyes again, and realize this question isn't all that difficult to answer, after all. A day ago, it would have been impossible. But after the conversation I had with Savage on Reed's patio a few minutes ago, I feel like there's a whole other side to Adrian Savage I didn't appreciate before.

"Well, I love how devoted Adrian is to his family," I say, looking into Savage's soulful, dark eyes. "His family is his top priority and he'd do anything for them. I don't think everyone knows that about him." Images of Savage from during the tour flash across my mind, making me realize I'd witnessed his softer side, many times. I just didn't give those aspects of his personality their proper due, up until now. I continue, "Savage will do anything for his friends." I chuckle. "Including drunkenly jumping naked into a hotel swimming pool as a friend's birthday gift."

Everyone in the room laughs with glee.

"He's also surprisingly goofy. The same as me, actually. He doesn't do it all that often—but, on occasion, Savage belly laughs with those closest to him. And when he does, it's the sweetest, most endearing sound you'll ever hear. It's like the clouds part when

Adrian Savage laughs from the depths of his soul, and the entire world is bathed in glorious sunshine."

Savage's chest heaves. His nostrils flare. His body language reflecting back to me how I'm feeling as I stare into his chocolate eyes.

I swallow hard. "Adrian is protective and supportive, too. He tells me to demand what I'm worth and not settle for anything less. He's also a thoughtful boyfriend. He knows I can't stand the smell or taste of cigarettes, so he quit smoking, just for me. When I was sick, he took care of me. Held my hair for me when I threw up." I bite my lower lip. "And, of course, it doesn't hurt that he's literally the sexiest man on Earth." I press my lips together, signaling that's all I've got, and Savage leans in and kisses me again—this time, even more passionately than before.

The crowd applauds, while Sunshine, our host, laughingly says, "Hey, it's a family show, guys."

Savage and I break apart, both of us breathing hard, and as the place explodes with raucous applause, Savage lays his palm on my thigh under the table, letting me know his arousal is most definitely *not* for show.

"Okay, before these two need a room," Sunshine says, "I think we'd better get our mentors out here. *Four* judges this season means *four* mentors! And here they are!" She motions to the side door and calls out each mentor's name, one by one, and they appear in order and stand behind their respective judge at the table.

There are a flurry of questions for the group—but, thankfully, no curveballs or surprises—and, finally, Sunshine wraps things up.

"Thank you for coming today! Full promo packages have been sent to you via email."

I look at Savage, ready to flash him a look of relief that the press conference is over, but he's eyeing my mentor behind me like he's plotting murder.

"Hey," I whisper sharply, squeezing Savage's thigh, and he turns around and smiles at the crowd again. But it's too late. His jealousy was on full display. Clearly, he's trying to figure out why the producers chose Colin, of all people—a drummer known more for his recent underwear campaign than his singing—as my mentor. And I must admit, I'm wondering the same thing. Colin and I have never been anything but friends. But there's no denying our chemistry. Also, I can't help remembering I offered up Colin on *Sylvia* as someone I've been wrongly linked with, right before I denied the rumors about Savage and me. Did the producers notice that little detail, too?

"Back to the greenroom, guys," a PA says to the cast. And, in short order, all eight of us exit the press conference and head back into Reed's game room. The minute we get to our destination, I begin walking toward Colin, intending to ask him what the producers said to him when they hired him. Did they mention what I said on *Sylvia* as one of the reasons they'd picked him? But before I've reached Colin, Nadine, the executive producer of the show, hugs me and pulls me over to Savage.

"You two are *geniuses!*" Nadine blurts, her angular face aflame. "We had *extremely* high expectations about you two this season. But now that I've seen the goosebumps you're capable of delivering, I can already tell we didn't aim nearly high enough."

THIRTY-NINE
LAILA

I'm sitting next to Savage in the backseat of a large, black SUV with tinted windows, headed toward whatever home the producers have secured as our fake love nest for the next three months. The same driver and bodyguard from yesterday are seated up front. Savage is looking out the window on his side of the car. *And I'm freaking out.*

Which parts of Savage's speech during the press conference—the one where he itemized all the things he supposedly "loves" about me—were based in truth? For my part, every word I said about Savage in *my* speech was tethered to truth. I don't *love* Savage, obviously, but now that I know about his devotion to his ailing grandma—like, seriously, where did *that* come from?—I realize he's not quite the monster I'd come to believe by the end of the tour. In fact, I think he might be a whole lot more like the dude I shared a bottle of whiskey with in Providence, than the asshole who tore me a new one in Atlanta.

Also, those two kisses Savage and I shared during the press conference are messing with my head. I've never swooned so hard in my life as I did during those kisses! My *brain* knew it was all for show, but my heart exploded like a nuclear bomb. I felt urgency and *need* in Savage's lips and tongue. I felt *passion*. And now, as I sit here next to Savage, driving to who-knows-where, I'm realizing, much to my dismay, I'm in for a very confusing three months, exactly as Aloha warned.

I look at Savage sitting next to me to find him tapping on his phone with a cute little smile on his face—the kind of grin I've seen on him only when he's interacting with one of his bandmates, but especially with Kendrick or Ruby.

"Are you texting with Kendrick?" I venture, looking for any excuse to start a conversation.

Savage looks up, still looking adorable. "My cousin, Sasha. She lives with our grandmother in Chicago. They watched the press conference and now my cousin is texting in all caps." He snorts. "She's so funny. Both Sasha and my grandma are losing it about the 'amazing girlfriend' I've never bothered to tell them about."

I glance at the two men at the front of the car and lean in to whisper. Surely, our companions are bound by an ironclad non-disclosure agreement, but better safe than sorry. "What are you telling your family about our 'relationship'?"

Savage flushes a deep crimson, telegraphing the answer to my question is: *I've let them believe we're an actual couple.*

"You haven't told them the truth?" I whisper.

He shakes his head, looking sheepish. "I was going to give my cousin a heads-up about us before the press conference, but I got distracted when I ran into Kendrick and found out he'd sent you the album. And now, they're both so excited about everything . . ." He exhales. "Mimi—my grandma—she's my father's mother—she always says she wants me to settle down and find the 'great love of my life,' the kind she had with her husband, Jasper, who died young. Apparently, after watching the press conference, Mimi told Sasha she felt like she could finally stop worrying about me, now that I've found a woman who can 'see past all that silly rock star business' to the 'real *me*.'" He chuckles. "Apparently, that comment you made about my laugh 'parting the clouds,' or whatever you said, made quite an impression on Mimi."

I chuckle with him. "Honestly, I'm relieved you haven't told your family the truth about us. It makes it a whole lot easier for me to ask you to lie to my family about us for the next three months."

Savage laughs. "You haven't told your family the truth, either?"

I shake my head. "I could tell my sister, but my mom is *always* on me about my supposedly horrible taste in men. I'm hoping our 'blissful relationship' will give me a breather from constantly hearing about how I need to stop falling for jerks and find myself someone 'nice' who 'treats me right.'"

"Your *supposedly* horrible taste in men?" Savage scoffs. "If Malik is any indication, there's no 'supposedly' about it, Fitzy."

I bite back a smile. Is it wrong of me to continue letting Savage think I had an actual relationship with Malik—and even more so that said relationship lasted well beyond Malik's horrible behavior in New York? If so, I don't want to be right. Not when Savage banged that flirty waitress in New York the very same night I kicked Malik to the curb.

"Are you sure your mom wouldn't think *I'm* further evidence of your horrible taste in men?" Savage asks, his eyebrow raised.

"Well, yes, *normally* you would be. You're exactly my type—which isn't a compliment. But after all that amazing stuff you said about me during the press conference, my mother and sister are convinced I've finally found the perfect man who totally gets the real me. So, if you don't mind, I'd be grateful for you to play along whenever I talk to my family, in exchange for me playing along when you talk to yours."

"Deal. Although I should mention, I sing Mimi to sleep on FaceTime, pretty much every night when I'm not on tour."

"Aw, that's so sweet. Don't worry. I'd love to say hi to your grandma, every single night."

Savage shoots me a smolder that flash-melts my panties. "Thank you."

"You're paying me two million bucks. It's the least I can do."

Savage grabs my hand. "Let's not talk about the money

anymore, okay? I'm over it. Your agent was right—this is an equal partnership. I was an asshole to whine about it."

I look into his dark eyes, feeling my heart beating like a hummingbird's. "No, you weren't. It was a huge and unexpected pay cut for you. It was only natural for you to feel upset about it. I tell you what. To help you recoup some of the money you're paying to me, why don't you leave my name in 'Hate Sex High' and make it your leadoff single? The song is amazing, and with all the publicity swirling around us, I bet that sexy little Easter egg buried in the mix will give the song even more buzz. It might even become your biggest hit yet."

Savage looks excited. "Are you sure you don't mind your name being in there?"

"Ha! You admit you sang my name!"

"No, I'm merely adopting your crazy megalomaniacal version of reality for the purposes of my question."

He's so full of it. Any sane human would hear my name at the end of those "la la" parts, as clear as a bell. But there's no point in arguing with him. He'll obviously *never* concede the point. "Yes, I'm sure," I say. "After what you said about me at the press conference, everyone thinks you're desperately in love with me. So, in that case, I'm now thinking it'd be kind of cool for people to think I'm not only the great love of your life, I'm also the freak in the sheets you made come three times. Plus, like I said, the smartest move in terms of marketing is making that song the leadoff single, with my name all over it."

He snickers. "Reed already picked that song as the first single. He was furious when I told him I needed to rerecord the 'la la' lines to take out the part some insane megalomaniac had interpreted as her name."

"You already told Reed about rerecording those parts? That was fast."

Savage makes a face like it's not a big deal. "You said you wanted it out and the album is set to drop soon, so . . ."

"I'm sorry if I freaked everyone out about changing it. Now that

I've had a minute to get used to the idea, I don't mind the world knowing the song is about me. In fact, I kind of like the idea of them knowing."

"Yeah, and I'm sure it thrills you to no end that I'm now going to look like as big a liar as you."

"Huh?"

"At the press conference, I said there are no songs on the album about you. And now, suddenly, I'm going to release an album that *some* people *might* interpret as containing the name *Laila?*"

I snort. "You're never going to admit you're singing Laila in those parts, are you?"

"I'm simply conceding there are probably lots more nutjobs in this world than you who'll wrongly hear your name in those same parts, the way you did."

I roll my eyes. "Well, it serves you right to look like a liar, seeing as how you *are* one, for denying you're singing 'Laila.' Plus, it's only fair, since I had to admit I was a liar on *Sylvia*. But don't worry, people will think you only lied during the press conference to protect my privacy, which only makes you an even more swoon-worthy boyfriend."

"*More* swoonworthy?" he says. "You admit I was *already* swoonworthy?"

"I admit nothing. I'm merely conceding there are probably plenty more nutjobs in this world than *you* who'd think so."

Savage belly laughs. "Touché, Fitzy. Too-fucking-shay."

Butterflies.

They've just now whooshed into my belly at the sound of his laughter.

With a little wink to me, Savage returns to his phone, so I look out the car window for a while, biting back a huge smile. After a few minutes of staring at the coastline, I realize our car has headed far enough north that we must be heading into Malibu. "Do you think we're going to be staying in Malibu?"

Savage looks up from his phone and looks around for a beat. "It sure looks like we're headed there."

"I hope that's where we'll be living," I say. "I *love* Malibu."

"Me, too. I love the ocean."

"So do I. I wish I could wake up every day of my life and see it, first thing."

"You can. By the end of the season, you'll have two million bucks in your bank account. Buy yourself a beachfront condo, if that's your pleasure."

I press my lips together. That's not going to happen, for several reasons. After taxes and commissions, and a few important things I want to do for my family, there won't be much left of that two million bucks. Certainly, not enough to upgrade my small condo in the Valley to something along the coast. Beachfront property isn't cheap. Plus, Savage is assuming I'll make it to the end of the season on the show. When in reality, that's not a certainty.

Unfortunately, when Daria and I finally got my contract from the show yesterday, it contained a buy-out clause that would allow the show to terminate me at any time for a payment of a hundred grand. Daria said the clause was non-negotiable. A dealbreaker. So, I signed on the dotted line. Luckily, Daria also assured me the chances the producers would exercise the buy-out were virtually nil. But, still, to be safe, I'm not going to spend a dime of my earnings from the show unless and until I'm positive I'm going to be around for the long haul. And even then, most of my salary will go toward helping my family in ways I've dreamed of doing for a while now, so a beachfront condo will have to wait.

The car makes a turn off the highway that makes it clear my Malibu guess was right, and ten minutes later, our SUV pulls to a stop in front of a large, gated home that's instantly recognizable to me—a cliffside mansion I've seen countless times on one of my favorite reality TV shows.

"Oh my gosh!" I blurt, my butt dancing on the car seat beneath me. "This is the mansion from *The Engagement Experiment*!"

FORTY

SAVAGE

As our SUV rolls to a stop in front of a large Mediterranean-style home seated on a cliff in Malibu, Laila shrieks, "My mom and sister are going to freak out we're living at the mansion from *The Engagement Experiment!*"

I've never watched the long-running reality TV dating show Laila's referenced, but I'm familiar with its basic concept, since Sasha watches it with Mimi sometimes. Also, my feed on Twitter is constantly filled with memes and tweets about that show, so I'm passively kept up to date on the gist of it.

"Is this where Savage and I will be living for the next three months?" Laila excitedly asks the driver.

"It sure is," the man replies, making Laila squeal and bop around in her seat.

The bodyguard in the passenger seat says, "Please wait here, while I do a sweep of the area."

When the bodyguard exits the car, the driver steps out, too, leaving Laila and me alone. Laila leans back and says, "Have you ever watched *The Engagement Experiment?*"

"No, but I know the concept. A bunch of fame-hungry women live in a big house, vying to get 'selected' by some random dude who's been anointed 'Prince Charming' by the show, for no discernible reason. At the end, the 'happy couple' rides off into the sunset, only to break up as soon as their contract allows, at which point, they become influencers who can charge upwards of fifty grand per Instagram post."

Laila makes a face like she's offended.

"Oh, come on," I say. "You can't possibly think anyone actually finds true love on that show."

"Some of them do," she insists. But when I look at her like she's naive, she adds, "At least, I think *they* think they do . . . for a little while. Whatever. The only reason I asked if you've seen the show is to explain that, at the beginning of each season, before the contestants start getting the boot, *thirty* women live in this house together, and there's plenty of room for all of them. So, I think we should be able to avoid killing each other over the next three months, if only barely."

"I'll believe it when I see it."

The bodyguard returns and says we're all clear, that there are no paparazzi or stalkers to be found, and Laila and I exit the car, where we're greeted by an attractive brunette in glasses.

"Hey, guys," the woman says brightly. "I'm Rhoda, a junior producer at *Sing Your Heart Out.* I'm here to give you a tour of the house and get you settled in your new digs."

Laila jumps for joy at the woman's news and then proceeds to chatter with her excitedly as we head toward the house. Inside the front door, Laila abruptly stops chatting when she beholds the large entrance foyer. "It's *exactly* like it looks on TV!" Laila gushes. "I can't believe this is my life!"

The producer laughs. "You mentioned in a recent interview that you and your sister always watch *The Engagement Experiment,* so we thought we'd surprise you. As luck would have it, the timing was perfect and the house is empty."

"That's so lucky!" Laila exclaims. She looks at me, her blue eyes wide and sparkling. "Aren't we lucky, Savage?"

I know Laila is looking for an exuberant reaction from me, but I can't supply it. Not when I feel like I got hoodwinked into pimping out not one but *two* reality TV shows—and for *half* the salary I'd originally negotiated. "This might be a stupid question," I say, walking behind the producer and Laila as they head into the living room. "But whenever Laila and I do our required 'happy couple' social media videos every night, won't fans recognize this house and think our relationship is nothing but a set-up?"

"We've got an easy solution for that," the producer says. "In your first video tonight, you'll explain the producers of *Sing Your Heart Out* supplied this famous house to you because, one, you didn't want to show your actual home on national TV, and, two, the producers heard *The Engagement Experiment* is one of Laila's all-time favorite shows."

"*Perfect!*" Laila squeals.

The producer continues, "With you two living here and filming your behind-the-scenes videos, we'll get some fantastic cross-promotion between the two shows. Plus, the audience will adore seeing you two living in this famous house. It's a win-win-win."

More like a singular win, I think. *For the network.*

But Laila is thrilled. "Genius!" she exclaims, twirling around. And even though I'm annoyed with the producers, I can't help smiling at Laila's obvious joy. The girl is a lot of things, but jaded ain't one of them. I've seen this bubbly, sunny side of Laila many times during the tour, but never with me. Always with someone else, from afar. And I must admit, finally getting to experience Laila's happy, sweet side, up close and personal, is making me forget I'm annoyed that the show is exploiting my valuable image and name to promote a cringey-ass dating show without my consent.

"Ooooh!" Laila coos, sprinting into the next room. "I'd know this kitchen *anywhere*. Ha!" She addresses the producer. "Remember that time those two guys from Jenny's season had that food fight in here?" She snaps her fingers, like she's trying to come up with something.

"Damian and Gregory," Rhoda replies, without missing a beat.
"Yes!"

Rhoda chuckles. "I worked on *The Engagement Experiment* that season. I even got mashed potatoes in my hair during that famous food fight."

"Shut up!" Laila shrieks, clearly enthralled.

The producer nods. "True story. I worked on that show five seasons—one through five, before getting promoted to help Nadine launch a certain singing competition that turned out to be the network's biggest hit, ever."

Laila grabs the woman's arm like she's gripping a flotation device during a plane crash. "Rhoda, you have to tell me every juicy detail from your five seasons on *The Engagement Experiment*. I have to know *everything* you know!"

The producer giggles. "I can't tell you *everything*. I've signed an NDA."

"Okay, just tell me this: was the food fight *real*—or did the show tell Damian to throw that first blob of mashed potatoes?"

"I really can't say."

"Shoot. That means it was fake?"

"I can't say."

Laila pulls at her hair comically, like she's a patient in an insane asylum. "Gah! I need to know! Please, please, Rhoda, come over here after work one night this week to hang out with me, so I can get you to spill *all* the tea. Thanks to *my* NDA, I wouldn't be able to tell a soul anything you tell me, right?—but I *have* to know *everything*!"

The woman looks thoroughly charmed by Laila, the same way everyone is when she turns on her mesmerizing charisma to full blast. "Okay, okay," the woman says, holding up her palms. "You make an excellent point about your NDA. I guess, since you're bound to secrecy, I could come over to tell you a *few* behind the scenes tidbits."

Laila hoots and dances and whoops from the depths of her soul, and I know, deep in my bones, this producer is now putty in Laila's pretty palm. *And there she goes again,* I think. *Adding to her collection of insta-friends.*

After a bit more chatter about the stupid dating show, we continue the tour. The producer opens a large, industrial-sized refrigerator, which makes Laila gasp at its neatly stocked shelves.

"As you can see," the producer says proudly, "we've stocked the fridge with everything you both mentioned you like snacking on." She looks at me. "And we got all the ingredients you requested to make tonight's meal, too, Savage."

"Tonight's meal?" Laila gasps out, her blue eyes wide. "You're cooking tonight?"

I wink. "I'm making you my grandmother's cioppino. I figured I should replace your false memories of our first date with some real ones."

Laila raises an eyebrow, perhaps understanding my ulterior motive here. When we talked about our fictitious first date, I told Laila our meal ended midway through with me eating her out and fucking her on her kitchen table. Surely, she knows that's my plan for tonight.

"Oooh, make sure you two look at each other exactly like that in front of the cameras tomorrow," the producer says. "That's sexy, guys."

We look away from each other, our faces flushed, and the tour continues. We head into a large living space with a glorious ocean view and a baby grand in a corner. Squealing happily, Laila makes herself at home behind the piano and plays the first few bars of one of her biggest hits. And, of course, as usual, her voice sends goosebumps skating across my skin.

When she stops playing, Laila leans forward and hugs the piano. "I love you," she purrs, making the producer and me chuckle. She adds, "I've always wanted one of these. The sound is so full and rich." She sits up and sighs happily. "I feel like Anne Hathaway in *The Princess Diaries.*" She looks at me. "Have you seen that one?"

"No."

"Then, put it on our list! We'll watch it after *Beauty and the Beast* and the high school one you mentioned."

"I'm not watching a movie called *The Princess Diaries,* Laila."

"Oh, yes, you are, or *else.*" She throws back her head and strikes an ominous-sounding chord on the piano, like she's the Phantom of the Opera on the warpath, and I can't help laughing at her goofiness.

"Your threats don't scare me, Fitzy," I tease. But I'm smiling like a fool.

"Well, you should be scared of me, *Adrian.* I'm a dangerous woman." She strikes another ominous chord, this time even more passionately. And this time, I not only chuckle. I belly laugh from the depths of my soul.

"Oh my gosh," the producer says. "Be sure to do this whole bit during a behind the scenes video at some point. This is pure gold."

I bristle. Is that what she thinks Laila and I are doing here—a *bit*? Because I'm certainly not. I don't think I'm even capable of laughing like that for pretend.

The tour continues upstairs. We see a home gym, an office we won't be using, and several bedrooms, before winding up in a large master.

"You can take this one," Laila says. "I'll take one of the other bedrooms down the hall."

My heart sinks. I know Laila requested separate bedrooms at Reed's house last night, but we've been getting along so well, I was kind of hoping she'd want to sleep with me during our three-month stay here. "No, you can have the master," I reply, not knowing what else to say. "I'm pretty easygoing when it comes to where I lay my head."

"No, no," Laila says. "You're the big kahuna here. I'm just the *opener,* remember?" She smiles broadly, without a hint of malice, letting me know her comment wasn't meant as a barb. But, rather, as self-deprecation. Clearly, Laila means to extend an olive branch for the tension we experienced during the tour, rather than starting yet another fight.

"No, no, we're equal partners this time," I insist. "Fifty-fifty. Honestly, I don't mind having one of the smaller rooms. I grew up sleeping in a closet, literally. And as a teen, I slept on a couch. For me, any room with an actual bed and a door feels like a palace."

Laila's face contorts with sympathy—which wasn't at all what I was going for. She says, "All the more reason for you to take this room. It's settled."

I shift my weight and say awkwardly, "Okay. Thanks."

The producer smiles broadly. "You guys are too cute. Why don't we shoot your first live video now, so I can hold the camera? We'll restart the tour, and Laila can react excitedly to the house."

"Great idea!" Laila says. She looks at me, her eyebrows raised. And it suddenly becomes clear I need to embrace this bullshit and give it my all, or I'm going to make Laila nothing but miserable for the next three months. Clearly, today is a thrilling day for her. Why drag her down by making her feel like she's dragging me along, kicking and screaming?

"Sounds good," I say, and Laila flashes me a smile that makes my heart skip a beat.

With the camera recording, we go back to the foyer and give our required speech about why we're living here. We redo our entrance to the kitchen, and then to the master bedroom we're supposedly going to share. We head into a small room we haven't already seen, and Laila is thrilled to find the producers have brought in a pottery wheel for her, much like the one she has at her own place. And, finally, we head outside and tour the large swimming pool, fire feature, and hot tub.

"Oh, man, I know that gleam in my boyfriend's eyes," Laila says suggestively when we reach the hot tub. "That's my cue to say goodbye for now, guys. We'll say hello again tomorrow when we get on-set for our first day of shooting. Until then . . ." She blows a kiss to the camera and slides her arm around my waist. "Say goodbye to the nice people, babe!"

I bristle. I've dreamed of Laila calling me babe for a very long time. *But not like this.* "Goodbye to the nice people, *babe*," I deadpan, making Laila laugh. Or, rather, making her *fake* laugh.

Finally, the producer lowers her camera and whoops happily. "Brilliant, guys. Perfect."

Laila removes her arm from my waist and exhales like she's just finished a workout. "What time will the car come for us in the morning, Rhoda?"

"Nine."

"Perfect."

We accompany the producer to the front door and say our goodbyes to her. And, suddenly, Laila and I are standing alone, in the foyer of our fake love nest—the house we're going to share for the next three months.

"So . . . are you hungry?" I ask.

"I could eat."

"Let's change into some comfortable clothes and meet in the kitchen in five."

"Cool." We start walking toward the staircase together, but Laila stops when her phone buzzes. "Oh, crap," she says, looking down. "My mom and sister saw our live video and demand I call them." She snickers. "As predicted, they're freaking out about the house."

"I'm sure my cousin showed Mimi our video, too. I tell you what, *babe*. Cioppino takes a half hour to prep and about an hour to simmer, before it's time to add a few last-minute ingredients. Why don't we get the broth simmering, and then we'll call both our families while it cooks?"

"You're a genius chef." She mimes a chef's kiss. "I'll meet you in the kitchen in five, *babe*." We walk up the grand staircase together and stop at the top. "If I'm forbidden to go into the West Wing," she says, "tell me now. Or I'm going there, first thing."

I look at her blankly.

"In your enchanted castle," Laila clarifies. "In *Beauty and the Beast*, the Beast forbids Belle from entering the West Wing. That was my way of saying you remind me so much of the Beast, I can't stand it."

"I told you I haven't seen that movie."

"I know. I said that to amuse myself." She smirks. "Do me a favor. Growl at me and say, 'I forbid you to go into the West Wing!'"

I pull a face that says, *Over my dead body.*

Laila snickers. "The Beast wouldn't do that on command, either."

"Just to be clear," I say, "you're supposed to *like* the Beast, right? He's the *hero* of that movie?"

Laila surprises me by stepping forward into my personal space and pulling me toward her. "Hell yeah, we're supposed to like the Beast. In fact, I didn't understand my reaction to the Beast as a little girl—the tingle he provoked on my skin and between my legs. But now, looking back, I understand that movie was my first foray into porn."

I bite back a smile and then growl and whisper-shout, "I forbid you to go into the West Wing!"

"Oooh, baaaaby," she purrs, like she's having a little orgasm, and I can't help chuckling in reply. "Just so you know," she says, "I'm the kind of twisted bitch who thought the Beast was a five-alarm fire . . . and the prince he becomes at the end when the spell is broken was a total disappointment."

"Thanks for ruining the ending for me, dude."

Laila slides her hand to my package to confirm what she already suspects: I'm finding this exchange hot as hell. "Aw, come on, Adrian," she says seductively, her hand cupping the bulge in my pants. "Nobody watches porn for the plot."

My breathing hitches. *This girl.* She knows how to hook me like nobody else. In fact, she's known it since the minute I laid eyes on her at Reed's party.

"Okay, you've convinced me," I say. "We'll watch *Beauty and the Beast* tonight."

She smiles seductively. "Fair warning, Beast? I always get what I want, one way or another. You'll find that out soon enough." With that, she releases me, winks, and sashays down the hallway, pointedly walking past the door to the master bedroom and disappearing into a bedroom a few doors away.

"You two are so beautiful together!" Savage's grandmother, Mimi, exclaims, beaming at Savage and me on Savage's phone. Mimi is in her bed in Chicago, while Savage and I are leaning over the island in our new kitchen. And if I thought Savage resembled the grouchy, snarling Beast during our tour of the house, he's turned into the sweet version of the Beast—the one who had the famous snowball fight with Belle—while talking to his grandmother on this call.

With his grandma, Savage is surprisingly gentle and easygoing. A man who smiles easily and chuckles often. A man who reminds his grandmother to "get plenty of rest" and "drink lots of water" and not to "overdo." Basically, he's the guy I've observed hanging out with his bandmates, with half the swearing and twice the adorableness.

"Don't take any of his crap, Laila," Mimi says.

"She never does," Savage says.

"Oh, I take *some* of his crap," I say. "But only because he's so charming."

"Yes, he is," Mimi replies wistfully. "That's why I still take some of his crap, too."

We giggle together.

"Oh, guess what, Mimi?" Savage says. "I checked the shooting schedule, and it looks like I'll be able to visit for Christmas. You'll be moved into the new house by then, so I'll get you a big ol' Christmas tree. The biggest tree you've ever had."

"How wonderful! Will you come to Chicago, too, Laila?"

I look at Savage and his eyes are saying, *Please, please, please.* "I'll be spending Christmas day with my mom and sister," I say. "But I'd love to come for a few days before then." I'm curious to find out some details about the house Savage bought his grandmother, but if I were truly his girlfriend, I'd already know all about it. So, I ask a question that seems pretty safe. "Are you excited to move into the new house, Mimi?"

"Very excited. But I feel guilty, too, that Adrian did this for me. When he told me what he did, I told him to return it. But he wouldn't do it."

"A house isn't like a pair of shoes," Savage says. "But even if I could 'return it,' I wouldn't do that. I bought the house for you, as a gift to *myself.* I want to see you in that house, Mimi. Now, please, let's not talk about this again. What's done is done."

Mimi addresses me. "See what I'm dealing with here, Laila?"

"He's incorrigible."

She flashes an adorable smile at her grandson. "Thank you, Ady."

"You're very welcome."

Mimi's dark eyes widen. "Ooh! Isn't it time to add the clams and mussels?"

Savage shrugs. "I have no idea."

"Well, what does your timer say?"

"I didn't set a timer. I forgot."

"*Adrian!*"

Savage laughs. "I got distracted." He pulls me into the frame and cups my face in his palm. "Wouldn't you get distracted, looking at this face, too?"

Mimi giggles. "Yes, I suppose if I were a young man, I most

certainly would. Now, show me the pot, sweetheart. I'll be able to tell if it's time by looking at the broth."

Savage points his phone at the pot on the stove, and Mimi confirms her hunch is correct: it's time to add the shellfish to the soup.

"Okay, now what?" Savage says after completing his task.

"You tell me," Mimi says.

"Mimi, come on. It's been forever since I've made this and I've had a long day."

"Okay, okay." She gives her grandson direction, while Savage repeatedly says, "Oh, yeah!" And I must admit, the entire exchange makes me giggle and swoon. They're adorable together. Endlessly entertaining.

"Laila?" Mimi says.

I peek my head onto the screen, my eyebrows raised.

"Next time Adrian makes my cioppino for you, please remind him to set a timer at each step. It'll work out fine this time because I'm here to save the day. But next time, he might not be so lucky."

I look at Savage and, not surprisingly, sadness washes over his handsome features at the implication of Mimi's comment—that she won't be around forever.

"I'll remind him, Mimi," I say, taking Savage's hand.

Finally, when the last ingredients are simmering, Savage says, "Okay, now that we've got everything added to the pot, let's get you to bed, Mimi. Close your eyes."

Mimi gets situated for the night, with the help of her caregiver. Sasha peeks onto the screen to say goodnight. And, finally, Savage begins to sing softly, in a hushed, soothing tone, "Mimi, Mimi, Mimi, I made you out of wishes. Mimi, Mimi, Mimi, and now I'm sending kisses. Hugs and kisses to you, I send them through the air. And when they reach you miles away, you'll feel how much I care." He sings the same refrain again, before finally whispering, "Sleep tight, sweet Mimi. I love you."

Mimi doesn't respond. Apparently, Savage's lullaby had its intended effect.

Savage whispers, "Stuart?"

Mimi's caregiver comes onto the screen, and Savage converses with him briefly before ending the call. As Savage puts his phone down onto the island, his Adam's apple bobs. He takes a moment to collect himself, and then takes a seat next to me at the kitchen table. When he doesn't speak, I rub his back in silence for a long moment, feeling the weight of his burden wafting off him. From what he said earlier today, I could tell he loves his grandmother. But watching him with her—watching his face as he sang to her—made me understand their bond in a whole new way. She's *everything* to him, clearly. A central figure in his life.

"I'm so sorry Mimi is sick," I say softly.

Without replying to my comment, Savage pulls me to him and kisses me deeply, with such depth of feeling, such passion, he takes my breath away. Without hesitation, I slide onto his lap and straddle him, kissing him sensuously. Finally, when we break free of our kiss, Savage looks flustered. Flushed. Disoriented. *Beautiful.* If he'd been born hundreds of years ago in Italy, I'd have no trouble believing he was Michelangelo's inspiration for *David*.

"I know for our first date I'm supposed to feed you first and fuck you on the kitchen table second," Savage says, his voice husky with arousal. "But I'm going to have to turn off the heat on the soup now and flip the script."

FORTY-TWO

SAVAGE

After turning off the burner on the stove, I return to Laila at the kitchen table. Practically panting with desire, I peel off her clothes, lay her naked body onto the table, and open her smooth thighs wide, until her glorious pussy is opened to me and her pink clit is calling out to be licked like a lollipop. With my mouth watering and my cock rock-hard, I lean down and get to work, eating Laila enthusiastically, with fervent swirls and swipes of my tongue and voracious movements of my lips. And all this while stroking her with my fingers and groaning and growling like a wild animal devouring his prey.

"Savage," Laila purrs. "Adrian. Oh, God." She arches her back and comes undone against my tongue in the best possible way, screaming and howling as her orgasm throttles her.

"God, I love that you're a screamer," I choke out, enthralled by the sounds of Laila's ecstasy.

When Laila's body goes slack and her screams die down, I grab a condom out of a nearby drawer—one of the many I stashed there while Laila was still changing her clothes earlier—and after getting myself covered, I rest Laila's calves on my shoulders, pin her wrists against the wooden table, and plunge myself inside her, balls deep.

As my tip slams her farthest reaches, we both moan with relief and excitement. As I start thrusting, and my tip slams her repeatedly, Laila grunts and moans with each and every movement.

It's a special kind of bliss, fucking Laila on this table. Knowing I'm going to be fucking her every day for the next three months. Knowing she's mine, all mine, at least for now. *Finally.* It feels so good to be railing Laila, in fact, after not too long, I have to slow my thrusts, and then pause altogether, to keep myself from coming too quickly. Nobody feels as good as this woman. Nobody tastes as good. Nobody looks as good. She's in a league of her own, in every way.

I didn't know I could feel quite *this* turned on—like I'm literally under a spell. As I pause with myself inside her, I massage her clit, slowly, methodically, relentlessly—and then resume fucking her, also slowly—while whispering dirty-talk to her. I tell her she feels amazing. Tastes amazing. That her tits are incredible. Her body perfect. Until, finally, Laila comes again, this time with my entire cock buried inside her, all the way. And there's no way to describe the ecstasy I feel as her body milks mine.

Somehow, I manage to hang on by the barest of threads through Laila's orgasm. I run my palms over her splayed body as she moans and writhes, and then begin fucking her, much harder. Harder and harder, I fuck her, my thoughts spiraling along with my pleasure. Why didn't Laila come to my room in Vegas, or any other city after that? Why didn't she break up with Malik in New York, when she *knew* I wanted her? Yeah, I mentioned Kendrick on that sidewalk, but Laila's not stupid. She knew I wanted her for myself. She *knew.* And she picked Malik over me. I slam her, over and over again, angry with myself for not saying what needed to be said back then. For not saying what needs to be said *now.* Fuck! I've wanted this woman so badly, for so long, but there's always something or someone standing in my way! Well, now I'm going to make her want me, as badly as I want her, even if I have to fuck her into submission. Even if I have to make her addicted to fucking me to get what I want.

When I'm on the cusp of losing it, I pull out and turn Laila around, bend her over the kitchen table, grab a fistful of her thick, sandy hair, and with one hand lodged against her scalp and the other reaching around to massage her clit in slow circles, I fuck my woman raw, with deep, unapologetic thrusts that make it impossible for her *not* to scream.

"I'm gonna come!" she shouts, her ass jerking and jolting against me.

Through sheer force of will, I pull out and kneel behind her, sensing her climax will be a straight-up gusher. A geyser of delicious goodness. The ultimate trophy. I eat her gently for a moment, letting her come down. Teasing her. Making her beg for more. And when I feel her ramping up again, I slide my fingers inside her and stimulate her G-spot as I eat her. When I feel her inner muscles shudder and tighten, I pull back and tease her again, until she's literally whimpering and begging me to fuck her. Over and over again, I take her to the edge and then back away. Over and over again, I pull her strings, letting her know I'm in control here. That every breath she takes, every moan she makes is exactly as I'm commanding.

Finally, I finger her while eating her with gusto. And when her body begins tightening sharply, when her moans become primal and pathetic, I let her go, pushing through those initial shudders without stopping, until I get what I want—a torrent of sweet, warm fluid gushing into my face. With a loud growl, I lick up my prize like a rabid dog, off her lips and inner thighs, the very taste of my trophy sending me to the bitter edge of ecstasy, without so much as a single touch to my cock.

When I've licked up the last drop of Laila's cum, I pick her up and carry her slack body into the living room and straight to the couch. On the night of the hot tub, Laila mentioned she likes being on top. Well, then, let the woman ride my cock until we're coming together.

I guide her on top of me as I lie on the couch and she immediately slams herself down and begins riding me like a feral animal.

As she fucks me, I devour her breasts and nipples. Her neck and lips. I whisper into her ear that she's mine now. That I own her body. I tell her she's a dirty little freak who's going to come for me again. And that tonight is just the beginning of what I'm going to do to her, while we're living here together. I tell her she turns me on like nobody else. I whisper all the things I can only say out loud while fucking her. The things I can pass off as dirty talk, even though they're the things I should have said on that sidewalk in New York. Or during the last month of the tour. Or backstage at the awards show. Or today in the fucking SUV. I say it all. And she groans and moans and throws her head back and fucks me hard.

When Laila starts making her most primal sounds, the ones I now recognize as the precursor to her losing control completely, I press down on her clit with my thumb while twisting her nipple, hard, with my other hand, and grit out, "Come, baby." And I'll be damned, Little Miss Freak comes again. For the *fourth* time. Like she's a goddamned sex doll with a written pamphlet of instructions. This time, with a roar so glorious, it flash-boils the blood in my veins.

When my orgasm comes, it's unlike any other I've experienced. So pleasurable, it momentarily blinds me. I'm not merely *seeing* God right now, I'm getting my cock sucked by him. And it feels fucking amazing.

With one last groan, Laila collapses on top of me, sweaty and panting, as my body finishes convulsing underneath her. I pull her head up by her hair and kiss her deeply and she grips my face and returns my kiss like I've just given her CPR after drowning.

When we break from our kiss, we stare at each other for a long moment, both of us dazed and breathless.

"Wow," she says.

I nod. "That about covers it."

She falls on top of me, breathing hard, and I stroke her back, half crowing to myself in victory and half freaking out. *That wasn't normal.* In fact, if I'm being honest with myself, it was so damned *abnormal,* so damned good, as to be terrifying. Now that I know sex can be *that* good—now that I know the night of the hot tub wasn't a fluke, but a *preview*—how will I *ever* want to fuck anyone else, as long as I live? The very thought makes me convulse with terror. Or, shit, maybe that's just an after-shock from my insane orgasm.

"I'm hungry," Laila says, sitting up. "Starving, actually."

I exhale a long breath. I need to make this woman *mine*. I need to make it so she doesn't want anything or anyone but me. I clear my throat. "Yeah, I'm pretty hungry, too," I say calmly, trying desperately not to sound like the raving lunatic I've become. The madman hell-bent on making this woman as addicted to me as I am to her. I smile brightly. Like a sane, normal man might do, and say, "Let's dig into that cioppino, eh? We'll need to fuel up for rounds two, three, and four."

FORTY-THREE

SAVAGE

"**I**t's soooo *good*," Laila coos, like she's in the midst of slowly riding my cock, rather than merely eating a bowl of Italian fish soup. "You didn't over-promise on this at all, Adrian."

I smile at her across our fancy dining room table. "I'm glad it turned out well. You never know. As you saw, I'm not particularly 'detail oriented' when I cook."

She snickers. "Honestly, I was surprised you were such a shit show while making this. I was under the impression you make this dish frequently."

I shake my head. "I don't have a kitchen, remember? Before tonight, I've only made this one time without Mimi standing right there to help me."

"What was the one time?"

"Mimi's seventieth birthday."

"How'd it turn out?"

"Not so great."

We both laugh.

"How old were you?" she asks.

"Seventeen. I'd just gotten my first job at a grocery store as a bagger, which meant I could afford all the ingredients, thanks to my fat paycheck and employee discount. I thought I was such a baller when I got that job. I thought I was Reed fucking Rivers."

She giggles. "I bet you got flirted with a ton while bagging nice ladies' groceries."

"I did. My co-workers used to tease me that whatever register I happened to be working always had the longest line."

Laila snickers. "Of course, it did." She takes another zealous bite of food, before saying, "So, what you're telling me is you discovered at an early age you're drop-dead gorgeous."

I feel my cheeks bloom. I know she's being light-hearted, but at her comment, memories of my early years flicker across my mind— times when, to put it mildly, I didn't feel 'drop-dead gorgeous' in the slightest.

Whatever Laila sees on my face, it causes her to furrow her brow. "I was just teasing you. Sort of. You can't help that's your face."

"No offense taken. I just . . ." I don't know how to finish the sentence, so I don't.

Laila shifts in her chair, obviously trying to read me. But when she can't crack the code, she looks down and takes another bite of food.

"So . . . you said Mimi is your dad's mother?"

"Yeah."

"Did your family go to your grandma's house and cook a nice meal for her on her birthday every year, or was Mimi's seventieth birthday an extra-special thing?"

I take a sip of water. "Mimi's seventieth was the only time I was stupid enough to try to cook a big meal for her. Like I said, I wanted to impress her, not only with my cooking skills, but with my deep pockets."

"That's so cute, Savage."

I pause. If I say this next thing, there will be no turning back. I'll open the door to talking about the real stuff. The shit I don't say in interviews. The stories I only tell Kendrick and Kai, since they were living in Mimi's apartment complex when I arrived on my grandmother's doorstep like a lost puppy.

I take another sip of water and decide: *Fuck it.* Laila's already met Mimi, and she's going to be talking to my grandmother every night for the next three months. I might as well give Laila a full picture of why Mimi means so much to me. "I didn't 'go' to Mimi's house for her birthday, by the way. I lived with Mimi. She was my only parent, beginning at age twelve."

"Oh. I didn't realize that."

"Mm-hmm." I take a bite of food.

Laila cocks her head to the side. "Why did you start living with Mimi? Did something bad happen to your parents?"

I take a long sip of water, gearing up for the conversation we're about to have. "Not in the way you mean. I'm sure if you asked my mom, she'd say *I* was the 'bad' thing that happened to *her.*"

Laila's features contort with sympathy. "Oh."

"Or, at the very least," I add, "I was the 'highly inconvenient' thing that made all subsequent bad things unavoidable. You know my band's song 'Sorry for the Inconvenience'?"

She nods.

"That song is a big 'fuck you' to both my parents."

Laila puts down her spoon. "You mentioned your 'asshole father' when we drank that bottle of whiskey in Providence. But I didn't realize you have an asshole *mother,* too."

"She's not an asshole. At least, she *tried* to raise me for a while, unlike him. She's just not a person who ever should have had a kid."

"I can't imagine. My mom is so grateful to have my sister and me. And now, my niece. She always says we're the best thing that's ever happened to her."

"That's what Mimi always says about me."

"Were your parents in a relationship?"

"No. It was a one-night stand. My father knocked up the bartender—my mother—at his favorite bar. Once my mom realized she was pregnant, she tracked my father down, but he denied I was his."

"No paternity test?"

I shrug. "I've never asked her about it. My hunch is she wasn't sure who the father was. By the time I was a toddler, though, it was a moot point. I looked just like him. She said she brought me to him when I was two or three and demanded he take me for a while, so she could have some fun again."

"*She told you that?*"

"My mother hasn't been shy about her lack of attachment to me. Anyway, she brought me to him, but he didn't want me, either. So, she did her best."

Laila is visibly floored. "I'm so sorry, Savage. Growing up, did you see your father, at all?"

"I saw him, now and again. Whenever he'd started feeling guilty about ignoring my existence. He'd come over, but only when he was drunk. Usually on my birthday or Christmas and we'd try to play happy family for a hot minute. But things always turned into a screaming match between my parents, and I'd run and hide in my closet. Which by the way, doubled as my bedroom, by choice. I've always liked small spaces. Anyway, fast-forward to Chicago, after I'd moved there and had been living with Mimi for a couple years—"

"Where did you live with your mom?"

"Phoenix."

Laila's eyebrows ride up.

"Yeah, you hate-fucked me in my hometown," I say. I wink. "It definitely made it extra special for me. Anyway, my sperm donor father got out of prison when I was fifteen or so. He showed up at Mimi's apartment, angry that she'd taken me in, when he wasn't sure I was his kid. He told her I was conning her. Planning to steal from her. So, I flattened his stupid ass." I smile. "I was fifteen and my father was three inches taller than me—and I took his ass *down.*"

"Whoa."

"It felt amazing when I was standing over him. That was the moment I realized how small he truly was—and that he had zero power over me. It was a huge turning point for Mimi and me. Until then, I'd been a little asshole to her. Always testing her. Trying to prove my theory she was going to throw me out at some point. But after that, I realized I loved her and that I'd do anything for her. *Anything*. And that's when I said to myself, 'Why not give her a real chance here? Why not stop being an asshole and start listening to her?' So, that's what I did. I started following her rules, and giving her the respect she deserved. And it was the best thing I've ever done. From that point, everything started falling into place for me. I befriended Kendrick and Kai, seeing as how I was going to be sticking around, and that's when I realized I could write songs and sing. Everything came together for me after that."

"I'm so glad you decided to let Mimi love you."

"I can't imagine who I'd be right now if I hadn't."

"Is it Sasha's mom or dad who's Mimi's kid?"

"Her father, Frank. He died in an accident at work when Sasha was eleven. Apparently, he was an amazing guy. Really sweet and kind. Thanks to Frank, Mimi knew she was capable of having a normal, loving son. Poor Mimi always blamed herself for my father, her second son, being such a dickbag. But at least Frank gave her some comfort that my father's assholery wasn't her fault. Mimi once told me she felt like my father was born without a complete soul. Like, he just didn't feel things the way other people did. She said it only got worse when his dad, Mimi's husband, died."

Laila looks down at her bowl of soup, looking distraught. "I'm sorry you've had it so rough, Savage."

"Nobody has it easy in life, really. Speaking of which, tell me about your asshole father."

Laila drags her spoon through her bowl of soup, gathering her thoughts. "My parents got married when my mom got accidentally pregnant with my sister. When things became rocky in their marriage, they decided in their infinite wisdom to have a second baby to 'fix' things."

"Brilliant plan."

Laila rolls her eyes. "Yeah. Obviously, my existence didn't fix a damned thing. I remember my dad often being loud and angry when Angel and I were little. He'd punch holes in walls. Smash plates and lamps onto the ground. And then, one day, my father did the unthinkable: he punched my mom in the face during an argument and broke a bone under her eye."

"Jesus."

"My mom took Angel and me to live with my aunt in Whittier. We lived there until my mom could afford an apartment of our own."

"Did you keep in touch with your father through all that?"

"Sort of. My sister was done with him the day we moved out. But I kept in touch for a while, by phone, and listened to him tell me how sorry he was. How much he'd changed. But one day, I heard my mom crying while talking to him on the phone, so I listened in. And the way he was cussing her out . . . That's when I knew he was still the same asshole who'd broken her face. And that's when I was done with him for good, too. I grabbed the phone and told him to fuck off and never speak to any of us again. Angel got on the phone and said the same. We told our mom we'd always take care of her and not to bother trying to squeeze any child support out of him, again. It wasn't worth it. And we've been a threesome ever since."

"Until he called to ask you for money," I say.

She looks up, surprised. "How'd you know about that?"

"It's always the same story, Laila. The same thing happened to me and to so many of my friends, once they started getting any kind of success and fame. You have no idea how common it is."

"Oh."

"So, did you give him money when he asked?"

She looks sheepish. "Did you?"

I nod. "I paid my father ten grand, in exchange for a comprehensive agreement. He's prohibited from talking about me to the press and can't sue me for the time I decked him. So, it was money well spent."

"Shoot. I didn't think to get an agreement like that. He's given several interviews about me. It's so embarrassing. He acts like he's been an amazing father to me—like my success is all his doing, simply because he got me a Fisher Price keyboard as a toddler. But he's not the one who sacrificed, constantly, to keep me going to piano lessons. He's not the one who listened to every new song I wrote, even the terrible ones, and cried tears of joy and told me I had a gift."

"Don't pay him another dime, Laila. Ever."

She sniffles. "I send him money a few times a year."

"Why?"

She shrugs. "I don't know. He was a heavy smoker and now he's sick. Helping with his medical bills makes me feel less guilty, I guess."

"Guilty for *what*?"

She twists her sultry lips. "I can't abandon him. He's blood. And I've been so lucky in my career."

Anger surges inside me. "No, Laila. Fuck him. You didn't ask him to have sex with your mom without a condom. And, yes, you've been lucky in your career. But luck is only one of the factors of your success." I motion to the half-empty bowl in front of me at the dining room table. "It's like this soup. There've been a whole lot of ingredients, besides luck, to get you where you are today. Hard work. Piano lessons. And most of all, like your mom said, your *gift*. Whatever luck you've had, it wouldn't have gotten you anywhere, without the rest of the ingredients along with it."

"Thank you," she whispers, looking moved. She swallows hard. "That means a lot, coming from you. I think so highly of your talent. You're an amazing artist."

My chest heaves. "Thank you. That means a lot, coming from you. I think the same of you. Your voice gives me goosebumps. When you hit those high notes, I literally get a tear in my eye."

She exhales a slow, long breath, like her heart is beating a mile a minute, and electricity crackles between us.

"He's a douchebag, Laila," I say, my eyes locked with hers, skin on fire. "Don't send him another dime."

"I probably will," she admits. "Because sending it is my way of controlling him—keeping him away from me and my family, for good."

The full extent of my assholery toward Laila hits me like a tsunami. "I'm so sorry for all the times I was a flaming dickhead to you during the tour, Laila. I'm sorry for any time I yelled at you or made you feel uncomfortable. I'm sorry for that time I said you didn't belong on the tour. You *did*. You're a genius with incredible talent and star quality and I was an asshole to suggest otherwise. I'm sorry for the times I've smoked around you, especially the times I've purposely blown smoke in your face, solely to piss you off. Please, forgive me for all of it. There were times during the tour when I felt irrationally rejected by you, or maybe I thought I couldn't make a play for you because Kendrick had a crush on you, and my solution to all of it was to lash out and/or push you away, with all my might. It was stupid of me. And I'm so sorry."

Her chest visibly rises and falls for a moment. Her blue eyes are practically glowing. "I accept your apology," she says. "I wasn't all that nice to you, on many occasions."

"It doesn't matter. There's something wrong with me, Laila. The same way there's something wrong with my father. Sometimes, I feel like I don't have a complete soul."

"That's not true, Adrian. I saw you with Mimi. I saw you with your bandmates for three months. I saw how respectful and sweet you are with Ruby. Trust me, you've got a complete soul."

"But what if I don't?" I say, admitting my worst fear, out loud, for the first time, ever. "What if I'm my father's son, in ways I don't want to be?"

Laila gets up and strides to me at my end of the table. "Stop. You're nothing like him." She stands over me and clutches me to her, and I lay my cheek on her belly, while she runs her fingers through my hair. She whispers, "You've got a beautiful soul, Adrian. You're just scarred by the stuff that happened to you as a kid, as anyone in your shoes would be." She kisses the top of my head and takes the seat next to me at the table. "Can I ask you something? That lyric in 'Hate Sex High' about punching a hole in the wall. Was that true?"

I nod. "After my run-in with Malik at the restaurant, followed by that argument we had outside on the sidewalk, I was angry and shitfaced. Feeling rejected and confused. So, I went back to my hotel room and punched a hole in the wall."

Laila presses her lips together. "I'm going to need you to promise not to do that sort of thing while we're living here together, no matter how much I might annoy or anger you."

"Of course, I won't. Ask Mimi or Sasha or Ruby. I'm not violent." I grab her hand. "I'd never hurt you. I'd protect you, yes. But I'd never hurt you."

"I don't think you'd hurt me. I'm just telling you that holes punched in walls and plates being smashed . . . those are the kinds of things that are triggering for me."

"I understand. You have my word."

Laila squeezes my hand. "How did you wind up living with Mimi at age twelve, given that you hardly ever saw your asshole father?"

I pause to gather my thoughts. To steady my racing heart. "When I lived with my mom, she used to run off with different guys for days at a time. She'd leave me with a few basic groceries and say, 'I'll be back soon.' So, this one time, right after I'd turned twelve, she was gone on one of her trips, and I wanted to make myself a grilled cheese sandwich on the stove. I don't know how it happened, since I'd made the same thing before, lots of times, but I somehow started a fire in the kitchen. I got it out, pretty quickly, without it spreading too much, thank God, but the fire department was called by a neighbor. And that's when they found out a twelve-year-old had been living alone in the apartment with no parent in sight for days and days—and that it was a common occurrence in my house. They sent me off to Child Protective Services while they looked for my mom. And when they couldn't find her, they contacted my dad, who was in prison at the time for assaulting someone. And that's when they found out my next of kin was one

Maria Savage Wilkes of Chicago, Illinois. They called and dropped the bomb on Mimi that she had a twelve-year-old grandson in Phoenix she'd never known about. She came and got me and brought me back to her little shoebox apartment, where I slept on the couch and acted like a raving asshole for almost three years, until I finally decided to give her a chance."

"Did your mother get in trouble for leaving you alone?"

I nod. "She got charged with reckless endangerment of a child after the fire, but she only got probation. To this day, she thinks I intentionally set that fire to get her into trouble."

"Oh my gosh."

"Maybe I did, subconsciously. I've certainly amassed a long track record since then of doing toxic, stupid shit as a backwards means of getting something I don't even know I want." I clamp my lips together, so I don't say something I'll regret. Something like, "Look at the way I treated you during the tour. Perfect example."

Laila knits her brows together. "I just realized . . . you go by Mimi's maiden name?"

"Yeah."

"So, your name is a stage name, after all."

"No, Savage has been my legal name since age fifteen. My mother gave me her name when I was born—Carter. But once I decided Mimi was my mother, I asked to change my name to hers. I didn't want Mimi's married name—Wilkes—since that's my father's name. Plus, Savage is a badass name."

"You're such a liar. You said you were 'born Savage.'"

I smile. "I was using a lower case 's.'"

Laila flashes me an adorable grin that sends a flock of butterflies into my stomach, and I can't help returning her smile with an even bigger one.

"You should copyright that smile, Fitzy," I say softly. "You'd make a mint."

She flushes. "There are no cameras here. We don't have to pretend anything."

"I'm not pretending a goddamned thing."

Laila's chest heaves. "Neither am I."

It's too much excitement for my body to handle gracefully. Physically twitching with arousal and excitement, relief that she's clearly beginning to trust me, I get up from my seat at the table, pull Laila up, and kiss her passionately. "Come on, beautiful," I whisper. "It's time for me to finally get to fuck you in a bed."

FORTY-FOUR

SAVAGE

As Laila rides my cock, I admire the curves of her body in the moonlight streaming through the bedroom window.

"You're gorgeous," I whisper, my pleasure ramping up and up. But I can't find the right words to convey how stunning she is to me. How perfect and addicting. Or, hell, maybe I do know the right words, but I'm too chicken to say them out loud to her. The only thing I'm sure about is that fucking Laila in this bed, in this moment, is a new level of rapture for me. I've never bared myself to a woman the way I did downstairs to Laila in the dining room. And somehow, knowing *she* knows all that shit about me, and is now riding my cock like none of it dampens her desire for me in the least, feels even hotter than the hottest hate sex.

"You feel so fucking good," I whisper, as Laila gyrates on top of me. I touch her clit and massage it round and round as she moves, and she begins snapping her hips back and forth with added enthusiasm. After a bit, Laila grips my chest and digs her nails into me, like she's hanging on by a thread. I make a guttural sound, as my eyes roll back from pleasure. She gasps out my name. My first name. Which feels amazing. That's a first during sex. And then, her interior muscles surrounding my cock release and ripple and squeeze fiercely, sending so much pleasure into my cock, I lose it, along with her.

When both our bodies have become quiet and still, Laila leans down and kisses me deeply. As her long hair falls on either side of my face, I inhale the scent of her shampoo. Revel in the taste of her lips and tongue. I run my fingertips down her bare back, feeling high. Drugged. Addicted. Gone.

"I feel high," she whispers into my lips, reading my mind.

"So do I," I admit. "Physically, like you're a drug."

We share a smile. This isn't a "hate sex high" we're feeling this time, and we both know it. Frankly, if I were to write a song about *this* kind of high, I don't know what the song would be called. This feeling is something I've never felt before. Something I can't name. Whatever it is, though, I never want it to end.

Sighing happily, Laila slides off me and lies alongside my naked body in the bed, cleaving every bit of her flesh into mine. "You really think I'm gifted as an artist?"

"One hundred percent."

"Why, exactly, did you step aside for Kendrick?"

"He had a crush on you."

"Yeah, I kinda figured. But so what? Why did you step aside for him?"

"He's my best friend. Plus, I knew he's boyfriend material, and I'm not."

"Yeah, but you don't pretend to be. Isn't that what you said in Providence, when you were bashing me for supposedly dating Malik?"

I furrow my brow. "*Supposedly* dating Malik? It sure felt like a whole lot more than 'supposedly' when he was throwing me against a wall, Laila."

Her cheeks flush. "No, yeah. I meant to say you act like you're *supposedly* not boyfriend material. You *supposedly* pretend not to be."

She's speaking gibberish all of a sudden. What am I missing? "There's no 'supposedly' about any of that, Laila. I've never pretended to be boyfriend material. I don't think anyone would make that mistake about me."

Her chest heaves. "Oh, I don't know about that. You did an awfully good impression of a guy who's grade-A 'boyfriend material' when you made me that amazing meal tonight." She swallows hard. "Listen, about Kendrick . . . I feel like I should tell you he never had a shot with me. Not with you on the tour. And probably not at all. Kendrick is the sweetest person who ever lived. But the minute I met him, I felt only platonic friendship for him. No lust. No heat."

I stroke her back. "Don't take it personally that I stepped aside for my best friend. It doesn't reflect on you. You were nothing but a vixen in a music video to me at that point. A fantasy. And Kendrick has been a better friend to me than I could ever explain to you. I wouldn't be here now without Mimi and Kendrick. They're the only reason I've got this life."

"I don't hold it against you. I think it's sweet you're a loyal friend to Kendrick."

"Plus, I hate to sound arrogant, but I knew I could have pretty much anyone else I wanted. So, why endanger my friendship with Kendrick over a girl I didn't even know, when someone else would surely catch my eye any minute?"

"Which is exactly what happened, many times over. I get it."

Fuck. That's what she still thinks? That all those groupies in her dressing rooms, that waitress in New York, all the ways I shoved my rockstar bullshit in her face, were real? Somehow, I thought she'd understood by now that I was only messing with her all those times—I thought maybe she'd understand I've only got eyes for her —and it's been that way for a very long time now—without me needing to explain it to her with words.

Fuck, fuck, fuck.

Should I come clean to her? Or would that be too big a confession on night one of our three months together? It was only yesterday that I swore I wouldn't "catch feelings" during this little charade, after all.

"Here's what I don't get," Laila says, before I've decided how much to confess to her, if anything. "Kendrick couldn't have had a crush on me when Reed first put me on the tour. I only met Kendrick at Reed's party, and the decision had already been made by then."

"Kendrick had a crush on you, even before he met you." *And so did I.* "You were his 'celebrity crush.'" *And mine, too.*

"No way." She makes an adorable face. "That's so sweet. Unfortunately, for him, though, you were *my* celebrity crush."

Hallelujah. "Well, that's convenient, because *you* were *mine.*" *There, I said it.* It's a small confession, considering what I'm holding back. But at least it's a start.

"No way," she says, her blue eyes sparkling.

"*Way.*"

Laila swats at my chest. "Okay, now I'm pissed at you for stepping aside for Kendrick—and especially that you objected to me being on the tour!"

I groan. "Laila, I only objected to you being on the tour out of self-preservation. Because I didn't want to watch you canoodling with Kendrick for three months. Because I'm that stupid and immature and selfish. Can we *please* forget everything that happened on the tour? Let's erase the whole damned thing from our memory banks and pretend none of it happened."

She's nodding furiously.

"From now on," I say, my pulse pounding, "we'll be the Savage and Laila we were downstairs in the dining room. The Savage and Laila who told each other about our dads. We'll start fresh and erase every last memory of the tour, and agree to only look forward from now on, okay?"

Laila looks bowled over. Surprisingly emotional and relieved. With a deep exhale, she throws herself at me, and I wrap her in my arms. "That sounds amazing," she murmurs into my shoulder.

"I'm so sorry, Laila," I whisper. "I fucked up right and left on that tour. I didn't know how to handle my attraction to you. Didn't want to betray my friend. I was jealous of Malik and pissed that you'd want an asshole like him over me. I was irrational and stupid, but that's me, unfortunately—irrational and stupid, a lot of the time."

"It's okay." She wipes her eyes. "The past is completely forgotten. We'll both press the reset button and start over and not mention anything either of us did, ever again."

"Thank you so much." I hug her to me. "Thank you, Laila."

For a long moment, we lie quietly, our bodies entwined in the moonlight. Suddenly, though, she lifts her head and says, "One tiny question about the past before we leave it for good. How did you know I played HORSE at Reed's party, and writhed around on the ground when I missed my shot?"

My stomach tightens. "Huh?"

"You mentioned that at the press conference, but you were nowhere near the basketball court when I did that. In fact, right after the game, I saw you hitting on a pretty woman by the pool."

I push Laila's long hair behind her bare shoulder. "I wasn't hitting on that woman. She was a reporter for *Rock 'n' Roll* and we were talking about my interview."

"I didn't know there were two reporters at that party!"

I nod. "While I was talking to the reporter, I glanced over at the basketball court, just in time to see none other than Laila Fitzgerald miss her shot and then drop to the ground like a goofball."

She giggles. "Why didn't you come inside and watch my performance with Aloha and the Goats, after I walked past you?"

"You mean, why didn't I follow you into the house, after you walked past me, flanked by Malik and Kendrick?"

"Oh."

I chuckle. "That's when I decided, once and for all, to give Kendrick a wide berth to take his shot."

Laila twists her mouth but says nothing.

"Any other questions before we leave the past and never, ever think about it again?" I ask.

Laila pauses. "No. I think I'm good. You?"

"I'm good."

She makes a goofy, cartoonish series of expressions and sounds, which I quickly find out, based on her next words, is her version of "erasing" the hard drive in her brain. She says, in a computerized voice, "Reed's party and the tour are now officially erased from the hard drive of Laila Fitzgerald's brain. *Goodbye.*" She closes her eyes and lets her tongue hang out.

I laugh. "You dork. I can't believe they hired *you* as *my* babysitter."

"I fooled them all."

"You sure did." When she yawns, I add, "Time for bed. We've got a big day tomorrow. We need our beauty sleep. Which, by the way, is what *you* should be saying to *me*, babysitter."

"Oh, I should put on my zit cream." With that, she hops out of bed and pads out of the room, much to my disappointment. And that's it. All hope I had Laila would sleep here in this room with me—

Oh. She's back. Carrying a toiletry bag and heading into my bathroom with a little wink. I hear a commotion in there. The shower turning on. And a moment later, the sound of Laila singing "Fireflies" by 22 Goats in the shower wafts into the bedroom.

My heart thumping, I head into the bathroom, step into the shower with her, and kiss her. And, instantly, my body makes it clear I'm damned happy to see her. I wash her wet, naked skin. Kiss her breasts. And when I can't resist any longer, drop to my knees and eat her out, with hot water running down my face and back.

After she comes, she returns the favor, while I press my palms against the plexiglass of the shower and groan like a yeti. When I come, we indulge in another round of washing, kissing, and caressing. But finally, she smacks my ass and tells me we need to get our beauty sleep, and we begrudgingly drag our asses out of the shower.

After drying off, I secure a white towel around my waist and watch Laila applying cream to her face.

"It's a crying shame condoms don't work in water, don't you think?" I say, leaning my hip against the bathroom counter.

Laila stops what she's doing and looks at me. "Is that your way of asking me if I'm on birth control?"

I grin. "It sure is."

Laila smirks. "Yes, I've got an IUD. But that's only to prevent me from getting knocked up accidentally. My firm rule is 'No wrapper, no dice, unless we're in a committed relationship and I trust you *completely*.'"

I furrow my brow, as Laila resumes her nighttime routine. I think she just implied she doesn't trust me completely. That's what she meant by that, right? "I've already promised I'm only going to have sex with you for the next three months," I say. "That's basically the same thing as a 'committed relationship.' And I promise you can trust me completely."

Not stopping what she's doing in the mirror, Laila says, "How shall I put this, Adrian? Oh, I know. *I don't.*"

"Trust me?"

"Correct. Not completely. But don't be offended. My complete trust is *very* hard to get. And you've got quite a reputation."

"I thought we agreed to forget the past."

"We did. But even so, I could google you right now, in the *present,* and instantly find out you're not the best bet to let raw-dog me."

"So, is your concern that I'm not clean or that I'm going to cheat on you? Because I've already promised I won't have sex with anyone else, and that's a promise you can take to the bank, ten out of ten times. On the other hand, if you're concerned I'm not clean, then I'm sure we could arrange for a doctor to test us both tomorrow, either on the set at lunchtime or here at the house after work."

Laila considers my suggestion for a long moment, making my heart thump in my ears with anticipation. Finally, she says, "Do you swear on your love for Mimi you won't sleep with anyone else, the whole time we're living together?"

I grimace. "Can we please leave my grandmother out of this conversation about raw-dogging you?"

She laughs. "Fair enough. Do you swear on your life?"

"I do. I won't touch anyone else while we're living together. I've already promised that in writing."

"To the *show*, in order to avoid the risk of a 'cheating scandal.' What I'm asking is for you to promise *me,* personally. And then, to keep that promise, no matter what."

I walk to her, cup her face in my palms, and look into her blue eyes. "I hereby promise, Laila Fitzgerald, that I, Adrian Savage, will have sex with you, and only you, and nobody else, for the entire time we're living together, so help me God."

Laila blushes. "Okay, let's do it, then, as soon as we get the 'all clear' from a doctor. And by 'doctor' I mean a real one—not an actor who plays one on TV."

I snicker. "I'll make it happen tomorrow."

"Cool. Now, come on. Your babysitter says it's time for bed." She takes my hand and pulls me into the bedroom. And then, to my thrill and relief, she guides me into bed under the covers and crawls in right next to me, obviously intending to stay with me.

I try not to smile too big. I try to act like I knew all along Laila was going to sleep with me here in the master bedroom. "Goodnight, Fitzy," I say casually. Like it's no big thing. But I'm smiling from ear to ear.

"Goodnight, Adrian," she replies. And even though she's now rolled onto her side, facing away from me, I can physically hear her wide, beautiful smile from here.

FORTY-FIVE

LAILA

"Welcome to the new season of *Sing Your Heart Out!*" Sunshine Vaughn, our famous host, bellows from the large stage, and the studio audience behind the judges' table bursts into applause.

My heart thumping wildly, I clutch Savage's thigh under the table and squeeze, letting him know I'm freaking out right now, and he places his hand on top of mine, letting me know we're in this crazy thing together.

"And now, let's say hello to our *four* judges!" Sunshine booms, gesturing to the panel. She introduces each of us, one by one, and each judge waves or blows kisses—or halfheartedly smirks like they'd rather be anywhere else, in the case of Savage—as their name is called.

Sunshine says, "Before we get started with the first audition, let's take a look at the journey our contestants have traveled to get here today—to be able to audition in front of our judges and a live studio audience!"

The live cameras cut out and a pre-taped package begins playing, and everyone at the judges' table exhales for a moment.

Savage leans into me and whispers, "You feeling okay?"

"Honestly, no. I'm suffering from major imposter syndrome right now."

"Bah." He squeezes my hand under the table. "Just pretend Sunshine is Aloha and each contestant a crew member and you'll be fine."

I pull a face of surprise. "That's great advice. Thanks."

Savage winks. "I get it right, once in a while."

"Actually, more than *once*, if last night was any indication." I wink suggestively, and that's all the invitation this horny man needs to lean in and kiss me.

Instantly, at the touch of Savage's lips to mine, the audience behind us bursts into wild whoops and cheers, and there's no doubt they're not reacting to the video.

The director peeks out from behind a monitor. "Savage and Laila!" He motions to the cameras, looking annoyed. "See how all the little red lights are *off*? We want you to make the audience react like that when one of the little red lights is *on*."

Nadine, our executive producer, appears out of nowhere, looking frazzled.

"I already told them," the director says, cutting her off at the pass. But, apparently, she feels the need to say it anyway. "Guys," Nadine says, looking at Savage and me. "The cameras have to be *on* when you whip the audience into a frenzy."

"We're sorry," I say, speaking for both of us, even though Savage's facial expression makes it clear he's not sorry in the slightest—that in fact, he's presently imagining both the director and Nadine eating a bag of dicks. I add, "We didn't mean to whip anyone into a frenzy. We simply got swept up in the moment and forgot about the audience and cameras for a second there. It won't happen again."

Nadine pauses, looking surprised by my explanation. And, suddenly, I realize I just admitted that Savage and I kissed off-camera, not because we're newbies who forgot to wait for the cameras to be trained on us, but because we kissed for real. For nothing but the sheer pleasure of it.

"Oh," Nadine says, her eyebrow raised. She smirks at the director before returning to Savage and me. "No worries at all. We know there will be a learning curve for you two, so we've folded that into the shooting schedule. We can do reshoots and edits throughout the audition shows, so it's no biggie. The problem will come later, when we switch to the 'live taping' format for the weekly singing competition. At that point, you two are going to have to be a well-oiled machine. But for now, we'll just have you redo the kiss."

Nadine and the director both leave, and the minute they're gone, Savage leans into me and says, "This is going to be even more painful than I thought."

"Nah, I'm sure it'll be lots of fun, once we get the hang of it."

He looks at me like I'm crazy. "No, it'll be flat-out torture, from beginning to end. All I can say is thank God you're here with me."

My heart skips a beat.

"Hey, everyone!" Sunshine says to the studio audience, after conferring with Nadine. "In a minute here, I'm going to chitchat with the judges. And when I get to Savage, he's going to kiss Laila again, the same way he did a moment ago. And when he does, will you folks please whoop and cheer, the same way you did the last time?"

The audience claps enthusiastically.

"I knew I could I count on you! Let's cheer even more loudly than last time, yes?"

I look at Savage and roll my eyes and he pulls a face like he wants to bang his head against the table.

A moment later, Sunshine begins going down the line of judges, chatting with Jon, and then Aloha, followed by me, asking us if we're excited to kick things off. Yes, yes, yes. We're so excited. When she gets to Savage, however, and asks him if he's excited about the season, he smiles at me and says, "I'll say this: I'm excited to be here with Laila."

"Aw," the audience says, along with me, just as Savage leans forward and kisses me. As promised, the audience combusts when Savage's lips touch mine, which prompts me to break away and act like I'm flustered and embarrassed by the crowd's boisterous reaction. For his part, however, Savage leans back in his chair and flashes a look that says, "Yeah, I fucked her three times last night." And the audience eats it up.

There's a bit more pageantry from Sunshine, until, finally, she introduces the first audition of the season—a blue-haired cutie named Addison Swain from Madison, Wisconsin, age eighteen. At the sound of her name, Addison walks onstage, looking nervous and adorable. She greets the judges and Sunshine and says this is a dream come true. After a little chatter, she performs a bit of "Titanium" by Sia—instantly establishing, in my opinion, she's the one to beat this season. I mean, holy hell, this blue-haired pixie can *sing*!

When Addison finishes her performance, the audience goes ballistic. As they should. On impulse, I bolt out of my chair and give Addison a standing ovation—which makes the girl burst into soggy tears. When the audience's applause dies down, Jon, Aloha, and I give Addison our effusive praise, with me being the most effusive. And, finally, all eyes turn to Savage, who's apparently already positioned himself as The Hard-to-Impress Judge.

"I agree with everyone else," Savage says calmly. "Addison, you've got some serious pipes and stage presence. You get an unreserved 'atta girl' from me."

The audience loses their collective mind. And, just this fast, it's clear Savage's opinion is going to hold more weight than anyone else's this season. Why? I don't know, exactly. All I know is that Savage's opinion has always held a whole lot of weight for me, too.

"Okay, judges," Sunshine says. "It's time to decide if you want to use one of your valuable tokens on Addison, in order to mark her as someone you want to haggle over on Draft Day!"

Jon and Aloha say they adored Addison's performance, but they're going to pass, since it's early days yet. But Savage and I both throw in our precious tokens, signifying we plan to fight over Addison, tooth and nail, when the time comes, and the audience claps and screams their approval of our choice.

And away we go, seeing audition after audition after Addison's, with varying degrees of success. Finally, the long day is over, and Nadine appears at the judges' table, bursting with enthusiasm. She tells Savage and me we "killed it" and that we should continue doing everything as we did today. I thank Nadine effusively, feeling the weight of the world lifted off my shoulders, while Savage, predictably, says nothing.

After a bit, Nadine asks Savage to come with her backstage. "My boss brought his thirteen-year-old to the taping today," she explains. "And apparently, she's a *huge* Fugitive Summer fan."

"I'm pretty tired, Nadine," Savage says, much to my shock. Dude. This woman is our boss and she's trying to impress *her* boss. Does Savage not understand workplace politics at all?

"It'll only take a few minutes," Nadine says. "I'd be grateful."

"Go on," I say in a casual tone, but my eyes are screaming, "Don't be an idiot! This woman signs the check you split with me!"

"Uh, okay," Savage says, peeling his gaze off mine. "I'd be happy to do it." He shoots me a look that says, *Happy now?* And I shoot him one that says, *Yes, I am, dumbass. Thank you.*

Savage leaves with Nadine, throwing over his shoulder as he goes, "I'll come to your dressing room when I'm done, *babe*."

"Okay, *babe*," I reply, and then giggle at the wink he shoots me, just before turning away.

"Laila."

I turn and discover Aloha standing before me, her famous green eyes sparkling.

"Hey, girl," I say. "What a day, huh? I'm exhausted."

"Every audition day is always exhausting," she says. "Hey, will you come hang out with me in my dressing room while I change? I'd love to chat with you about your first day."

"Great."

As we walk, Aloha and I talk casually about the day. Mostly, about the amazing talent we've seen. But the second we get into Aloha's dressing room, and she's closed the door behind us, she whirls around and whisper-shouts, "What the hell is going on with you and Savage?"

FORTY-SIX

LAILA

"What do you mean what's going on?" I say to Aloha, taken aback.

She drags me to a couch on the far side of her dressing room. "I mean you and Savage couldn't keep your hands off each other all day, even when the cameras were off. You exchanged googly-eyed looks and goofy smiles, *even when the cameras were off*. And you giggled at *everything* that man said, even when it wasn't funny, even when the cameras were off. So, I'm asking you, 'What the heck is going on between you and that man that you haven't told me,' because I know you and this is exactly how you act when you're gone, baby, gone!"

I flop onto the couch and rub my face. "You nailed it. I'm gone, baby, gone."

"Oh, girl."

"I'm in big trouble here, Aloha." I throw up my hands. "Savage is The Beast and I'm Belle and last night was our snowball fight!"

Aloha gasps. "No."

"*Yes!*"

"Holy hell, Laila. The boy gives you a few orgasms and

suddenly you've got amnesia about all the times he made you cry during the tour?"

"Well, it wasn't just a *few* orgasms," I mutter, snickering. And when Aloha chastises me nonverbally, I add, "Okay, look, I know Savage was a colossal jerk to me during the tour. But I wasn't exactly a saint to him."

"You didn't deserve what he did to you, though. That tirade in Atlanta. The groupies he brought to your dressing rooms. The groupie he fucked in Vegas, mere *hours* after having sex with you."

"I know. But I found out he'd gotten some terrible news the morning of his tirade in Atlanta. And he thought I was dating Malik when he brought all those groupies into my dressing rooms. And it's not like we'd agreed to be *exclusive* when he banged that groupie in Vegas. So, all things considered—"

"He'd sent you a text, begging you to come to his room, mere minutes before banging that groupie, Laila!"

I pout. "Yes, I know, Aloha. But we've both agreed to forgive and forget all sins committed during the tour by either of us. We're going to press the reset button and see what happens and I'm excited about that."

Aloha raises her eyebrows. "You think you can do that?"

"I do. Now that I've had a chance to get to know him on a deeper level, I think I can forgive and forget and move on. I've told him that I expect and require monogamy while we're living together, and he said he totally understands and promises to be with nobody but me. And not because of his contract or the fake romance. But for *real*. And I believe him."

Aloha looks skeptical.

"What's the downside?" I blurt. "He's hot as hell and I'm stuck with him in a fancy house for three months. I might as well enjoy myself."

Aloha smirks. "Well, that's true. I just don't want you getting hurt, that's all."

"I'll be fine. Thank you."

"Regardless, I think you should bring it down a notch, on-camera, just to give yourself a little headroom, so to speak—room for the on-camera romance to grow."

I furrow my brow. "Nadine said she was thrilled with what we did today."

"Yeah, I heard. But let me offer some unsolicited advice. I've been in this industry my whole life, so trust me when I say you can't give the suits everything they want on day one, or there's nowhere for your performance to go. Trust me, they always want more, more, *more*, until their expectations feel impossible to fulfill. You and Savage should leave yourselves some room for your 'romance' to blossom each week on the show, or else, by the finale, they're going to want you to give birth on-air."

I laugh.

"I'm only half-kidding."

I process that for a moment. "Here's my predicament, though. The producers slipped a cheap buy-out clause into my contract, and I'm worried if the romance storyline isn't a ratings bonanza out of the gate, the producers will axe me from the show."

"Shoot, Laila. Daria was okay with a buy-out clause?"

"We had no choice. The producers wouldn't do the deal without it, and I wanted to do the deal. Daria said the chances of them invoking the clause are almost nothing, because she thinks we'll pull in record ratings. But, still, just knowing that clause is in my contract like a ticking time bomb is messing with my head. It makes me not want to give anything less than a hundred percent, right out of the gate."

Aloha pats my arm. "Don't worry, Laila. Like you said, Nadine is thrilled with you and Savage. I'm probably just being paranoid. Nadine was the executive producer of *The Engagement Experiment* when it first launched, so I know for a fact she's hard-wired to wring every drop of romance she can out of every situation, at full blast."

"I'll keep that in mind and maybe try to pace myself a little bit more, on-camera."

"And also maybe try to keep your wits about you a tiny bit, off-camera, too?" She smiles. "Honey, I want you to be happy. And I want this thing with Savage to work out great for you. I'm just saying you cried a whole lot during that tour. And I don't want that boy to make you cry again, this time around."

I pat her arm. "I hear you and appreciate what you're saying. But it's going to be okay. Like I said, we're both pretending the past doesn't exist and taking each other as we are now. Trust me, that strategy absolves me of almost as many sins as Savage."

Aloha looks at me for a very long moment with nothing but kindness in her eyes. "Well, that sounds like a great thing, then. I'm happy for you."

"But you think I'm pulling a 'Laila.' Sprinting ahead with blinders on and ignoring every red flag."

Aloha pauses. "No. I mean, yes. But I don't blame you. What I think is that you're a gorgeous, passionate, horny-ass woman who's stuck for three months in the mansion from *The Engagement Experiment* with a rock star who regularly gives you multiple orgasms that make you scream in ecstasy. Frankly, I don't think you're pulling a 'Laila' this time, as much I think you're pulling a 'red-blooded human.'"

FORTY-SEVEN
LAILA

"Cheers!" I say, holding up a glass of champagne in one hand and my phone in video mode in the other. While recording a live video, Savage and I are sitting side by side on the couch in our living room, toasting our first day of shooting with a bottle of Dom Perignon sent home with us by Nadine. Despite the sobriety clause in Savage's contract, Nadine gave us the bottle on two conditions. One, we had to promise we'd open the champagne in a live video tonight and joyfully toast on-camera to our first day as judges. And two, Savage had to promise no photos of his dick or bare ass would join his already robust collection on the internet.

"Cheers, baby," Savage says, clinking my glass with his and kissing my cheek.

We sip our champagne and talk about the day's shoot, telling everyone watching we can't wait for them to see the amazing talent we witnessed today when the first episode airs in a few weeks. We trade playful banter about who's going to wind up with the best team after Draft Day—the notorious day on *Sing Your Heart Out* when the judges haggle and jockey to wind up with the best contestants from those they've given a precious token. And, finally, we wrap up our video with a little kiss on the mouth and a joyful "See you next time!"

When I turn off my camera, I plop my phone onto the coffee table in front of us and exhale. "I think it's distinctly possible by the end of the season, these daily videos will feel like a colossal pain in the ass."

"By the *end* of the season?" Savage says, his expression making it clear he already feels that way.

A buzz simultaneously emanates from both our phones on the coffee table, and we grab them, curious to see who's texted us. It's Reed Rivers, telling us he wants us to write a "sappy, classic love song" as soon as possible—a single we'll perform in the show's finale and release that same day. Reed writes, "Send me the bones of the song within a week or so, to give us enough time to get it fully produced before the finale."

I look up from my phone and wait a beat for Savage to finish reading. When he looks up, I say, "I think a week to write one song is doable. Do you?"

"In theory, yeah. But I've never written a 'sappy, classic love song' before. I've never even written a straight-up love song."

"You've heard my songs. Sappy love songs aren't exactly in my wheelhouse, either." It's the truth. I'm known for writing breakup songs. You-did-me-wrong songs. Or, on occasion, damn-boy-you're-so-fine songs. But never the kind of song Reed has requested. "I still think we can do it, though," I say. "All we have to do is treat this like a creative writing project. We'll write the song as if we're writing it about some other couple—a perfect, sweet one who's 'couple goals.'"

Savage scowls. "'Perfect and sweet' isn't my goal, Laila."

I roll my eyes. "It's not mine, either. But you know what *is* my goal? Making a whole lot of money off this song. And 'perfect and sweet' is the world's couple goals, so that's what we'll write. God help us, if we infuse too much of our actual personalities into the lyrics, the song will be about a couple fucking in a shower."

Savage's face lights up. "And in a bathtub, a hot tub, a pool . . . a rainstorm . . ."

I snicker. True to his word, Savage arranged for a doctor to come to the set today during one of our breaks—a real one, not a dude who plays one on TV—and we both got our "all clear" results during the drive home.

"You know what I think we should do to get into the mindset to write this song?" I say. "We'll pretend we're writing the soundtrack to a romantic movie—like, you know, something unapologetically sweet. Like, I don't know, we'll pretend we've been asked to write the 'big song' for a remake of *Ghost*."

"I haven't seen that one. But I get your drift, I think."

"You haven't seen *Ghost*?" I shout incredulously.

Savage shrugs. "I think this is going to be a running theme, Laila. So I'd ration your outrage, if I were you."

"But *Ghost* is one of the greatest movies ever made! I got my pottery wheel after seeing that one. It's so romantic. A total tear-jerker."

"Yecch. I hate tear jerkers."

"Well, too bad, because we're watching it now. *Ghost* is the *perfect* movie to inspire our song!" I pick up the remote control exuberantly. "Fire up the popcorn maker, Adrian! We're going to snuggle up and watch the most romantic movie ever made, and then sit down and write the sweetest, sappiest love song ever written in fifteen minutes flat!"

So much for writing a love song after watching *Ghost*. The only thing that movie inspired Savage to do was demand that I immediately teach him how to work my pottery wheel. And I'm such a dork for my wheel, I leaped off the couch and sprinted up here with glee to get the thing fired up. Yes, I'm well aware Savage's request was nothing but a ruse to be able to make out while using the wheel, the same way Demi and Patrick do in the movie. But I don't care. I'd never pass up the chance to watch Savage's talented fingers molding wet, spinning clay. Plus, bonus points, Savage is shirtless as he works, and his face is wearing an expression of extreme concentration. In short, he's fatally gorgeous right now.

"How are you already so good at this?" I say, mesmerized by the bowl taking shape underneath his fingertips. He's making it for Mimi, of course, as a Christmas present, he said, even though he's already bought the woman a house for Christmas.

"It took me weeks to get anything to take shape that symmetrically," I marvel as Savage slowly continues coaxing the clay into form. "You've done this before, haven't you? You lied."

Savage chuckles. "I swear I've never done this. I've always been pretty good with my hands, though. This feels intuitive to me."

Damn straight, you're good with your hands, I think. I watch for a moment longer, before putting up my palm. "Okay, I think that's enough. You should stop now."

Savage doesn't stop.

"Adrian, seriously," I say. "Stop now. If you make the clay too thin on the edges, it'll flop over."

"I just want to make the top rim a bit thinner."

"If you overwork the clay—"

"Nooo!" Savage shouts dramatically as the edge of his creation flops over and then wobbles asymmetrically on the wheel, before abruptly turning into nothing but a marred, spinning blob. Savage lifts his bare foot from the wheel's pedal, bringing the turntable to a stop, and looks at me. He grimaces adorably. "Sorry, what were you saying?"

I giggle. "It shouldn't be too hard to fix. If it is, we'll start again. That's life. In the meantime, though . . ." I get up and move to him, spread his thighs wide, enough to accommodate me kneeling between them, and then look up at him and say, "As it turns out, watching you making pottery is a huge turn-on for me."

Savage smolders down at me, his face awash in lust. "That's a good thing, since it turns out, you watching me making pottery turns *me* on."

"What *doesn't* turn you on, Adrian?"

He touches my face, smearing clay onto my cheek. "Nothing, as long as you're nearby." He bites his lower lip. "Take off your clothes for me, unless you want me to get clay all over them. One way or another, I want those clothes off."

I rise and comply with his request, while he proceeds to peel off his own clothes, his clay-covered hands be damned.

When we're both naked, Savage resumes his chair before me, his cock straining. So, I resume my prior kneeling position and take his erection into my mouth. As his pleasure ramps up, Savage reaches behind me, and a moment later, I feel the sensation of wet clay being smeared onto my bare back. And then, my left shoulder. My skin alive and my heart racing, I stop what I'm doing, pulling my mouth off him with a loud pop—and then dip my hand into the wet clay on the wheel behind me. When I turn back around, I smear clay across the grooves and ridges of Savage's cut abs, while swirling my tongue across the tip of his cock.

When I'm finished painting his abdomen with clay, I lick him from his balls, all the way to his tip, and then purr, "Now you're a real-life version of the *David*."

"And you're my *Venus de Milo*," he replies, not missing a beat. He adds, "With arms, of course." To emphasize that last point, he smears clay down my left arm, and then my right. He grabs more clay, takes my face in his palms, and kisses me. After that, he pulls me to standing along with him and smears even more wet clay across my belly and ass. He bends down and devours my breasts and nipples for a bit, making me shudder and moan softly, before smearing those areas with wet clay, as well. "You're a work of art, Laila," he whispers, his dark eyes blazing and his tone passionate.

I feel like I've got a jackhammer in my chest, as well as one between my legs. Breathing hard, I guide Savage back to sitting, gather some wet clay onto my fingertips, and smear it onto the bridge of his perfect nose. Shaking with arousal, I straddle him in his chair—he's the hottest I've ever seen him right now, and that includes the times I've had drool running down my chin while watching him onstage—and then take Savage's big, thick, gorgeous cock inside me, all the way, making him groan loudly as I slide down. I know when Savage suggested we get tested by a doctor, he wasn't envisioning this particular scenario. But I can't imagine a better way to kick off our condom-less adventure.

As my palms cup Savage's cheeks, leaving clay all over them, Savage grips my back, leaving more clay on me. I move my body energetically on top of him, rubbing myself against him in just the right way—and soon, I find myself erupting with a delicious orgasm that causes me to scream loudly with pleasure.

As my body releases, Savage's does too. He growls as he comes and clutches me, hard. For a long moment, we remain intertwined, our clay-streaked bodies slack. Our lungs working hard. Our hearts beating in tandem.

"So . . ." he says on an exhale. "Did you get inspired to write a sappy love song while I was railing you?"

I laugh. "I believe I railed *you*, sir."

"And quite well, I might add."

Smiling, I reach behind me and grab a handful of wet clay and then caress every inch of Savage's smooth forehead, sculpted nose, chiseled cheeks, and steel chin with both sets of fingertips, like I'm a facialist at a fancy spa, and Savage is my client. "You're so freaking beautiful," I whisper, and his body underneath me physically shudders in reply. I nuzzle his nose with mine, stealing some of the clay I've wiped on him. "I feel drugged by you, Adrian," I whisper. "I feel high as a kite when I'm around you."

"Laila," he whispers. And for a long moment, we stare into each other's eyes, neither of us moving.

"Wait here," I say. "Before this moment ends, I want to get a photo of you."

He grabs my forearm. "No, Laila. Don't go."

"I'll be right back."

"Don't take a photo."

I knit my brows. "But you look so beautiful—like a statue. I want to remember this moment."

Savage's usual swagger is nowhere to be found. He's earnest now. *Vulnerable.* And breathtakingly beautiful. "For your own memories?" he asks. "Not to post? Because I don't want you to post a photo of me like this with some cringey caption that says, 'Look what happens when I try to teach my boyfriend to use my pottery wheel!'"

Oh, my heart. The look on his gorgeous face is making my heart feel like it's physically twisting. "I only want a photo for *me*," I assure him. "Not to post. Not to brag. Just to remember."

Savage exhales and shoots me a lopsided smile that says more than a thousand words ever could. He drops his hand from my arm, freeing me to go, and whispers, "Only if you'll let me take a photo of you, too, for the exact same reason."

FORTY-EIGHT
LAILA

"Can you believe we're heading into the final day of auditions?" Sunshine Vaughn says into the camera. We've been shooting auditions for the past two weeks now, assembling enough footage for the show's editors to cobble together the first four episodes. Throughout the shoot thus far, Savage and I have been sitting side by side at the judges' table, barely able to keep our hands off each other. If we're not physically touching, we're shooting each other lascivious looks and flirtatious smiles. When we're offering our feedback to whichever contestant onstage, we almost always wind up playfully teasing each other or laughing at each other's jokes. Basically, we've behaved on-camera the same way we do when we're home alone. We act addicted and head over heels *on*-camera because that's exactly how we're both feeling, in real life.

As a matter of fact, real life with Savage has been the most fun I've ever had. When we get home from work, we eat whatever fancy meal our private chef has made for us. And then, after doing our required live video for fans, we call our families and say hello, and then plug our phones onto their chargers and leave them there for the rest of the night. After that, we attack each other, basically.

Usually, in order to check off another box on our proverbial bingo card by having sex in yet another room or area of our massive house. So far, we've been making incredible progress in our game. Thank God, "Let's Have Sex in Every Room of the House" isn't a drinking game, or Savage and I would be blitzed out of our minds every night.

Amazingly, though, sex isn't even the best thing Savage and I do together, as great as it is. The best thing is just . . . hanging out. We work out together in our home gym. We watch movies while snuggled on our couch. Besides watching *Ghost*, we've watched *Fast Times at Ridgemont High*, too, which was hilarious. We've also watched some fabulous porn. And by that, I mean we watched *Beauty and the Beast* for me and *Mean Girls* for Savage. Oh, and we've played cards, as silly as that sounds. The games Mimi taught Savage as a boy and loves to play with him whenever he visits her.

The only thing not going amazingly well for Savage and me? Writing the duet. Try as we might, we can't write that damned love song. I thought it'd be easy to do, considering how prolific Savage and I usually are as songwriters, but, for some reason, we can't come up with an idea that leads to anything good. It's frustrating, to say the least. Not to mention, anxiety-producing, since we're now a full week past the deadline Reed initially gave.

Speaking for myself, I haven't been able to write the damned song because, every time I look into Savage's dark eyes, I feel anxious that whatever idea I might be thinking about, whatever sappy and sweet suggestion I might make, will hit too close to home. Be too honest. Too vulnerable. Something Savage will know is the truth, rather than part of a "creative writing assignment," which is what we've both agreed the song should be. And, just like that, I can't come up with an idea I'm willing to speak out loud to save my life.

I have no idea why *Savage* has had writer's block, as well, but I admit I'm hoping he's been running up against the same dilemma as me. Or maybe that's just wishful thinking. He said, right from the start, sappy loves songs aren't his thing. So, more likely than not, he's simply waiting for me to take the lead.

Sunshine's cheery voice yanks me from my reverie. Looking into a camera, she says, "Another batch of auditions, and then we'll move on to Draft Day, when our judges will get to finalize their teams. After that, we'll have Mentor Day, and then . . . *finally* . . . our live weekly singing competition will begin!"

The audience roars with excitement.

Sunshine looks at the judges' table. "Are you excited for everything that's coming, judges?"

The first three judges reply, like good soldiers, that we're excited and raring to go. Whoop-de-doo! But Savage being Savage, he gives Sunshine nothing but a half-hearted thumbs up and an expression that says, "If I must." Of course, the studio audience is enthralled by Savage's disdain, since by now, that's become his *thing* on the show—acting like the whole exercise causes him physical pain. It works so well for him, I think, only because, on occasion, he unexpectedly breaks free from his usual disdain to grace the world with a beaming smile or effusive praise, usually saying something so perfect on those rare occasions, he makes whatever contestant he's speaking to burst into tears and the entire audience swoon.

Our host returns with a huge smile to the camera aimed at her. "Until next time, I'm Sunshine Vaughn, reminding you to . . ." The studio audience joins in on the show's famous sign-off: "*Sing. Your. Heart out!*" And then, as the audience applauds, we four judges do what we always do at this point—we stand and applaud and dance to the theme song blaring in the studio.

Finally, when the theme song ends, we four judges stop celebrating and swiftly head backstage with some bodyguards, so we won't get mobbed with requests for selfies and autographs from the studio audience. But as our foursome makes our way backstage, Nadine approaches the group, stopping our movement.

"Savage and Laila?" Nadine says. "Can I talk to you for a moment—perhaps in Savage's dressing room?"

My stomach drops into my toes. When the big boss says she wants to talk to you, in private, it's probably not a good thing, no matter how well the past two weeks of shooting have gone. I have to think that's especially true when you're a newbie cast member who strong-armed her way onto the show in the first place, and the producers insisted on reserving an early termination clause in her contract that's not in anybody else's.

When we get to Savage's dressing room, Nadine closes the door behind us and gestures to the couch. "Please."

Savage and I take the couch, our body language stiff, while Nadine sits in an armchair across from us, her body language confident and unapologetic. This woman has been the big boss on this show since its inception, and *The Engagement Experiment* before that, so her demeanor not surprisingly communicates power and confidence in no uncertain terms.

"So, guys," Nadine says on an exhale, clasping her manicured hands in her lap. "First off, I want to compliment you on your performance these past two weeks. You've both *far* exceeded our expectations."

I sigh with relief and grab Savage's hand. "Thank you. I'm so glad you're happy."

"We're *thrilled*. You've been selling the romance beyond our wildest dreams. You're either amazing actors, or . . ." She raises her eyebrow and lets her facial expression finish the sentence: *Or you're not acting at all.*

I look at Savage, who isn't looking at me, and can't help noticing his breathing has become noticeably stilted and his jaw tight. I return my gaze to Nadine, my cheeks radiating with heat.

"Either way," Nadine continues, "we've been blown away by how convincing and authentic you two have seemed, both here onset and in your behind-the-scenes videos from home. When the first episodes begin airing in a few weeks, nobody could possibly doubt the authenticity of your relationship. Which, of course, was *initially* our primary goal."

Initially.

Oh, fuck.

Something about the way she emphasized that word unsettles me. If that was only the *initial* goal, then what's the goal . . . *now?*

"Now that we've got our *initial* bases covered so well," Nadine continues, once again emphasizing that same word, "we're going to shift course. Add a little conflict to the love story, to make all the sweetness and happiness feel all the more special for the audience."

Fuck.

Fuck.

Fuck!

In a flash, I know Aloha was right. We've given the suits too good a love story, right out of the gate, with nowhere to go but a live birth in the finale . . . or, in the alternative, a little trouble in paradise.

Nadine leans forward in her armchair. "Remember how you two were at each other's throats during our very first conference call? That's the dynamic we want to see during the last batch of auditions tomorrow, and then during Draft Day and Mentor Day, too. Sound good?" Her question is rhetorical. She barrels ahead without pausing. "During our break for the holidays, my team and I will pour over all the footage while editing together the first batch of episodes, and at that point, we'll decide what direction we want to go next during the 'live' singing competition."

I look at Savage, my heart crashing and my eyes wide with panic, and discover he's every bit as poker-faced and cool as a cucumber as I am freaking out. Which makes sense, I suppose, since he has no idea about the early termination clause in my contract. To him, this is all white noise. A request he isn't going to grant. While to me, this is catastrophic. Plainly, the producers are trying to figure out the best storyline for The Savage and Laila Show—which actually means, when you boil it down, they're trying to figure out if maybe The Savage and Laila Show should become The Savage Show, sans Laila, like they'd initially wanted in the first place.

Nadine says, "We want to see 'hate-lust' from you guys! We

want to see the same 'I want to fuck you to death!' energy that was in your famous meme! Bring us some of the fire from that viral video of you two fighting on the sidewalk. Bring us *heat*. Anger. *Danger!*" She chuckles with glee. "We want sniping, banter, and combativeness—the kind of hostility that'll make our audience imagine you fighting at the judges' table by *day* . . . and having angry but amazing hate-sex by *night!*"

My mouth hangs open. "But . . . Nadine, we don't hate each other anymore. We did all that stuff when we did."

"I never hated you, Laila," Savage says, speaking for the first time during this conversation.

"It doesn't matter what you feel. Fake it! The truth is that every passionate relationship straddles a thin line between love and hate. Or *lust* and hate." She raises an eyebrow, letting us know she thinks the word "lust" is a far more appropriate descriptor than "love," when it comes to Savage and me.

"But . . ." I say. I look at Savage again, but he's no help. So, I return to Nadine. "Are you *sure* that's what the audience will want to see from us? During that first conference call, you said it was your top priority to make sure our romance was *totally* believable. You wanted something that would make the audience 'swoon.' And I think we can agree that's what we've delivered."

"Absolutely. Although, to be clear, our top priority was never making the romance believable. That was a means to an end. Our actual top priority was, and still is, and always will be, supplying a show that captures maximum ratings. Now that we're confident the initial footage we've gotten will convince everyone your relationship is real, we feel the next batch of episodes should offer a plot twist that will keep viewers glued to their TVs and coming back for more. We want the audience to worry a bit that your relationship might be on the rocks. We want them rooting for you to find your way back to each other—and tuning in, breathlessly, each week, to see if, in the end, you two make it to a happily ever after."

I press my lips together, feeling flabbergasted.

In the face of my silence, Nadine addresses Savage. "Do you understand what we want?"

Savage snakes his arm behind me on the couch in an apparent show of solidarity. His jaw muscles pulse briefly, before he licks his lips and says, "I understand the meaning of your words, yes. But as far as I'm concerned, Nadine, I'm contractually obligated to be a judge on a reality TV singing competition and Laila's devoted boyfriend. I'm *not,* however, contractually obligated to become, nor am I interested in becoming, a pawn on a dating show. I'm not a contestant on *The Engagement Experiment,* Nadine. That was never the deal."

Nadine's dark eyes flicker. "You both signed on to 'sell' the romance to a television audience. And, trust me, I know better than anyone on this planet, literally, how to do that. Based on my expertise, I've determined the audience will enjoy a bit more 'Vintage Savage and Laila' for a few episodes, as a foil to the 'Blissfully Happy and In Love Savage and Laila' we've come to know and love these past few weeks." She flashes me a pointed look that telepathically screams at me to convince Savage to pivot with me. "You get it, don't you, Laila? This is reality TV, not reality. We need to keep the audience entertained."

"I understand the meaning of your words, yes," I reply, echoing Savage's comment a moment ago. His arm is still around my shoulders and I want to show him the solidarity he clearly thinks he's showing me. But when Nadine's eyes harden, I can't help adding, "I'm willing to do my best to deliver what you want, if I can. I'm just not sure, at this point, that I can."

"Oh, I have faith in you," Nadine replies, and her tone makes me feel like there's a subtextual "or else" hidden in her statement. With a plastic smile, she slaps her thighs and rises from her armchair. "Show us 'Vintage Savage and Laila' tomorrow, during the last round of auditions, and then during Draft Day and Mentor Day, too. After that, we'll take the long holiday break to regroup and figure out where we want to take things from there."

"Mm-hmm," I say, as my stomach twists and clenches.

I look at Savage to find him silently staring Nadine down.

"So," Nadine says brightly, "do either of you have any fun plans for the holidays?"

As a matter of fact, during our three weeks off, Savage and I have lots of fun plans. The morning after shooting ends, Savage and I will head to Chicago to visit Mimi and Sasha. After spending three days with Savage's family, I'll fly back to California to spend Christmas day with my family, while Savage remains in Chicago with his. A few days after that, Savage and I will reunite in LA for a couple days before flying to Cabo to relax and celebrate the new year. The trip is Savage's generous Christmas gift to me, and I can't wait. After that, as the first episodes of the show begin airing, Savage and I will return to our fake love nest in LA to relax and gear up for the weekly singing competition to come. But sitting here now, I don't know if Savage would want me to mention any of that to Nadine. In fact, based on the way Savage has reacted to Nadine during this conversation, I'm quite certain he wouldn't want me telling her a damned thing about our private life.

"We're just going to relax and spend the holidays with our families," I reply.

Nadine looks at Savage and he nods.

"Sounds fun," Nadine says. She tells us about her holiday plans —she's taking her family to Hawaii. She's getting her daughter a puppy for Christmas. Blah, blah. As Nadine speaks, I can barely breathe, as my mind races along with my pulse. Finally, Nadine bids us a good evening and heads toward the door of Savage's dressing room. Before exiting, though, she turns around and shoots us a smile that doesn't reach her eyes. "Thanks again for doing such a great job, guys." She looks at Savage. "Especially you, Savage. The audience is going to fall even more in love with you when these audition episodes air." With that, she turns and leaves. And I'm suddenly positive my days on the show are numbered, if I don't deliver precisely what Nadine has requested. Maybe even if I do.

FORTY-NINE

SAVAGE

"This is a disaster!" Laila whisper-shouts as we tumble into the backseat of our SUV. We shot the final batch of auditions today, during which there's no doubt we didn't deliver "Vintage Savage and Laila," as requested by Nadine yesterday. Not even close. On the contrary, we were every bit as enamored and enthralled with each other, as ever. And now, Laila is freaking the fuck out.

If I'm being honest, I didn't actually *try* to change course or deliver any semblance of what Nadine asked for yesterday. Why would I? I have no desire to return to any sort of toxic, angry dynamic with Laila—to mess with the blissful happiness I've found with her these past weeks. Not for any reason. But certainly not to please the executive producer of some reality TV singing competition that's contractually obligated to pay me, regardless.

Even if I were only "pretending" to be a dick to Laila again, I worry I might genuinely hurt her feelings somehow. And I don't want to risk that. So, all day long, I've sat back and let Laila take the lead in delivering the "hate-lust" dynamic Nadine requested yesterday. And guess what? Laila has followed *my* lead. She's returned my every smile, laughed at my jokes, and squeezed my hand every time I've squeezed hers. And before I knew it, the shooting day was done, and Laila and I had given the audience a whole lot more of the same—a blissfully happy couple that adores each other, can't keep their hands off each other, and laughs at each other's jokes. Even the stupid ones. And I'm not sorry about it. Not even a little bit.

Our usual bodyguard closes the door behind Laila as she gets settled into the back seat of the SUV next to me. "It's a disaster," Laila mutters, repeating her earlier refrain. "A total and complete *disaster!*"

I chuckle and pull her to me. "I think you should pick another word besides 'disaster,' babe. Repeating the same word, over and over, makes it lose its punch."

"Catastrophe. Calamity. Crisis. Any word you want to use, today wasn't good."

"Fuck Nadine. The audience will love seeing us happy and the ratings will reflect that. And if not, oh well. You and I will get paid the same amount, either way. We'll flip Nadine the bird on our way to the bank, baby."

The car heads toward the exit of the studio's parking lot, and Laila looks out her window, her body language stiff and encumbered. In fact, she looks like she's carrying the weight of the world on her shoulders.

"You worry too much, Fitzy," I say. "I'm telling you, the audience will *love* us being happy."

I wait for her to reply, to smile and exhale and say I'm right. And when she doesn't, I sigh and pick up my phone to reply to some texts from throughout the day. I deal with a group chat from Reed Rivers about my band's imminent album release. I text Sasha to confirm my upcoming travel plans and shoot a quick selfie video for Sasha to show Mimi when she wakes up in the morning, since I've unfortunately missed singing Mimi to sleep again, the same thing that's happened the past few nights, thanks to Mimi's exhaustion from the move into the new house, my busy shooting schedule with the show, and the time difference between Chicago and LA.

And, finally, last but not least, I reply to a text from my best friend, who's expressed excitement about joining the show tomorrow afternoon for Mentor Day.

Me: I can't wait for you to see the bullshit dog and pony show for yourself, KC. This show is everything I hate, all rolled into one. Thank God for Laila sitting there with me.

Kendrick: Speaking of Laila, I've acquired some fascinating information that relates to her supposed fling with Charlie the Fitness Trainer during the tour.

Me: It's not a supposed fling. Laila confirmed it herself when I saw her at the awards show.

Kendrick: She lied. In the middle of our training session today, Charlie got a phone call from his HUSBAND. I guess it's possible Charlie is a bisexual adulterer, but I think the more likely scenario is that you're a paranoid nut job and Laila is a liar who knows how to push your buttons to maximum effect. LMFAO!

My heart lurching into my throat, I look at Laila sitting next to me in the car, to find her texting away on her phone, and an unexpected torrent of conflicting emotions floods me. Anger, relief, *rejection*. Anger that Laila took my jealousy and paranoia and stoked it, solely to mess with me. Relief that Laila didn't fuck Charlie on the tour, as I've thought for so long.

But, mostly, I'm feeling acute *rejection* in this moment. As jealous as I was to think of Laila choosing Charlie over me during the last month of the tour, a piece of me found weird solace in that idea. If Laila hadn't jumped into something with me after the amazing night of the hot tub, then I had to come up with some reason for that. Someone else had caught her eye. Someone else

LAUREN ROWE

had stolen her away from me. Someone else had made it possible for her to resist me. Well, why not Charlie? He's handsome and buff. A good guy, from what I can tell. And Laila made it clear, every time she was near him in my vicinity, that she liked him.

So, if Charlie isn't the reason Laila didn't come to my room, not even once, then what the fuck! I'm right back to feeling literal madness at trying to figure that woman out! How and why did she stay away from me for so long after Phoenix? If Laila didn't start fucking Charlie after the night of the hot tub, then . . . does that mean she stayed away from me . . . simply because she'd lost interest in me? Because I hadn't rocked her world, the way she'd rocked mine? Because she simply didn't *want* me, the way I so desperately wanted her? Every single thought I'm having in this moment feels like a dagger not only to my ego, but to my heart.

With my pulse thumping loudly in my ears, I tap out a reply to Kendrick:

Me: *I didn't see that one coming. Gotta go. See you at the studio tomorrow.*

Kendrick: *Hold up. Call me now.*

Me: *Can't. Sitting next to Laila in a car.*

Kendrick: *Don't do it.*

Me: *Don't do what?*

Kendrick: *Whatever scheme is already taking root inside your twisted brain. I only told you about Charlie's husband to free you from the batshit jealousy you've been holding onto since the tour. Don't turn around and throw this in Laila's face. Don't try to coax her into a conversation about Charlie so you can catch her in another round of lies. Let bygones be bygones, Savage. You're happy now. BE HAPPY.*

Me: *I'm not going to throw this in Laila's face. I'm not even going to mention it to her.*

Kendrick: *You lied to Laila, too, remember? In fact,*

you lied first about that waitress in NYC, and then about all those women you brought into her dressing rooms. Call it even and let it go. Otherwise, if you bring this up to her, you'd better be ready to tell her all the shit you lied about, too. And WHY you lied to her. The FEELINGS you were having when you did all that. Are you ready to open up about how obsessed and crazy you were, behind the scenes?

Me: Not even a little bit.

Kendrick: That's what I thought. So, keep your big mouth shut.

Me: I will. Thanks for the info. Gotta go.

I plop my phone down onto the seat, facedown, between Laila and me, while Laila keeps tapping away on her phone. Why didn't she want me the way I wanted her, during that last month of the tour? I just don't get it.

"Who are you texting with?" I ask, when she still hasn't looked up.

"Aloha."

"You were with her all day."

Laila calls up to our driver. "Hey, Mike, could you turn up the music, please?" When music starts blaring loudly, Laila looks sheepishly at me. She says, "I have something I need to tell you. It's something I'm contractually not supposed to tell you or anyone else. But, screw it. I've already told Aloha and I don't want to keep this from you any longer."

My stomach twists. "Okay."

Laila takes a deep breath. "I kept this from you because I didn't want to burden you with it, or make you change the way you acted on-camera. I thought if you knew what I'm about to tell you, you might act differently on-camera, in a way that didn't seem natural."

"Spit it out, Laila."

She bites her lip and exhales. "There's a termination clause in my contract. A buy-out clause, by which the show can send me packing, at their sole discretion, at any time, without prior notice, by paying me a hundred grand."

"A hundred grand? Jesus, Laila. *No*."

She nods.

"A hundred grand is *peanuts* to them!" I whisper-shout, running my hand through my hair. "No wonder you've been so stressed out about what Nadine said yesterday."

"I'm obviously on the chopping block, especially after we didn't deliver today."

"You should have told me about this the minute Nadine left my dressing room last night, Laila!"

"I didn't want to force you to do anything you didn't want to do. Plus, I thought I could handle this on my own. But after today, when you were so sweet to me and I didn't have the heart to be anything but sweet back to you, I realized I can't do this alone. Everything depends on me delivering 'Vintage Savage and Laila' tomorrow. It's my last chance to hit a homerun before the long break. After shooting was over for today, Nadine popped into my dressing room while I was changing and made it clear she was pissed about our 'happy couple' routine today. She didn't say this, explicitly, but her demeanor made me think they're going to fire me during the break if we don't hit it out of the ballpark tomorrow, exactly like she's requested."

My heart feels like it's exploding. "They can't fire you. They're contractually obligated to let you perform in the finale, remember?"

"Okay, so maybe they'll invite me back to let me sing. Yet another chance for huge ratings."

"But we're picking *four* teams tomorrow. The whole audition process has been built around you being one of the judges."

"That'd be an easy fix. They could fire me during the break, say we broke up and I didn't want to return to the show. And then, they'd parcel off the contestants on my team to the three remaining judges

HATE LOVE DUET   379

and finish out the season with three judges, like always. Just think about the ratings if they did all that, Savage! They'd have a self-created 'scandal.' A big 'mess' they'd have to scramble to fix. Don't you think everyone would tune in to see that? Not to mention, to see how poor Savage is doing after his breakup with Laila? I haven't slept a wink since Nadine talked to us in your dressing room, and I've looked at it from every angle. I've decided I'm not paranoid. They're going to fire me during the break, Savage. I can feel it. Unless we deliver what Nadine asked. And even then, I might be toast, regardless."

"Well, fuck that. I won't let them fire you," I say, my jaw tight. "If that's what they ultimately decide to do, then I'll tell them I won't do the show without you."

Laila's face melts with affection for me. She touches my cheek gently and smiles ruefully. "Thank you, but I'd never let you do that. You're contractually obligated to do the show. You'd have a lawsuit on your hands."

"I don't care. I'm not doing the show without you, Laila. That was a basic condition of me doing the show. Doing it with you."

"No, it wasn't. You agreed to do it, long before you knew I'd be anything but Aloha's one-episode mentor. Plus, the whole reason you signed onto the show was for *Mimi*. And that reason still stands today, more than ever."

I feel flooded with panic. But I manage to say, "Okay, let's not panic here. I'm not supposed to tell you this, but I know something you don't. Something that proves, beyond a shadow of a doubt, they won't fire you, whether we deliver 'Vintage Savage and Laila' tomorrow or not."

She looks at me hopefully, her blue eyes wide and brimming with hope.

I glance toward the front of the vehicle, to make sure our driver and bodyguard can't overhear me, despite the loud music. And when it's clear they're enmeshed in their own conversation, I return to Laila and grab her hand. "There's a dangling carrot in my contract, baby. They'll pay me a fat bonus—a quarter mill—if I get down on bended knee and propose to you, right after we perform our duet in the finale."

Laila gasps. "*No.*"

I nod. "They didn't want me telling you about it, to ensure you had an 'authentic reaction' on-camera. And, honestly, I've never told you about it, anyway, because there's no way I'm going to do it. But the mere fact the bonus is hanging out there proves you've got nothing to worry about. Why would they offer me a bonus to propose to you in the *finale*, if they're not planning to keep you around until the finale?"

Laila's shoulders slump. The hope in her eyes a moment ago fades. Clearly, she doesn't find my logic as compelling as I do. "I don't think we can rely on that clause to protect me, honey. I think they're preserving themselves all sorts of potential storylines, depending on what happens, from week to week. You know, hedging their bets. *If* I'm still around for the finale, then *maybe* you'd choose to earn that bonus. But *if* they don't keep me around, then that's fine, because they've got a Plan B that will work, too. That's what Rhoda told me they do on *The Engagement Experiment*, all the time. She worked on that show with Nadine for five seasons, remember? When she came to the house and spilled all the tea, her stories made it clear the producers of that show always hedge their bets. They manipulate the contestants in lots of different ways, and then run with whatever storyline begins taking shape. Savage, you wouldn't believe the stuff they do to people to manipulate their emotions and actions on that show. I think Nadine has taken a page out of her old playbook."

I process that for a moment. "Okay, then. If you're genuinely worried about this, then I'll do my best to be more of a dick to you tomorrow, so you can fight fire with fire, and we can deliver 'Vintage Savage and Laila,' like Nadine wants."

Laila sighs with relief. "Thank you. I don't know if I'm capable of scowling at you anymore, let alone being a bitch to you. I'm sorry, but you're going to have to pick a fight with me tomorrow to get the ball rolling."

"Hell no! You'll have to be a bitch to me *first*, or I'll come off like a misogynistic asshole. Like I'm punching *down*. I'll play along and give *almost* as good as I get, but you're going to have to be the one to get the ball rolling." Laila snuggles into me and I put my arm around her. "It'll be fine, baby," I coo softly. "You'll be a bitch to me and I'll fight fire with fire, and we'll be everything Nadine wants and more."

She sighs like there's a hundred-pound weight resting on her chest, and my heart pangs in reply.

"I don't know if I'm capable of being a bitch to you anymore, Adrian. You fucking bastard. You've tamed the shrew."

I can't help chuckling. "You say that like it's a bad thing."

"It *is*. I can't even imagine how mortified I'd be if I got fired from the show. The list of fired judges, forevermore, would be me and Hugh Delaney." She makes a guttural, disgusted sound. "Let's face it. The word 'disaster' really does say it best."

We sit without speaking for a long moment, listening to the loud music in the car. The song, by chance, is "Fireflies," by our friends 22 Goats. Finally, Laila sits up and breaks the silence. "What if you told them you're planning to propose to me in the finale? Maybe that would make them want to keep me around!"

My heart explodes. "I . . . I don't think I could do that convincingly, Laila."

She pauses. "You couldn't *tell* them convincingly . . . or fake-*propose* to me convincingly?"

"I couldn't fake-propose convincingly. I've never once imagined myself proposing to someone. Never once imagined myself even wanting to get married. I think I'd stumble through it, red-faced and stammering, and wind up doing more harm than good."

Laila's chest heaves. "You don't think you could do it convincingly for a quarter million bucks? That's a lot of money, especially when you're already paying half your salary to me."

"We've agreed not to talk about the money anymore, remember?"

"No, you asked me not to talk about it. But I never said I wouldn't."

"I'm over it, Laila. You negotiated for an equal partnership, fair and square. And that's exactly what we are."

Boom.

For some reason, saying those words out loud—acknowledging the now-obvious fact that Laila and I truly are an equal partnership—makes me think maybe I *could* convincingly perform a fake proposal in the finale, after all. Not for the money, as Laila's suggested. But because Mimi would be thrilled to see it. That's all she's ever wanted for me—to see me settle down with a woman who loves me for *me*. So, why not give my grandmother all the bells and whistles, and also save Laila's job on the show while I'm at it? I think, up until now, I've been dismissing the idea of ambushing Laila with an on-air proposal, partly because I was scared she'd turn me down on national TV. Talk about public humiliation. And by the same token, I didn't want to risk ambushing Laila and having her say *yes* to me on national TV . . . only to find out afterwards the proposal wasn't real—that it was made by me, solely in exchange for a quarter-million bucks.

As if reading my mind, Laila says, "Now that you've told me about the bonus provision in your contract, I don't see why you wouldn't do it. Why not take their money? I promise I'll act totally surprised when you kneel down and ask me. I'll make this face." She gasps, widens her eyes, and brings a shaky hand to her mouth, like she's a newly minted beauty queen who's just heard the good news. In a heartbeat, she drops the beauty queen act, and flashes a mischievous smile. "Pretty convincing, huh?"

"Masterful," I concede.

"So . . .? I'd be thrilled for you to get a little extra money out of this gig, after I've taken half your salary. All I ask is that you give me a heads up the day before you 'propose,' to confirm you're going ahead with it, so I can warn my mom and sister it's coming. If they saw you pop the question on TV, without me telling them the real deal beforehand, they'd crap their panties with excitement, and I wouldn't want to do that to them. Telling them after the fact it was all a money grab would break their poor little hearts."

Fuck. My heart squeezes. In a flash, I have the preposterous impulse to propose to Laila for real. It's a stupid thought and I chastise myself for having it the moment I do. I'm not husband material, any more than I'm boyfriend material. But, man, it would be fun to give the Fitzgerald women that kind of thrill. A happily ever after, after all the shit they've been through with Laila's father.

"It's okay," Laila says, apparently reacting to my facial expression. "I'm sure the idea of fake-proposing to me gives you hives. It was just an idea to make some money for *you* and give *me* an insurance policy. But don't give it another thought."

I don't know what Laila saw on my face to make her say that. Yes, I'm feeling conflicted and confused about the idea of fake-proposing to Laila. But in the end, the thing that doesn't feel confusing at all is the notion that Mimi would love to see that.

"You know what?" I say. "Now that I've told you about the bonus provision in my contract, I think the proposal is probably doable."

Laila's blue eyes ignite.

"For Mimi," I clarify quickly. "Not for the money. More than anything, Mimi wants to see me settle down with the great love of my life, the way she did with her husband, Jasper. If, incidentally, me doing this silly thing for Mimi would *also* help you, then why wouldn't I do it?"

Laila's face is glowing with excitement. "Are you sure?"

My heart is racing. "Pretty sure. Can I have a little time to think about it? My contract says I don't have to give them advance warning to earn the bonus. The clause states I can decide, right up until the last possible moment. So, maybe, let's see how things shake down tomorrow with our newfound commitment to being dicks to each other again. If things look like they're going well for you after that, it'll be a moot point. But if it looks like you're still on the chopping block, then I can always swoop in and make it known that I'm planning to propose in the finale."

"Fantastic plan. Thank you so much."

"Of course."

I kiss her, and as I do, our phones buzz in unison with an incoming text. We break apart and pick them up to find we've both got the same message from Reed Rivers:

Reed: Due to time constraints, I've asked Fish and Alessandra to help you write the duet. I know you're both heading out of town for the holidays on Saturday, so I've asked them to meet at your house tomorrow night at 7. I'll take the lead on getting the song produced during the holidays, and you can add your vocals to the track in the new year. RR

"What do you think?" Laila says, putting down her phone.

"It doesn't matter what I think. The all-powerful Oz has spoken. Reed always does whatever he wants, no matter what I, or anyone else, wants."

"Yes, I know, but that doesn't mean you don't have an opinion. What do you think of Fish and Alessandra helping us get the song written? That's two more people earning royalties, at the end of the day."

"True, but what's the alternative? We've tried, many times, and we can't write this damned song to save our lives. Honestly, I think Reed is a genius for putting Fish and Alessandra on the project. Fish let me hear some of the rough cuts from the album he's co-writing with Alessandra, and every song they've written for her is the sweetest, purest, most classic little love song you've ever heard. I'm confident whatever they help us write will be perfect for what we're trying to accomplish here."

Laila nods. "Okay, so this is good news, then. Once again, Mr. Rivers knows exactly what he's doing."

"Yeah, I'm no fan of Reed's. But I have to admit this is a good call, even if it means you and I will get a smaller percentage of royalties. If you ask me, it's better to have a smash hit, with four co-writers, than to have only two writers on a shitty attempt at a love song that doesn't even make the charts."

"Great point. So, I'll tell Reed we're in agreement, then?"

"Not that he'd care. But, sure."

Laila taps on her phone and sets it down, and then looks out her side of the car like she's in deep thought again. And, suddenly, I know what I need to do. I pull out my phone and tap out a quick text, and then pull Laila to me after pressing send.

I kiss the side of Laila's head. "Stop worrying, baby. Everything is going to work out fine."

"I hope so."

"When we get home, we're going to open a contraband bottle of wine. And you're going to drink a glass or two or three."

"I promised I wouldn't drink, while you're not allowed to drink."

"Desperate times call for desperate measures. You're going to drink some wine and relax. You're going to get nice and horny and loose, while we eat whatever the chef left for us. And when you're feeling really good, and *really* naughty, I'm going to take you upstairs and fuck you like I *hate* you."

She giggles. "Oooh. You're going to help me 'get into character' for tomorrow, are you?"

"You've already figured me out. Yep, I'm gonna fuck you so hard, you'll remember what it feels like to want to fuck me to death. And tomorrow, when it's time for you to tap into your inner bitch, all you'll need to do is remember the way I fucked you like a dirty little whore the night before, and you'll be off to the races."

FIFTY

LAILA

With "Hate Sex High" blaring—which is creating a kinky kind of "life imitating art imitating life" energy between Savage and me—Savage is fucking me hard, doggie style, in our bed. So damned hard, I feel like the tip of his cock is going to poke out my mouth with the next beastly thrust. I grip the sheet beneath me, as the top of my head bangs against the headboard, and do everything in my power not to come. Throughout this entire, raucous session of sex with Savage, which has involved multiple positions thus far and a whole lot of groaning and screaming by me, Savage has repeatedly forbidden me from coming. "Not unless I've given you permission," he keeps saying. And, holy hell, it's been a tall order, thanks not only to the wine I had earlier with our meal, but the way Savage has been fucking and eating and fingering me, masterfully, for the past hour. Time after time, he's gotten me right to the edge. And then, he backs off and switches things up. Time after time, I've cried out with pleasure, and begged him to say the word. But each time, he's pulled out, or stopped whatever he was doing and told me to shut up and do as I'm told.

"Please," I beg, feeling myself, yet again, on the bitter cusp of release.

"Not yet," he barks, making me moan. Without warning, he pulls my head back by my hair and growls into my ear. "Now put your vibrator against your clit again on low. *And don't come.*"

We've been playing with my toy, now and again, all night. I packed it in my suitcase in the first place, thinking I might need it, occasionally. But this is the first time I've used it since moving in. And what a way to reconnect with my loyal and efficient "ex-boyfriend"—by having a threesome with it and the best lover I've ever had, by a long mile.

"I'm gonna come," I announce. "Oh, God."

"Nope."

Savage pulls me upright, onto my knees. His frontside pressed against my backside, he roughly spreads my thighs apart and orders me to return the vibrator to my tip. "On low again. *Now.*"

Trembling, I press the vibrator between my legs, as instructed, while Savage runs his palms greedily over my torso. He gropes my breasts and nipples. Bites and licks and kisses my neck. I feel his dick against my ass and feel the quiver of his body as he holds back his own release.

I let out a garbled sound. "I'm gonna come," I choke out.

"Not yet."

With a loud growl, he flips me over, throws my legs up, and enters me. He rolls his hips as he thrusts, making my eyes roll back into my head so hard, I feel like they're rubbing against my brain.

"You're mine, Laila," Savage says, as his body plunges into mine, over and over again. As his large dick impales me. "I own this body," he says. "It's all mine."

"*Savage.*"

"Not yet."

I feel my inside walls clench. My eyelids flutter. I make an inhuman sound.

"You can come now, baby," he coos, almost inaudibly. And that's it. I immediately come undone. With a loud scream, I come harder than I ever have in my life. As I writhe and moan in ecstasy, Savage pulls out of me . . . and a second later, I feel the sensation of warm wetness splattering across my face.

As I lie there, processing the fact that Savage just shot his load into my face, he crawls between my legs and does the same thing he always does after I've had a gushing orgasm. He licks up every drop of his trophy.

"You're delicious," he murmurs, after finishing his work. With a wink, he leaps off the bed and pads into the bathroom, leaving me cum-streaked and exhausted and staring at his hot backside in retreat. When Savage returns to the bed, he's not only got a towel in his hand, but a huge smile on his face. In fact, the boy is grinning as big and wide as a Cheshire cat. He slides his fingertip through the warm streak on my face and offers it to my lips, so I take his finger into my mouth and suck.

"Good girl," Savage says softly, like he's talking to a baby bird. With another wide smile, he wipes my face with the towel. "Are you feeling ready for tomorrow now?"

"You can't possibly think what we just did has helped me remember how to hate you. It was *incredible*."

Savage's smile broadens, even more. "Aw, come on. It had to have helped you get into character for tomorrow a *little*." He sits on the edge of the bed and counts off his supposed sins on his fingers. "I wouldn't let you come. I bossed you around and pulled your hair. And then, I topped it all off with a sperm facial." He smirks. "How rude of me. How *degrading*. How *infuriating*." His expression is pure snarkiness. He knows full well what he did to me was hot as hell, top to bottom, and that I loved every minute of it.

"This is so classic you," I say. "The same thing as when you sang my name in 'Hate Sex High,' but buried it slightly in the mix, just enough to preserve yourself some deniability. You wanted to have dirty sex and come in my face. Period. But you *said* you were doing it to help me 'get into character,' so you could hide behind your suit of armor, if it turned out I didn't like it. *Classic Savage*."

Savage smiles wickedly. "Well," he says. "Even if I haven't

made you remember to hate me, at least we had a damned good time."

"We sure did." I peck his cheek and then hop out of bed and head into the bathroom. I wash my face and brush my teeth, and soon, Savage joins me for his usual bedtime routine.

"Don't worry too much about tomorrow," he says, his toothbrush sticking out of his mouth and his naked, massive dong hanging low. "I have faith you'll figure out a way to convince yourself you're highly annoyed with me tomorrow—if not downright infuriated."

"I don't know," I say. "It's a tall order these days. Look at you. You're perfect. Gorgeous. Talented. Sweet. How could I possibly remember what it feels like to be annoyed with you—let alone *infuriated*?"

Savage lifts an eyebrow, his expression practically screaming, *I've got a secret.*

"What?" I ask.

"What *what*?"

"That look."

"What look?"

"You just did it again. It's full of mischief. Like you know something I don't."

Savage spits his mouthful of toothpaste into the sink and grins adorably. "You're a drunken, paranoid lunatic. Now, come on, baby. It's time for bed. You need to sleep off all that contraband wine, so you can wake up tomorrow and, against all odds, remember how to tap into your inner bitch with me."

FIFTY-ONE

SAVAGE

"Wake up, Fitzy," I say. As I say the words, I tap Laila's forehead repeatedly, like a woodpecker pecking holes into a dead pine tree. Today's mission? Operation Annoy Laila, with the higher goal of helping her recall, vividly, the sensation of hating my guts, so she can take the lead on delivering the combativeness Nadine has demanded. Obviously, I don't want to push Laila so hard as to make her *genuinely* hate me again. The very thought of regressing to those dark days with this gorgeous woman makes me physically recoil. But, for the greater good, I'm more than willing to aggravate the crap out of Laila today, in ways big and small, if it will help her get into character for today's long shooting day.

Tap, tap, tap. "Wake up!" I bellow into Laila's beautiful, sleeping face. "Up and at 'em, baby!"

All things considered, this ought to annoy her pretty well, right out of the gate. Laila isn't a morning person on a good day, the same as me, and I'm waking her up a full two hours before her alarm. Plus, Laila drank three goblets of wine last night, before we headed upstairs to screw, so I'm betting she's feeling a particular need for some extra sleep this morning.

Without opening her eyes, Laila bats at my hand as it continues tapping her forehead. "Stop it," she murmurs.

Tap, tap, tap. "There shall be no stopping!" I boom. "I've got a big surprise for you! Wake up!"

Laila squints at me. "My alarm hasn't gone off, has it?"

Tap, tap, tap. "No. It. Has. *Not*! It's only six!"

"*Six*? What the fuck!"

"Six is the time for my big surprise!" *Tap, tap, tap.*

Laila swats at my hand again. "What's wrong with you?"

Tap, tap, tap. "Nothing's wrong with me, baby! I'm all kinds of right. We're going to work out this morning before heading into work."

"Have fun with that. Bye now."

I laugh with glee. "Get dressed and meet me in the gym in five, or I'll physically drag you." *Tap, tap, tap.*

Laila's fully awake now. Scowling, she pulls the covers to her chin and rolls onto her side. "I'll work out tonight after work. I drank too much last night."

"Fish and Alessandra are coming over tonight, remember? It's now or never."

"Never, then."

Without warning, I yank the covers off Laila's near-naked body, subjecting her to the brisk early-morning air in the room, and she shrieks and curls into the fetal position. I pull out my phone and aim it at her. "Say good morning to everyone, babe. We're *live*."

Laila shrieks and covers her face with her hands. "Please, tell me you're joking."

I don't blame her for second-guessing me. In all the time we've been posting daily "happy couple at home" videos, it's *always* been Laila, not me, who's initiated our videos. And only when Laila is good and ready and has checked her makeup in the mirror.

"Not joking. Look." As she peeks out from behind her hands, I turn my phone around to show her the screen. "See? Now, say hi to the nice people."

She waves halfheartedly and says hello. "Sorry, guys," she says. "We'll come back after I've had my coffee. Say goodbye, Savage."

I turn the camera lens on myself. "Isn't Laila adorable when she first wakes up? So cranky! Ha! So, here's the deal, guys. I woke Laila up *way* earlier than her alarm, so we could squeeze in a workout before heading off to work today, since we've got plans with friends tonight. So, would you guys do me a big favor in the comments and help me convince Laila to work out with me? Only positive comments, please. Give her a pep talk. No trolling. And if it works, we'll come back later and show you part of our workout." I return the camera to Laila's angry face. "Say goodbye to everyone, babe."

She waves. "When you guys leave your comments, be sure to tell Savage he's annoying as hell."

Ha. Operation Annoy Laila is already off to a fantastic start.

I turn off my camera and spank Laila's ass. "Now, get dressed and meet me in the gym to see your surprise." With that, I exit the room, and head back to Charlie the Fitness Trainer, who's waiting for me in the gym.

"Charlie," Laila gasps out, freezing just inside the doorway of the gym. Her blue eyes shift to me. Confusion. Anger. *Betrayal.* Those are the emotions flickering across Laila's frozen face as she stares at me in disbelief.

Charlie reaches Laila and gives her a warm bear hug, unaware of his status as my unwitting pawn, and Laila peeks over his broad shoulder to shoot me the kind of scathing look I haven't seen from her in a very long time. Well, that's weird. I haven't even gotten to the annoying part yet—the part where I supposedly find out, in front of Laila, that Charlie is gay and married. And she's already shooting me murderous daggers? Well, that feels a bit premature . . . and vaguely worrisome. But, oh well. I've got a job to do. And I'm going to do it.

"It's great to see you again, Laila," Charlie says.

Laila returns the compliment, her face flushed.

Charlie says, "I've been following you and Savage on Insta-gram. Looks like you two are having a blast, living together and shooting the show. Emma can't wait to see you as a judge. When will the first episode air?"

"Right after New Year's," Laila replies.

"Sorry, who's Emma?" I ask. "Your daughter?"

"My stepdaughter. She and my husband came to visit me during the tour—and when Emma met Laila, she was starry-eyed. And then, when Emma saw Laila perform, forget about it. An obsession was born."

"Tell Emma to join the club," I say. But my eyes are on Laila's, letting her know the full implication of Charlie's story hasn't escaped me. *Charlie is married. And not only that, he's married to a dude.* Frankly, it was a lot easier than I thought it'd be to pull that information out of Charlie. I thought I'd have to ask him all sorts of awkward, uncharacteristically personal questions to get him to mention any of what he just said. But, no, right off the bat, I've hit a grand slam homerun.

Laila's plainly furious with me. It's not hard to see. Which makes sense, since I've just outed her as a liar, unless, I suppose, Charlie is a bisexual adulterer and Laila the kind of girl who'd have a tour fling with a married man. But, come on, I think we both know, in this moment, the jig is up. Her lie revealed. Yes, I was the one who jumped to the wrong conclusion in the first place about Charlie and then went on and on about my theory backstage at the awards show. But Laila confirmed her fling with Charlie and stoked my jealousy, mercilessly. So now, as far as she's concerned, I've just figured out the truth about all of it.

"Hey, you know what, Charlie?" Laila says, peeling her blazing blue eyes off my smug face. "Savage didn't know this when he invited you here to surprise me, but I've got plans this morning I can't reschedule."

"Oh, no," Charlie says.

"Yeah, it's a bummer. Hopefully, we can do this another time. But you two go ahead." She looks at me, her blue eyes homicidal. "I'll have Mike come get me now and come back for you later."

And that's it. Before I've replied, Laila turns on her heel and strides toward the exit of the gym.

"Wait!" I shout, my heart thrumming wildly in my chest. I feel panicky. Like I've made a misstep. Something is off. Laila was pissed the *minute* she saw Charlie. Yes, her anger seemed to escalate when Charlie mentioned his stepdaughter and husband, thereby proving her a liar. But I can't shake the feeling there's something I don't know at play here. Some land mine I've stumbled into that just blew my arms and legs off, without me realizing it. "Laila, wait!"

To my surprise, she turns around in the doorway, her blue eyes blazing and her cheeks on fire. "What?" she says.

"Maybe we should . . . do another live video to let people know you made it into the gym."

She smiles, making my stomach twist. That wasn't a happy smile. That was a murderous one. "Great idea," she says. "Record it now. We'll tell everyone you got exactly what you wanted this morning."

I grimace, unsure what to do.

"Go on," she prompts, motioning. "Wouldn't want to keep everyone in suspense."

Fuck. She looks genuinely enraged. Capable of murder. And not for show.

"Uhh . . ."

"I'll do it myself." She grabs her phone out of a side pocket in her leggings, trains the camera on herself, and plasters a huge, fake smile on her face. She says, "Hey, guys! You did it! You convinced me to get in here and work out! I'm in the gym with my boyfriend now. He's right there. Say hi, Savage."

I wave feebly, feeling the hair on the back of my neck standing up.

"And that's Charlie Ford right there. The world's most amazing personal trainer. Say hi, Charlie!"

"Hey, everyone!"

Laila returns the camera to herself. "I'll put Charlie's links below so you can follow him. He's *amazing*, guys. And easy on the eyes, too. I can honestly tell you there's not a mean, selfish, self-centered, thoughtless, *hypocritical* bone in Charlie's body. Which is more than I can say about the other guy in this room. Man, don't you hate hypocrisy? When someone says one thing and does another? I especially hate it when the thing that person said was deeply meaningful to me. When I relied on it, totally. And in fact, *needed* it to be the truth, or everything else would fall apart." With that, she trains the camera on my astonished face and shouts, "That's the face of a hypocrite, guys! Not so pretty, is it?" With that, she lowers her phone, flips me off, and stalks out of the room.

"*Whoa*," Charlie says, obviously taken aback by what just transpired. "What just happened?"

My heart is crashing. "Hell if I know," I say. And, unfortunately, it's the truth. For a second there, I thought Laila figured out what I was trying to do and played along, a little *too* well. But the look in her eye at the end there felt all too real. Like genuine white-hot *rage*, the likes of which I haven't seen from Laila since the tour. "That had nothing to do with you, Charlie," I choke out. "Laila and I were having an argument before you got here, and I guess I didn't read the situation right."

"You should go."

I take a deep breath. "No. Let's work out. She obviously needs a little 'alone time.'"

Charlie shakes his head. "No, I think you should follow her, Savage."

My heart wants to run after her. To take her into my arms and tell her I did this for her—to get her into character for today's shooting day. But my head tells me that's exactly what I *shouldn't* do. "No, trust me," I say, "it's for the best if I leave her alone to stew and get as angry as possible at me. Let's work out. I'll talk to Laila about everything tonight, when we get home from work."

Charlie looks at me like I'm crazy. "I realize I don't know Laila nearly as well as you do, but we got to be pretty good friends during the tour. And I think she wanted you to follow her, Savage. Did you see the way she lingered in the doorway for a minute? It seemed like—"

"You need to trust me on this, Charlie. The best thing I can do for Laila is leave her alone, let her get pissed as hell, and throw myself on her mercy later tonight after all shooting has wrapped for the day. Now come on. I want you to really make me sweat."

FIFTY-TWO

LAILA

"Where the hell is Savage?" Nadine barks at no one in particular.

It's Draft Day at *Sing Your Heart Out*. And all the judges, minus Savage, are seated at a large, round table, surrounded by the entire crew and staff, ready to start shooting. Savage's ass should have been sitting in the empty seat next to mine a full fifteen minutes ago, but he's nowhere to be found.

Nadine looks at me, her dark eyes fierce. "Where's your boyfriend, Laila? He's *your* responsibility, remember?"

"He'll be here any minute . . ." I say reflexively, even though I haven't heard from my ward all morning. Not since I left him in our home gym with Charlie. I've texted Savage, repeatedly, in the last few minutes, asking him where the heck he is, but he hasn't answered. I look beyond the nearest camera, toward the backstage area, praying I'll see Savage walking toward the set at the last minute, the way he always does in situations like this. But, no. There's no sign of him.

"I'll give him a quick call from my dressing room," I say. "Be right back."

Before anyone can reply, I bolt away and sprint down the

hallway leading to my dressing room. How could Savage do this to me—*today*, of all days, when he knows I'm freaking out about my head being on the chopping block? Savage promised to help me today, and so far—

Oh, Jesus.

That fucking idiot.

Savage thought he was *helping* me this morning by inviting Charlie over, didn't he? And yet, as I know full well, inviting Charlie to the house to interrogate him, and find out the truth, once and for all, about my supposed tour fling with Charlie, was actually something Savage needed to do for *himself*. Yes, I'm sure Savage told himself he invited Charlie for my benefit. But in reality, whether Savage realizes it or not, he was pretending to wear a suit of armor for me, in order to get something he desperately wanted for himself, all along.

I poke my head into Savage's dressing room, and when he's not there, I head to mine, figuring I'll do what I said I'd do—give him a call. But when I swing open the door of my dressing room, there he is. Adrian Savage. Languidly lounging on the couch, like he doesn't have a care in the world.

"What the hell is wrong with you?" I bellow. "Everyone is waiting for you!"

"Oh, hey, Fitzy," he says. He puts his arms behind his head. "Turns out you *didn't* fuck Charlie during the tour! I wonder why you didn't tell me that."

"We'll talk about it later," I grit out through my teeth. "As your babysitter, I *order* you to head to the set now. I told you I'm on the chopping block today. How could this possibly help me, when the producers consider your misbehavior as *mine*?"

Savage stands and winks at me. "Don't worry about today. I've got a good feeling we'll deliver everything Nadine asked for, and more."

So, that's it. Savage has convinced himself he's helping me out —being an asshole in order to inspire me to slap the shit out of him on-camera today—when in reality, he's been dying to scratch this particular itch for months. That's so Savage, it makes me want to punch his gorgeous face. "I'm not *faking* my anger toward you, if that's what you think," I say. "I'm not 'playing along.' I'm genuinely pissed and *hurt* about the stunt you pulled this morning."

He looks shocked by my word choice. "*Hurt?*"

"We'll talk about it later. Right now, I need you to act like a professional."

"What do you mean you're *hurt?* You mean you're *annoyed.* Pissed off. Miffed. Frustrated. Maybe even embarrassed I caught you red-handed in a lie. But *hurt?*"

"Don't tell me what I'm allowed to feel, Adrian. Trust me, I'll be happy to explain my emotions to you, in full, later. Unfortunately, if I start explaining myself to you now, I won't be able to stop. In fact, it's fifty-fifty I'll burst into tears."

"*Tears?*" Savage blurts, looking horrified. "*Why?* Laila, what's going on?"

"I can't, Savage. Not with everyone waiting on us and my makeup done and a fucking buy-out clause hanging over me." I point. "Just, please, get your clueless ass in there and don't say another word about this morning until the cameras are off for the last time tonight."

Savage stands, looking uncertain. "I was trying to help you by inviting Charlie to the house. Surely, you've figured that out."

"Go."

His brow furrowed, he walks past me, out of the room, and I follow him into the hallway. When he stops and inhales like he's about to speak, I cut him off.

"No," I say. "Don't talk about it. Just *go.*"

"I don't understand you," Savage mutters. "No good deed goes unpunished."

"Shut the fuck up and *go.*"

He takes a few steps, his body language reflecting confusion . . . and then stops in the hallway, turns around, and flashes me a huge smile. "You're fucking with me. Ha! Okay. Good. This is good."

"*Go.*"

He winks. "You got it, Fitzy. Bring it, baby. I can take it."

As he turns around, his demeanor shifts. He's lighter now. Unencumbered. Clearly, he's convinced himself on a dime I couldn't possibly be genuinely upset with him. But he's wrong about that. Very, very wrong.

We reach the sound stage and Savage whoops out a big hello to the crowd, like he's just waltzed onstage at Madison Square Garden.

"Thank God," Nadine mutters. She claps her hands as Savage and I take our assigned seats at the round table. "Okay, folks, we've got *two* episodes to shoot today, back to back, as you know, and time is tight." She glares at Savage and then me. "We're already running late today, so let's try to be as efficient as possible."

I lean sharply into Mr. Rockstar Cliché next to me and command, "Apologize to everyone for being late."

"Nah," Savage says, leaning back into his chair and spreading his thighs. "I think I'll let my babysitter do that for me. She's the one being paid half my salary to make sure I'm on time."

"Asshole," I whisper, before saying loudly to Nadine and the crowd, "Hey, everyone. Sorry about that. Savage was on a phone call with his grandmother." I glare at Savage, who's smirking infuriatingly at me. "We're very sorry and both promise, it won't happen again."

FIFTY-THREE

SAVAGE

"**D**raft Day is a wrap, folks!" the director shouts, and in response, everyone around me on the stage—the three other judges, crew, and staff—sigh with relief and/or applaud. It's only lunchtime and we've still got Mentor Day left to shoot this afternoon. But, at least, after hours of bantering, bartering, haggling and fighting—that last one being mostly between Laila and me—all four judges now have their final teams. I didn't want to be the one to pick a fight with Laila today, but once she started giving me hell about that blue-haired pixie she wanted the most, Addison Swain, I actually enjoyed giving Laila as good as I got.

And it worked. Midway through the morning, Nadine came over to Laila and me and flashed us a huge smile and thumbs up. Which means, if Laila ever had cause to worry that her job was on the line today—which I'm not convinced was ever the case—I'm now positive she's in the clear. And that means whatever genuine anger my stunt this morning might have provoked in Laila, all will be forgiven by the time we leave the studio tonight. In fact, I'd bet dollars to doughnuts Laila will give me the blowjob of my life when we get home to thank me for knowing her better than she knows herself.

"Hey, everyone, before we break for lunch," the director says, and the room quiets down. "Why don't we get all four mentors out here real quick to shoot the full-cast round table discussion. We'll do some trash-talking about the teams and then break for lunch."

"Sounds great," Nadine says. She addresses a production assistant. "Wrangle the mentors from the greenroom, Gina."

"Yes, ma'am."

As crew members hustle-bustle around me, setting up whatever is coming next, I lean back in my chair and wink at Laila, who's sitting next to me at the table. "What'd I tell you, Fitzy? *We nailed it.*" I hold up my hand for a high-five, but she leaves me hanging. "Aw, come on. You can drop the act now. Our scenes together are almost done. After this little round-table thing, you'll be shooting with Colin and your team for the rest of the day." I hold up my palm again. But, again, Laila leaves me hanging. Chuckling, I grab her limp hand and thwap her palm against mine, like a parent showing a toddler how to high-five. "'Thank you, Savage,'" I say on her behalf. "'You're a genius and I'm grateful to you.'"

Laila yanks her hand from mine. "I told you not to talk about this until we're done for the day. I can't get into this right now."

"Into *what?* You know why I invited Charlie over this morning."

She leans forward and whisper-shouts, "*Stop. Talking. Now!* Somehow, I need to get through the rest of the day without screaming at you, bursting into tears, or murdering you."

I'm flabbergasted. "Bursting into *tears?* There you go again. What the hell is wrong with you?"

Her nostrils flare. "Trust me, I plan to enlighten you, in great detail, when my job is done and we're alone. For now, however, I'd appreciate you kindly pretending I'm not here."

"Laila, the only reason I invited Charlie to the house was to help you get into character today. Surely, you've figured that out by now."

"You want to know what I've 'figured out'? You're a hypocrite and a liar. Which I knew, of course. But I thought I could overlook the red flags and learn to trust you completely. I thought you'd changed. But now I know I was deluding myself."

My heart explodes with panic. "What are you talking about?"

"Quiet on the set!" the director yells, glaring at me. "Okay, let's cue the mentors! And . . . roll cameras! Mentors?"

After flashing me a little snarl, Laila plasters a fake smile on her face and turns her attention toward the entrance of the stage, where two seconds later, the show's four mentors enter.

My heart racing, I look down at the table. How does Laila not understand my ulterior motives here? Obviously, I pulled this morning's stunt to *help* her. But even if I didn't, even if there was no early-termination clause in her contract and I invited Charlie to the house this morning to find out if Laila did, in fact, screw him during the tour, then so what? Would that have been such a horrendous crime? Yes, it would have been a bit immature of me. Obsessive, maybe. But would it have been enough of a misstep to undo all the goodwill and trust I've built with Laila since living with her? If so, then I guess what we've been building is a whole lot less sturdy then I've been thinking.

"Okay, judges, let's have you get up and greet your respective mentors," the director calls out. And we four judges dutifully spring into action.

When I reach Kendrick, he grips my palm in a sideways handshake, the same greeting he usually gives me, and I can't help sneaking a peek at Laila to find out how she's greeting Colin. Well, that figures. She's kissing Colin's cheek. Probably trying to get a rise out of me. Classic Laila.

I look away, and by chance, discover Aloha greeting Fish with a kiss to his cheek. *See?* I say to myself. *There's no reason to panic. Laila doesn't want to jump Colin's bones any more than Aloha wants to jump Fish's.*

"Okay, got it," the director says. "Now, everyone take seats at the round table, with judges and mentors next to each other, and we'll do a few minutes of trash-talking about the teams before breaking for lunch."

All eight of us take seats, as instructed, and proceed to banter and hype up our teams for the next fifteen minutes or so. Until, finally, the director yells cut. "Before I release you for lunch," he says, "let's get some pickups and close-ups with each judge-mentor duo. Laila and Colin, you're up first!" The director points toward a mark on the other side of the soundstage, and Laila and Colin get up and head to where he's indicated, with Laila not even bothering to look at me before she leaves.

"You're freaking out about Colin again, huh?" Kendrick says in a whisper, the minute Laila and Colin are gone. "Dude, Laila's only doing what the director tells her to do. The same as the photographer during that photo shoot."

I run my palm down my face. "I messed up today, KC." I tell him the gist of this morning's stunt involving Charlie, and then add, "I thought I was helping Laila and now she's pissed at me in a way that feels disproportionate. For a while, I thought she had to be playing along, but now it seems she's genuinely pissed at me. She keeps saying she's 'hurt' and that she's trying not to burst into 'tears.' And I'm like, '*What the fuck is going on?*'"

Kendrick shakes his head. "I told you not to do anything with that information about Charlie. I told you to let bygones be bygones, Savage! But did you listen to me? *No.*"

"I was *helping* her, man."

"No, you were being a vindictive dick."

"Not this time! I swear to God."

The director yells, "Okay, let's have Kendrick and Savage over here next!"

With a long exhale, I get up with Kendrick and walk to the middle of the soundstage, passing Laila and Colin as they return to the table. Of course, Laila doesn't look at me as she passes. On the contrary, she pretends to be deep in conversation with her assigned mentor who just so happens to be an underwear model, as well as a kickass, tatted drummer. And suddenly, I feel like everything I've ever done to show Laila who I really am doesn't matter. I'm right back at square one with her. So why even bother to try?

When we reach our mark, the director tells Kendrick and me what to do, and we go through the motions, after which the director moves on to shooting the other two remaining judge-mentor duos while I resume my seat next to Laila. Finally, lunchtime is called. The director shouts, "After lunch, let's start with Laila and Colin and Laila's team, while the other judges and mentors rotate through some B-roll with their teams. Take forty-five, people!"

There's a commotion around us, as people begin scattering, and Aloha and Fish head over to Colin and Laila sitting to my right. There's a brief conversation I can't make out because that Penelope fucker—Jon's mentor—has waltzed over to Kendrick on my left and is talking way too loudly to him in my ear.

"Yeah, sounds good," I hear Laila saying, just before she and Colin rise from the table.

"Oh, is everyone headed to lunch together?" I ask, thinking I'll invite myself and Kendrick to join Laila and her group, whether Laila likes it or not.

"No, Colin and I are going to grab box lunches and eat in my dressing room, instead of joining Fish and Aloha in the cafeteria. Colin wants me to give him the 4-1-1 about each of my contestants before he meets them after lunch. Hi, Kendrick."

"Hi, Laila."

"I'm so happy to see you. Let's catch up later."

"Sounds good."

Without a word to me, Laila heads off with Colin, leaving me watching her departing frame like a dog pressing his nose against a window as his owner heads off to work.

"Ooph, she's definitely pissed at you," Kendrick whispers once Laila is out of earshot.

"I told you. I thought she'd understand what I was trying to do for her. I actually thought she'd be *grateful* for what I did, but she's gone off the deep end."

"Well, it's not like you came into today with a clean slate."

I turn my head sharply to scowl at Kendrick. "What the hell does that mean?"

Kendrick looks unfazed by my death glare. "It means the stunt you pulled this morning was the same kind of shit you pulled throughout the tour. Maybe she's thinking the past weeks were a blip—an act—and now you've reverted back to true form."

I roll my eyes. "That can't be it. Laila's been living with me, night and day, Kendrick. She's seen me sing Mimi to sleep. We've had deep conversations and watched movies and eaten meals together. She knows who I am. She knows what I'm really about. Or, at least, I thought she did."

Kendrick shrugs. "That was my best guess. I mean, Laila's not crazy. Passionate, yes. Does she have a bit of a temper? Yes. But she's not legit *nuts*. So there's got to be *something* logical behind her reaction."

I look toward the exit again and exhale, feeling every cell in my body vibrating with the need to understand what's going on. To fix it, whatever it is. "I'll go to her dressing room now, and ask her—"

"No, no, not now." Kendrick sighs from the depths of his soul. "I wish I had a recording of me saying that to you, so I could press a button and save my vocal cords."

"I can't sit here and play it cool, KC. Laila is in her dressing room with Colin, feeling far more pissed off at me for what I did than is logical. God only knows what that crazy woman is thinking —what she'd do to torture me, if she thinks I've got it coming. For all I know, she's blowing Colin in there, as we speak!"

Kendrick rolls his eyes. "Would you stop being a jealous lunatic for a minute and listen to me? I swear, when it comes to Laila, you're a madman."

"Yes, I am," I admit. "That goddamned woman turns me into a *madman*. But even so, I'm not crazy this time. I can feel in my bones Colin wants her. He didn't suggest they eat lunch in Laila's dressing room, alone, to talk about Laila's contestants. He asked her in there so he could finally make his move."

"Oh, for the love of fuck. Even if you're right about that, don't you trust Laila? She wants *you,* man. Not *him.* You."

I run my hand through my hair. "But does she, though? Right

now, I feel the same way I did when Laila didn't come to my room during the tour! I thought she wanted me then, too, Kendrick. I would have bet any amount of money. But she never came to me and ignored me and blocked my number, and to this day, I can't understand why! And now, here I am wondering why she's spinning out of control, simply because I invited Charlie to our house—"

"To prove she's a liar."

"To help her get into character!"

"Okay, calm down." Kendrick sighs. "I'm sure she'll explain herself tonight. But for now, let's get some lunch and let the girl do her job, okay? She and Colin are up first after lunch, so they really do have work to do before then. Let's let them do it."

I place my elbows on the table and my head in my hands. "I swear, that woman has taken *years* off my life."

Kendrick pats my back. "At some point, you've got to decide to trust her, Savage. That's what this all boils down to—you finally deciding to trust a woman, completely. To let your guard down with Laila, once and for all, and *trust*."

Emotion surges inside of me. "How can I trust Laila when she didn't come to my room, when I was *so* sure she would? How can I trust a woman who wanted to be with Malik fucking Wallace after he so *clearly* showed her and everyone at that restaurant what a flaming asshole he is? How, how, how, Kendrick?"

"And how can *Laila* trust *you* when she thinks you're the guy who fucked that waitress and all those groupies? You weren't her boyfriend at the time, true, but she thinks she knows how you roll, man."

"She has to know I was full of shit about all that stuff by now!"

"But does she, though? Have you come clean to her about everything yet?"

I rub my forehead. "No. Once I get started talking, it's gonna be a *lot*. I want to be sure I'm all-in before I head down that road."

"Well, then, if you ask me, you can't be too surprised when she doesn't trust you any more than you trust her. My advice? You two need to sit down and talk this out, from top to bottom. Just talk to her and tell her everything."

I throw up my hands. "You specifically told me *not* to tell her a goddamned thing until I was positive of my feelings for her, or else you'd beat me up."

"That's still true." He smiles sympathetically. "But it seems to me you're pretty fucking sure about your feelings at this point, man."

I process that for a beat, and then lean back in my seat, feeling overwhelmed. "Kendrick, I'd crawl over a hundred miles of broken glass for that woman. I'd do *anything* for her. Literally *anything*. And yet, clearly, no matter what I do, she doesn't trust me as far as she can throw me. *And I don't understand why.*"

FIFTY-FOUR

LAILA

I take a seat next to Colin on the couch in my dressing room and begin opening my box lunch. "Thanks so much for meeting with me about my team," I say excitedly. "I can't wait to hear your thoughts about—"

"I didn't ask you here to talk about your team," Colin interrupts. "Sorry. I only said that to get you away from Savage."

My eyebrows shoot up. "Oh?"

"There's something I need to talk to you about, Laila. Something confidential." Colin places his box lunch on the coffee table in front of us. "I'm breaching my NDA with the show to tell you about this, but, as your friend, I can't keep it from you. Please, don't tell the producers I told you. Also, don't tell Savage. That guy's a loose cannon."

I nod and wait, my stomach tight with dread. I'm not sure I won't tell Savage whatever Colin is about to tell me, but I'm too nervous to speak, one way or the other.

Colin runs an anxious hand through his dark hair. "I found out yesterday the producers want me here to create the potential for a love triangle with you and Savage. They want me to create the impression that I'm your ex during our scenes together. I guess there's some chatter about that, online, and they don't want me to dispel it."

"Well, it's not true, obviously, so we'll just be ourselves, and—"

"That's not the part that made me feel like I needed to talk to you. I'm just giving you background." He sighs. "The big thing is the bonus they've offered me. During a break this afternoon, they want me to lure you to that patio in the back of the studio and make a move on you. They said they'll pay me a hundred grand if I do it today. Fifty grand if you're seen leaving my place in the early morning hours over the next two weeks. They didn't say it, but the implication was they'd arrange a photographer, who'd then 'leak' the photo to a click-bait farm. Or maybe they have faith someone out there in the world would organically take a photo of us. I guess that's pretty realistic, considering how much press you and Savage get. Basically, they want it to look like it's at least *possible* you're cheating on Savage with me. Or that you're tempted. Or maybe I'm your ex and you're not totally over me. They hit me with a lot of weird shit, Laila. I don't even know if *they* know what they want. All I know is they're looking to screw you over, and I'm not going to be a party to that or let it happen on my watch."

I touch his arm, trembling with adrenaline. "I can't thank you enough for telling me about this, Colin."

"Of course. I couldn't believe my ears."

"Who talked to you about this?"

"Nadine. She's the mastermind here. And she's ruthless."

I exhale. "I should have known this job was too good to be true. They never wanted me here. They wanted their usual three judges for the live shows—the same format they've always had. In fact, when that Instagrammer's video first hit, they only wanted me as Savage's mentor and fake girlfriend for three episodes. They never wanted me as a judge, but my agent strong-armed them. I guess they've figured out a way to make lemonade out of the Laila lemons they never wanted in the first place."

"They're idiots," Colin says. "You're incredible, Laila. So talented and beautiful. Funny and witty. I watched you guys shooting Draft Day on the monitors while I was waiting in the greenroom, and I was so impressed with how natural and charismatic you're able to be on-camera. You're totally yourself, other than pretending you give a shit about Savage."

My heart pangs sharply. "I'm not pretending anything when it comes to Savage," I confess. "Our relationship was fake when I first told you about it at Reed's. But it's not anymore. It's as real as it gets." Colin looks skeptical, so I add, "At least, it's real for me."

Colin looks sympathetic. Like he thinks I'm a fool. And that's all it takes for the image of Savage walking down that hallway in Las Vegas with that groupie, one arm around her shoulders and the other holding a bottle of booze, to pop into my head and make me realize Colin is right: *I'm a fool.*

Colin assesses me for a long moment. "You're in love with him?"

My breathing hitches. Savage and I have never labeled what we feel, and I don't think I've admitted the full depths of my feelings for Savage, even to myself. I blink and a tear leaks out of my eye and streaks down my cheek. "Before today, I would have answered that question, yes, without a doubt. But today, he did something that made me realize it's probably not going to work out between us." I sniffle and wipe my cheek. "It's too bad, honestly. I've had the time of my life with him. I was feeling pretty swept away."

"Aw, Laila. Come here. Cry on my shoulder."

"Thank you."

Colin opens his muscled arms and I scooch over to him on the couch and let him wrap me in a warm hug, just as soggy tears begin falling down my cheeks.

"What'd he do?"

"It's too much to explain. Bottom line, Savage can't handle being happy. If he's feeling too happy, he has this weird compulsion to mess it up, one way or another, even against his own interests."

There's a knock at the door and I lurch away from Colin, worried someone is going to burst in with a camera and snap a photo that makes me look like I'm doing something I'm not. But thank God, it's only one of the PA's calling to me from behind the closed door. "Fifteen minutes, guys!"

"Thank you!" I call toward the door. And when I hear receding footsteps, I smile with relief at Colin. "For a split-second, I thought someone was going to barge in here and snap a photo of me crying on your shoulder."

"Aw, Laila, you poor thing," he says. And there's no doubt in my mind he's being sincere . . . but also, semi-hitting on me. Thankfully, however, Colin has the emotional intelligence not to do anything too overt in this moment.

"It's interesting they offered you a hundred grand to 'lead me astray' today," I say. "That's the same amount they'd have to pay to buy me out of my contract. Sounds like they want me gone, one way or another, for a hundred grand. I'm sure if they're not successful convincing you to do their bidding, they'll move on to Plan B and get rid of me in a much less exciting way. Either way, I'm guessing I'll be gone during the break."

"That sucks."

I shrug. "It was fun while it lasted."

"So . . . are you planning to stay with Savage when the show is over for you, or is this more like a tour fling—the show ends, and the relationship ends?"

"I don't know what the future holds for Savage and me," I admit. "But I feel like I should tell you . . . either way, you and I probably aren't destined to be more than friends, Colin."

He grins. "I'm that transparent, huh?"

"I had a hunch."

"Thanks for letting me know. I appreciate that."

"I appreciate you thinking I'm worthy of you. You're an amazing guy."

He pauses. "Are you turning me down because of your feelings for Savage, or because you're not attracted to me, regardless?"

I consider my answer for a moment and realize I like and respect Colin too much not to answer him with complete honesty. "I don't think the word 'regardless' is in my vocabulary anymore, in this context, because I can't imagine a world where I wouldn't want Savage. Even though he did something today that pissed me off and made me think I'm an idiot to want him, I still do. In fact, it's impossible for me to imagine wanting anyone else. So, given that, it's pretty hard for me to tell you if I'd be attracted to you, *regardless* of my feelings for Savage, when the truth is my heart and soul and body belong to him."

"Wow," Colin says, looking shocked.

"Before you tell me I'm a fool," I add quickly, "I already know that. My brain knows this won't end well for me, but I guess I need to let it run its course, or my heart will never give up on him. Never get over him." Tears prick my eyes again and I wipe them. "Shit. My makeup is going to be a mess."

Colin pats the couch next to him and I scooch over again, grateful to let him comfort me. I lean into Colin's open arms, saying, "Thank you for telling me everything, Colin." But midsentence, as the second half of my comment falls out of my mouth and my body falls into Colin's waiting arms, Savage bursts into the room, his dark eyes blazing and bugging out.

"Savage," I blurt, leaping off the couch to standing.

"What the fuck?" he blurts. He looks between Colin and me. "*Laila?*"

"Nothing happened! I was upset. Colin is a friend who offered a shoulder to cry on."

"*Yeah, he did*," Savage spits out, looking murderous. He marches toward Colin, looking homicidal, his fists clenched. And in reply, Colin leaps to standing next to me, ready to defend himself. I lurch in front of Savage, blocking his progress, and, thankfully, he stops and shifts his weight from foot to foot, his energy like a live wire that's come loose and is now zapping wildly on the ground.

"You hit on her," Savage barks at Colin. "When you *knew* she was with me!"

"I thought your relationship was *fake*," Colin says. "And by the way, she turned me down. So now what, Savage? You're gonna beat the shit out of me for taking my shot? I didn't beat the shit out of *you* when you *fucked* my woman, but you're gonna throw down when I've done nothing but give yours a shoulder to cry on?" Savage's dark eyes shift to mine, looking guilty as hell, as Colin adds, "Maybe you should be more worried about *why* Laila needed a shoulder to cry on, than about who offered her that shoulder, you dumbass."

Savage looks like a caged animal as I flash him an enraged look. *He fucked Colin's girlfriend?* And the man has the nerve to freak out about me *talking* to Colin?

"There you are!" a male voice says, as Savage opens his mouth to say God-knows-what, and thank God, Kendrick appears a second later and grabs Savage's tense shoulders. "Come on, man. Don't do this."

Savage shakes off Kendrick's grip and looks at me plaintively, like he's on the cusp of a total and complete breakdown. "Do you want him?" he rasps out, motioning to Colin. "Is that why you didn't want me? Have you wanted Colin all along?"

"No!" I yell. "Colin is my *friend,* as I've told you many times— the same way *Ruby* is yours!"

"Yeah, well, I've never dragged Ruby into a room alone so I could hit on her!"

"Fuck you," Colin says. "I didn't do anything wrong."

"And neither did I!" Savage booms. He returns to me. "I was trying to *help* you this morning by inviting Charlie over. I don't understand why you're—"

"Of course, you don't understand!" I shout, anger flashing through my nerve endings. "Because you have the emotional intelligence of an amoeba and the impulse control of a gnat! Now, please, go, Savage. I need to wash my face and touch up my makeup before Colin and I start shooting with my team in five minutes. Kendrick, please." I point toward the door, nonverbally begging Kendrick to drag his best friend out. "I'm in charge of babysitting this boy's stupid ass, so if he disrupts the shooting schedule again, that's on *me.*"

"Come on, Savage," Kendrick says, gripping Savage's arm. "Leave her alone to do her job."

Thankfully, Savage lets Kendrick guide him toward the door. But before Savage exits, he shakes off Kendrick's grip, turns around, and flashes me one last tortured look, followed by a white-hot, murderous one at Colin. And then, Adrian Savage, the man who can't get out of his own fucking way, turns around and stalks out the door . . . but not before leaving a lovely parting gift for me: *a fist-sized hole in the wall next to the doorframe.*

FIFTY-FIVE

SAVAGE

"You had sex with Colin's girlfriend?" Laila shouts, the minute the door closes behind us in the SUV. Draft Day is in the can. Mentor Day is in the can. And now, finally, we're alone and headed home to our fake love nest to begin a much-needed three-week break from shooting—time I've been eager to spend with Laila. First, in Chicago, then, in Cabo, and finally, back at home in LA for a week of relaxation while the show begins airing. But after today, I'm not sure Laila is still planning to spend a minute of the break with me, let alone travel to see my family or drink piña coladas with me on a Mexican beach. I'm not even sure if Laila is planning to continue living with me for the remainder of the season, even for the sake of our written contracts.

In response to Laila's angry question about Colin's "girlfriend," I call out to our two usual escorts at the front of the car and ask them to turn up the music—and the minute the volume in the car ratchets up enough to swallow my voice, I reply to Laila. "No, I didn't have sex with Colin's *girlfriend*. I had sex with Colin's *ex-girlfriend*."

Laila scoffs. "Gee, I wonder why they broke up."

"It had nothing to do with me. They'd already broken up when I got with her."

"Colin said 'I didn't beat you up when you fucked my *girlfriend.*'"

"No, he said, 'when you fucked my *woman.*' Which means, apparently, Colin thinks his *single* ex was off-limits to me and every man on the planet—a concept I'm sure you strongly disagree with, as an independent, sex-positive woman."

"He didn't mean 'every man on the planet,' Savage. He meant *you.* I'm sure Colin considered you a *friend* when you nailed his girlfriend."

"*Ex*-girlfriend. And no. Colin and I travel in the same circles, but we've never been anything more than acquaintances. Ask any of my *actual* friends, Kendrick or Kai or Titus, ask Fish or C-Bomb, and they'll *all* tell you I'm as loyal as the day is long. Laila, I stepped aside from hitting on *you*—despite my *huge* crush on you— for a *friend.* But with Colin's *ex*, I was supposed to say, 'No, no, sorry, I can't have sex with you because you dated a guy whose band is *also* signed to my label?' Give me a break."

Laila pouts but doesn't reply.

"They'd been broken up for a full week," I mutter. "She was a free woman."

"A week?" Laila shouts. "Savage! You were her rebound fuck? No wonder Colin is pissed at you."

"Aaah. I see what this is about. You're jealous you're not the only woman who's enjoyed my services as a rebound fuck. You wanted to be the only one, eh?"

Laila grunts with anger. "No, Adrian, this isn't about me being jealous of Colin's ex. This is about me realizing I've ignored way too many red flags with you. This is about me realizing I can't trust a word you say!"

"What the hell are you talking about?"

"You looked me dead in the eye at Reed's house and told me Colin didn't like you because you're buddies with C-Bomb! You said Colin must be taking Dax's side in their beef. And then you had the audacity to chew me out in Reed's laundry room for supposedly *flirting* with Colin, while not bothering to mention to me, 'Oh, gee, come to think of it, Colin *might* be pissed at me because I banged his ex-girlfriend, rather than because he's siding with his best friend in a stupid beef with C-Bomb'!"

"I didn't *lie* to you. I just didn't tell you the whole truth because I didn't want you thinking Colin was flirting with you to retaliate against *me*."

"Oooooh, so let me get this straight. You *lied* to my face—oh, sorry, 'didn't tell me the whole truth' to my face—in order to protect my sensitive feelings?"

"I shaved the truth a bit to protect your feelings, yes."

"And once again, you prove, without a doubt, you're a liar. The truth is you wanted to get laid that night, and you figured telling me about the time you railed Colin's ex a week after they'd broken up wasn't going to help your cause."

I pull a face that concedes she's got a point. "I suppose it could've been that, at least in part."

Laila throws up her hands. "See what I mean? I can't believe a word out of your mouth!"

"I just copped to wanting to get laid that night!" I shout. "Jesus, Laila! I feel like you're looking for things to be mad at me about, when what you're really mad about is Charlie, for reasons I can't comprehend, since I only invited him over to help you tap into your inner bitch! Which, by the way, you *did*—brilliantly, all day long. *You're welcome.* But guess what? You can stop being a bitch now, Laila, now that the cameras are off!"

Laila gasps, and I immediately regret my comment. *Come on, Savage. You're trying to make amends here. Not fan the flames.*

"You 'can't *comprehend*' the reason I'm mad about *Charlie?*" Laila booms. "Okay, then, amoeba boy, let me explain it to you in terms your amoeba-sized brain can understand. *You're* the one who said we should put the past behind us and press the reset button. *You're* the one who said we should forget the past and move forward—so, that's what I've tried to do, with all my might. And you have no idea the mental gymnastics it took to do that! But I did! And then, what did you do? The boy who can't help self-sabotaging couldn't resist dredging up the past this morning, despite what *he* suggested we do, because he couldn't resist finding out, once and for all, if I'd let Charlie plow me during the tour!"

"Oh, my fucking God. Laila, I already knew about Charlie's family situation when I asked him to come to the house. Kendrick told me about Charlie's husband *yesterday*. I only invited Charlie over when you started freaking out about your job being on the line. I thought me supposedly finding out that Charlie is married and gay, right in front of you, would give you something to chew on during today's shoot. *And I was right about that!*"

Laila shakes her head. "Don't you see? You bringing Charlie into our *new* life, after we explicitly agreed to forgive and forget the past, made me realize you're still that guy from the tour, the one who wanted groupies more than *me*, no matter how much I try to—"

"I didn't want groupies, Laila! I only wanted *you*. All those groupies were a set-up! I thought you knew that. The same with that waitress in New York. I never even called her, Laila! I only got her number to piss you off, because I was so jealous of watching you and Malik!"

To my shock, tears prick Laila's eyes. "I saw you bringing a groupie to your room—and that was most definitely *not* a set-up."

"What? Where?"

"The fact that you don't even know which city I'm referring to isn't a good sign, Savage."

My heart is stampeding. "Laila, no. Whatever you saw, it wasn't what you thought. Women throw themselves at me, all the time, but that doesn't mean I *catch* them. I wasn't with anyone but you on that tour, Laila. Nobody but you."

She scoffs and a dam of panic and despair breaks inside me. I've been so happy with this girl. So fucking happy. How is everything falling apart so fast and suddenly?

"What happened today?" I shout, my frustration and panic

boiling over. "Do you want Colin, so you're trying to get me to break up with you? Is that it?"

She wipes away a tear. "No. I've just realized I'm in way too deep with you. At your core, you're still the same guy from the tour. The Beast from *before* the snowball fight. I've realized I need to slow this thing down before I get myself really, really hurt."

"I'm not going to hurt you, Laila."

I try to grab her hand, but she yanks it away.

"You already did!" she screams. "I told you about my father! I told you how scary and horrible he was! I asked you not to punch holes in walls or—"

"Oh, God, Laila. I'm so sorry. Please forgive me. That was so stupid of me."

"How could you do that, when I told you how much that kind of thing triggers me?"

I open and close my mouth. But there's no excuse. No words I could possibly say to make it better.

"You did it to *hurt* me!" she says. "Plain and simple. So, tell me, Savage, why would I want to be with a man who *wants* to hurt me?"

My heart feels like it's physically shattering. I didn't plan to punch that wall. I didn't make a conscious decision to do it. But I suppose it's only fair to say I knew, deep down, somewhere inside me, that punching that wall would scare the shit out of Laila. And I did it, anyway. Did I punch that wall to push her away, to make her leave me *now*, rather than later, when losing her would wreck me all that much more? Did I subconsciously do it to see if doing the unthinkable would make Laila finally leave me, the same way I did horrible shit at first with Mimi, to see if there was something, anything, that would make *her* leave me, too? For fuck's sake, did I set that kitchen fire at my apartment in Phoenix on purpose, like my mother always says I did? Despite everything, despite all the love Mimi has given to me, all the lessons she's tried to teach me, was it all for nothing because, at my core, I'm my father's son—*and always will be?*

"I'm sorry, Laila," I choke out, my emotions hanging on by a thread. "I'd never harm a hair on your head. I'd die to protect you. I'd do *anything* for you. But you're right: punching that hole in the wall was unforgivable."

Her lower lip trembles. "I don't feel physically threatened by you, Adrian. But I do think you need some sort of therapy. Anger management, maybe. You made a promise to me and you should have been able to control yourself and keep it."

I clench my jaw. My knee-jerk reaction is to reply, "Well, if I need therapy, then you do, too, sweetheart, because you're definitely a few bricks shy of a load." But, luckily, I'm not stupid enough to give voice to my honest thoughts. My next thought is, "Please forgive me, Laila. I'll do whatever it takes to make you stay with me. To make you happy. *To make you love me.*" But those words don't come out, either.

"For what it's worth," I mumble. "I think my brain didn't connect the promise I made to you at the house to your dressing room. It's stupid, I know, but I think maybe not being at the house made me forget . . ." I stop talking, based on the incredulity I'm seeing on Laila's face, and whisper, "Regardless, I made a promise to you and I broke it. I'm sorry."

Laila holds my gaze for a long beat and then looks out the window on her side of the car at passing traffic, effectively letting me know this conversation is over, and that she emphatically does *not* forgive me.

I pick up my phone and murmur, "I need to call Mimi, before it gets too late. I've missed bedtime the last three nights." I pause, hoping the mention of Mimi's name will prompt Laila to tell me if she's still planning to come to Chicago with me tomorrow. But when Laila doesn't say a word, but continues silently staring out her side of the car, I add, "While I'm talking to Mimi, I'd appreciate you pretending you still like me. My grandma still thinks we're blissfully happy and I'd like her to keep thinking it for Christmas— and for however long she's got."

Laila looks away from the window, rolling her eyes. "I won't scream at you or flip you off while you're speaking to your ailing grandmother, Adrian, if that's what you think. And you know why? Because I've got this weird thing called *impulse control*. Ask a therapist about it sometime."

Annoyance floods me. I think, "Yeah, Laila. You're a paragon of maturity." But thanks to *my* impulse control, I don't say it. After taking a few deep breaths, I press the button to FaceTime my cousin—and the minute Sasha picks up, even before saying hello, she says, "What's wrong?"

"Nothing," I reply. "We just got done with a long shooting day. Can you put Mimi on, so I can sing to her? I'm in a bad mood and not wanting to chat."

"Mimi's already asleep. I texted you an hour ago to let you know it was now or never."

I rub my face with my palm. "I didn't see your text. I was shooting and didn't have my phone."

"It's okay. You'll be here tomorrow."

I glance at the time on the dashboard of the SUV. "She fell asleep an *hour* ago? That's awfully early, Sasha."

"The move has been exhausting for her."

I furrow my brow with concern. "But she likes the house, right?"

My cousin smiles broadly. "She *loves* the house. Of course, she does, Adrian. You gave her an incredible gift. Mimi says she sees Jasper in every nook and cranny."

My heart skips a beat. "I can't wait to carry her around from room to room and hear all her stories."

"Mimi is so excited you're coming. That's all she's been talking about—getting to see you and Laila, in person."

I glance at my fake girlfriend next to me to gauge her reaction to Sasha's comment, and instantly surmise Laila is feeling conflicted. "Hey, I need to put you on hold for a sec, Cuz," I say, before muting the call. I look at Laila. "Are you still coming to Chicago tomorrow? If not, I need to give Sasha a heads-up so she can break the bad news to Mimi when she wakes up in the morning."

Laila pauses and I hold my breath, bracing myself. "I'll come," she finally decides. "*Mimi* didn't say we should leave the past behind us and then turn around and invite Charlie to the house, and *Mimi* didn't punch a hole in the wall, after promising she wouldn't."

"Thank you."

"I'm not doing it for you."

"Any drop of happiness you bring to my grandmother is a huge gift to me. So, thank you." With that, I unmute the call with my cousin. "Sorry about that. Laila and I will be landing around five tomorrow. I'll text you when we're driving to the house."

"Perfect. See you soon."

"Oh, hey. I ordered a bunch of groceries to be delivered to the house tomorrow morning—everything for Mimi's famous raviolis. I thought Mimi could show Laila and me how an expert makes pasta from scratch tomorrow."

Sasha pauses, ever so briefly. But it's long enough to make the hair on the back of my neck stand up.

"What?" I ask.

"I wouldn't get your hopes up too high about Mimi cooking with you during your visit, Ady. Mimi's been really tired lately."

My breathing catches. "I'll make sure Mimi gets plenty of rest, I promise. But I have to see her cooking like a boss in that huge gourmet kitchen."

Sasha smiles thinly, but says nothing.

I take a shallow breath. "Okay, well. Gotta go. See you tomorrow."

"Sleep tight and travel safe," Sasha says. "Is Laila there?"

"Right here."

I shift the camera to capture Laila and she waves.

"I can't wait to see you in person," Sasha says.

"Same here," Laila replies. "Thank you for taking such good care of Mimi."

"Thank you for taking such good care of Adrian."

"Okay, bye now," I say, abruptly shifting the camera back to myself. "Love you, Sash."

I hang up the call, feeling physically ill. If I hadn't messed up today, that call would have been one of the most exciting of my life. If I hadn't messed up, I'd be on the cusp of taking a girl home to meet my family, for the first time in my life. For *real*. And, man, I would have been excited about that. Proud to show Laila off, as my gorgeous, talented, brilliant girlfriend. As it is, however, for reasons I still don't fully understand, it seems like we're hanging on by the barest of threads, if at all.

Our SUV reaches the iron gate in front of our reality TV mansion and our driver punches in the code—and when we roll into our driveway, we see a car already parked in front of the house.

"Fuck," I say, suddenly remembering. "Fish and Alessandra. We're writing our sappy love song tonight, remember?"

"Fuck," Laila replies. She shakes her head. "Well, all I can say is thank God for Fish and Alessandra. Because as hard as it's been to write a song about our 'undying love' the past few weeks, it'd be fucking impossible now."

FIFTY-SIX
LAILA

When Savage and I enter our large kitchen, Fish and Alessandra are already there, seated on stools at the island while our private chef prepares something on the stove.

Savage and I greet Fish and Alessandra and the chef. We thank our friends for coming here to save our asses and chat about today's long shoot, since three out of four of us were there. And through it all, I can't bring myself to look at Savage, even once.

After some more small talk, we sit down at the kitchen table and eat the meal our chef has prepared. As we eat, I keep catching Savage staring at me, his eyes begging for forgiveness. And I must admit, despite everything, my anger thaws a bit every time I look into his dark, tormented eyes. My solution? I try to avoid looking into Savage's eyes, as much as possible. However much living with Savage in this TV mansion has made me swoon, today made me realize there's too much baggage between us, too much jealousy and hypocrisy and popcorn lies, for us to move forward together, as a real couple, outside of this carefully curated bubble. Which means I'd better get my heart extricated *now* from this situation, before it's too late.

After our meal ends, our foursome heads into the living room to get to work, with Savage and Fish grabbing acoustic guitars, Alessandra taking an armchair with her laptop, and me taking a seat behind the baby grand.

"Okay," Fish says on an exhale, tuning the guitar in his lap. "Reed said this song should be a 'classic love song.' He said he wants it 'sweet and romantic.'"

"Pure, gooey goodness," Alessandra chimes in.

Fish looks at Savage and me. "Is that your understanding, too?"

"Yep," Savage says.

"Cool," Fish replies. "Let's write a hit love song, guys."

"Thank God you and Alessandra came over to help us out," I say. "Left to our own devices, Savage and I couldn't write 'pure, gooey goodness' to save our lives."

Savage looks like I've slapped him in the face. "Well, I wouldn't go *that* far," he mutters, and I quickly look away from his pained expression.

"It shouldn't be too hard for the four of us geniuses to write something, on-brand, if we put our heads together," Fish says. And Alessandra concurs. But when the pair looks at Savage and me for confirmation . . . they get crickets. Nothing. In fact, with each passing second of silence, the air in the room is becoming increasingly thick and stilted.

Alessandra clears her throat. "So, have you two worked up any ideas to get us started, or . . . ?"

"We've got nothing," I reply, letting my eyes return to Savage's. And when the words leave my lips, he physically winces in reply, like I've lashed him with a whip. Crap. Maybe that was a bit harsh of me. My heart aching, I peel my eyes off Savage's tormented face and return to Fish and Alessandra. "We've tried to write this song, over and over again. But everything we've come up with has been all wrong. Way too intense and passionate and angsty for the assignment."

"I think a little angst would be okay, here and there," Alessandra says.

"Yeah, well, angst is all we've got, unfortunately."

Alessandra looks at Fish. And then back at me. "I do think the song should feel authentic to you two, regardless of the assignment, since you're the ones who'll be singing it. And you're both extremely intense and passionate people. Why don't you guys let Fish and me get the ball rolling, to lay the groundwork for something on the lighter side, and then we'll let you two sprinkle in some details in the verses that are more personal to you. Little details here and there that will make the song feel tailored to you?"

"Love it, babe," Fish says. He looks at Savage and me, but we say nothing. "Is that approach cool with you guys?"

"Great," I say, while Savage strums his guitar and mutters, "Whatever you want to do."

Alessandra and Fish look at each other again for a long beat, their expressions clearly saying, "What the heck?" But after her nonverbal conversation with Fish, Alessandra turns to the group and suggests everyone think about a person we love unconditionally and without complication. "Not necessarily in a romantic way," Alessandra prompts. "I want you to think about the purest, easiest form of love in your life and meditate on the way that kind of love makes you feel, deep in your soul."

I quiet my mind and think about my infant niece, Everly, who's already the light of my life in the most uncomplicated way possible. I look at Savage and instantly know who he's thinking about. *Mimi.* And, damn it, despite everything, my heart swells for him, as I think about how much that poor man loves his grandmother and can't stand the thought of losing her.

I lay my fingers on the piano keys and play the little melody Savage always sings to his grandmother at bedtime and Savage's attention snaps to me, his face as beautiful and heartbreaking as I've ever seen it.

"I love that!" Alessandra says. "Let's build on that!"

"Yeah, that's a perfect riff for the chorus," Fish agrees. "It feels like a lullaby."

"Exactly!" Alessandra says excitedly.

And that's all it takes. The minute we've got some mutual inspiration going, the song basically writes itself. In a flurry, we brainstorm some themes for our lyrics, based on our ideas about uncomplicated love. We shout out words like unconditional and endless. Eternal and infinite. And Alessandra notes everything on her laptop. We jam for a bit, building on that little lullaby sequence, and faster than I would have thought possible, the musical structure for the song and vocal melody begin taking shape.

As suggested by Alessandra earlier, Savage and I throw in a few angsty lyrics to complement the gooey-sweet ones we've already written. But, nonetheless, in the end, the song the group creates feels far more about the sweet love shared by Fish and Alessandra than about anything felt by Savage and me. But that's okay. The assignment was to write a classic love song that will make us truckloads of money after we perform it on *Sing Your Heart Out*. And I'm pretty confident we've done exactly that.

We run through the song several times, making tweaks, here and there, until, finally, everybody agrees we wouldn't change a thing.

"Let's record a quick demo and send it off to Reed for his feedback," Fish suggests. "If we need to change anything after Reed's notes, we can do that remotely while you guys are out of town."

"Sounds like a plan," I say. And when my eyes flicker to Savage, it's clear he's deeply relieved by the implication of my comment: I'm still planning to travel with him to Chicago, like I assured him earlier in the car.

We record a rough demo of the song on Fish's iPad, with me playing piano and the guys on their guitars—and Savage and I barely look at each other as we sing our parts. Fish says he'll add a few bells and whistles to the demo—stuff like programmed drums and a bassline—in order to give Reed an idea of the general vibe we're envisioning for the full production. And, finally, after Fish and Alessandra have gathered up their stuff, Savage and I walk them to the front door.

We say our goodbyes to our friends. Give them high-fives about the song. And, finally, Fish and Alessandra head out the door and into the starry night, to drive to the home they share together on the beach—to enjoy the sweet, uncomplicated, gooey goodness that is their love story.

I close the front door behind our friends and lean against it, exhaling. "What time is our flight?"

"Noon."

"Thank goodness it's not at the crack of dawn. Today was a long day." I press my lips together and wait. Savage looks like he's going to say something—something important. But in the end, he closes his mouth, bites the inside of his cheek, and sighs.

"Okay, well, goodnight," I say. "I'll wake you up when I get up, so don't worry about setting an alarm."

"Laila."

I turn around.

Savage's Adam's apple bobs. He clears his throat. "I'm so sorry I punched a hole in that wall. I can't believe I did that. I hope you can find your way to forgiving me for that, at some point. I promise on my love for Mimi I'll never, *ever* do that again, or anything else that would scare you. I'll never break a promise to you again, Laila. I'm giving you my solemn word on that."

I twist my mouth. His promises don't mean a whole lot to me. But I don't feel like fighting right now. I just want to go to sleep. "Thank you for that," I say calmly. "I need to get some sleep now. We can talk some more about that another time, maybe."

He nods. "Any time you want."

"Goodnight, Adrian."

"Goodnight, Laila."

As I walk away, I bite my lip, and somehow keep myself from crying until I get safely into one of the bedrooms down the hallway from the master. Which is where I throw myself onto the bed and cry myself to sleep.

FIFTY-SEVEN

LAILA

Evanston, Illinois

"Is this still Chicago?" I ask Savage, looking out the window of our limo. After pulling away from the curbside at O'Hare, we've been driving about thirty minutes now, and the view out my window has become decidedly suburban and upscale.

"No, we're in Evanston now," Savage replies. "Mimi's house is a few blocks away."

"It's so pretty here."

"This is where Mimi lived as a teenager."

"Oh, I thought you lived with Mimi in the City."

"I did. In an apartment. But Mimi lived here with her mom when she was young."

I return to the window on my side of the car. "Was Mimi's family wealthy, or did this neighborhood become posh more recently?"

"Mimi grew up poor. Her dad died when she was twelve or

thirteen, so her mom got work as a housekeeper in this neigh-borhood."

"Ah."

"I'll let Mimi tell you the whole story, but, basically, Mimi's mom went to work for a rich family in Evanston, and that's where Mimi met her husband, Jasper, a teenager. He was one of the rich family's teenaged sons."

It's the longest, and most relaxed, conversation Savage and I have had all day. We didn't speak at all during the drive to the airport this morning, though Savage's dark eyes pleaded with me to speak first. We barely spoke during our flight, other than to ask polite questions about legroom and the shows we were separately watching. But now that we're here, and on our way to Mimi's new house, the cold air feels too super-charged with excitement and adventure for my heart to remember to be closed off.

The limo turns onto a residential street lined with stunning mini-mansions. And when the car makes another turn, the passing homes turn from mini-mansions to actual ones—massive homes with meticulously sheared hedges and tidy walkways and iron gates. Stunning homes that look straight out of a bygone era.

"Whoa," I breathe. "These homes are gorgeous." I gasp and point. "Look at that one!"

To my shock, I've no sooner said the words than the car comes to a stop in front of the very house I'm indicating—a breathtaking mansion with countless windows framed by green-painted shutters, sprawling gardens, and brickwork walkways.

I open my mouth wide in shock. "*This* is the house you got for Mimi?"

"This is it," Savage confirms, his beautiful face radiating with pride.

As the driver exits the car and begins unloading our luggage from the back, Savage and I start bundling up for the short walk from the street to the front door. I don't know anything about archi-tecture, so my brain can't conjure the right words to describe this home. All I can say is it looks like a "Victorian mansion" to me. Or maybe a Civil war era house? Yeah, I don't know what I'm talking about. All I know is it looks old, but painstakingly restored, and gorgeous. No wonder Savage wanted to keep his full salary from the show! I don't know how much this fancy house cost him, but I have to think Savage was depending on his full salary from the show when he decided to buy it.

"Who lives here with Mimi?" I ask, as we begin walking up the front pathway with our luggage.

"Sasha is staying here, for the time being, and Mimi's got a rotation of caregivers who stay here, too."

"I'm not sure there's enough room for everyone," I joke.

"Just barely," he replies.

"It must take a day just to vacuum the downstairs."

"I've got a maid service coming, twice a week, to keep it from getting dusty."

"Wow. I would have given anything to play hide and seek in a house like this as a kid."

Savage flashes a crooked smile. "I'd be happy to play with you during our stay, if you'd like." There's sexual innuendo buried in his tone. Knowing him, he's probably imagining himself nailing me, wherever he finds me.

"Let's not get ahead of ourselves," I say. "We're here for Mimi."

His face falls. "Yeah. Okay. Thanks again for that." He reaches for the doorknob, but stops and takes a deep breath, like he's gearing up for something.

"What?" I ask.

He bites his lip. "I know intellectually you're only here for Mimi's sake. But, still, my heart is racing. Even if this is fake, it's still a first for me—bringing a girl home to meet my family. I've never done that before, and it's kind of exciting."

Oh, crap. In a torrent, I feel the urge to throw myself into Savage's arms and kiss the hell out of him. I want to tell him to forget yesterday—to say we'll press the 'reset' button, *again*. But, this time, as much as my heart wants to ignore the red flags and bury my head in the sand and enjoy the ride, my head won't allow such foolishness.

"Just so you know," Savage says. "When we walk through this door, Mimi is going to fling her little hummingbird body at you like a missile." He chuckles. "I'm sure she's sitting on the couch, watching TV right now. And the minute she hears our voices in the foyer, she's going to hobble over to us and lose her ever-loving mind."

I giggle. "Sounds amazing. I think I can handle being attacked by a hummingbird. Bring it, Mimi."

With a huge smile, Savage takes a deep breath and opens the front door. We walk inside the house and into a beautiful foyer, where we're surrounded on all sides by splendor—a huge wooden staircase directly in front of us, and two well-appointed rooms to either side.

"Whoa," I say. "It looks straight out of a movie! Did you hire a designer?"

"No, I bought it this way. It's amazing, isn't it?"

"It's perfect."

"Hello?" Savage booms. "We're here!" He pauses, a huge smile on his face. And then, when the house remains quiet as a mouse, he yells, "Sasha? Mimi? We're here!" We wait. But nothing happens. "She must be watching TV in the family room. It's hard to hear back there. Come on." He grabs my hand, and off we go through a fancy living room into another room appointed with more modern-looking, comfy furniture and a large-screen TV. But it's empty. We head into the next room—a huge, modern kitchen. And, again, there's nobody here.

"Where the hell is everyone?" Savage mutters. "Mimi always watches TV around this time—and never in bed. Mimi says it makes her sleep better at night if she spends most of the day outside her bedroom."

"Adrian," a voice says behind us. And when we turn around, it's Savage's pretty cousin, Sasha Wilkes—a Mother Earth type I've spoken to several times on FaceTime. Not surprisingly, given that she shares genes with Savage, Sasha is a beauty with dark hair and eyes. Also, from what I've seen, she's someone who's earned Savage's full trust and admiration.

"Sasha! Whew. I was getting nervous." He bounds across the room toward his cousin and hugs her. "Is Mimi watching TV upstairs?"

Sasha swallows hard. "Yeah, she's in her room. Sit down, sweetie."

Savage's body stiffens. "What's wrong?"

"Sit down."

His chest heaves. "Just tell me, Sasha."

"Sit down. Hello, Laila. It's so good to see you."

"You, too." I hug her and take a seat on a couch next to Savage, who looks like he's suddenly having trouble breathing.

After taking a chair across from us, Sasha says, "Adrian, Mimi hasn't gotten out of bed in over a week."

"*What?*" Savage whisper-shouts.

Sasha's face contorts, like she's holding back tears. "She hasn't been doing well, Ady. Even before the move, she was in a state of rapid decline. But now that she's here, it's like she's exhaling with relief. It's like she thinks she's reached the finish line."

"*No,*" Savage says, his voice tight. "No, Sasha. That's not why I bought Mimi the house—for her to give up! I bought it so she'd have a reason to keep going!"

"It doesn't work that way, honey. She says she's ready to go now."

"No!" he shouts, this time not whispering. "No! We'll tell her *no.* Have you told her no?"

Sasha smiles through tears. "Actually, I've been telling her *yes.* I've told her she's free to go, whenever she wants. I've told her we'll be okay and she'll always be with us."

"No, Sasha!" Savage pulls on his hair, his body convulsing. "Why the fuck did you tell her that shit, without asking me first? I never agreed to you telling her that! You should have consulted me!"

"She's in pain. I don't want her to feel pain anymore."

"Well, neither do I, obviously! But Mimi can't go yet." He chokes up. Pauses. Pulls himself together. And finally says, "I still need her, Sasha. You don't. *But I do.*"

I scootch over to Savage on the couch and put my arms around him and he pulls me fiercely into him, his body wracked with tremors.

Tears spill down my cheeks as I hold him.

"Why didn't you at least tell me she hasn't been getting out of bed?" Savage chokes out, his voice tight and pained. "You let me think everything's been fine. You said she was tired because of the move. You didn't say she's ready to *go!*"

"I didn't want to worry you. I knew you were coming today. So, why worry you before then?"

"Because you promised you'd tell me when it was time for me to drop everything and come! You swore to tell me that, Sasha!"

"I'm telling you now. You both have had a busy shooting schedule for the show and I didn't want you dropping everything for nothing. I knew Mimi was determined to hang on to see you both, in person. I knew that."

"But I would have had more time with her, Sasha! Fuck the show! I only signed on to do the goddamned show in the first place for Mimi—so she could watch me on her favorite show while lying in bed in the master bedroom of *this* house." He's shaking. Fighting tears. "Are you telling me she won't even make it to see the first episode?"

Sasha swallows hard. "I doubt she'll still be here by then."

Savage makes a garbled sound that breaks my heart. His body quaking, he pulls out his phone, pushes a button, and brings the phone to his ear. His chest heaves. His Adam's apple bobs. And then, "Nadine Collins, please. This is Adrian Savage. It's an emergency. Thanks." He waits. And as he does, Sasha and I look at each other, both of our cheeks wet with tears. Savage inhales sharply before saying, "Hi, Nadine. Thanks for taking my call. Listen, I've got a family emergency on my hands. I'm in Chicago with my sick grandma. She's like a mother to me. The only mother I've ever known. And I've just been told her time is a whole lot shorter than I realized. *Sing Your Heart Out* has been her favorite show since the beginning. She's never missed an episode. So, I'm calling to beg you, literally, *beg* you, to please send me the first episode, so I can sit down and watch it with her right away. I'll sign whatever you need and promise whatever you want. But I need this favor from you, Nadine." His chin trembles as he listens to whatever Nadine is saying on her end of the line. His shoulders soften. His chest lurches. He whispers, "Thank you. I appreciate that. Thank you. Bye."

Savage hangs up and takes a deep breath. "She's sending it now."

"That's good," Sasha says. "Mimi will be so happy to share that with you."

Savage opens his mouth, but whatever he was planning to say gets lodged in his throat. He hangs his head and breathes fitfully for a moment, while I rub his back and look at Sasha through tears.

"Ady, she's at peace," Sasha says. "She wants to see you and Laila together. She wants to hear you sing to her. She wants to kiss you and hug you. But then, she's excited to get to see Jasper and my dad again. So, please, don't make a tearful plea for her to stick around. This isn't about you. It's about *her*."

Savage inhales a deep breath and raises his head. "I understand," he says softly, resolve settling in his jawline. "I'll make sure Mimi knows I'll be okay."

"Good. Thank you." Sasha rises and extends her hand to her cousin. "Come on, sweetie. Maybe you can carry her around the house, so she can point out all the little nooks and crannies where she and Jasper fell in love." She looks at me. "Did Adrian tell you this is where Mimi met her husband, Jasper—when Mimi's mom worked here as a live-in housekeeper?"

"He told me a little bit," I say. "But no details."

Sasha says, "Mimi and Jasper were both sixteen when they fell in love here, in this house. She got pregnant with my father, so they ran off together to get married, against the wishes of Jasper's family. In fact, Jasper's family disowned him."

"Oh, no. Did they ever come around and accept Mimi and their baby?"

Sasha shakes her head. "They never did. They acted like Jasper, and his family, were dead to them."

"Oh my gosh."

"Even after Jasper died, way too young, they didn't help his young widow with her two young sons—my father and Adrian's. They pretended Mimi and her two little boys didn't even exist."

"That's terrible." I look at Savage, suddenly understanding his motivation to purchase this sprawling house for Mimi, during the last weeks of her life. He wanted revenge against Jasper's family, obviously. He wanted Mimi to get the last laugh against her cruel in-laws. He wanted Mimi to be the mistress of this grand home, if only briefly, and perhaps get to enjoy a torrent of memories, too, about the beginning days of her love story with Jasper.

"Jasper's family tried to pay Mimi off to ditch Jasper," Sasha says. "But when she refused, they tried to pay off Jasper to leave Mimi and deny the baby was his. Jasper was their first-born son, and, apparently, they'd had an heiress in mind for him, ever since birth. But Jasper and Mimi said they'd rather be poor, but happy together, and that's precisely what they were."

Savage motions to the grandeur around us. "And now, fuck 'em all. Mimi owns their fancy fucking house. She sleeps in their fancy fucking bedroom. She's queen of this entire fucking castle, and they can all rot in hell."

FIFTY-EIGHT

SAVAGE

"Mimi," I whisper, plastering a smile on my face as I race to her bedside, past her caregiver, Stuart. How did I not realize how much my grandmother has been deteriorating during our recent phone calls? Now that I'm seeing Mimi in person, it's clear how pale and whittled away she's become. No wonder Sasha looked downright pained when I talked cluelessly last night about my plan to cook raviolis with Mimi in her fancy kitchen tonight. Based on the way Mimi looks right now, it's clear I've been willfully blind these past few weeks. Seeing what I wanted to see.

"Ady," Mimi breathes with an exhausted smile, as I lean down to hug her.

"Merry Christmas," I whisper into her white hair. "I love you so much, Mimi."

"I love you, too," she whispers. "Forever and always, my sweet boy."

When we disengage, Mimi's dark eyes find Laila, who's standing tentatively a few feet away, her body language suggesting she doesn't want to intrude.

"Come," Mimi says. "Sweet Laila. Welcome."

Laila steps forward, swallowing hard. Somehow, she manages to squeak out a heartfelt little "Merry Christmas, Mimi," before bending down and taking my beloved hummingbird into her warm embrace. "I'm so happy to be here," Laila whispers. "I love you so much, Mimi. I already do."

It's more than my already beleaguered heart can take. I turn away and breathe deeply, determined to stuff my emotions down. But when I see the faces of Sasha and Mimi's favorite caregiver, Stuart, reflecting my own heartbreak back to me, I lose it. With my back to Mimi, as Laila continues chatting with her, I put my hands over my face and try to regain control.

"Are you and Adrian happy?" Mimi says behind me.

"We're so happy," Laila replies. "We couldn't be happier."

Mimi exhales, like the weight of the world has been lifted from her tiny shoulders. "Ady?"

I take a deep breath and turn around. "I'm right here. And I've got great news for you." I pull a second chair to Mimi's bedside, next to the one Laila is now sitting in. "Mimi, I was able to get a copy of the first episode of *Sing Your Heart Out*, so we can watch it together."

"Oh, how exciting."

"Oh, come on, honey, tell Mimi our *really* good news," Laila says, her eyebrows raised. And when I look at her blankly, she leans into my ear and whispers, "Tell her we're engaged."

My heart lurches. "Ooooh, yes. Of course." I shoot Laila a grateful smile and she winks at me. And then, I take my grandmother's hand in mine and say, "We were going to wait to tell you this on Christmas, but I think Laila's right—we shouldn't wait." I smile broadly. "Laila and I are engaged, Mimi."

Mimi gasps and her eyes prick with tears, as Sasha behind me whispers, "Oh my God."

I continue, "I asked Laila to marry me three nights ago at our house. We were having a nice dinner and, suddenly, I realized I don't want her to be my girlfriend. I want her to be my *wife*. So I asked, and she said *yes*."

"Of course, I did," Laila says, gripping my free hand. "And it was the easiest decision I've made in my life."

Tears flood Mimi's dark eyes. "Praise God," she whispers. Her eyes drift to Laila's hand, presumably looking for a ring, so I say, "We don't have a ring yet. We're going to get one when we get back home."

"Adrian figured I'd want to help pick the ring out," Laila explains.

"Well, that and I asked Laila, spur of the moment, without a plan. You know me, Mimi."

The skin around Mimi's eyes crinkles, letting me know she's thinking, *Yes, I do.*

And just like that, it hits me like a ton of bricks I wish this story were real. I wish I'd asked Laila to marry me, spur of the moment, over dinner the other night. I wish I'd been smart enough to realize, back then, that I can't live without her. That I don't want her to be my girlfriend—I want her to be my *wife.*

"I did have one condition for Adrian," Laila says. "One thing I told him he'll need to do before we say 'I do.'" She looks at me. "I told him, 'You're the most amazing man I've ever met and I don't want anyone else, ever. But if we're going to have a shot at living happily ever after, without some of the traumas of our childhoods getting in our way, then I think we should both agree to go to therapy.' I think Adrian could use some help with anger management, honestly. And I could certainly use some help dealing with a few things from my childhood, as well."

My heart is galloping. "I had no problem saying yes to that, Mimi." I look at Laila. "I told her, 'No problem. I'll do anything to make this work.' I wanted Laila to know she can always trust me—that I'd never hurt her or do anything to push her away or scare her. I wanted her to know I screw up sometimes, yes, but I want this more than I've ever wanted anything, ever, so I'll do whatever it takes."

"Holy fuck," Sasha whispers.

Laila's flushed. She says, "When Adrian said all that, I told him, 'Well, it's not like I'm perfect or anything. I've got some major hang-ups and insecurities I haven't dealt with very well. So, I think this idea would be good for both of us.'"

"I'm so proud of you both," Mimi says, patting Savage's hand. "Don't let the past rob you of the future you both deserve."

"We won't, Mimi," I say.

"Good." Mimi looks at Laila. "I'm guessing you've started to figure this out, sweetheart, but, still, it's worth mentioning. When Adrian promises something, he sometimes messes up and breaks his promise. But once he does that, if he promises *again*, that's when his word becomes unbreakable. He sometimes needs to make a mistake, *once*, to figure himself out."

Laila looks at me and says softly, "Yeah, I'm starting to realize that about him."

"Don't put up with his crap, Laila," Mimi says quietly. "But when you can, show him patience and grace, and you'll be greatly rewarded." With that, Mimi's eyelids flutter, and it's clear she's exhausted her energy for now.

"Sleep now," I say, gently caressing her cheek. "When you wake up, we'll watch the first episode of the show." I sing softly to her—the little lullaby I always sing to her—and soon, it's clear Mimi has already drifted off to sleep.

I address Stuart, Mimi's caregiver. "She's gonna wake up, right?"

"I'm sure she will," Stuart replies.

I exhale a long breath and look at Laila and my cousin. "Do you two ladies want to go downstairs, drink some whiskey, and smoke a big, fat blunt with me? Because fuck me, I need to unwind."

"Hell yeah," Sasha says.

I look at Laila. "You're not gonna rat me out to the producers for breaching the sobriety clause in my contract, are you, babysitter?"

"Dude, fiancée trumps babysitter."

Smiling, I pull Laila to me and plant a little peck on her lips, and, to my relief, she puckers and returns my kiss. With a deep exhale, I rise along with Laila, and accept a big hug from my cousin. When Sasha releases me, I walk out of the room with her, my arm around my cousin's shoulders, and with Laila trailing behind. As we head down the grand staircase, I tell Sasha how much I've missed her. I thank her for taking such good care of our grandmother and apologize for my initial reaction when I first heard the news about Mimi's decline.

"It was a lot to process," Sasha replies. She squeezes my trapezius muscle, the one near my neck that always tightens up the most, and says, "Ooph. You're knotted-up like crazy."

"This is the worst I've been in forever. The show is killing me."

"Well, let me at that famous body!" Sasha says, like she always does. "And I'll fix you right up!"

I chuckle and reply the way I always do: "Knock yourself out, Sasha."

When we get to the base of the staircase, I turn around to say something to Laila. But she's not there. On the contrary, she's frozen in the middle of the staircase, looking like she's just seen a ghost.

"Laila?" I say, my heart in my throat. "What's wrong?"

Laila's mouth is hanging open. Her face is pale. For a long moment, she doesn't reply. "*Sasha*," she finally whispers. "It was *Sasha*."

"What?" I say.

"Sasha is a massage therapist," she murmurs.

"Right," I say. "I told you that."

"I'd be happy to massage you first," Sasha says. "Fuck Adrian. He gets enough attention, right?"

"You'll be in good hands," I say. "Sasha is the best."

Laila remains frozen and pale on the staircase, not moving a muscle.

"I know it's weird," Sasha says, filling the awkward silence, "but my favorite thing in the world is working out knots."

Laila blinks a few times in rapid succession, exhales, and slowly begins descending the steps. As she walks, I disengage from Sasha to meet her in the middle, perplexed by the expression of pure shock on her face.

"What is it?" I ask.

Rather than replying to my question, Laila takes my face in her hands, pulls me to her, and kisses me deeply. Passionately. Without holding back. Like she's kissing her actual fiancé. The great love of her life.

I have no idea what's prompted this reaction, especially on a day when Laila has barely spoken to me. Was it something Mimi said? Maybe that thing about me tending to fuck up once, but not twice? Or did Mimi's frail condition remind Laila that life is short—that we're all mortal and imperfect and flawed—and should therefore not sweat the small stuff, but, instead, grab happiness, wherever we can find it?

There's no way to know, in this moment, what's inspired Laila to kiss me like she forgives me. Like she *loves* me. And, honestly, I don't need to know. All that matters is I've realized I've found the great love of my life, exactly as Mimi's always wanted for me. And this kiss tells me Laila believes she's found hers. And so, without asking why, or how long it'll last, I take Laila, the woman I love, into my arms and kiss her in return with everything I've got. Everything I am. And everything I can't wait to become, with her by my side.

FIFTY-NINE

LAILA

Sasha blows out a plume of smoke from the joint she's sharing with Savage and me and says, "I'm so glad you're here."

The three of us are chatting while smoking pot and drinking booze in Mimi's comfortable family room. I'm sitting next to Savage on a couch, my legs draped across his lap, while Sasha is sprawled across a nearby armchair. And it's blowing my mind to realize, the whole time I'd been certain Savage was some kind of sex addict player, his cousin was the "groupie" I saw him with that fateful day in Las Vegas. *Sasha* was the one walking arm-in-arm with Savage, saying she was thrilled to be there with him. *Sasha* was the girl who wanted to get her hands on his famous body. *Because Sasha is a massage therapist.* Holy hell. If I hadn't seen Savage with his cousin that day, and hadn't misinterpreted their conversation, where would I be right now? Would I be sitting here with Savage and his cousin, feeling swept away by my feelings for Savage? Or would our tour fling have ended when the tour did?

"So, tell me the truth, guys," Sasha says, putting down her wine glass. "Are you two really engaged or did you tell Mimi a beautiful lie?"

Savage takes the joint from me. "The engagement part was a beautiful lie, but we really are together and totally committed." He looks at me, his expression saying, *Please, let that be a true statement.* And when I smile and nod, Savage grins and exhales in relief.

Sasha takes the joint from Savage and sucks on it. "I figured the engagement had to be a lie for Mimi's sake. If you'd actually proposed to Laila, you would have spammed me beforehand with a thousand texts. 'Sasha, how should I ask her?' 'Sasha, where should I ask her?' 'Sasha, what should I *wear* when I ask her?'"

Savage chuckles. "I was *sixteen* and had never asked a girl on an actual date before, dude. You always give me hell about that."

"It was cute the first *ten* times."

"It wasn't ten times. Three or four, tops. And that was back in high school when I had no game. I'm a grown-ass man now. A rock god, if you haven't heard."

"Wait, *what*?" Sasha deadpans.

"I'm on magazine covers and everything."

"Wow."

"I'm also a judge on *Sing Your Heart Out.*"

"No."

"True story."

"Impressive."

"If I wanted to propose nowadays," Savage continues, "I wouldn't need to ask for your or anyone else's help to do it, any more than I need help walking onstage and performing for *tens* of thousands of people who've paid good money to come see *me.*"

"Gosh, you're so fancy."

"I am. If I wanted to propose, I'd slay that shit, dude, all by myself."

"Well, pardon me, Mr. Famous. My bad." Sasha looks at me, her dark eyes sparkling. Clearly, bantering with her cousin is one of the great joys of Sasha's life. But I can barely function in this moment. Does the cheeky speech Savage just gave signal he's thinking about proposing to me in the finale, in order to grab that bonus the producers offered him? I mean, assuming I'm still around by then. Frankly, I wouldn't blame him if he did it. In fact, I *want* him to do it to earn himself some easy money. Plus, I can't deny the idea that I might get to look into The Beast's eyes and hear him say those magical words—"Will you marry me, Belle?"— is incredibly exciting to me. Even though my brain would understand the fakeness of the moment, my heart would nonetheless enjoy getting to feel, if only fleetingly, like a princess in a fairytale.

Sasha picks up her wine glass again, while I pick up my whiskey. "Well, I'm glad you told Mimi such a lovely lie. I can't remember the last time I saw her smiling that big."

Savage replies to his cousin, and an entire conversation ensues, but my attention is flickering in and out. I'm bursting at the seams to tell Savage about my epiphany on the staircase—namely, that I saw him with *Sasha* in Las Vegas, and every action and reaction of mine since then has been tainted by that misunderstanding. I should wait to tell him everything in private, I decide, since my revelation about Sasha will undoubtedly make a whole lot of other dominos fall—dominos that will surely whip up quite a bit of emotion inside me. But, still, I can't resist asking Sasha a few pointed questions about that fateful day.

I wait for a lull in the conversation between Savage and his cousin, and then ask, "Sasha, did you ever visit Adrian during our tour?"

She nods. "Once. Your show was brilliant, Laila."

"Thank you. Which show did you see?"

"Las Vegas. It was Adrian's birthday weekend. Our birthdays are five days apart, so he flew me and a couple of my friends to Las Vegas to celebrate, as a birthday gift to me."

"No, flying you to Vegas was my birthday gift to *me*," Savage corrects.

Sasha rolls her eyes. "See what I'm dealing with here? This year, he flew me and my friends to Vegas. Last year, he bought me a *house* for my birthday. And all I ever give him as a birthday present is the same thing, every year: a bottle of his favorite whiskey and an extra-long massage."

"That's all I ever want," Savage says.

"Speaking of me giving you a massage," Sasha replies. She raises her palms and kneads the air, like she's massaging invisible shoulders. "Let me at that famous body!"

Savage chuckles. "I think I'll take a rain check, actually." He looks at me and his dark eyes flicker with heat. "No offense, but I'd rather get my knots out a different way tonight."

"*Oh*," Sasha and I say at the same time.

Savage stands and extends his hand to me. "Come on, Fitzy. Time for bed." As I take his hand and rise from the couch, Savage says to his cousin, "I don't care what time it is, or what X-rated noises you might hear coming out of my room, if Mimi takes a turn or wakes up and needs me—"

"I'll get you," Sasha interrupts. "I've already told Stuart the same thing. If Stuarts knocks on my door, then I'll immediately knock on yours."

"Thanks." Savage grips my hand. "Goodnight, Sasha."

"Goodnight. Thank you for coming, Laila. Mimi was so excited to hug you."

"There's no place I'd rather be," I say. I smile at Savage, letting him know my words are sincere, and then we walk hand in hand through the large house to the bedroom where Savage stowed his suitcase earlier.

"Wait here," he commands, guiding me to sit on the end of the bed. When I'm situated, he wordlessly leaves the room, leaving me whispering to myself, "Okay, then, goodbye." But a moment later, Savage returns, carrying my suitcase, which he pointedly sets down in a corner. It's his way of telling me I'm staying with him during this trip, obviously. And he'll get no argument from me.

"Thank you," I say.

"No. Thank *you*," he replies, taking a seat next to me.

He reaches for me, obviously intending to kiss me. But I stop him with my palm.

"You're not going to ask me why I'm not mad at you anymore?"

"No," he says flatly. "I don't want to look a gift horse in the mouth."

With burning eyes, he begins fiddling with my shirt, clearly intending to remove it, but I touch his hand, stopping him.

"Hang on," I say softly. "I need to explain myself to you. There's something important I figured out when I saw you walking down the staircase with Sasha."

Savage looks confused by that comment, but he whispers "okay" and waits for whatever is coming next.

I clear my throat. My heart is racing. "When you texted me your room number in Las Vegas and asked me to come to your room after the show—"

"More like I *begged* you to come."

"I did, Savage. I came to your room. And not after the show, but within *minutes* of receiving your text. In fact, I practically sprinted to your room."

"*What?*"

"When I got to your floor and started walking down the hallway toward your room, you happened to get off an elevator in front of me. You had your arm around a beautiful brunette, who I thought was a groupie—"

"*Sasha,*" he whispers.

I nod. "I assumed you were bringing her to your room for sex, the same way you'd brought those groupies to my dressing rooms."

He palms his forehead. "Oh, God."

"Only this time, you couldn't possibly be flaunting her in my face to get a rise out of me. This time, there was no mistaking your intentions. It was the real deal. Or so I thought. In my mind, you were taking a woman to your room for sex, mere *hours* after having amazing sex with me, and mere *minutes* after you'd begged me to come to your room."

Savage exhales loudly and groans out, "I can't believe it."

"I wanted to believe it was some kind of misunderstanding," I say. "So, I tiptoed closer and eavesdropped on your conversation.

And that's when Sasha said, 'Let me get my hands on that body!' Or something along those lines. And I lost it. I sprinted away and texted Charlie to meet me in the gym. And then, during my workout with Charlie, I got a second text from you, telling me you couldn't stop thinking about me—that you were lying there thinking about me."

"I was! I sent that right after my birthday massage!"

I groan. "When I got that second text, I was so grossed out. I thought, 'Okay, this guy is a sex addict or a sociopath or both. Did he text me while that groupie was riding his cock, or did he have the decency to wait for her to go into the bathroom?'"

"Oh my God. Finally, everything makes sense!"

"I blocked your number after I got that second text, and I promised myself I'd never speak to you again. That's why I got so mad about Charlie yesterday. I've been turning myself into a pret-zel, trying to forgive and forget about that 'groupie' in Las Vegas. Trying to reconcile the Savage I've come to know with the asshole who brought a groupie to his room, mere minutes after begging *me* to come there. I was angry you—a hypocrite who'd fucked a multi-tude of groupies on tour—couldn't handle the thought of me having a nice little tour fling with the fitness trainer on tour!"

Savage looks absolutely floored. "Everything would have been so different, if only you'd come to my room two minutes later. I would have already been in there with Sasha. I would have intro-duced you. I would have told Sasha to leave."

"She said she wanted to get her hands on you! She squealed and said she was excited to be there. After all the groupies I'd caught you with prior to that, there wasn't a shred of doubt in my mind what I was seeing."

Savage runs his hand over his chin. "Laila, I waited up all night after that Vegas show, positive you'd come to your senses and come to me. Every noise I heard in the hallway made me leap out of bed and peek through the peephole. Every time, I was positive you'd be standing there. But you never were. Rinse and repeat, in each new city. I'd lie awake in bed, alone, every night, praying you'd finally show up. When you seemed so cozy with Charlie, I figured that had to be the reason you didn't want me. Otherwise, I couldn't understand. How was it possible that night in Phoenix hadn't rocked your world the way it'd rocked mine?"

My heart is crashing my chest. "I'm so sorry."

"I've been a madman, Laila. Totally and completely obsessed with you, and trying to understand the enigma that is your brain. I've been so confused. Feeling so rejected."

"Oh, baby." I touch his face. "You sat alone in your room every night for the entire last month of the tour?"

"Not only the last month. I did the same thing the first two months of the tour, as well." He smiles. "Sweetheart, I haven't been with anyone but you since I laid eyes on you at Reed's party."

I gasp. "But . . . what about that waitress in New York?"

"I didn't even call her. And all those groupies were a set-up, too. I sent them packing right after you caught me with them. I was an asshole, Laila. Pissed I'd decided to step aside for Kendrick. Jealous you wanted an asshole like Malik, instead of me."

"No. I only wanted you, from the second I saw you at Reed's. I lied about Malik. We never had an actual relationship. Just one date before the tour and some texting. We never even came close to having sex. You're the only one I've been with since I first laid eyes on you at Reed's. The only one I've wanted for so long."

Savage looks like his brain is melting. "But . . . you and Malik couldn't keep your hands off each other in New York—and you were constantly on the phone with him after that."

I shake my head. "My 'relationship' with Malik was a lie that kept snowballing on me. On day one of the tour, I could tell Kendrick was interested in me, but I already had my sights set on you. So, when he mentioned he'd seen a photo of me at Malik's game, I went with it. I said Malik was my boyfriend. But it wasn't true. That game was our only date. During the tour, Malik texted me pretty persistently, but I wasn't interested. And then, he told me he was coming to the show in New York—and not because I'd invited him, by the way. So, I said he could be my plus-one at

Reed's dinner party afterward. But I only brought him there to get a rise out of *you*. I couldn't understand why you always ignored me. Why you *never* hit on me. I thought maybe if you saw a guy like Malik all over me, it'd *finally* spur you into action. But all you did was get that waitress's number and scream at me to give *Kendrick* a shot."

"Oh, fuck."

"Babe, I kicked Malik to the curb right after dinner—literally, during the car ride from the restaurant to our hotel."

"No!"

I nod furiously. "I told Malik to fuck off and never contact me again. And I haven't spoken to him since."

"You faked *all* those phone calls with Malik after New York?"

"Every single one. The same way you faked *all* those groupies, apparently."

"Holy fuck," he whispers. "Kendrick said we're the same person in male and female forms . . ."

"I thought for sure you had sex with that waitress in New York!"

"Nah, I only got her number to piss you off. After our fight on the sidewalk, I stumbled back to my hotel room, punched a hole in the wall, barfed my guts out, and passed out."

"And then dragged your sorry ass to Alessandra's music video shoot the next day."

"Only because I knew you'd be there, without your asshole boyfriend. That's the only reason I showed up, Laila. Not for Reed. Not for Alessandra or Fish. But to see *you*, without Malik hanging all over you. I kept my word and showed up because I wanted you to like me."

"How was I supposed to like you when all you talked about when you got there was the hot sex you'd had all night and day with the waitress?"

"I was fighting fire with fire! You went on and on about your hot night with Malik!"

"Because I was jealous about the waitress!"

"Well, I was jealous about Malik."

"I'm positive you bragged about the waitress first."

"No, it was the other way around."

We both burst out laughing.

"Wait, what were you doing in that hot tub in Phoenix at three in the morning? I assumed you were drowning your sorrows about that video of Malik getting head."

"I *was* drowning my sorrows," I admit, "but not about *Malik*. I mean, yes, that video of him did embarrass me. I'd been romantically linked to Malik online, thanks to that photo of me cheering him on at his game. So, yes, it was embarrassing to think the world was wondering if he'd cheated on me. But, mostly, I was sitting there thinking about *you*. Kendrick had invited me to your birthday party earlier that night, and I was sitting there feeling bummed that things had gotten so bad between us, I didn't even feel like I could come to your birthday party. I was drowning my sorrows that my hot crush had turned out to be a rockstar cliché asshole who hated me, and I couldn't understand why."

Savage smiles wickedly. "You sneaky little freak. You let me think we had *revenge* sex that night."

I return his smile. "That was your assumption, so I let you keep thinking it. It made the sex extra hot, didn't it?"

His dark eyes flash with heat. "It sure did. Hot as hell."

I run my fingertip up his forearm. "If it makes you feel better, we really did have *hate* sex that night. I didn't fake that part." I wink. "Or any of my *three* orgasms."

"Well, duh." He bites his lip. "I'm so hard right now, baby. I feel like a five-hundred-pound elephant has finally gotten off my chest."

"Me, too."

"Laila, I'm so sorry I punched a hole in the wall in your dressing room. It's no excuse, but I've been slowly going insane since the tour, trying to understand why you didn't want me the way I wanted you. Trying to understand pieces of a puzzle that just didn't fit together. When I saw you with Colin, I thought I'd lost you for good. I promise I'll never do that again, or anything else to scare or hurt you."

"I know you won't. I trust you, Adrian. But I do think you should get some therapy, like I said to Mimi. There's no shame in that. You've been through a lot. Maybe a professional could help you work through some stuff."

"I'll do whatever it takes to make this work."

"So will I."

"Please forgive me for all the ways I've screwed up," he says.

"We've both screwed up. Please forgive me."

"You were fighting fire with fire. I was the bigger asshole."

"We were both assholes," I say. "Can we please press the reset button, for real now?"

Savage nods and leans in and kisses me. And that's all it takes to light our fuse. In a frenzy, we begin pulling our clothes off, both of us desperate to consummate our new beginning by fusing our bodies. Once naked, we tumble onto the bed and kiss passionately. We grope and grab and caress and stroke. Until, finally, Savage sinks himself inside me, all the way, and begins gyrating enthusiastically on top of me in a way that feels totally new. Now that we're finally *free* of the past, it's clear to me how much it was weighing us both down. How much it was holding us back. Speaking for myself, all my walls are down now. I'm no longer protecting my heart. In fact, I'm giving it to Savage in this moment, with both hands. *Take my heart, Savage. Take me. I'm all yours.*

"You're the only one I want, Laila," he whispers into my ear, as his body invades mine, over and over again. As our chests rub together with each thrust.

"I'm all yours, Adrian," I whisper back. I grip his face and kiss him deeply as he comes. He's the only one I want. The one I've wanted for so long. In fact, I can't imagine wanting anyone else, ever again.

SIXTY

SAVAGE

Even before opening my eyes, I sense sunlight on my face. Yawning, I roll onto my side and reach out next to me on the mattress, thinking Laila must have scooted to the edge of the bed in her sleep. But I feel nothing there—not even a warm spot.

I open my eyes. "Laila?" I look toward the bathroom, figuring she's in there. But when I say her name again, silence answers me. I look at the time to find it's a few minutes past seven. And that's *Chicago* time. Laila's body clock still thinks she's in LA. So, what's a night owl like her doing up so early, with nowhere she needs to be?

Mimi.

The thought hits me like a ton of bricks. Did Sasha knock on our door and I didn't hear it? *Shit.* I leap out of bed, quickly brush my teeth, wash my face, and throw on a pair of sweats and a hoodie —fuck, it's cold in this old house!—and then bolt out of the room. But when I enter Mimi's room, what I find there makes me exhale from the depths of my soul. *Calm. Quiet. Peace.* That's what I find in Mimi's room, along with Laila holding Mimi's hand at her bedside.

"Good morning, ladies," I say brightly, determined not to let my tone betray the near-panic I was feeling a moment ago. As my pulse comes down, I give both women a kiss on their foreheads and begin pulling up a chair next to Laila's. But when I notice Mimi's facial expression as I take my seat, I get the distinct impression I've interrupted something.

"Oh. Would you two like me to step out while you finish your conversation?"

To my surprise, Mimi nods, while Laila looks sheepish and apologetic.

"Not a problem," I say quickly. I address the caregiver on duty now—a sweetheart of a woman named Felicia—the one who always relieves Stuart in the early morning hours. "Let me know whenever Mimi is ready for me to come back. I'll be in my room."

"Yes, sir."

My heart thumping, I return to my room and jump in the shower. And that's where I let myself wallow in the full extent of the dread and pain I've been feeling since my conversation with Sasha last night—the one in which my cousin told me Mimi is ready to go. I didn't want to believe it when Sasha said that, but, just now, I could see it in Mimi's eyes when she told me to leave. *Sasha was right.* Mimi would never tell me to leave any room, ever, unless she felt she was saying something urgent and confidential. Which, in this instance, must have been Mimi giving Laila some sort of advice about *me.*

Finally, after I've stayed in the shower for far too long, I get out, dry off, and get dressed. Grabbing my phone off the dresser, I head to my bed, intending to text Kendrick the latest about Mimi. But when I pick up my phone, I've got a missed call from Nadine Collins, the executive producer of the show. Damn. What's she doing up so early in LA, during the break—and why the hell is she calling *me?*

"Savage!" Nadine says, answering my call. "Thanks for calling."

"You're up early on a day off."

"No rest for the wicked," she says brightly. "I've got a conference call with the entire team in an hour, so I'm getting ready for that. Oh, how's your grandmother?"

"Hanging in there. Thanks for sending that link. I'm going to watch the show with her today."

"Wonderful. Enjoy. Listen, Savage, there's something important I'd like to talk to you about. We've got a couple options, in terms of the direction we want to go for the remainder of the season. A few storylines we're considering. Some of which depend on *you*." She pauses. "Can you tell me if you're planning to earn that bonus with a proposal in the finale? Have you come to a decision on that yet?"

I don't hesitate, even though I'm not technically required by my contract to give Nadine a firm answer on that, in advance. "I'm not going to propose in the finale," I reply flatly. And I have no doubt it's the right decision as I say it. Mimi was the primary reason I was considering doing it. But now that Laila and I have already told Mimi we're engaged, what would be the point? In fact, I can't imagine anything more cringey-ass and embarrassing to me than getting down on bended knee in front of my actual girlfriend and fake-proposing to her on a reality TV show.

"Is there any way I can entice you to change your mind about that?" Nadine asks. "Maybe sweeten the pot to get an affirmative commitment from you right now?"

There's nothing Nadine could say to change my mind, but, still, I figure I'll hear the woman out. "What do you have in mind, Nadine?"

"What if I told you there's a jeweler who's willing to supply a ring to you, in a value up to half a million bucks, in exchange for a sparkling shot of the ring during the proposal and a post on Instagram afterwards by you and Laila. All you have to do is remain 'engaged' to Laila for six months after the finale, and the ring is yours. When you and Laila 'break up,' you can sell the ring and keep the proceeds! Split them with Laila, if you like, or keep them for yourself. Totally up to you."

She's high if she thinks this scenario sounds even remotely attractive to me. "Not interested," I say simply.

"Okay, then. I've got authority to add another quarter mill to the bonus we've already put on the table—which brings our offer to a half-million bucks, if only you'll agree *now*, in writing, to commit to making the proposal in the finale. All we'd require is that you and Laila continue playing happy couple for six months after the finale, including making daily social media posts, and after that, you two can do whatever you want. Date whoever else. Or ride off into the sunset for real, if that's how you're feeling. At which point, you'll have a ring to keep or sell and half a million bucks."

Listening to Nadine talk, it dawns on me there's no amount of money, no dangling carrot, no free diamond ring, that would ever make me fake-propose to Laila. And not because the moment would be cringey-ass, which it would be. But because I love Laila. Because after all the puzzle pieces have *finally* snapped into place for me, thanks to our amazing conversation last night, a dam has broken inside me and there's no turning back. I love that girl, with all my heart and soul, and I'm one hundred percent sure of it. And guess what? I'm positive getting down on bended knee, looking up at Laila with a ring in my hand, and saying those sacred words to her, without truly meaning them, will fuck things up for us beyond repair. Maybe not that same day. But down the line.

Likewise, if I get down on bended knee, ring in hand, and ask Laila to be my wife—and actually *do* mean those sacred words— then blowing that once in a lifetime memory by doing it on reality TV would haunt me for the rest of my days. I don't know if I want to get married one day. I don't know if I'm capable of being anyone's husband. Not even Laila's. But if I decide to propose to Laila in the future, then I'm going to do it right. And not because Nadine Collins wants me to do it, as some sort of ratings grab.

"I tell you what," Nadine says, apparently interpreting my silence as a "no." "We'll let you tell Laila about the proposal in advance. That's what's concerning you the most, right? That you'd propose to Laila and she'd think it's real—and then, you'd have to tell her the truth afterwards?"

Yet again, Nadine's words are helping me understand my feelings. Contrary to what Nadine thinks, I'm not worried about Laila thinking my proposal is *real*. I'm worried about her thinking it's *fake*. I'm worried about having to tell Laila, after the fact, "Oh, no, that was really me asking you to marry me." Obviously, telling Laila about the proposal in advance wouldn't solve that problem. If I told Laila in advance about my plan to get down on bended knee, Laila would assume the proposal would be fake. And then, wouldn't she feel at least a little bit disappointed about that, after everything that passed between us last night? On the other hand, if, somehow, I got to the point two months from now where I felt certain I *genuinely* wanted to propose to Laila, then I sure as hell wouldn't tell her that in advance. Not for all the money in the world. So, really, how could a proposal in the finale, real or fake, *not* end badly for me? "I'm not going to propose to Laila in the finale," I declare. "Not for any amount of money."

Nadine doesn't speak for a long moment, but I can hear her wheels turning over the phone line. Finally, she says, "I was hoping for a different answer from you, Savage. The truth is, in the absence of a confirmed proposal in the finale, we're going to need to shake things up a bit."

Goosebumps erupt on my arms and neck. "Shake things up *how?*"

"You and Laila are going to break up this week. And we're going to terminate her contract."

Fucking bitch. Laila was right. "You can't do that, Nadine."

"Actually, I can. There's a buy-out clause in Laila's contract. And in the absence of a confirmed proposal on the horizon, we're going to exercise it. We might bring Laila back for the finale. In fact, we hope to do that. But we'll have to play it by ear and see how the new storyline unfolds."

"Laila was promised a performance slot in the finale, in her *written* contract. We relied on that and wrote a song to perform together."

"I'd be happy to show you Laila's contract. Invocation of the early-termination clause expressly renders all other promises in the contract null and void. So, technically, if we were to terminate Laila, we'd be released from our promise to give her that performance slot. We'd love to give her that slot, regardless. Which we'd do, if you were to call me, at least two weeks before the finale, and say you've 'gotten back together' with Laila and now plan to propose to her in the finale. Of course, you could avoid that entire rollercoaster ride by agreeing now, in writing, to propose to Laila in the finale."

I argue Laila's case for a while—talking passionately about Laila's incredible talent and charisma. I talk about how good she is with people, and insist the contestants on her team, as well as the audience, will love her. And as I say that last bit—about the contestants and audience loving Laila—my heart swells and solidifies with my *own* love for Laila.

But it's no use. No matter what I say, Nadine has made her decision. She's hell-bent on getting that proposal out of me, one way or another. Or if not, making people tune in to watch me overcome my supposedly broken heart on national TV.

"Okay, Nadine," I finally say. "You've made an offer to me. Now, let me make one to you. I'll let you keep a half-mill of my salary, if you'll promise, right now, to keep Laila on the show for the rest of the season and leave us alone to be happy. In that time, I promise I'll consider proposing to Laila in the finale. If I do, you wouldn't need to pay me any bonus. I'd do it for nothing."

In truth, I won't be proposing to Laila on reality TV, no matter what. But by then, what could they possibly do to me if I don't get down on bended knee like they want?

I add, "That'd be a net positive to you of a million bucks, Nadine. You'd keep the bonus you just offered me *and* keep a half-mill of my salary, too."

Nadine pauses, which means she's considering my offer. She

says, "Let us keep a *million* bucks of your salary now, and you've got yourself a deal."

I close my eyes. *Fuck.* "Do you promise to leave Laila and me alone—no more demands for 'Vintage Savage and Laila'? No attempts to create any kind of love triangle?"

"Ah, Colin told Laila about our offer to him, and Laila told you? I *knew* he'd run and tell her."

I press my lips together. My "love triangle" comment was purely hypothetical. I was grasping at straws. But clearly, my instinct about why they hired Colin as Laila's mentor was correct. Were they planning to create the storyline in the editing room? I'm sure there's plenty of footage to allow them to stitch together a saucy little narrative. Hugs and smiles between Colin and Laila. Daggers between Colin and me. Not to mention, Laila and I delivered a whole lot of spicy "trouble in paradise" footage on Draft Day.

"Yeah, Laila told me everything about your plans with Colin," I lie. "And one of my conditions, if I pay you that million bucks, is that you stop chasing any 'love triangle' storyline that involves Colin or anyone else."

"Well, that's a moot point now, seeing as how he said no."

No to what? "Yeah, but you guys are geniuses in the editing room. I don't want you to stitch something together to create even the suggestion that Colin or anyone else has come between Laila and me."

Nadine sighs. "Look, I'm going to need you to pledge your full salary as collateral, in order to agree to this side deal. If you wind up proposing in the finale, then I'll release a million back to you. If you don't propose, then we'll keep the full two mill."

Fuck, fuck, fuck! I run a palm down my face, my mind whirring, but quickly decide I've got no choice. "Okay, Nadine, but only if you meet three conditions. One, you'll call Laila within the next twenty minutes to tell her she's doing a bang-up job on the show, better than your wildest dreams, and you want her to know you're going to keep her on for the entire season. You'll say, 'We're tearing up that early buy-out clause. We can't imagine doing the show without you.'"

"Fine."

"Two, I hope this goes without saying, but Laila and I will be performing our duet in the finale, as planned."

"Yes."

"Three, you'll never tell Laila about this side deal of ours. *Ever.*"

"Wouldn't you want Laila to know you're her knight in shining armor?"

"No. She already feels guilty enough she's getting half my initial salary. She doesn't need any reason to feel even guiltier." I hear footsteps in the hallway, getting closer. "So, do we have a deal or not?"

Nadine sighs. "Yes, we have a deal."

"Great. I've got to go. Don't forget to make that call to Laila."

"Will do. Happy holidays."

"Bye, Nadine."

The door opens as I'm saying "Nadine," and Laila steps into the room. As she approaches, I toss my phone onto the nightstand. "Hey, baby. Is Mimi ready to see me now?"

Laila sits on the edge of the bed next to me and takes my hand. "No, Sasha is in there. You were talking to Nadine?"

My heart lurches. "Yeah, she called to wish me happy holidays and tell me how thrilled everyone is with us. Apparently, our 'fight' on Draft Day quenched their thirst for drama, and now, they want us to go back to being a happy couple for the entire rest of the season."

Laila's jaw drops. "Nadine said that?"

"She did. Oh, and she also said she's looking forward to our performance in the finale."

Laila looks flabbergasted. "And I was so positive they were going to fire me during the break! I wasn't going to tell you this, but when Colin and I were alone in my dressing room, he told me something confidential—something that made me all the more certain my days on the show were numbered." She tells me her story, which makes my blood boil, and wraps up with, "See? I told you Colin is a good guy. He came straight to me with the information, rather than ambushing me for an easy hundred grand."

"That was cool of him," I admit. "I'm a little surprised you didn't march outside with him, right then and there, and kiss the hell out of him for the cameras, just to get back at me for the Charlie thing. You were so pissed at me."

She looks shocked. "Adrian, I would *never* do that to you, no matter how upset I was about the Charlie thing. That would have been way beyond the pale for me to do to you. Plus, why would I do that to *myself*? Forevermore, I'd have been The Girl Who Cheated on Adrian Savage. God help me if ever I ran into one of your diehard fans on the street after that."

I pause for a long time, before saying, "I feel like I owe Colin a phone call. If I'm completely honest with myself, I think Colin and I were a bit more than acquaintances when I hooked up with his ex. I see Colin all the time. We have mutual friends. Colin isn't like Kendrick or Kai to me, obviously. Not even close. But he was a friend, and I did betray him. But, despite that, when he had the chance to take that bonus, and use you to get back at me, he didn't do it. He looked out for you, no matter what."

"And for you, too, indirectly. Even if that wasn't his motivation, he did save both of us from quite a bit of humiliation."

"True." I process everything for a moment, and then ask, "So, what did Mimi say to you? You two looked as thick as thieves."

Laila smiles. "She just wanted to give me some advice about you. She's so happy we're 'engaged' and wants to make sure we have a long and happy marriage." She squeezes my hand and smiles. "But guess what? I already knew pretty much everything Mimi told me about you, all on my own."

"What'd she tell you?"

"She didn't phrase it this way, of course. This is my own interpretation. But, basically, she told me you're a prince who was sadly turned into an unruly beast a long time ago by a mean woman who held a grudge, for no good reason."

My heart skips a beat.

"Again, that's not how Mimi put it, but listening to her, I felt like everything she was saying was basically a retelling of *Beauty and the Beast*."

"Well, aren't you clever."

"I'm a genius." She grins. "So, did Nadine mention that bonus they've offered to you?"

"She did. I told her it's a non-starter. I'm not going to propose on national TV. Making Mimi happy was the only thing that made me consider it. But now that we've told Mimi the deed is done, and Nadine is so happy with you on the show, there's no reason for me to even think about that."

"A quarter-million bucks is a lot of money. Especially when you're giving half your salary to me, and you've bought houses for Sasha and Mimi."

"Please, Laila, don't feel guilty about the salary thing. You negotiated your share, fair and square."

"I wish I'd said yes to ten percent, like you first offered. I think that was fair."

"Stop, please. We're going to make bank on the duet. And my album is releasing next week. Honestly, I don't want to talk about the money again. We've pressed the 'reset button,' remember? The money is part of that."

Laila sighs. "You promise you're not secretly mad about the money?"

I kiss her cheek. "Baby, I'm not even capable of being mad at you."

As I'm saying that last sentence, there's a knock at the door.

"Adrian?" Sasha's wobbly voice says. My cousin sniffles behind the door, making my breathing halt, before adding, "Honey, Mimi is ready to see you now."

SIXTY-ONE

SAVAGE

As I enter Mimi's bedroom, I nod at the caregiver, Felicia, in the corner, lay my laptop on a table, and slide into a chair next to the bed. "Hey, Mimi," I whisper, taking her hand. She looks impossibly frail under her covers. Exhausted like I've never seen her before. "I'm here, Mimi. I'm right here."

My grandmother opens her eyes and purses her lips, asking for a kiss, and I lean forward and give her one, before settling back into my chair and cupping her slender hand in both of mine.

"Would you like me to carry you around the house, so you can tell me stories from when you and Jasper were young?" I whisper.

Mimi shakes her head, turning me down. And I realize talking has become difficult for my sweet grandmother.

Swallowing hard, I gently squeeze Mimi's frail hand. "Would you like me to sing to you?"

This time, Mimi nods. So, I launch into singing the lullaby that's become part of our ritual, and when I reach the end of that simple song, and Mimi is still awake and attentive, I sing another. This time, one of my all-time favorites by one of my favorite singer-songwriters: "Grace" by Jeff Buckley. Buckley was a genius, if you ask me, who died way too young, well before he'd graced the world with the full extent of his gifts. And the song of his I've chosen is about accepting mortality in the face of true love—a song about letting go gracefully. Frankly, I can't imagine a better song for this moment.

Grace.

It's the word, more than any other, that describes what Mimi has always shown to me. The gift of unconditional love and acceptance.

When I finish singing, Mimi whispers, in a barely audible voice. "I'm ready, Ady."

Tears flood my eyes. Sasha warned me last night that's what Mimi's been thinking, but I didn't expect Mimi to say it to me so bluntly. So starkly, without warning or lead-in.

The words "Not yet, Mimi!" form on my lips. But I bite them back and swallow them down. Of course, I want my grandmother to stay here with me. I can't imagine a world where she isn't here to chastise me with a gentle "*Adrian*" when I'm being a shithead. To smile at me when I'm being goofy. And most of all, to love me, no matter what stupid thing I do or say. But I know all of those desires are selfish—that now it's my turn to show Mimi *grace*.

Still cupping Mimi's slight hand in mine, I rest my elbows onto the mattress and say, "If you're ready to go, then go. Cross the bridge to Jasper and Frank. Have a picnic with them. Give them lots of hugs and kisses. I'll miss you so much—more than I could ever say in words. But I promise I'll be okay, and that I'll spend the rest of my life doing my best to be the man you've tried to teach me to be." I wipe a tear from her cheek. "Oh, how you've tried to teach me. I was quite a project, huh?"

Mimi smiles weakly.

"You did good, Maria Savage," I whisper, caressing her white hair. "I'm going to be okay, thanks to you. You taught me how to love with all my heart and soul. You taught me, Mimi. And I listened and learned. I know it didn't seem like it sometimes, but I promise I did. I understand everything now, Mimi, so you can go now, without worrying about me."

Mimi smiles, letting me know my words have touched her, and then she looks at her caregiver in the corner.

"Now?" the woman says. And when Mimi nods, her nurse walks to the dresser, pulls out a tiny box from the top drawer, and brings it to me, its lid opened. There's a simple ring inside—a band with the tiniest of diamonds at its center.

"Your grandfather slipped this ring onto your grandmother's finger the day they got married," the nurse says. "Mimi wants you to take the diamond out of this ring and use it somewhere in the setting of Laila's engagement or wedding ring."

"Oh, Mimi," I say, feeling overcome with guilt. I felt justified in lying to Mimi about my fake engagement with Laila yesterday, given the situation, but accepting Mimi's treasured wedding ring from Jasper today, to give to my fake fiancée, feels wrong. "I shouldn't accept this," I say reflexively, but add quickly, "Sasha should have it, in case she gets married one day."

Mimi looks exasperated with me—which, I must admit, makes me grin. How many times have I seen this same look of exasperation on Maria Savage's face over the years, when talking to me? Too many to count. And every time, it makes me smile.

The nurse says, "Mimi's already talked to Sasha about this ring, and told her she wanted you to have it for your future wife one day. This was weeks ago, before she knew about you and Laila. And Sasha said that sounded like a lovely idea. Mimi's given Sasha all her other jewelry, and Sasha is thrilled with that."

I exhale, feeling a bit better about the situation. If Mimi wanted me to have this ring before I'd lied to her about Laila, *and* Sasha's not bummed to miss out, then I suppose I can take the ring, as Mimi wishes. "Thank you, Mimi," I say, slipping the box into the pocket of my hoodie. "This means a lot."

She nods weakly.

Once again, I stroke her white hair. "Do you want to see me as a judge on *Sing Your Heart Out*? I've got the first episode cued up on my laptop over there."

Mimi nods and smiles.

I ask softly, "Should I call Sasha and Laila to come in here and watch with us?"

Mimi shakes her head and whispers, "Just you and me, Ady."

My heart squeezes. "Okay. That sounds good, Mimi. Just you and me."

Trembling, I grab my laptop and connect it to the large television on the far wall. And when I've got the show cued up, I crawl into Mimi's bed alongside her, reposition her frail body until she's lying comfortably in my arms, and press play.

The familiar theme song of *Sing Your Heart Out* begins and Mimi makes the tiniest cooing sound in my arms. It's a far cry from the whooping and laughter and shrieks I expected to hear from my grandmother when I've imagined this moment. I never envisioned Mimi watching me on the show while lying in my arms, unable to speak without significant effort. But even so, that little cooing sound was enough. It tells me she's conscious, able to understand what she's seeing, and thrilled about it.

At the end of the day, all I wanted was for Maria Savage to get to see that the little twelve-year-old asshole she took into her home —and into her heart—has grown up and made her proud. I wanted her to see that, thanks to her, and her ability to dream so fucking big for me, that little asshole is now sitting at the judges' table on her all-time favorite show. I wanted her to see *she* did this. *She* took an angry and distrustful pile of shit and turned him into something golden. Someone people actually care about. All because *Mimi* cared first and so fucking well.

About fifteen minutes into the show, I glance down to find Mimi's eyes closed. I look in panic at the monitor next to the bed and exhale with relief when the neon line marking her heartbeat is still bouncing up and down, albeit slowly.

"Is this it, Felicia?" I ask the caregiver. "Will she wake up?"

"I think she will," Felicia says. "But she's close now, Adrian. Very close."

I swallow down the lump in my throat and kiss the top of Mimi's head. I whisper, "You can go now, Mimi. Have a picnic with Jasper and Frank. I'll be right here the whole time, holding you, so you won't be alone as you cross the bridge." A sob catches in my throat, but I take a deep, halting breath that somehow chases it away. I clear my throat. "Felicia, will you do me a favor and let Sasha and Laila know I've had my alone-time with Mimi, and they're welcome to come in now? In and out, if they want. Any time. But tell them I'm going to stay right here with my grandma, without letting go of her, for as long as it takes."

SIXTY-TWO

SAVAGE

Los Angeles, California
Two weeks later

I stop my car in front of Reed Rivers' iron gate, roll down my window, and press the intercom button.

"Adrian!" a female voice says.

"Hey, Abu!" I say, recognizing Amalia's sweet voice. I smile into the camera on the box. "What's shaking, woman?"

Amalia giggles. "Reed isn't here, Adrian. He and Georgina are out to dinner. Was he expecting you?"

"Nope. I came to steal you away from Reed, as a matter of fact. So pack a bag and let's *gooo!*"

Amalia laughs. "I've told you I'll never leave Reed. But I can offer you some tea and conversation."

"I'd rather steal you away, but I guess some tea and conversation would be a nice consolation prize."

The gate buzzes and slowly begins opening, and I drive

through and park near the front door—and by the time I get out of my car, Amalia is already standing there waiting for me.

I hug Amalia in greeting and squeeze her tight, and as I do, every bit of pain I've been holding in and stuffing down since Mimi died surges inside me.

When the time finally came the day before Christmas, Sasha, Laila, and I were at Mimi's side. After that, Laila remained in Chicago with me through Christmas and beyond, as Sasha and I threw together a small funeral for our grandma, which my band-mates attended, as did some of Mimi's old neighbors, her caregivers, and Sasha's mother.

After that, I insisted Laila take the trip to Cabo we'd originally planned to take together, but with her mom, sister, and baby niece. I told Laila I could use a few days to grieve with Sasha in Chicago, and then on my own in LA. And it was the truth when I said it. But the minute Laila left Chicago, I felt like I was missing my right arm. And when I walked into that stupid reality TV mansion in LA, all by myself, I felt like I was missing not only my other arm, but both legs, too. As it turned out, I didn't want to be alone, like I'd thought I would. *I wanted to be with Laila.*

I release Amalia from our warm hug, made even warmer by the cool night air.

"My grandma, Mimi, died," I say softly. "The day before Christmas."

Sympathy washes over Amalia's elegant face. "Oh, Adrian. I'm so sorry." She hugs me again and then guides me inside. In Reed's kitchen, I sit at the table while Amalia puts the kettle on. And we talk, every bit as easily as we did the last time, even though I'm not shitfaced this time.

As we drink our tea, we talk about Mimi, at first. After a while, however, we talk about spirituality, in general. The fact that we both believe Mimi is still with me, and always will be. And, finally, I tell Amalia about Laila. Specifically, I admit I've fallen desper-ately in love with her, but haven't had the nerve to say the magic words to her, just yet.

"I guess I'm waiting for the perfect moment," I say.

"Don't wait for a 'perfect moment,'" Amalia advises. "Just let it blurt out of you, whenever you can't hold it in any longer."

"Maybe I'll get lucky and she'll say it first."

Amalia looks at me the same way Mimi always did whenever I'd said something stupid. "Don't worry about being first, Adrian," she says. "Tell Laila you love her whenever you're ready, whether Laila has said it or not. Better to have spoken what's on your heart and risked it all, then wonder 'What if?' later."

I nod. "That's good advice, Abu. Thanks." I bite my lip. "I've got a favor to ask you. Laila is out of town until Tuesday, and all my friends are scattered for the holidays. I don't want to spend the night, all alone, in the huge house I share with Laila. So, I was wondering if I could stay here with you?"

"Of course, you can."

My heart leaps. "You don't think Reed will mind?"

"Reed would insist on it."

My shoulders soften. "It'll only be two nights. And I won't bug you. I'll just say hi to you, here and there, in between whatever you're doing."

Amalia smiles. "You can stay as long as you like."

"Thank you. I've got a bag in the car. If you'd said no, I was going straight to a hotel."

Amalia scowls. "No more hotels for you, Adrian, unless you're on vacation. If ever you need a place to stay, you'll *always* come here. Do you understand?"

My heart bursts. "Yes, ma'am. Although I'm sure Reed will have a slightly different opinion."

"No, he won't. I've mentioned to him how much I adore you, and he was highly supportive of me taking you under my wing."

"He was?"

"Of course. Reed thought it was very sweet that we bonded when you stayed here with the show."

I run my finger over the rim of my mug for a moment, trying to imagine Reed and Amalia's conversation about me, but it doesn't compute. The Reed Rivers I know would cut off my balls, dip them in eggs and breadcrumbs, bake them at four hundred degrees, and eat them with a nice aioli sauce. "Reed must be a lot nicer behind closed doors than he seems, huh? I mean, if you like him so much."

"Reed is a prince among men and also a shrewd businessman. A man can be both."

"I wouldn't know. I'm neither."

She chuckles. "I don't know about that. You seem like a prince to me. At least, a prince in training. I'm sure Laila would agree."

I smile shyly. "Laila calls me The Beast, actually. You know, like in *Beauty and the Beast?*"

Amalia's dark eyes sparkle. "I'd bet anything that's Laila's highest compliment."

"Yeah, when she says it, she gets a naughty little gleam in her eye that gives me a little zap where it counts, if you know what I mean."

"*Adrian.* That's not what I meant."

I laugh. That's exactly how Mimi used to say my name when I'd said something kind of naughty. I ask, "Will you say that again for me, Abu?"

"Say what?"

"My name. Like I've gravely disappointed you."

Amalia pauses, looking lovely. But, finally she humors me and repeats my name. This time, looking positively charmed by me.

"Thank you. I like hearing you say my name like that. You sound just like Mimi."

Amalia lays her hand on mine. "I'll always be here for you, Adrian."

"Thank you." I look down at my mug of tea. "I realized something after Mimi died. Even if you're lucky enough to leave this earth with white hair and wrinkled skin, there's still far too little time. And I don't want to waste mine. Not a second of it." I run my fingertip over the rim of my mug again. "Last week, I was able to sell a house I'd bought for Mimi for a tidy sum. So, I've decided to use that money to buy a place of my own and ask Laila to move in with me, when the show is over."

"How exciting. Congratulations."

"Hopefully, I'll get the courage to say the magic words to her before then. If not, that'd be pretty awkward, huh?"

Amalia chuckles.

"I don't want to ask if I can move in with Laila at her condo. That'd feel like me mooching, you know? Like me asking Kendrick if I can sleep on his couch, rather than The Beast turning into The Prince and inviting Belle to live at his castle."

Amalia puts her palm on her heaving chest. "Maybe you're not a prince in *training*, after all."

I shrug. "I'm a little nervous Laila will turn me down, only because she loves the little condo she bought herself. She's super proud of it. So, I think I should buy a place that'll knock Laila onto her ass, you know? Some place that's a huge step up from her condo, where she'll be excited to live with me."

"I'm confident Laila will say yes to you, and it will have nothing to do with the house itself. She'll say yes because she wants to be with *you*."

"Well, that would be preferable," I admit. "But I'm not taking any chances. You should have seen her excitement when she saw the fancy mansion we're living in now. I don't want a place as big as that. I don't like big spaces. But I do want whatever house I get to have some kind of 'wow' factor. Maybe an ocean view. Laila said she loves the ocean. I'd want a home gym and hot tub, too. Oh, and a living room that's big enough for a baby grand piano."

"You play piano?"

"No, but Laila does."

Amalia smiles. "That sounds lovely."

"So I guess what I'm asking is will you help me find a house like that? My manager gave me the number for a real estate agent, but the whole thing feels overwhelming to me. I've never bought a house for myself, and certainly not one I'm planning to surprise my girlfriend with."

"Oh, you're not going to ask Laila to help you look for the perfect place?"

"No. Going house hunting with my girlfriend feels like way too big a *thing*. I just want to find the perfect house and surprise her with it. And when she's feeling blown away by my new digs, I'll surprise her by asking her to live there with me."

"That sounds wonderful. But I'm not the right person to help you buy a house. Reed, however, is an expert when it comes to real estate. I'm sure he'd—"

Movement at the entrance to the kitchen attracts our attention, and speak of the devil, Reed enters the room, along with his fiancée, Georgina, both of them dressed to kill.

"Savage," Reed says, sounding surprised, but not upset, to find me sitting at his kitchen table.

"Adrian needs a place to stay for a few nights," Amalia explains. "His grandmother passed away recently and Laila is out of town. He'd rather not be alone."

"Of course, you're welcome here," Reed says. He and Georgina offer their condolences about my grandmother and take seats at the kitchen table.

Amalia says, "Adrian, do you mind if I tell Reed about your house hunting?"

"Feel free."

Amalia gives Reed the scoop, after which Reed enthusiastically offers his assistance, even without any prompting by Amalia.

"Wow, Reed, thanks," I say. "I appreciate that."

"Don't look so surprised," Reed says. "I told you in New York I'd owe you a personal favor if you appeared in Alessandra's music video. Well, consider this that favor."

"Don't tell Laila about this, okay? I want to get a kickass place as a surprise and invite her to move in with me when the show is over."

"Aw," Georgina says. "That's so sweet."

I bite my lip. "Hey, Georgina, I feel like I should mention . . . I didn't *actually* hit on you at that party. I mean, I did. But on a dare.

It was Kendrick's birthday, and Kendrick, Kai, and I have played 'Birthday Truth or Dare' for years now. We all knew Reed wanted you, even back then, so Kendrick thought it'd be funny to make Reed want to murder me."

Reed chuckles.

"Sorry," I say to Georgina. "That's in no way meant to imply you're not worthy of being hit on. But I know better than to step on the big boss's toes. Plus, regardless of Reed, I'd already seen Laila that night. And from then on, she was the only one for me."

"Oh my gosh," Georgina says, swooning with Amalia. "That's so lovely."

"Reed," Amalia says. "May I ask a favor of you?"

"Anything."

"When Adrian has found his new home, could you spare me once a week for a few months, so I can get him and Laila nice and settled?"

"Sure," Reed says. "As long as he doesn't try to steal you away from me."

"I've already tried, repeatedly," I admit. "And she keeps saying she'll never leave you."

"Never," Amalia confirms.

"That's a loyal woman right there," Reed says.

"And wise, too," I say. "Why do you think I keep trying to steal her?"

We sing Amalia's praises for a bit longer, until, finally, Reed gets up from the table and extends his hand to Georgina.

"Make yourself at home," Reed says to me. "Stay as long as you like."

"Thanks. I'll be heading back home the second Laila is back in town."

Reed stops in the doorway with Georgina. "Hey, I could move a few meetings around tomorrow so we can check out some places, if you're free."

"Free as a bird. I'd love it."

Reed looks at Georgina. "Are you free tomorrow?"

"I can make myself free."

"Please do. You make everything more fun." Reed flashes his fiancée a beaming smile, the likes of which I've never seen on his face before. And in reply, Georgina pats Reed's scruff playfully, causing the huge diamond on her finger to sparkle under the kitchen lights.

Out of nowhere, the sparkle on Georgina's finger has me imagining me slipping a similar rock onto Laila's hand. Not only asking Laila to live with me in whatever fancy house Reed helps me find, but to *marry* me, too. Suddenly, I realize the idea of proposing to Laila doesn't even freak me out! Actually, whoa, yes, it does. But only a little bit. Not as much as I would have thought. And that's a pretty mind-blowing development.

". . . or in the hills?" Reed says from across the kitchen.

"Huh?" I say. "Sorry. My mind was wandering."

Reed says, "I asked if you want to live by the coast or in the hills."

"Coast."

"Okay, I've got the perfect real estate agent in mind. I'll text her now and tell her to drop all her silly plans for tomorrow."

"Thanks so much, Reed."

"What's your budget, so I can tell her?"

"You know my financial situation better than anybody. What should my budget be?"

"With all the exposure you're about to get from the show, the new album and your duet with Laila will both be smash hits. So, even if it doesn't feel like it right now, in the near future, I think it would be very realistic for you to get a place in the range of seven to nine mill."

"*Whoa.* Seriously? I bought a house for my grandma in Chicago for five mill, and I had to take out a huge loan."

"You won't have to do that this time. How much is the show paying you?"

"Zippo."

"What?"

"They're not paying me a dime. They were initially going to pay me four mill for the season. But through a series of events I don't particularly want to talk about, I'm now making exactly zero dollars for being a judge on the show."

Reed looks flabbergasted. "What the fuck, Savage?"

I laugh, realizing I'm not mad in the slightest about the money I've paid to Laila, or about the money I'm letting the show keep to ensure Laila remains on the show. In fact, I'd do it all again, if it would ensure I'd be right back here in my life, head over heels in love with Laila, wanting to move in with her. "What can I say? I traded money for love," I say. "And I'd do it again."

Reed chuckles. "Goodnight, Savage."

"Goodnight."

Reed and Georgina exit the kitchen. And when they're gone, Amalia turns to me and says, "Adrian, I don't know what you did to 'trade money for love,' but whatever it was, I know Mimi is smiling down on you, feeling very, *very* proud of you for doing exactly that."

SIXTY-THREE

SAVAGE

"Savage!" Laila shrieks happily from the foyer of our massive reality TV mansion.

At the sound of Laila's voice, the ache that's been ravaging my heart since Mimi's death and Laila's departure on her trip feels instantly soothed. In fact, as Laila gleefully screams my name again, my heart feels as gleeful as she sounds. I feel *happy*. Relieved. And certain of the path I've been sprinting down the past couple days in Laila's absence.

Having returned to this house from Reed's only a few minutes ago, I've been sitting here on the couch, excitedly skimming the offer Reed's real estate agent just submitted for me on the house of my dreams. It was a dream I didn't even know I had a week ago, but now that I've seen *that* house, and Laila is back, and I can so clearly envision how happy I could be with Laila, I know in my bones Mimi was right all along. *This* is what I've always needed and wanted. Love. Acceptance. Trust. Family. Stability. *Grace*. And I'm going to have it all with Laila.

Quickly, I slam my laptop closed and sprint through the house toward the foyer. When I get there, I find a tanned and sparkling Laila, surrounded by far too many pieces of luggage for her short trip to Mexico. When she sees me, she barrels to me, and then launches herself into my waiting, open arms like a missile. Somehow, I catch her without falling over, and as she wraps her legs around my waist and peppers my face with kisses, I squeeze her tightly, clutching her to me, groping her ass, breathing her in, and, finally, kissing her deeply, without holding back. For the first time since Mimi died, I suddenly, in this moment, feel like *me* again. Only better. I feel at peace now. I feel whole, despite the Mimi-sized hole in my heart.

I love you, I think. But what I say is, "I missed you." Once I start saying the magic words to Laila, I'm sure they'll pop out of my mouth as easily as "good morning" and "goodnight." I certainly had no problems saying them to Mimi. And I say them to Sasha all the time, too. But saying them to Laila feels different. Monumental. I want to be sure, totally sure, when the words come out of my mouth, they'll be met in kind.

"I missed you, too," she gasps out.

We've got plenty to talk about. I'm sure she'll tell me all about her trip and show me photos. And I'll tell her that I've been doing a lot better, in terms of handling my grief about Mimi. I'm sure I'll tell her some of the cool stuff Reed's got lined up for my band's album release next week. But right now, I don't want to talk. I need to get inside her.

I put her down where we're standing, pull up her sundress and yank down her undies, grab her hot little ass, and indulge in the pussy that owns me. When she's wet and moaning, even before she's come, I back her up to the nearest wall, pull my cock out of my jeans, pick her up, and impale her. I'll make sure she gets hers before we're done. But in this moment, I feel a primal, urgent need to get inside her and fuck her hard. To claim her by leaving my load inside her and marking her as mine.

My thrusts are animalistic and raw. With each hard thrust of my body, we both growl and grunt. Moan and groan. She takes my bottom lip between her teeth and grits out, "Yes!" And I fuck her with everything I've got. With each movement of my body, I'm slamming into the farthest reaches of hers. Invading her. Conquering. With each thrust, I'm leaving a piece of myself behind. Giving all that I am to her. All that I could be, if only she'll promise to love me in return. Now that my walls are down and my heart is bare and vulnerable—beating, totally unprotected, in Laila's palms—I realize just how guarded and scared I was before now. How much I held back, for fear of rejection. The same rejection I *thought* I'd suffered during the last month of the tour.

"Laila," I grit out, impaling her against the wall with every ounce of force I can muster. I've fucked her against a wall before. And those times, I've whispered into her ear, "I'm pinning you against the wall because you're a work of art." But this time, there's no way I could make a quip like that. In this moment, I can't be smooth or funny. Dirty talk isn't a possibility. I'm raw. Wrecked. In love. Desperate. I need her to understand I'm hers now. Mind, body, and soul.

"Adrian," she replies. And the tone of her voice, the fact that she's used my first name, for some reason, that one word has said it all. She's mine. Every bit as much as I'm hers.

"I love you," I choke out. "I love you, Laila."

She bursts into tears. "I love you, too." I feel her body rippling around mine. Milking mine.

A sensation of white-hot ecstasy consumes me, as my body quakes and convulses. When my body quiets down, I set Laila on her feet and kiss the hell out of her.

"How have you been doing?" she asks softly, cupping my face in her palms. And it's plain from her tone she's referring to my grief about Mimi.

"I'm a whole lot better, now that you're here."

"I shouldn't have left you."

"I insisted, remember? And, honestly, it was for the best. Being without you . . . it made my feelings so obvious. So *indisputable*. I don't only want you, Laila. I *need* you. I love you. I can't live without you. I can't be happy without you. I can't be *me* without *you*."

Her eyes water. "I feel the same way. And it became so clear to me when we were apart. I realized . . ." She stops herself. "Actually, I have a much better way of telling you what I realized. During my trip, I wrote a little song that will tell you exactly what I realized."

I smile. "You wrote a song for me?"

"Yes and no. I wrote a response to 'Hate Sex High'—a sloweddown version with new lyrics. It's your song, done my way."

"Oh my God, Laila."

"There was a piano at the hotel and I'd go down there every night and play for a bit before bedtime. You know me. My favorite way to unwind. And one night, when I was missing you so much, I started playing 'Hate Sex High,' just to feel closer to you. And when I got to my name in the song, I switched things up a bit. And, suddenly, all new lyrics for the entire song started flooding me. I jotted them down on my phone, so I could maybe sing you my version of the song one day, if ever I mustered the courage." She chuckles. "I didn't think in a million years I'd be playing the song for you right after returning home from my trip. But now, I can't stand the thought of this moment passing without me playing it for you."

"I can't wait to hear it."

She grabs my hand and leads me into the living room. While Laila takes a seat at the baby grand, I stand next to the piano, watching her, my heart crashing with anticipation.

Smiling, Laila lays her fingers onto the keys. "Wow. This feels even more nerve-wracking than performing on *Sylvia*."

"Take your time."

She looks into my eyes for a long beat, apparently mustering her nerve. "I can't believe I'm about to play this for you. I'm so happy, Savage. I love you so much."

"I love you, too."

We share a huge smile. Until, finally, Laila begins to play her song:

True Love High

Yeah, yeah

I've fallen, fallen deep into love with you
  I'm feeling something so beautiful

You saw me with him at the show
  I was a liar
  I played it cold to your face
  I was on fire
  I said I was his all along
  Knew you wouldn't like it
  I wanted you desperately
  But wanted you only on your knees

I've fallen, fallen deep into love with you
  And I'm feeling something so beautiful
  I've fallen, fallen deep into love with you
  And I'm feeling something so beautiful

La la la la la I love you, I love you
  La la la la la la I love you, I love you

I saw you so clearly that night
  Like it was the first time
  You made me a bowl of fish soup
  And sang with a sweet smile

I swore not to catch any feelings
But couldn't resist
Now I'm a slave to you, boy
And you're stuck with this bitch

I've fallen, fallen deep into love with you
And I'm feeling something so beautiful
I've fallen, fallen deep into love with you
And I'm feeling something so beautiful

La la la la la I love you, I love you
La la la la la la I love you, I love you

You fucked with my body, baby
Then stole my heart
I said you meant nothing to me
I was yours from the start
Yours from the start
Yours from the start
All along, been chasing a
True Love High

As Laila sings out the last high note of her song, I feel a tsunami of love and certainty crashing into me. Pure euphoria. But even more than that, I feel a deep sense of completeness. I've found the great love of my life. The woman I'm going to spend the rest of my life with, without a doubt. I've found true love, exactly the way she just sang to me.

I scoop Laila up in my arms and kiss her deeply. And then, as words of love and adoration flow from my lips, as the last remnants of fear and indecision leave my body, as certainty and peace and grace flood me, I pick my woman up like a bride, carry her up the staircase and to our bedroom, and worship her body for the next two hours, stopping only when we're both too physically exhausted to keep going.

Go to
http://www.laurenrowebooks.com/laila-f-true-love-high
to hear Laila sing True Love High to Savage

SIXTY-FOUR

SAVAGE

"Wake up!" Laila shouts. She taps on my forehead. *Tap, tap, tap.* "Time to wake up, Adrian! Wakey, wakey!"

I squint at her. "What the fuck are you doing?"

"I have a surprise for you!"

I look at the clock on the nightstand. It's just past eleven in the morning. Which wouldn't be an unreasonable wake-up time, normally. But, in this instance, Laila and I stayed up until sunrise, talking and making love. Rummaging through the refrigerator. Sharing a contraband bottle of whiskey while soaking naked in our hot tub. Basically, reveling in our true love high.

"Laila, go back to sleep," I mutter. "You can give me this 'surprise' later."

"I can't wait." *Tap, tap, tap.* "The most important part of my gift finally arrived a minute ago and I *cannot* wait another second to give it to you!"

I rub my eyes and yawn. "You got me a gift?"

"I did."

"Why?"

"Because I love you and you sent me and my family to Cabo

and treated us to the fanciest vacation, ever. Because paybacks are a bitch, bitch! So get up!"

I sit up. "I don't need a present from you."

"Too bad. I already had a little present in the works for you, when I left for Cabo. But while I was there, I realized it wasn't nearly enough, so I started making some other arrangements. And now, I've finally got all of it and I can't wait to give it to you!" She grabs my face and kisses me. "Stay right here and don't move a muscle and don't you dare go back to sleep!" She rustles my hair, squeals, and sprints out of the room, leaving me feeling dazed and confused and highly intrigued.

A moment later, Laila returns to the bedroom, carrying a large cube wrapped in bright paper, as well as a book-sized wrapped gift lying on top of the cube. She tosses the small gift onto the mattress and shoves the large cube at me. "Open this one first."

"You shouldn't have gotten me anything," I say.

"Fuck right off with that. I have more money than I know what to do with and a man I love with all my heart. Of course, I'm going to buy you a gift or two, especially after you sent me and my family on such an extravagant trip."

"Laila, it was Cabo. Let's not overstate the extravagance here. Plus, I sent you on that trip as a *gift*. Gifts don't require *payback*."

"Would you shut up and open my gift, motherfucker? I can spend my money any way I see fit, whether you like it or not. And what I want is to give my man this *gift*."

"*Jeez*. So feisty." Chuckling, I take the large gift and begin unwrapping it and soon discover it's an old-school guitar amp.

"Oh, wow. This is so cool!"

Laila shrieks, "*It belonged to Jeff Buckley!*"

My jaw drops. I don't think I've mentioned my near-obsession with Jeff Buckley to Laila. Not that I was keeping it a secret. It just never came up. Did she hear about it from Kendrick? "Laila," I breathe, my heart pounding. "He's one of my all-time favorites."

"Yes, I know. Hence, the gift."

"Laila," I say stupidly, feeling overcome. "Wow. Thank you." I hug her tightly and sputter, "This is the best gift I've ever gotten."

"Check it out," she says. "It's super cool."

I turn my attention to the amplifier, running my hands over it. Twisting its knobs, each touch of my flesh on places where Jeff Buckley's hands also touched giving me goosebumps. All traces of sleepiness gone, I hop up from the bed, shouting, "I'm gonna get my guitar and plug it in!"

"Not yet!" she yells. "Wait, Adrian! There's more to the gift!"

I dance around like I've got ants in my pants. Like I'm four years old, wearing my Christmas jammies, and just got a toy train that needs its caboose. "Babe, I want to get my guitar. *Please.*"

She giggles. "Before you do that, there's more to this gift." She motions to the spot I just left. "Please."

"Whatever more there is, take it back," I say, shuffling toward the bed. "It's only downhill from here. This is *literally* the best thing you could have gotten for me, in the history of time." I resume my seat on the mattress next to her. "Did Kendrick tell you how much I love Jeff Buckley?"

"No, *you* told me, without actually telling me." She winks. "You always sing Jeff Buckley in the shower."

"I *do?*"

She nods. "All the time. And, of course, besides that little lullaby you always used to sing to Mimi, you often sang little snippets of Jeff Buckley to her, too. I could tell how meaningful his songs were to you."

My heart is bursting. "Still, though, it's a giant leap that you'd think to shell out the kind of money it'd take to buy one of Buckley's *actual* amps. I'm blown away."

"I love you. That's worth more than all the money in the world."

I grin broadly, thinking about the money I've given up to keep Laila on the show. And once again, like I told Reed the other night, I'm positive I did the right thing. In fact, I'd do it again and again, every single time, if my life were *Groundhog Day*. If it meant I'd be here with Laila this morning, with "True Love High" still ringing in my ears, and Jeff Buckley's amp sitting on my bed . . . and, most importantly, Laila's beautiful smile lighting up my bedroom.

Laila points. "The amp's got papers certifying it was Buckley's. I taped them to the bottom of the amp. Check 'em out."

I turn the amp over, as requested, and I'll be damned, there's a folded-up piece of paper taped to the bottom. I detach the paper and unfold it, excited to see Buckley's name in black and white. Which I do. But I also find a small envelope with the certificate. I open the envelope and find a USB flash drive inside. I hold it up to Laila, a question on my face, and she smiles as big as the Grand Canyon.

"Adrian Savage, my love," she says. "On that flash drive, you will find . . . a rare treasure." Against all odds, her smile somehow finds a way to widen even more. She says, "That flash drive is loaded with the pro tools multi track stems . . ."

"No."

"Of the entire album . . ."

"Oh my God, Laila."

"Of *Grace!*"

"Laila!"

"Every single track from every single song on *Grace*, your favorite album by your favorite artist, the original owner of that guitar amp."

I feel like I'm going to faint. Or have a heart attack or stroke. All while being simultaneously shot out of a cannon. It's unthinkable that she's acquired this impossible treasure for me. It's beyond my wildest dreams or fantasies or imaginations. In my palm, I'm holding something priceless. Something that can't be bought on the open market: the *actual* raw files from the recording sessions which were then layered and edited and seamlessly woven together to create the songs on my all-time favorite album. In other words, she's given me the Holy Grail. A magical gift only a fellow artist would ever give—a gift only a fellow artist would possibly *understand* to give.

I thought the amp was the best gift, ever. And it was, a moment ago. But now, this is, by far, the most boner-inducing, heart palpitating, perfect, mind-blowing gift Laila could ever, ever, ever have given me. And to think she did it not only because she loves me. But because she knows me, so well. Because she's figured me out, without anyone, not even Kendrick, telling her this would be the best gift I could receive. Honestly, I don't think even Kendrick would come up with this idea, if tasked with finding the perfect gift for me. Only Laila could or would do something so magical for me. So amazing. And the effect on me is like she's given my very soul the most amazing blowjob in the history of time.

I swoop her into my arms and kiss the hell out of her, thanking her profusely. I tell her I love her, over and over again, as I take off her clothes. And she tells me she loves me, too, over and over again, as she slides her naked body onto my cock and rides me like there's no tomorrow. I devour her breasts and nipples. Massage her clit. We fuck and laugh and kiss, our euphoria palpable. I didn't know love could feel like this. I thought love like this was a fairytale. And love songs about it were bullshit. But now I know this kind of love is not only real, it's the only thing that matters.

When we're done making love, we lie in bed for a bit, kissing and laughing. But soon, I can't resist grabbing my laptop and inserting the flash drive, as Laila cuddles up to me and lays her cheek on my shoulder. As the files unfurl on my screen, I "ooh" and "aah" like I'm watching a fireworks display on the Fourth of July, and Laila giggles at my reaction.

"How did you get your hands on this?" I ask, clicking around through the files like a madman.

"Reed said he owed me a big favor for doing the music video for Alessandra. So, I called in the favor."

"I could weep."

She laughs, not realizing I'm not joking.

I pull her to me and silently hug her close for a very long moment, long enough to gather myself. Finally, I feel in control of myself enough to pepper her gorgeous face with kisses, before taking her face in my palms. "Laila Fitzgerald, if I'm ever so much as cranky toward you, if I'm ever even remotely close to being an asshole in your presence, ever, please, *please*, say 'Buckley multi track stems' and I promise on my life I'll instantly stop whatever shitty or immature thing I'm saying or doing, drop to my knees, and kiss your feet."

She makes an adorable sound of pure joy. "I'm gonna hold you to that."

"And rightly so."

We kiss again. But, suddenly, Laila says, "Oh! There's one more gift you need to open."

"No. Stop. No more."

"This one is a small token. It cost me approximately twenty dollars."

She grabs the book-sized wrapped gift from the corner of the bed, and hands it to me. "I had this made for you when we were in Chicago. But I decided to wait a little bit to give it to you."

My heart thumping, I open the wrapping paper to find the inside of an old birthday card, given to me by Mimi on the first birthday I spent with her. My thirteenth. Laila's gotten the card framed behind glass like it's an exquisite work of art. Which it is, to me.

The handwritten note on the card from Mimi reads:

My dearest Adrian,

Happy 13th birthday, my love. I thank God everyday he brought you to me, so you could light up my life like a shooting star. Whenever you get frustrated or angry, if you're feeling like the world is against you, take a deep breath and remember you're never going to be alone again. You've got me now. And I'm not going anywhere. Even when I'm gone from this earth, my love for you will remain. You're the light of my life, Adrian. I love you, forever and always.

Love,
Mimi

SIXTY-FIVE

LAILA

One month later

It's around nine in the morning on my twenty-fifth birthday. I'm sitting at the baby grand in the corner of the living room while Savage sleeps upstairs. For the past hour or so, I've been working on a song for my third album that came to me in a dream.

Ever since I got back from Mexico a month ago, and Savage and I shared that incredible, magical night, during which we must have said "I love you" to each other a thousand times, I've been flooded with musical inspiration. All of it, about love. Or if not that, directly, happiness and joy. And it's no surprise, considering how great everything has been going in my life. Not only with Savage, but with the show, too. When it started airing, the ratings hit record numbers and never dipped. Which, thankfully, has insulated Savage and me from any more meddling from Nadine. In fact, she's left Savage and me alone to be happy and authentic on-camera, exactly the way she said she'd do when she called me in Chicago.

And now, I can't write one of my usual "fuck you!" kind of songs to save my life.

"Happy birthday," Savage says, entering the living room, and I quickly stop playing the song I was working on—the passionate love song about Savage that came to me in my sleep.

When Savage reaches me, he kisses me in greeting and then makes me scooch over on the piano bench so he can join me. "The big two-five," he says, settling himself next to me. "I should have gotten you a walker for your birthday."

"You didn't? Darn."

Savage tickles the ivories playfully. "Nope. Unfortunately, all I got you was a baby grand, just like this one, that'll be delivered to your place when we're booted out of here in a few weeks."

I gasp. "*No.*"

Savage grins. "Happy birthday, baby."

Squealing, I hug him and thank him profusely, and we talk about my exciting gift for several minutes. "So, hey," I say, "speaking of us being booted out of here in a few weeks." I take a deep breath. I've been wanting to broach this topic with Savage for a few weeks now. He's told me in the past he hates feeling "tied down" or "locked in," but we've been so happy together, I can't stand the thought of not waking up to his face every morning after we leave here. Savage couldn't possibly want to live apart when our contractual relationship is over, could he? I walk my fingers up the piano keys, mustering my courage. "When we leave this house, where are you planning to live?"

When he's silent, I gather the courage to peek at Savage's face and find him red and flustered.

"A hotel?" I ask, returning to the piano keys.

"Uh . . . yeah. A hotel."

"I figured. I've been thinking, though . . . maybe it would be fun if you came to live with me at my condo." Savage says nothing, so I peek at him again. This time, he looks like his mind is racing. Like he's been caught with his hand in a cookie jar. "Uh oh, did I scare you away?" I've tried to make my tone sound light and bright. Like this is no biggie. Ha, ha. Just a wild idea. But, truthfully, I feel disappointed he hasn't replied with a quick and simple yes. But oh well, at least he hasn't given me an immediate no. So, that's something.

Savage's features soften when he sees whatever look of anxiety has crept onto my face. "Of course, you didn't scare me away, Fitzy," he says. "Nothing you could say or do could possibly scare me away. I just don't want to be a mooch, that's all."

I sigh with relief. "Don't think of it like that, babe. I have a place and you don't. This makes sense. One plus one equals two."

Savage bites his lower lip. "You know what? You're right. Of course, we should live together after the show, since I don't have a place of my own."

"Exactly."

"It makes perfect sense."

"I couldn't agree more."

Savage snickers.

"What?"

"Nothing. I'm just excited. Thanks for asking me to live with you."

"Thanks for saying yes." I shudder with excitement. "This is going to be so *fun*!"

Savage smiles broadly. "Yes, it is. 'A grand adventure,' as Mimi always used to say."

"Indeed."

We seal the deal with a kiss, after which I squeal again and say, "I can't wait to play my new piano in my condo! It'll be a tight fit, but I can get rid of a couple chairs and make it work."

"What were you working on when I came in? I heard a snippet. It sounded amazing."

I shake my head.

As Savage knows, I don't reveal my works in progress until I'm certain the song is worthy of being born. And that's especially true of the song I was just working on about Savage. It's the most honest, passionate song I've ever written in my life. A song I'm nervous might freak Savage out a bit, to be honest, if I play it before its time, since it contains some lyrics that will express things to Savage we haven't yet said to each other. I've told Savage I love him many times. But telling him I'm going to love him *forever*, that my love is "infinite and everlasting," as this song does, repeatedly, feels like taking our relationship to the next level, and I'm not sure he's ready for that yet.

"Okay, then, if you won't play me whatever you were working on when I came in," Savage says, "then play me *something*. You can't whet my appetite like that and then leave me hanging."

"Sure. Any requests?"

"How about one of your cool Laila Fitzgerald covers?"

I can't help smiling. Savage loves it when I transform one of my favorite songs by another artist into a slowed-down, piano cover. I pause, considering my options, and then start playing the intro to "Fireflies" by our friends, 22 Goats—one of my all-time favorite songs to sing. But since I'm playing the song much slower than the recorded original, and also on nothing but piano, Savage only recognizes the song when I start singing the famous first line: "Fireflies, you've got me feeling 'em/never before or since."

"I've got goosebumps!" Savage blurts. "Just like the ones I got when I heard you singing this song with Aloha and the Goats at Reed's party!"

I stop playing on a dime, my jaw hanging open. "You heard me singing this song at Reed's party? But you told me you didn't come inside and see the performance."

"I didn't. I was standing outside on the patio and could hear the first part of the performance from there. Don't stop. Sing me the whole thing. I love your voice on this one."

"Your wish is my command." I return my fingers to the keys and start from the beginning again, turning "Fireflies" into a piano ballad, with a few tweaks to the original lyrics, especially for my love:

. . .

Fireflies
You got me feelin' 'em
Never before or since
All my life
Been chasing butterflies
And in
Just one night
One perfect night . . .
Boy, you made butterflies your bitch

Oh, Fireflies
Oh, In your eyes

Don't know if you're feeling it
These wings and lights
Or if everything's all in my head
But there's one thing I know
One singular truth:
I need you
I need you
Boy, I need you so bad
In my life
In my bed

Oh, Fireflies
Oh, in your eyes
Oh, Fireflies
Oh, in your eyes

Fireflies
Fireflies

You got me feelin' 'em
With you
And nobody else
You're a savage
A puzzle
My destination
Would give my soul to the devil
My soul to the devil
To never stop feeling
Those
Fireflies
With you

When I finish singing my version of "Fireflies," Savage looks absolutely blown away, the same way he always does whenever I sing for him. He kisses and hugs me, whispering, "You sound even more amazing on that song than you did at Reed's party. I love it when it's just you and your piano, and no other instrumentation."

"I can't believe you heard me singing this song at Reed's party. I thought for sure you hadn't."

"I heard half of it. I left midway through the song."

"I looked for your face in the audience during the entire performance! And when I didn't see you, I decided, 'Screw it, when I'm done performing, I'll put my ego aside and find him, and be the first one to say hello.' But when I got offstage, and did a lap of the party looking for you, you were nowhere to be found."

Savage chuckles. "I heard you singing 'Fireflies' and couldn't stay at the party a second longer. Your voice was so gorgeous, so mesmerizing to me, it made me want to cock-block Kendrick the second you walked offstage. So, I left the party, right then, to keep myself from hitting on you."

"Oh my gosh," I say. "I was positive I couldn't find you because you'd left the party with whichever lucky lady you'd decided to bang that night. Georgina, or the woman you'd been talking to by the pool, or whoever else."

He shakes his head. "I didn't want to be a dick to Kendrick. By the way, I didn't hit on Georgina that night. I mean, I *did*, but only because that was Kendrick's birthday dare for me. Although, admittedly, I was thrilled to do it to get you back for flirting so brazenly with Cash in front of me."

I snicker. "I wasn't remotely interested in Cash." I wink. "But I sure did enjoy the look of molten jealousy in your eyes when I flirted with him."

"You're an evil woman," he says with a lopsided grin, but his tone feels like he's giving me his highest compliment.

I shrug. "I wanted you to hit on me, and you weren't. All's fair in love and war."

"Hell yeah, it is. Too-fucking-shay, Fitzy."

I bite my lip. "Speaking of 'Birthday Truth or Dare' . . . Will you let me play tonight at my birthday party?"

Savage shakes his head. "Only Kendrick, Kai, and I are allowed to play. We've never even let Ruby and Titus play on their birthday —and trust me, Ruby's held a grudge about it for a long time."

"Well, that's a simple fix. Let me play tonight and let the twins play on their next birthday. The more the merrier, right?"

Savage pauses. And for a second, it's like his hard drive is rebooting. Like, he's truly never considered it could be just that simple to change a longstanding tradition.

"I mean, no worries," I add quickly. "I'm cool with not playing. I'm just saying you *could* let me play, if that's what you want to do. The past is the past. The future is whatever you want it to be."

Savage stares at me, dumbfounded, making me laugh.

"Don't worry about it, honey," I say, patting his hand. "It was just an off-handed remark. You don't have to change a thing."

Savage's face is flushed. I don't know what just happened inside his brain, but I know him well enough to know he's having some deep thoughts. "You know . . ." he begins. "You don't need to be playing 'Birthday Truth or Dare' to get me to do something for you—or *to* you. Whatever you want, your wish is my command, every day of the year. You know that, right?"

I grin. "Yes, I do. I'm not sure it works that way when it comes to getting you to tell me the truth, but, yes, I know I don't need a birthday dare to get you to do something for or to me."

"Well, if 'Truth' is what you want, then you wouldn't get that, even if we let you play. There's no 'Truth' option in our game."

"But it's called 'Birthday *Truth* or Dare.'"

"That's a misnomer. We deleted the 'Truth' option years ago, when we realized truth is boring as hell."

"I don't think it's boring. In fact, if you ask the right question, then 'Truth' is far more interesting—and scary—than any dare could possibly be."

Savage considers that. "Huh." He looks at me blankly for a long moment. And then, "Well, either way, you don't need the game because I always tell you the truth."

I snort. "No, you tell me whatever truth you're ready to share. I'm not calling you a liar, babe, just saying I think I could get a whole lot more out of you if you *knew* you had no choice but to tell me the whole, unvarnished truth, so help you God, about a particular topic." I raise an eyebrow. "You want to try it now—play a private little game of 'Birthday Truth or *Truth*,' just you and me?"

"I can't think of anything I'd like to do . . . *less*." He laughs. "But you know what I *would* like to do, as a private little game for your birthday? Can you guess?"

"Eat the Birthday Girl's Pussy?" I ask coyly. Because I know that gleam in my man's eyes. The swipe of his tongue over his lower lip. It's what Savage *always* does when he's got a boner and his tongue is craving the pleasure of a pussy well eaten.

"Ding, ding, ding!" Savage shouts. "We've got a winner!"

With that, my hot boyfriend stands, guides me onto my back on the piano bench, pulls off my panties, and with dark, burning eyes, proceeds to kick off my twenty-fifth birthday in the most delightful, toe-curling way imaginable. *Happy birthday to me.*

Go to
http://www.laurenrowebooks.com/laila-f-fireflies
to listen to Laila's cover of "Fireflies" along with Savage.

Go to
http://www.laurenrowebooks.com/22-goats-fireflies
if you're curious to hear 22 Goats' original version of "Fireflies."

SIXTY-SIX
LAILA

"What do you mean you're not *drinking?*" Rhoda, the junior producer from *Sing Your Heart* Out who's become my friend—the one who gave Savage and me a tour of our love nest on day one—gasps out. She's just arrived at my birthday party and found out I'm drinking club soda tonight. I'm standing with Rhoda in the already-crowded living room of the reality TV mansion I share with Savage—and Rhoda is beside herself with exasperation to find out I'm not drinking tonight in solidarity with Savage. Rhoda yells above the din, "But it's your own damned birthday party! You at *least* need to sip a glass of champagne on your own freaking birthday!"

I shake my head and hold up my glass. "I promised Savage I wouldn't drink while he's contractually not allowed to drink."

Rhoda looks surprised.

"You don't know that's one of the terms of Savage's employment?" I ask. "That he can't drink during the season?"

"I had no idea."

"Nadine doesn't want to see Savage's dick trending on Twitter again."

Rhoda snorts. "It's nothing the world hasn't already seen."

"Tell that to your boss."

"I will." Rhoda pulls out her phone. "With the ratings you two have been pulling in, Nadine should at least give Savage a one-night dispensation to get drunk off his ass, at his own fake house, to celebrate his very real girlfriend's quarter-century."

"Make it happen, Rhoda!" I shout. "I believe in you!"

"I'm going in!"

As Rhoda begins tapping on her phone, I look around the crowded party and notice a group coming through the front door: Fish and Alessandra, Dax and his wife, Violet, and Colin with a pretty date. I race over to the group and exchange greetings with everyone. I meet Colin's date, who seems sweet. And, of course, everyone wishes me a happy birthday.

For a few minutes, I stay and chat with the group, glancing occasionally at Savage across the room. At present, he's doing that thing I love the most: belly laughing with Kendrick and Kai. All of a sudden, a feeling of delicious *déjà vu* washes over me. I can't believe my celebrity crush, whom I watched laughing with those very same bandmates across Reed's crowded party months ago, has now become the great love of my life.

"Okay, Laila, I made it happen," Rhoda, the producer, says, diverting my attention from Savage across the room. She says, "Nadine said Savage can have a *one*-night dispensation to get shit-faced for your birthday, as long as you *personally* guarantee his dick won't make a single new appearance on Twitter."

"Woohoo! Tell Nadine thank you and I accept her terms." I turn and shout into my party, to no one in particular. "Somebody get Savage and me some booze! *Savage!*" Someone taps his shoulder and says something to him, and he looks at me from across the party, just as Rhoda is handing me a champagne glass. I hold it up and point, since the party is noisy, and then motion to him and me, him and me—and then to Rhoda. For her part, Rhoda holds up her phone by way of explanation and nods, and that's all Savage needs. With a loud whoop, my boyfriend grabs a full drink right out of Kendrick's hand, throws it back in one fell swoop, and shouts something I can't make out above the loud music.

Someone turns the music up, even louder, drinks are poured, and less than an hour later, I'm buzzed to perfection and dancing like a fool in the middle of my living room with Savage and a rowdy group of our best friends—Savage's bandmates, some of my musician friends, and, of course, Aloha and her entire crew: her husband, Zander, and the guys from 22 Goats with their dates.

I can't help noticing there's been a complete lack of tension between Colin and Savage tonight, and I'm glad about it. In fact, I've caught the men sharing a laugh here and there. Perhaps, Colin showing up to my party with a date has put Savage at ease. Or maybe the therapist Savage started seeing last week, with plans to see her once a week, has already rubbed off on him. Or maybe Savage finally feels secure enough in our relationship to trust our love for what it is: rock solid.

When the current song on Alessandra's party playlist ends, none other than "Hate Sex High" begins blaring. And of course, the entire party goes ballistic. When Fugitive Summer's album released a few weeks ago, this particular song, which was released as its leadoff single, went straight to number one. And not just in the United States—in countries all over the world.

It was a first for Fugitive Summer to have a leadoff song capture that much global success, and Savage and his fellow band members have been thrilled about it. And not just for the pure accomplishment of it, but because of . . . the *money*. Oh my God, the *money*. Savage isn't a particularly money-driven person, but, still, money means freedom, and it's now clear Savage will be free as a bird for the rest of his life, along with his bandmates, provided nobody does anything too stupid. The one-two punch of "Hate Sex High," along with Savage's high profile on the show, has caused interest in Fugitive Summer and its entire catalog to skyrocket, which, in turn, has launched Fugitive Summer to a whole new level of success.

As "Hate Sex High" hits its first verse, the members of Fugitive Summer find each other on the dance floor and sing the song together loudly, throwing their heads back and jumping around like lunatics, while the entire party sings and laughs along with them. There are a whole lot of musicians and music industry types here tonight, so we all know the success Fugitive Summer is currently having is lightning in a bottle—quite possibly, never to be repeated, no matter how successful they might be in the future—and we're all thrilled to celebrate this amazing time with them. Nobody more than *me*. The muse for the song. La La La *Laila*. The woman who came three times while chasing a "hate sex high."

Fugitive Summer has never confirmed or denied the widespread belief that the song is about *me*. But it's awfully hard to miss my name at the end of those "la la" lines, no matter what Savage has always stupidly insisted. And so, when the song blaring in the party gets to that part in the song, everyone in the room screams my name at the tops of their lungs, making Savage pick me up and spin me around, while singing along with his own blaring voice. "Laila, Laila."

Even if someone hearing this song for the first time had never heard of Laila Fitzgerald, or had never seen that viral video of Savage and me fighting on a sidewalk or watched my interview on *Sylvia*, they'd know this song is about some chick named *Laila*. Some chick named *Laila* who wanted to "ride" Savage, and did. Some chick named *Laila* who came *three* times in hot pursuit of her "hate sex high." And now, finally, by singing along with the recording at the top of his lungs along with all of our friends, Savage is finally tacitly admitting what the world already knows: yep, he's most definitely singing "Laila" and not "la la" on those parts.

Of course, when the line "You came three times" comes up in the song, the party sings it even louder than anything else, and then goes ballistic around me. When Savage speaks that same line in the middle of the song in a smug, sardonic tone—"You came three times"—the entire party shouts it along with him, while looking straight at me, every single person playfully chastising me along with Savage's snarky voice for claiming sex with Savage had meant "nothing to me."

If my party guests think they're going to make me blush by serenading me on that line, however, they're dead wrong. I'm too drunk to be embarrassed about my sexual appetites at this point. Too in love. In fact, I'm so in love with the man dancing with me right now, the man who threw me this party and earlier today agreed to live with me at my condo when the show is over, I can't do anything but raise my arms in victory and celebrate joyfully. Fuck yeah, I came *three* times with my hot boyfriend, bitches! And since then, I've come a whole lot more! What, *you* don't come three times, or more, with *your* man? Well, that's a pity, sis. I guess my boyfriend is a whole lot hotter, and a whole lot better at putting his fingers, tongue, and dick to use than yours. Ha!

When the song reaches its last, spoken lines: "Did *he* make you come *three* times? Yeah, didn't think so," the party yells the line, yet again. And as they do, my drunk boyfriend bends down and motorboats my rack on the outside of my dress, claiming his prize. Making it clear *he* made me come three times, and *nobody* else. In response, I throw my head back and laugh hysterically, reveling in the fact that Savage feels every bit as unleashed and in love in this moment as I do. I'm in love with Adrian Savage. Riding a true love high. And I'm positive, even when the booze that's coursing through my bloodstream is gone, I'll never *ever* come down.

When "Hate Sex High" ends, and Savage is done motorboating me, he lays a deep kiss on me, making the party cheer and whoop. As his tongue slides into my mouth, I slide my arms around him and devour him, the whiskey on his tongue reminding me of our first kiss at Reed's house.

"I have a birthday present for you," Savage says, grabbing my hand. "Come on."

I hold my breath as he leads me through the crowd. *Is he going to propose?* I can't believe it, but that's the first thing that's popped into my head. That's a crazy thought, right? An unthinkable one. But I've thought it, distinctly, and now, as Savage leads me through the crowded room to parts unknown, I can't *stop* thinking it . . . and *hoping* for it.

When Savage stops, we're standing in front of Kendrick and Kai. He says, "Guys, I demand we let Laila play 'Birthday Truth or Dare' tonight. I won't take no for an answer."

Oh.

Well.

That's incredibly sweet. And I should be thrilled. It's a romantic gesture, considering our conversation this morning while seated at the piano. But I can't help feeling vaguely disappointed, even though there's no logical reason for me to feel that way. Savage once told me he's not boyfriend material. So, come on, Laila, give the guy credit for how far he's come and leave it at that.

In response to Savage's "demand," Kendrick and Kai look at each other like, "What the fuck?"

Kai says, "If we say yes to Laila, then Ruby and Titus will never forgive us. Especially Ruby." He looks at me. "It's nothing personal, Laila, but we've never let *anyone* but the three of us play the game."

"Oh, I understand," I reply.

But Savage is determined. A dog with a bone. "You have to admit we've been running out of good ideas for a while now," he says. "The best Kai could come up with for me last time was a naked swan dive into a swimming pool? I mean, come on! The whole world had already seen my dong by then. And yet *that's* what he thought would humiliate me? *Please.* I vote we invite not only Laila, but Ruby and Titus into our game, too, from now on. But if you can't handle that much change, all at once, then at least let the three of them in for one year, as a test-run, to see if it makes the game more fun. If not, they're out again. We'll make that clear to them up front so there are no hard feelings if we wind up booting them."

Kendrick and Kai consult briefly, before declaring their verdict.

"Okay, but only this year on a probationary basis," Kai says. He looks sternly at me, "You understand the terms? This is a one-shot deal, for now."

"So you'd better make it good," Kendrick adds with a wink.

"I understand. Thank you!" I whoop and do a happy dance. "Are there any rules or limitations?"

"Hold up," Kai says. "Let's get Ruby and Titus over here to give them the good news. Ruby's been demanding to be included for years."

Kendrick retrieves the twins and brings them to our group. And when Ruby hears the good news, she loses her ever-loving mind, like she's just found out Fugitive Summer has been nominated for a Grammy—which, by the way, is something I predict is in Fugitive Summer's near future. When she finishes hugging all three of her benefactors, Ruby hugs me and we laugh and squeal together, while Titus looks at us like we're lunatics. Obviously, Ruby and I are overreacting here. But what I've learned in life is this: overreacting to good news is a whole lot more fun than underreacting to it. Plus, we're drunk and happy and surrounded by a whole lot of happy people, so why not wring every drop of fun out of the situation?

"Okay, Laila, let me tell you the rules," Kai says. "Ruby, Titus, listen up. You won't be performing dares tonight. You'll be admitted into the game, officially, on your birthday."

"You think we don't know the rules by now?" Ruby mumbles, but when Kai nonverbally chastises her, she mimes zipping her lips.

"Rule number one," Kai says. "Your dare can't be something that would maim, kill, or send any of us to prison."

"Shoot," Ruby says, snorting, while I think to myself, "You're assuming I won't pick *Truth*?"

"Two," Kai says, counting off on his fingers. "The dare has to be something the person can do, right here and now. You can't demand we perform some complicated prank that would take hours or days to perform. We have to be able to do it, spur of the moment."

"Dang it!" Ruby says. "There goes my idea of making all of you bitches get a Brazilian wax."

Rolling his eyes, Kai addresses me again. "As long as you follow those two rules, Laila, then the third rule of the game is that your minions have no choice but to do *whatever* you say. We're your loyal subjects, Birthday Queen. Powerless to say no."

Ruby raises her arms to the ceiling. "My prayers have been answered!"

"Dude," Titus says to his sister. "Why are you so excited? Only Laila is doling out dares this time."

"No shit, Sherlock," Ruby replies to her brother. "I'm *vicariously* excited for Laila. For what this means for *womankind*." She turns and massages my shoulders, like she's my cornerman in a prizefight, about to send me into the ring in a title bout. "Okay, Laila. You gotta *represent*, girl. Make womankind proud."

"I'll give it my all, coach!" I say, dancing from foot to foot like a boxer. And when Aloha happens to walk by, an idea pops into my head. Kai Cook is a "too cool for school" type. The last person in the world who'd ever "fanboy" over *anyone*, least of all a Disney-star-turned-pop-princess. I remember Kendrick once telling me about the time he made his big brother "fanboy" over Keane Morgan, the actor from Alessandra's video shoot, during a game of "Birthday Truth or Dare," so, I decide to follow Kendrick's expert lead for my first foray into the game.

"Kai, you're up first," I say. "I dare you to fanboy over Aloha, until you get her to sing the theme song to 'It's Aloha!' for the entire party. If you can't convince her to sing it, then *you* have to do it."

Our entire group, other than Kai, breaks into raucous laughter. As we all know, Kai doesn't sing. *At all*. He's a fantastic bass player. One of the best in the business. But God did *not* bless him with dulcet vocal cords. Which is why, fun fact, Kai is the only member of Fugitive Summer who never supplies background vocals on any of their songs. Not even the singalong "la la's" in "Hate Sex High."

Predictably, Kai looks tortured as the rest of us laugh with glee. Scowling, he says, "You're girlfriend's a savage, Savage."

Savage smiles at me. "She sure is. It's my favorite thing about her."

In the end, though, as torturous as the dare sounds, it turns out to be a softball. Not surprisingly, Aloha wound up refusing to sing the theme song to her long-running Disney show—after ten years of hearing it everywhere the poor girl went, she now *hates* that song with the passion of a thousand suns. But when Kai finally dragged himself to standing on a chair, poised to sing the hideous song for the entire party, and Ruby turned off the blaring music and got everyone's attention while I sat at the piano to accompany Kai, my victim didn't get two words into the first verse before the *entire* party started singing loudly along with him. In fact, thanks to the iconic theme song being burned into our generation's gray matter, everyone at the party couldn't help singing along with Kai, the same way a knee can't help kicking forward when batted by a doctor's rubber hammer. In fact, by the song's end, even Aloha had started singing along with Kai and the crowd, despite herself. Which tells me she's drunk as hell or an awfully good sport.

When the singalong led by Kai finishes, the entire party applauds and whoops and asks for another singalong. And so, seeing as how I'm sitting at the piano, and 22 Goats is here at the party, I play one of my all-time favorite singalongs—"Fireflies"—the same one we performed at Reed's party. The song I performed for Savage this morning, before he gave me some mighty fine birthday oral sex. And, immediately, it's clear I've picked well. On the iconic line, "Girl, you made butterflies your bitch!" the crowd sings at the tops of their lungs. And in each easy, singalong chorus, the party practically blows the roof off our reality TV mansion.

When our collective performance ends, the crowd demands *another* song. But this time, I stand on the piano bench and tell everyone to put a cork in it because I'm playing my first ever game of "Birthday Truth or Dare" and won't be distracted from it a moment longer.

"That performance from Kai kicked off our game," I explain. "And now, it's time for my dare for Kendrick!" The crowd cheers, apparently already feeling as invested in the game as I do. With a wide smile, I address Kendrick. "KC, I dare you to hit on Reed Rivers over there, to the very best of your abilities, stopping only after you've successfully made him *smile*."

Everyone but Reed claps and hoots in response to my edict. Reed shouts, "Leave me out of this, Fitzgerald!" But his tone is playful.

"Aw, come on, Reed," Savage yells. "It's her birthday!"

The crowd goads Reed on, enthusiastically, until, finally, the music mogul relents.

"Okay, fine," Reed says, and, in response, the crowd cheers like their team just scored a goal at the World Cup.

"Don't go easy on him, Reed!" I shout across the room. "You have to make Kendrick work for that smile!"

"I know of no other way," Reed deadpans.

And away we go. To the great pleasure of the crowd, Kendrick saunters over to Reed. But he doesn't stop when he reaches him. He walks right on by. Immediately, though, Kendrick doubles back, looks Reed up and down lasciviously, and says, "Oh, hey there, baby. Do you believe in love at first sight . . . *or should I walk past you again?*"

Of course, the crowd loves it and reacts accordingly. But Reed doesn't look even tempted to smile. In fact, Reed replies flatly, "No, you can keep on walking with a piss-poor line like that, moth-erfucker."

Kendrick snorts. "It's not gonna get much better than that, unfortunately." As the crowd laughs and applauds, Kendrick puffs out his cheeks, contemplating his next attempt. But when it's clear Kendrick is ready to try again, the crowd goes quiet with anticipa-tion. "Hey, baby," Kendrick says to Reed. "Do me a favor. Feel my shirt."

"Because it's made of 'boyfriend material'?" Reed supplies. "Sorry, you're gonna have to do better than that."

"Fuck."

Everyone in the room, other than Reed, guffaws again.

But Kendrick won't be denied. Squaring his shoulders, Kendrick flashes Reed an incredibly hot smolder and says, "Hey there, sexy . . . I seem to have lost my phone number. Can I—"

"Have mine?" Reed interrupts. "No. Fuck off."

There's another round of laughter, before Kendrick swipes his thumb over his nose, winks at Reed, and says, "Hey, gorgeous, are you a parking ticket? Because you've got—"

"*Fine* written all over me." Reed shakes his head. "Amateur. Bush league. Weak. Try again."

And on and on it goes, pretty much just like that, through four more rounds. Until, finally, Reed breaks. But not in response to anything *Kendrick* has said—but in response to something *Reed* himself has said. Kendrick asks, "Can I follow you wherever you're going, Reed? Because my *momma* always told me to—"

"*Follow your dreams*," Reed interjects, his expression set in stone. And then, he takes a step forward, getting into Kendrick's handsome face, and says, "Do me a favor, KC. Tell your momma I said, 'Fuck Kendrick. Fuck his dreams. And thanks for sucking my cock last night.'"

"Reed!" Georgina shouts, as the party explodes with shocked laughter. And that's when Reed throws his head back and guffaws at his own inappropriate joke.

"That doesn't count!" Kai shouts, as his brother raises his arms in victory. "Kendrick didn't make Reed smile! *Reed* made Reed smile!"

But the rest of the party agrees it did, indeed, count. And, quickly, the group's attention turns to Savage. *My last victim.*

Someone yells, "Make him show us his cock!"

"Just google him if you want to see that," I fire back, and the party hoots with laughter.

"No more dick pics from Savage!" Rhoda, a producer from *Sing Your Heart Out*, yells.

I quickly assure Rhoda, and the boisterous crowd, I've got no desire to add to Savage's online dick pic collection tonight. "Actually . . . ," I say from my perch on the piano bench. I smile at Savage below me. "For Savage, I pick *Truth*."

"Truth isn't an option," Savage says quickly. But his bandmates desert him instantly, with all of them saying I can pick any damned thing I want, since I'm the Birthday Queen.

"*We* never pick Truth because we know everything there is to know about you," Kendrick explains to his best friend. "But as the Birthday Queen, Laila is all-powerful."

I return to Savage and realize anything worth asking him, I'd want to hear his answer in private. Also, like Savage said to me this morning, there's no need to "dare" the man to do a damned thing, since, one, he'd do any important thing I asked, whether it's my birthday or not, and, two, any not-important thing I might dare him to do, in order to humiliate him in front of a crowd, wouldn't be fun for me. I have no desire to humiliate my sweet boyfriend, even for fun. And even if I did have that urge, it wouldn't outweigh my desire to ask Savage an important question and *know,* without a doubt, he felt required to tell me the *whole* truth, without spinning or half-truthing it.

"I tell you what," I say. "I'll pick Truth *and* a rain check. We'll finish this game later, behind closed doors, when it's just you and me, as long as you agree that Truth is an option."

The crowd boos.

Ruby is beside herself.

The Cook brothers tell me that's not allowed.

But I'm firm in my decision and can't help noticing Savage looks deeply relieved.

"You've got yourself a deal, Fitzy," Savage says, his dark eyes sparkling.

The faux-angry crowd begins throwing napkins and empty Solo cups at me, but I don't care. I hop off the piano bench, straight to the love of my life, and kiss his sensuous lips.

"Don't think I'm letting you off easy," I murmur. "Whatever I ask, you'll need to tell me the whole truth, so help you God."

"That's the game," he says. "All I can say, though, is be careful what you wish for."

Go to
http://www.laurenrowebooks.com/hate-sex-high-music
if you'd like to listen to Fugitive Summer's number one hit, "Hate Sex High" again.

SIXTY-SEVEN
LAILA

The house is finally empty. All partygoers have left. It's the wee hours of the morning on the day after my twenty-fifth birthday—the best birthday of my life—and I'm presently sitting on my boyfriend's face on our couch, having an intense orgasm.

When my body stops warping and rippling, and my groans come down, Savage guides me off him, flips me onto my hands and knees, and fucks me from behind like I'm nothing to him but a blow-up doll he purchased online. *And I love it.* He calls me his "dirty birthday girl" and grips my hair. He tells me I'm hot, and his, and that watching me dancing to "Hate Sex High" earlier tonight, and owning that shit like a boss, turned him on like crazy. Until finally, Savage is coming hard inside me, followed by him fingering me until I do, too.

When both our bodies are spent and we're way too exhausted to keep going for now, we cuddle naked on the couch for a long moment, catching our breath. For a fleeting moment, I have the impulse to spring up from the couch and play him the song I've been writing for him. "Savage Love." But I quickly decide, no. First off, I'm not finished tinkering with the song. But, more importantly,

I'm not ready to say all that "infinite and everlasting" stuff to Savage, just yet.

When I spoke to Mimi in private, during those last days of her life, she explained that Savage has always suffered from extreme anxiety, though the world would never guess that about him, based on his swagger and showmanship. She told me the thing that helps him keep his anxieties in check is taking things one day at a time. Not making firm commitments about the future. Not feeling tied down.

"That's why Savage proposing to you is especially wonderful," Mimi said to me. "It's a huge breakthrough, to know he loves you enough to be able to envision, and promise, *forever* to you."

Obviously, it wasn't true. Savage had promised no such thing to me. And the weight of that lie hit me like a ton of bricks at the time. But nonetheless, that conversation with Mimi has helped me understand Savage better, which has helped me keep my expectations about him in check. For now, the boy has agreed to move into my condo with me when the show is over in a couple weeks. Surely, if Mimi were here and somehow found out we aren't actually engaged, she'd nonetheless feel Savage's agreement to move in with me, on its own, was a huge breakthrough for him. A massive commitment, standing alone. And I'm determined to be satisfied with only that, without also dreaming about exchanging promises of "forever" with him, as well.

"So, what 'Truth' do you want to know, Fitzy?" Savage asks, pulling me from my thoughts.

"Hmm?"

"Birthday Truth or Dare," he says. "What's this all-important question you have that's more important than getting to watch me make a fool of myself in front of all our friends?"

I pause, considering my options, and finally settle on the one thing that's been nagging at me the most lately—actually, ever since the press conference, and then even more so after our conversation in Chicago, when Savage admitted he hasn't slept with anyone else since first laying eyes on me at Reed's. *What's the whole truth about what Savage said to that Instagrammer at Kai's birthday party?*

I haven't talked to Savage about that, since those very first days when he swore, up and down, he didn't mention my name to her, simply because I've been certain he wouldn't give me a straight answer, even if I asked. Or maybe I haven't asked Savage recently about this because I've been afraid the truth wouldn't be as romantic as I've come to hope. If Savage *did* tell that woman he had to "lay low" for the show, and nothing more, I'd rather not hear that now. On the contrary, I'd rather continue fantasizing about a fairy-tale where my gorgeous Beast told that Instagrammer he couldn't sleep with her that night because he had his sights set on someone named *Laila*.

I stroke Savage's naked chest and the grooves in his abs for a moment, keeping him in suspense. And finally say, "Okay, here's my question—and I want the whole truth. Tell me whatever you can remember about your conversation with the Instagrammer at Kai's birthday party. I know you were drunk and don't remember *everything,* especially now that so much time has passed, but—"

"I remember every word of that conversation. At least, every word *I* said to *her.*"

My breathing hitches. I look up from his chest and something in his moonlit expression makes me sit up, all the way on the couch, and brace myself for whatever is going to come out of his gorgeous mouth next.

Following my lead, Savage sits up, too. "You want the whole truth? Well, here it is. When I saw her video the next morning, and heard her tell the world I'd said your name *twice,* I was scared shitless she'd outed me—but also relieved as hell. I felt like I'd dodged a huge bullet. Because the *full* truth is that I said your name at least *ten* times to that woman during our short conversation."

"*What?*" I whisper.

Savage's dark eyes flicker with heat. "I was totally and completely obsessed with you by that point. Tortured you hadn't answered any of my texts during the tour, or after it. Tormented you hadn't come to my room in a single city, despite how much I'd begged you. I'd been dreaming about you, pretty much every night. Pulling out my hair, trying to understand how the night of the hot tub wasn't as big a game-changer for you as it had been for me. So, when I saw that woman, and she looked so much like you—although, to be clear, you're *way* hotter than her—I lost it. I told her she looked like you—that she reminded me of *Laila*. And finally saying your name out loud to someone broke the seal on my madness, so to speak. And, suddenly, I couldn't stop myself from confessing everything. *Laila, Laila, Laila.* I poured my heart out to her. Told her how obsessed I was with you. How tortured I'd been. But I guess she didn't hear most of it, due to the noise at the party. When she asked me to take her upstairs, I was shocked. I'd just told her, in no uncertain terms, that I only wanted *you.* And this bitch's response was to think I'd fuck *her* as your stand-in? It pissed me off to think she, and the whole world, assume I'm *that* big a player. So, I told her no, I didn't want to go upstairs with her or anyone else. I told her I'd made a *promise* to myself not to have sex with anyone but *Laila*, ever again. Until the end of time. And that she should feel free to tell the whole world I'd said so."

I gasp.

"I knew who she was the whole time. I'm not stupid. She was constantly tagging me and the band in her posts and videos. So, I drunkenly *told* her to post a video outing me because I wanted *you* to see it. Because I wanted you to know how much I wanted you. Because I wanted you to finally put me out of my misery and contact me, even if only to tell me why you didn't want me the way I wanted you."

I can't speak or breathe. My jaw feels like it's resting in my naked lap. The world feels like it's warping around me.

Savage says, "When I woke up the next morning, my sober brain realized how stupid and reckless my drunk brain had been. So, when Eli gave me a plausible interpretation of what I'd said the night before, I ran with it. But it was *Eli* who said I must have said I had to 'lay low' because of the show. Not me. I didn't use the word 'promise' in relation to my contract with the show, Laila. I said everything that Instagrammer claimed I did and much more. I wanted you so badly, it physically hurt by then, and I couldn't figure out, for the life of me, why you didn't want me, too."

"Oh, Adrian."

I kiss him, passionately. And when our kiss ends, he strokes my cheek and looks deeply into my eyes. "You want to hear a few more Truth bombs?" he asks, his dark eyes on fire. "Because now that I'm confessing the whole truth to you, I don't want to stop."

I nod furiously. "I'll take as many Truth bombs as you've got."

Savage drops his hands from my face and takes one of mine in his. "I watched your set every night during the tour. I sneaked into the wings and hid behind this huge speaker at stage right so you wouldn't see me, and I watched every minute of every performance. Unless, of course, I left a little early to drag some random groupie into your dressing room at precisely the right time for you to walk in and find me."

I bite my lip. "I did the same thing, basically—minus the groupies. I could have left the venue every night after my set was finished. But I never did. Half the time, I listened to your set in my dressing room, with a glass of wine. I'd touch myself and listen to your voice singing 'Come with Me.' And it never failed to make me come, no matter how much I hated you."

"Oh, my God, Laila. That's so hot."

"Other times, I'd creep into the wings during your set and hide behind that same huge speaker at stage right, so you wouldn't see me. And your performance never failed to blow me away. It's how I knew, deep down, I didn't hate you. If I did, you never could have given me goosebumps—which you did every time I watched you."

Savage's chest heaves. "The Video Music Awards. I bet you thought we got put together as presenters, by chance? Or maybe by the producers on purpose, thanks to that viral video of us fighting on the sidewalk in New York?"

I nod, as a mischievous grin spreads across Savage's gorgeous face.

He shakes head. "*I* did that. When the show called to ask me to present an award, I said I'd only do it if they paired me with *you*."

I bite my lip, feeling turned on by this latest revelation.

"I was desperate. You weren't answering my texts and I had to see you again. By then, I'd convinced myself you were in love with Charlie. It was the only thing that made sense. And I had to know."

"The chorus in 'Hate Sex High'?" I ask, breathlessly. "Was the 'something' you didn't want to feel a kernel of truth or a popcorn lie?"

"You already know the answer to that, Laila. The 'something' I was feeling was straight-up obsession, which wasn't something I wanted to feel—and definitely not something I wanted to admit to you."

I kiss him fervently, but abruptly break free of his lips, my breathing ragged. "I already know the truth about this next thing, but I want to hear you say it. You're singing 'Laila' at the end of those 'la la's.' Admit it."

Savage chuckles. "Of course, I am. As a matter of fact, I was hard as a rock the whole time I was recording the vocals to that song. I closed my eyes and thought about you and practically came in the recording booth."

"That's so hot." I kiss him again. And when my clit begins pounding too insistently to ignore, I stroke Savage's cock to hardness, and then slide myself down on it. I fuck him, slowly, while kissing his gorgeous lips. And as our bodies move together, I whisper that I love him. That I'll *always* love him. I've never used that word before with him. Never confessed the endlessness of my love for him. Never been brave enough to pledge my forever in words. But I do it now, as my body moves with his. And to my thrill and joy and relief, Savage whispers that he'll love me "forever," right before coming beneath me.

SIXTY-EIGHT

LAILA

Two weeks later

"How's that?" my makeup artist, Susanna, says.

I open my eyes and look at myself in the mirror. "Gorgeous. Love it."

"I added a little extra glitter to your lids this time, so your eyes will sparkle like crazy as you look lovingly into Savage's eyes during your duet."

"Brilliant. The glitter gives off a 'fairytale princess' vibe."

"Along with a little splash of 'He's all mine, bitches!'"

I giggle. "Well, with this face, that's unavoidable."

We've made it to the last episode of the season—the "live taping" of the finale, during which this season's winner will be crowned. I'm in my dressing room with Susanna, awaiting my cue to perform with Savage in about fifteen minutes. Currently, the top ten contestants of the season, other than the two finalists vying for the crown—my quirky, blue-haired crooner, Addison, and Savage's powerhouse belter, Glory—are onstage with Aloha, performing a cheesy group rendition of Aloha's latest hit.

I look at a large clock on the wall of my dressing room and realize I've got a solid ten minutes before I'll need to hit my mark. "I think I'll watch the show from the wings," I say. "I'm too amped to sit still." For more reasons than one, if I'm being honest.

Yes, I'm nervous to perform the duet for the first time. But Savage and I have rehearsed relentlessly, so I'm pretty confident our performance will go off without a hitch. Plus, the song is fantastic—catchy and swoonworthy—a textbook hit, even if it's far more about Fish and Alessandra's uncomplicated love story than mine and Savage's. No, I think the true source of my nerves is the fact that, since Chicago, Savage has never again mentioned that bonus the show offered him. The one where he'd earn a cool two hundred fifty thousand bucks, merely for *faux*-proposing to me after our performance. And I can't help thinking maybe, just maybe, he hasn't mentioned it because he's decided to do it . . . *and maybe even for real.*

I know I'm crazy to think it. To *hope* it. But I can't help myself. Even if the odds are low, I think there's a small chance he'll get down on bended knee the minute we stop singing, and the very thought makes every cell in my body electrify with giddiness.

When I arrive at the wing of the stage, I look around for a PA, or someone with a headset, to make sure the production staff knows where I am. These "live taping" shows are an intense juggling act for the crew, since they're shot precisely as the show will air, with no editing or re-dos. So, given my upcoming performance, it's critical everyone knows where to find me at all times.

As I'm looking around for someone in a headset, I spot Nadine, the executive producer, standing with her back to me alongside Rhoda, the junior producer who's become a good friend. Given that Rhoda and Nadine are both wearing headsets, I head over to the duo, intending to tap one of them on the shoulder and wave, as if to say, "Here I am." But when I get close enough to overhear the women's conversation, I stop short and listen in.

"Who knows if Savage will do it?" Nadine is saying as I come to a stop behind her. "Unfortunately, his contract states he can decide, yes or no, if he wants to earn that bonus, right up to the last moment. So now, all we can do is wait and cross our fingers."

"I'm betting he'll do it," Rhoda says confidently. "And not for the bonus—but for *real*."

Nadine snorts. "I wouldn't hold my breath on that, Rhoda."

"You didn't see him at Laila's birthday party. He's head over heels in love with her, Nadine, for real. Anyone could see it. But, hey, if his love for her doesn't convince him to propose to her on national TV, then maybe a quarter-million bucks will tip the scales for him."

"Try a *million* bucks."

"*What?*" Rhoda gasps out, as I clamp my hand over my mouth to keep my own gasp from becoming audible.

"I made a secret side deal with Savage," Nadine says. "But don't worry, I'm not stupid enough to have agreed to paying him a million bucks out of pocket. He let me keep his full salary, two million, in exchange for me promising *never* to terminate Laila and to leave them alone to be 'happy' without any meddling. If he proposes tonight, like a good little boy, then he'll get a million bucks of the money we've withheld from him."

I clamp my palm over my mouth again, this time to keep myself from screaming.

"Did you give him the ring?" Rhoda says.

"Yeah, a few minutes ago," Nadine replies. "I told him to put it in his pocket, so he'd have it, just in case. And I'll be damned, he took it. So who knows? I'm hoping that's a good sign." Nadine scoffs. "Or maybe he's just fucking with me."

"No. I'd bet anything he's going to give her that ring. A million bucks, a free ring, *and* the chance to propose to the woman he loves on national TV? What rational man *wouldn't* leap at a deal like that?"

"I think we both know Adrian Savage is anything but rational."

I've heard enough. Plus, now that the group song onstage is

wrapping up, I'm scared to death these two women will turn around and catch me crouching behind them in the dark. I turn on my heel and sprint away on my tiptoes, as Sunshine Vaughn announces a commercial break.

When I reach my dressing room, I shut the door behind me and lean against it, my eyes wide and my chest heaving. There's so much to unpack here, my brain feels like it's exploding. Out of every shocking thing Nadine just said, however, the thing that's rising to the top of the heap is the part where Nadine said Savage forfeited his *entire* salary in exchange for Nadine's promise not to fire me. *When the hell did that happen?*

I pace circles in my dressing room, too freaked out to sit. I'm insanely grateful Savage swooped in to protect me like that, but I wish he hadn't. I already felt bad enough that he had to give up two million bucks to get me onto the show, in the first place. And now I find out he gave up two million *more* to *keep* me on the show?

All I can hope and pray is that Savage realizes his best bet is to get down on his knee after our performance is done, and fake-propose. Obviously, I'd love to hear those amazing words out of Savage's mouth one day, for *real*. And, selfishly, I'd love to hear them tonight, even if it's only for pretend, solely to have a beautiful, false, fairytale moment with Savage, however fleeting and fake. *Laila, will you marry me?* Just imagining those words coming out of Adrian's mouth gives me goosebumps, even if it's only for show. But, truly, the main thing here is that I want Savage to get himself paid.

I stride toward the exit of my dressing room, determination flooding me. I'm going to hunt Savage down and tell him I know everything. I'm going to demand he fake-propose to me in a few minutes to earn that bonus, and *also* tell him I've decided to return every penny he's paid me this season. I've felt guilty about taking half Savage's salary for a while now, and what I overheard from Nadine was the last straw. It's not like I don't have the ability to make an incredible living on my own now. Thanks to my exposure on the show, I've become a household name, which my agent,

Daria, has already started leveraging for all sorts of new projects and ventures. Regardless, though, even if I'd be penniless after returning Savage's two million bucks, I'd do it, anyway, simply to get this elephant off my chest, once and for all.

Before I get to the door of my dressing room, however, someone knocks on it. "Laila?" a voice I recognize as belonging to a PA shouts. "Time to take your mark for the duet!"

"Coming!"

As I follow the production assistant through the backstage area to the spot where I'll await my cue to walk onstage, I look around frantically for Savage, so I can tell him everything that needs to be said. *But he's nowhere to be found.*

Finally, when the PA and I arrive in the wings, I see Savage standing across from me in the wings on the other side of the large stage. Crap. I forgot the director decided at the last minute he wants Savage and me to start singing from opposite ends of the large stage, and then walk toward each other during the first verse. I'm sure that blocking will make for a delightfully dramatic performance and all, but, unfortunately, it means I won't have a chance to talk to Savage before we start singing.

"Okay, Laila, stand by," the PA whispers, a hand on her headset. "Three, two . . ." She gestures toward the outer edge of the stage, and I take my mark in the dark, my heart thrumming. I accept a live mic handed to me by a crew member and inhale deeply, just as Sunshine Vaughn bellows, "And now, it's Savage and Laila, performing the world premiere of their duet, 'Perfect for Me'!"

The audience applauds wildly, the lights come on, the band kicks off, and Savage and I begin walking slowly toward each other across the large stage, as planned. I sing first in the song—a line about Savage being imperfectly perfect. Blah, blah. And he replies that I'm a "Picasso"—a bit of a mess, with my colors bleeding outside the lines, yet always a "work of art" to him. Blah, blah. And by the time we sing in unison in the chorus about being imperfectly perfect for each other, we've both reached the middle of the stage.

I'm giving the song my all, which thankfully quiets the raging storm in my head. And I can tell Savage is giving it his all, too, even though he's been clear he thinks the song is a "gigantic cheese-fest." And by the time we reach our final, soaring notes, there's no doubt the audience is transfixed.

After we sing our last note together, the band plays the song's melodic outro, and, just like that, everything I was thinking before the music started playing crashes into me, all over again. I lean forward, intending to say, "Get the bonus, Savage!" . . . but freeze when Savage touches his pocket like he's about to slide his hand inside and grab something.

I wait. Hold my breath. And as the music ends, Savage touches his pocket *again* . . . and then unceremoniously drops his empty hand to his side.

Fuck!

I lean in and whisper to him through my smile, like I'm a ventriloquist who's speaking through a dummy, "Bonus. Now." But Savage remains frozen and smiling at me as the audience applauds wildly.

I lean forward, intending to repeat my command, but when I do, Savage goes in for a kiss, making the audience applaud even more wildly. Flustered, I break away from his lips and whisper into his ear, "Get the bonus!" And in reply, Savage grabs my hand and raises it with his, like we're actors executing a Broadway curtain call.

When the audience roars again, Savage puts his arm around me and pulls me close, making it pretty damned clear he's *not* about to kneel before me.

I'm shocked at how long the lights and cameras have remained trained on us, without turning off or the show cutting to commercial. The director is letting this post-performance moment go on for much longer than usual, isn't he? But finally, the bright lights in our faces fade to black. The little red light on the camera directly in front of us turns off. And the director yells, "And we're clear!"

So, that's it.

In the end, Savage decided not to propose. Not even for

pretend. Not even to recoup a million bucks out of the four million he forfeited because of me. Not even when he was offered a free freaking ring from some fancy jeweler. I have no doubt Savage loves me with all his heart. For crying out loud, the man secretly paid two million bucks to keep me on the show, netting him literally *nothing* in salary for three months of hard work. But the fact remains, no matter how much Savage loves me, proposing to me—even if only for pretend—was a bridge too far for him.

I shouldn't feel disappointed about that. But if I'm being honest, I do. I desperately wanted Savage to earn that bonus. But even more so, I want Savage to want to marry me! Yes! My feelings are so clear now. More than any amount of money or fame or success in my career, I want to marry Adrian—and I want *him* to feel the same way.

When the lights turn off, a PA immediately escorts Savage and me offstage, before I've had a chance to say a word to him. She compliments our performance and instructs us to wait with her in the wings while Sunshine announces this season's winner. "Once Sunshine makes the announcement," the PA explains, "the winning judge will run onstage to congratulate their contestant for a moment, before the remainder of the cast joins the winning judge and contestant onstage for the 'big celebration.'"

"It's gonna be Addison," Savage whispers to me, referring to the blue-haired cutie who's amassed an unprecedented army of fans since the first audition episode aired.

I take a deep breath. That's what he wants to talk about, after what he just decided *not* to do out there—who's going to be crowned this season's winner on the show? "It'd better be," I whisper, even though there are a thousand other things I want to say, if we were alone. Or maybe, if only I had the courage.

"And the winner this season is . . ." Sunshine, says onstage, as the two finalists—mine and Savage's—huddle together next to the host, both contestants looking like they're going to barf. Sunshine looks up from the opened envelope in her hands and shrieks, *"Addison Swain!"*

As streamers and glitter burst from the ceiling above the stage, I feel swept away in my excitement for Addison and forget about my own concerns for a moment. I hug Savage standing next to me, crying tears of joy for my blue-haired favorite, and a moment later, the PA nudges me and says, "Go congratulate Addison now, Laila! Go, go, go!"

As the house band begins playing an upbeat, celebratory dance song, I stride gleefully onto the stage to my darling pixie and take her into my arms. For a long moment, we cry together. I don't know about Addison, but this feels like the finish line of a legit marathon to me.

Out of nowhere, Sunshine shoves a microphone in Addison's face, and she breaks from our hug to thank me profusely for making her win possible. She goes on to thank the audience at home for voting for her, week after week. And her family for their support, too. She thanks the writer of every song she's ever performed, and Sunshine and the producers of the show, and I laugh and cry with her, through it all.

When it's my turn to take Sunshine's microphone, I tell Addison she was already a star the minute she walked onstage that very first time and blew me away. "Your victory today has nothing to do with me, honey," I say, and I mean it with all my heart.

Once I've made my little speech, the whole cast descends onto the stage—the other three judges and all four mentors—and we commence a not-so spontaneous dance party in celebration of Addison's win, as well as yet another successful season of the show. The most successful season yet, as a matter of fact, in terms of ratings and popularity. In fact, from what Daria has told me, Nadine has already indicated her fervent desire to have Savage and me return next season. And not only that, to sign both of us to a multi-year deal.

As music and dancing and laughter continue swirling around me onstage, I glance at Savage across the crowd to find him laughing with genuine abandon with Kendrick, Fish, and Colin, and my heart skips a beat at his easygoing demeanor. It's especially gratifying to catch him, once again, looking comfortable and friendly with Colin. After my birthday party, I asked Savage if he'd said something to Colin to bury the hatchet, and Savage confirmed he had, and that Colin had been extremely receptive and appreciative.

While I'm still looking at my boyfriend, his gaze finds mine. For a moment, time stops as we smile at each other from across the crowded stage, both of us basking in not only our love, but also our newfound freedom from the pressure-cooker of the show. The constant social media posts we've been required to make. The fishbowl nature of it all. On the one hand, it's been the happiest three months of my life, living and working with Savage. And I know Savage feels the exact same way. But I'm also more than relieved to move onto the next phase of our relationship, a much more private one that's not for show, but only for us. I can't wait to find out who we are when we're living together in my tiny condo, rather than a sprawling reality TV mansion. I can't wait to find out who Savage and Laila are when nobody is watching.

The director yells, "We're clear!" and a loud cheer rises up onstage.

Without hesitation, Savage beelines over to me, weaving in and out of happy people. When he reaches me, he swings me around, whooping with joy.

"Free at last!" he booms, before pulling me into him for an exuberant kiss.

"I love you!" I shout amidst the din. And he returns my words, as well as my beaming smile. In the midst of our canoodling, Savage and I are interrupted by Aloha and her husband, Zander, both of whom hug me, and then Savage, and congratulate us on our first season.

"Have you signed on for next season yet?" Aloha asks, putting her palms together in prayer. "Daria told me they're rabid to have you."

I look at Savage and say, "We're still thinking about it." But, in reality, I know it would take a miracle to make Savage say yes to another season—an offer he truly can't refuse. I add, "Our agents are haggling with Nadine, probably as we speak."

"Well, don't sell yourselves short, guys. They had their best ratings, ever, this season. And that certainly wasn't because of *me*. It was because of you two." Aloha addresses Savage, specifically. "Laila and I share an agent, Daria, so she already knows what I make on the show, since Daria's the one who negotiated my deal. But if it helps your agent in negotiations for you, tell him or her I've got a five-year deal, ten mill per season. You and Laila are both worth the same as me now. So, tell your agent not to accept a penny less." She looks at me. "That goes for you, too, girlie. Get yourself paid."

"Holy fuck," I blurt, simply because it never occurred to me to tell Daria to demand what Aloha makes. Aloha is already a legit icon in the industry, after all, and I'm still a relative newbie next to her.

To my surprise, Savage reacts calmly to Aloha's suggestion. "Thanks for the intel," he replies smoothly, his tone tacitly admitting he agrees with Aloha's assessment. "I'll pass it along to my agent."

My chest tightens at the idea of me ever being *that* rich. Growing up, my mom, sister, and I saved our spare change in a jar to afford my piano lessons! But, regardless, it's a moot point because Savage has told me repeatedly he's got *zero* desire to continue as a judge, and I'd never continue as a judge without him. Not that the show would want me without Savage, anyway.

"Are you going to the wrap party now?" I ask Aloha and her husband, eager to change the subject.

"No way, dude, I'm outta here," Aloha says. She snuggles her gorgeous husband. "All I want to do is go home with my man, crank up the fireplace, and have a quiet night, just the two of us."

"That's our plan, too," I say, snuggling into Savage's side in the same way Aloha is doing with Zander. "It's our last night at our fancy mansion. Tomorrow, we're moving into my little condo. So, I've asked our chef to make our favorite meal—cioppino—and get a nice bottle of champagne for us. We're going to eat and drink and relax in our hot tub."

Aloha shoots me a little wink, letting me know she's well aware I've ended my sentence before getting to the best part of all—the part where Savage makes me scream the way she overheard that night, from across the hall. It's crazy to think that drunken night at Reed's house was only three months ago on the calendar, considering it feels like a lifetime ago. Savage and I have not only fallen deeply in love since then, which is earth-quaking news, in and of itself, but we're also *irrevocably* in love. Committed to nurturing and safeguarding our love, always. No matter what. *Forever.* If I'd had a crystal ball three months ago, and saw where our relationship would end up, I never would have believed it. Not in a million years.

After a bit more conversation, Aloha and Zander head off, hand in hand, while Savage and I do the same. We change clothes in our respective dressing rooms for the last time and gather our stuff. We say goodbye to staff and crew and administer hugs here and there. We thank Nadine and a couple other producers we run across, all of whom say basically the same thing: they're eager to put together a multi-year deal with us for many seasons to come. And what does Savage say to that? A noncommittal, "Send your offer to our agents and we'll have them take a look."

Finally, we head to the back of the studio and slide inside our usual SUV to begin our drive to our reality TV love nest for the very last time. As our car pulls away from the curb, Savage looks at me and exhales a long, slow, deep breath. "We did it, Fitzy. Hallelujah."

Leaning my head on his broad shoulder, I whisper, "What a ride."

"Baby," Savage says, kissing the top of my head. "I promise the best of our ride is yet to come."

SIXTY-NINE

SAVAGE

Laila and I are sitting in the backseat of our SUV with our usual driver and bodyguard, supposedly heading to our reality TV mansion in Malibu for the last time. In actuality, though, we're headed a few miles down the road to my new, kickass pad—the fully furnished, four bedroom, cliffside home Reed helped me find and purchase, and which Amalia and Georgina helped me personalize and perfect. *And I'm losing my fucking mind.*

When we arrive at my new house, I'm not only going to tell Laila the shocking news that the place is mine, and that I want her to move in with me, I'm also going to get down on my knee and ask Laila to be my wife. Not for pretend. Not for a bonus. And certainly not with a ring supplied to me by a sponsor of *Sing Your Heart Out.* No, I'm going to ask Laila to marry me for *real*, with a million-dollar rock I personally paid for and picked out for her, although I admit I made my final decision about which ring to purchase with the help of Amalia, Georgina, and Sasha on Face-Time. Because, for fuck's sake, a guy's got to put it *all* on the line when he asks the woman of his dreams to marry him, including laying down his own goddamned money. Plus, I never would have forfeited the chance to see Mimi's little diamond shining like the most beautiful star in heaven in the setting of my future wife's ring.

"... during the celebration," Laila is saying, pulling me from my thoughts.

"Hmm? Sorry. I was zoning out."

Laila smiles. "I said I liked seeing you having fun with Fish and Colin during the celebration. It seems like you've buried the hatchet with Colin."

"Yeah, you were spot-on about that whole thing. Plus, Dr. Reynolds told me I should mend fences whenever I can, so . . ."

Laila's smile broadens. She's already made it clear she's beyond thrilled I've started seeing a therapist once a week.

"I think you'd like seeing someone, too," I say, reacting to Laila's smile. "After only a few sessions with Dr. Reynolds, I'm already realizing my childhood has affected me far more than I've ever understood. I bet it'd be the same for you."

Laila nods. "Aloha has a therapist she adores. I'll ask her for the name."

"Good."

Our phones buzz at the same time, and we look down to find a group text from Reed, sent not only to Laila and me, but to Fish and Alessandra, as well, letting us know our cheeseball duet is now sitting at number one on the daily singles downloads chart.

"*Yes!*" Laila says, laughing.

"I have a feeling that sappy love song is going to make us a boat-load of money, Fitzy."

"Woohoo!" Laila says exuberantly, and we high-five. She bites her lip, contemplating something for a moment. "Is it weird I don't feel any emotional connection whatsoever to that song?"

"I feel the same way. That's because the song isn't about us."

"I'm glad it's not," Laila replies. "I wouldn't have wanted to bare my entire soul and the deepest depths of my love for you for the first time on national TV."

I furrow my brow, as the implication of what Laila just said hits me. "You're saying you haven't bared your entire soul to me yet?"

Laila shakes her head. "I've told you how much I love you in *words*. But telling you how I feel in a *song* would be a whole other level." She smiles shyly. "I've actually written a love song to you. I've been working on it for a while now, but haven't felt ready to play it for you . . . until now." She bites her lip. "Now that we've finally got the duet behind us, I'm suddenly dying to play it for you when we get home."

My heart skips a beat as tingles skate across my skin. I've been feeling close to positive Laila will say yes when I propose to her tonight, but, somehow, hearing her say she's written a love song to me, and is now ready to play it for me, obliterates any last irrational shreds of doubt I've been harboring. Laila is a true artist. Which means, although she's damned good at expressing herself in words, it's when she sings and plays her piano that her truest voice can be heard.

I take Laila's hand and squeeze it. "I can't wait to hear the song."

My phone buzzes in my lap and I look down. This time, the incoming text is from my manager, Eli. When Laila and I first got into the car, I relayed Aloha's message about her compensation package, and now, Eli is telling me he's already in the midst of a back-and-forth with producers that makes him feel confident their next written offer, which will be coming shortly, will be in line with Aloha's deal.

I plop my phone onto the car seat. "Eli says he's sure the producers are going to offer me a deal in the range of Aloha's."

"Holy shit," Laila gasps out.

"Have you told Daria what Aloha said?"

Laila shakes her head. "There's no need. Daria is the one who negotiated Aloha's deal. I trust Daria to get me whatever I'm worth."

"No, babe." I motion to Laila's phone in her lap. "Text Daria and tell her you won't take a penny less than what Aloha makes. Make that clear to her."

Laila scoffs.

"Yes, Laila. Tell your agent to coordinate with mine before she responds to any offer. Tell her I'm instructing Eli not to take any deal unless the exact same package is offered to you."

Laila's eyes are wide. Her chest heaves, but she doesn't pick up her phone.

"*Laila*," I say, picking up her phone and shoving it at her. "Do it. Tell Daria not to respond to any offer until Eli gives her the green light. I'll instruct Eli to get the best possible deal for me, nothing less than Aloha's, and *then* tell the producers I'll only take their offer *if* they give the exact same one to you."

Her face flushed and her hand trembling, Laila takes her phone from me. "So . . . does that mean you're willing to say *yes* to doing the show again—and for multiple seasons—if they pay you the same as Aloha?"

I shrug. "If they were to agree to pay me and *you* the same as Aloha, and also to leave us alone and not require any social media from us, then, yes. That is, if doing the show again, and for multiple seasons, is something *you*'d want." That last part is a bit of theater. I'm one thousand percent certain Laila wants to continue doing the show. But why not give her the chance to talk it through?

Laila's face is the portrait of a woman going out of her mind with excitement who's pretending she's not. "Well," she begins, "I had a blast working with you this season. And I loved getting to spend time with Aloha, too. I thoroughly enjoyed working with my contestants."

"You were a natural with them."

"When Addison won, it was one of the best moments of my life."

"I could tell."

Laila sighs happily, apparently reliving the joy she felt for Addison when the young singer's name was called. She continues, "Aloha loves doing the show and says it's the easiest money she's ever made. So, I think if we just had to show up each week and do the judge thing, the same way Aloha does, without having all that other crazy stuff hanging over our heads, we'd probably have a great time. The shooting schedule wouldn't get in the way of our music. I've written my entire third album this past month, while still doing the show."

I take in her sparkling blue eyes and hopeful expression. I'd never stand in the way of Laila getting to do this, and the producers have already made it clear they want *both* of us, as a package deal. Plus, if the producers truly do come back with money in the range of what Aloha gets, I'd be a fool to turn it down. Not only for myself, but because my continued exposure on the show will wind up lining my bandmates' and manager's pockets, too.

Laila adds, "I'd never want to force you to do something that would make you miserable, though."

I squeeze her hand. "I could never be miserable doing anything, if I was doing it with you." I pick up my phone and begin tapping out a text to my manager. "I'm telling Eli to be sure to coordinate with Daria on this. And not to bother me until they've offered everything I want."

"Sounds good," Laila says. She starts tapping on her phone. "I'm telling Daria to sit tight until she hears from Eli." When she puts her phone down, she looks beside herself with excitement. In fact, she can barely sit still. "Well, damn," she says, "I feel a whole lot better now about you not earning that bonus tonight. If we get this deal, that bonus will feel like chump change, huh?"

Shit. I was hoping Laila wouldn't mention that stupid bonus tonight. Not when, unbeknownst to Laila, I'm going to propose to her for *real* in a matter of minutes.

When I say nothing, Laila fills the awkward silence. "Were you even tempted to earn the bonus tonight?"

Damn. She's obviously not going to magically drop the subject, without me responding. "Uh, no. Once we told Mimi we were engaged, proposing to you on the show was a moot point."

Laila presses her lips together for a long moment, during which I literally pray she drops the subject. But nope. A moment later, Laila says, "Did the producers give you a ring to give to me? I thought I saw you touching your pocket a couple times, right at the end of our song."

Fuck. "Yeah, they did. Some jeweler supplied a ring for promo, and Nadine made me put it in my pocket before I walked onstage, in case I suddenly became overcome by the impulse to get down on bended knee." I chuckle. "I knew Nadine would be watching me with bated breath when our song ended, so I touched my pocket a couple times, just to fuck with her." I flash Laila a wicked smirk, thinking she'll laugh along with me, but she doesn't. In fact, she looks downright stressed. "Aw, come on," I coax. "Nadine deserved that. She's a master at messing with people's emotions. Two can play at that game."

Laila shoots me a tight smile but says nothing, which tells me she's got something big on her mind.

"What is it, Laila?" I ask.

She pauses an eternal beat before blurting, "I know what you did, Savage! I know *everything*."

Every hair on my body stands on end. What, *exactly*, does she know? Does she know about my new house? About the engagement ring in my pocket? Thankfully, Laila speaks again before I've stupidly started confessing everything to her.

"I overheard Nadine talking to Rhoda before we went onstage," Laila explains. "Nadine told Rhoda she'd made a side deal with you that let them keep your *entire* salary—two million bucks!—in exchange for them not firing me."

Well, shit. I wasn't expecting that. I didn't want Laila knowing about any of that, ever. I open and close my mouth, feeling tongue-tied, and Laila forges ahead before I've choked out a single word.

"Nadine said she thought there was a good chance you'd propose after the song, in order to get back half the money you'd let them keep. She said they gave you a free ring *and* promised you could earn back a million bucks by proposing to me. But you didn't do it!"

I'm still opening and closing my mouth like a fish on a line, incapable of forming words.

"You gave up an easy *million* bucks, Savage!" Laila shouts. "How could you do that? I don't care how much you might be making on the new album or on future seasons of the show, that's still a *ton* of money. Especially when you've already paid *me* two million bucks! I wish so badly you'd told me you'd forfeited your entire salary for me, because I never would have let you do that. Thank you so much. Thank you from the bottom of my heart. But I was already feeling so terrible about taking half your salary—"

"Laila, stop. We agreed not to talk about the money, remember?"

"No, *you* agreed. When did you make that side deal with Nadine?"

"In Chicago. Right before Mimi died. And I'd do it again. I have zero regrets."

"Why didn't you tell me what was going on?"

"Why make you feel stressed and guilty, when it was something *I* wanted to do, for my own happiness? Don't you see? I made that deal with Nadine for the same reason I bought that house for Mimi. For the same reason I bought a house for Sasha. Because I love you and want to take care of you. And, also, because, selfishly, I couldn't stand the idea of being stranded on that stupid fucking show without you."

"*Selfishly?* Savage, what you did is the most *selfless*—"

"Please, don't make this a thing, Laila. I did it because I love you and wanted the best for you—because I knew Nadine would be making a huge mistake to get rid of you. And I was right! The show had its best ratings *ever* and now they're *begging* you to sign a multi-year deal. Fuck Nadine! We got the last laugh, baby!"

Her nostrils flare. "Well, I hope you know I'm going to pay you back every dime you paid me this season. That's non-negotiable, Adrian."

I trap my lower lip between my teeth. Laila looks incredibly beautiful right now. Fierce and determined. Feisty and self-righteous. It dawns on me there's no need to argue with her about this right now, considering that, before the night is through, Laila will

be my fiancée. And soon after that, my wife. Which means everything I have will be hers, including the two million bucks she's now
insisting on repaying me.

"Okay, baby," I concede. I bring her hand to my mouth and kiss
it. "Pay me whatever makes you feel good, as long as your repay-
ment buys me the freedom of never, ever having to talk about that
two million bucks again."

She grins. "Deal."

We shake on it.

"I'm grateful for what you did for me," she says, her eyes
pricking with tears. "Thank you."

"Laila, did you hear a word I said? *I did it for me.*"

She chuckles, and a tear falls down her cheek. She wipes it and
sighs. "Would you ever have told me what you did for me, if I
hadn't overheard Nadine and Rhoda tonight?"

"No. Never."

"I don't understand."

"Would you have done the same thing for me, if the situation
had been reversed?"

"In a heartbeat."

"Then, you *do* understand."

We share a huge smile, and two seconds later, our car takes a
different turn than our usual route.

"Where are we going, Mike?" Laila calls to the driver.

"I've asked him to take a detour, so I can show you something,"
I interject. "I've got a little surprise for you."

"How long will the detour take?" she asks. "I've arranged for
dinner to be waiting for us at home."

"Only a few minutes," I say, even though I'm thinking, "*Only
the rest of our lives.*"

The car makes a turn, and then another, before coming to a
stop in front of my new house.

"Surprise," I say, gesturing out the car window.

Laila follows the trajectory of my gesture and looks straight at my house. But it's clear from her facial expression she has no idea what she's seeing. "Where are we?" she asks. "Who lives here?"

I try not to smile too big. "Let's go inside and find out."

Laila's jaw drops. "Did Kendrick buy a house?"

I chuckle at Laila's shocked reaction. If she's this excited for Kendrick to buy himself a new, beautiful house in Malibu, she's going to have a straight-up aneurysm when she finds out the true owner of this beauty. "You guessed it," I say. "Nothing gets past you. Do you like it?"

"I *love* it. It's *gorgeous*. Wow. Good for Kendrick."

"Let's go inside and say hi."

"Yes! How exciting!"

We get out of the car and walk, hand in hand, toward our new home, as Laila babbles happily about the beauty of the house and its spectacular location. As she rambles, it takes all my willpower not to interrupt her to scream, "The house is ours, you fool! I want you to live here with me, forever!"

My new house isn't huge, like Reed's place. It's not small, by any stretch. But nobody would ever call it a mansion. Which suits me perfectly. As far as I'm concerned, the place is the perfect size for Laila and me and our needs. We've got enough room for ourselves and any guest we might have—Sasha or Laila's family. Plus, some extra rooms for music- and pottery-making. And best of all, there's a perfect place in the living room for Laila's baby grand —a spot in a corner overlooking the ocean. The house is so perfect for Laila and me, in fact, I wanted it the second I walked through the front door. The minute I entered the house, I said to Reed and Georgina and Reed's real estate agent, "We're done for the day. I'm home." And that feeling only grew and solidified as we visited subsequent houses throughout the day, just in case, none of which held a candle to the cliffside house that had instantly felt like home to me.

When Laila and I arrive at the front door of our new house, she rings the doorbell. And when I punch a code on the box by the door, she rolls her eyes and says, "Of course, Kendrick gave you the code. You two are so cute."

I open the door and follow her inside, and while she gushes about how gorgeous it is, how spectacular the view, how much she loves the furnishings, I say, "I'm glad you like it. Because it's not Kendrick's new house. It's *ours*."

"*What?*" she shrieks.

"I bought it for us, baby. So we could live here together. Please say yes."

She throws herself at me and screams, "Yes!" And I laugh and hug her to me.

We kiss and hug for a long moment. She asks me a thousand questions about when I bought it, how long I've kept this secret. Until, finally, I laugh and say, "Come on, baby. Let me give you a tour of your fancy new house."

SEVENTY

SAVAGE

"Our living room. Obviously." I gesture toward the room we're standing in. "You won't believe the ocean view in the daytime. It's a little slice of heaven."

Laila rushes to the floor-to-ceiling windows on the far side of our living room, and when she gets there, she presses every inch of her body against the glass, like she's one of those rubber lizard toys that adheres to glass with suctions cups. Of course, I can't help belly laughing at her exuberance.

"It's *gorgeous*," she whispers. "Oh my God. I can see so many stars!" She turns around, her face aglow. "I can't wait to sit out on the balcony and watch the sunset with you!"

"My thoughts exactly."

She sprints across the room and flings herself at me, almost knocking me over. "I love it!" Her eyes land on the baby grand piano in a corner behind me and she gasps. Squealing, she disengages from me and lopes over to it, bounding across the room with exaggerated movements, like she's a gazelle bounding through tall grass. And, once again, I belly laugh at her enthusiasm.

"I hope you don't mind I had it delivered here, rather than to your condo," I say, even though her body language makes it clear she's thrilled.

"Thank you!" she shrieks happily, hugging and kissing her beautiful new instrument like it's her long lost child. "I love you, baby!" she coos. But she's not talking to me. She's talking to her new piano.

Without hesitation, Laila slides onto the piano bench and whips off the introduction to one of her biggest hits. "Listen to that sound! It's glorious!" She gasps. "Should I play you the song I wrote for you?" I open my mouth, but before I've said a word, she answers her own question. "No, let's wait. I'm way too excited to see the rest of the house. I won't even remember my lyrics. Come on!"

She leaps up and takes my hand and drags me into the adjacent kitchen. And then proceeds to hug the island and every professional-grade appliance. She opens cupboards and drawers and fawns over every little detail. She holds up a cheese grater. And then a can opener. A couple pots and pans. All of which make her "ooh" and "aah" like she's watching a spectacular fireworks display.

"How do you have *all* this stuff already?" she says.

"I bought it fully furnished, with Reed's help, and then Amalia and Georgina helped me with the finishing touches." I tell her the story of how I wound up staying a couple days at Reed's house after Mimi died, while Laila was still in Cabo. "Great news," I say. "Amalia said she'll come over once a week to hang out with me. I mean, *technically*, she said she'll come over to 'help me with the house.' But I'm going to make her sit down and hang out with me whenever she comes."

Laila giggles. "I can't believe you've kept this secret from me, all this time."

"It's been excruciating," I admit. "I've almost blown it, like, a thousand times." I kiss her cheek. "Sorry about the meal we're not eating back at the mansion. I'll text the chef and tell him to take it home to his family."

"Why don't we order cioppino to be delivered from Salvatore's?" she asks.

"I already did."

Laila laughs at that coincidence, that we've both planned the same celebratory meal for tonight, while I pull out my phone and send a text to our chef. We finish the tour of the house, with Laila reacting to each and every room with even more excitement than I'd hoped. And, finally, when the tour is done, I realize it's time. *This is it.*

"While we wait for the food to arrive," I say, "I have a little surprise for you, out on the balcony."

"So many *surprises!*" Laila gushes, taking my hand and letting me lead her.

When we get to the balcony, I tell her to stay put at the railing. And then, with my heart crashing even louder than the waves in the nearby ocean, I grab a rectangular, wrapped box from behind a chair and bring it to her.

"For you," I say, handing her the wrapped box.

After thanking me, Laila rips open the paper . . . and immediately bursts into tears when she beholds the token of my affection inside. It's a rose encased in glass. The real-life version of the enchanted rose from *Beauty and the Beast.*

"Oh, Adrian."

"Laila," I say, my voice becoming thick with emotion. "Thanks to you, I've learned to love and to be loved, before the last petal has fallen. Thanks to you, I've transformed from The Beast into your prince. Hopefully, the kind of prince who won't disappoint you."

She touches her heart and whispers, "You could never disappoint me."

"I hope this goes without saying, but I promise to keep fucking you like a Beast, forevermore, even if I'm going to be the Prince now, in all other ways."

Laila laughs and nods with tears in her eyes. "I love you so much."

I inhale a deep breath, take the box from Laila and put it down, and then take both her hands in mine. "Laila, what I'm trying to say with this Beast metaphor is that, from this day forward, you're not only 'allowed' to go into the West Wing, it's *yours*. Because the entire castle is *yours*. Literally and figuratively. Everything I own, everything I *am*, it's all *yours*. Forever."

"Oh, Adrian. I love you."

Shaking, I pull a ring box from my pocket—the one containing the million-dollar rock I bought for Laila with my own money. The one *I* chose for her, that wasn't supplied to me by some jeweler looking for a promotional opportunity.

When Laila sees the box, she gasps. And when I open the lid and she sees the rock nestled inside, she lets out a garbled sound of excitement and shock, the likes of which I've never heard from her.

I swallow hard. "I didn't propose to you on the show tonight because I didn't want you thinking, even for a second, my proposal was fake. And I didn't want to do it for *real* for a TV audience. I'm sick of sharing our love story with the world, Laila. I'm not doing this for money or fame. None of that stuff matters to me, if you're not there with me, enjoying it all, right by my side, forever."

With that, I sink to my knee, making Laila burst into sobs. I hold up the ring and smile up at her, emotion turning into a hard lump in my throat. "Laila Fitzgerald," I whisper. "Not too long ago, I felt coerced into a fifty-fifty partnership with you. But I want you to know, I'm now one hundred percent yours, voluntarily. With this ring, I give you all of me. I want you to take everything I am and everything I'm going to be. It's all yours, just as long as you say yes to being my wife." My hopeful smile broadens. "Laila Fitzgerald, will you marry me?"

"Yes!" she screams. "Yes!"

Tears threaten my eyes, but, somehow, I swallow them down while standing and sliding the ring onto her finger. The ring in place, and our agreement made, I pull my fiancée into me for a deep kiss, and then wrap my arms around her and hold her tight.

After a moment, when I've gathered enough control of myself to speak again, I take Laila's hand and point at a cluster of diamonds nestled around the central rock. "See this little diamond here? That's from the ring Jasper gave to Mimi—the diamond that was in her wedding ring."

"Oh my gosh." She physically convulses with emotion.

"Mimi wanted you to have that diamond in your ring, so you'd always know she was smiling down on us from heaven."

Laila throws her arms around me. "I love it. And I love you. Thank you so much." She pauses. Pulls back. "But what about Sasha? Shouldn't Sasha have Mimi's diamond?"

"No, Sasha wants you to have this."

Laila returns to hugging me and loses herself to sobs.

I hold her shaking, quivering body for a long moment, feeling happier in this moment than I've ever felt in my life. I feel Mimi's love and guidance all around me. I feel certain I'm on the right path, with the great love of my life—a woman I'm going to love and protect, forever. I pull back and look into Laila's tear-filled eyes. "I love you, Laila, and I always will. I can't wait to spend the rest of my life with you."

"I love you, too." She wipes a tear. "I've got a savage love for you, Adrian Savage. It's infinite." She touches my cheek. "And *everlasting.*"

EPILOGUE

LAILA

Kendrick, as Savage's best man, raises his champagne flute to Savage and me, and everyone in attendance at our small wedding, which we're having at Reed's sprawling home, follows suit.

"To Savage and Laila," Kendrick says. "You two are perfect for each other. I sincerely believe that. Laila, you make Savage a better man." Kendrick looks at his best friend, the groom, and smiles. "And, Savage, you make Laila make you a better man."

Everyone laughs.

Raising his glass even higher, Kendrick bellows, "Cheers to the bride and groom!"

The party erupts and Savage and I kiss.

We're outside on Reed's large patio, underneath twinkling lights. Savage and I both have shiny new rings on our third fingers and perma-grins on our faces. Our wedding this evening has been a fairly simple affair, attended by our closest friends and family. And it's been perfect. Straight out of a fairytale.

We pulled our wedding together a bit faster than we maybe envisioned when Savage proposed four months ago, once we realized how busy we were going to be in the coming year. My third album just released and it's already soaring. "Savage Love" is my biggest hit, by far, and I've been hard at work on designing a makeup line, too.

Savage and his band are working on their next album. And I have no doubt it's going to be another smash hit. Soon, my husband and I begin shooting the next season of *Sing Your Heart Out*. Our first of four seasons we signed on to do. And once shooting on the show ends, Fugitive Summer and I are going to participate in a "festival style" tour with a slew of other artists, including 22 Goats, Aloha, and Alessandra—a new touring concept that will make the process of bringing live music to our fans a whole lot more fun and less of a grind for everyone involved.

All things considered, Savage and I realized we had to get married pretty quickly, and in a relatively simple fashion, or else wait another year and a half to do it in grand style. So, here we are. And, frankly, I wouldn't have it any other way. The past four months in our new house have been magical for us, to the point where we've both felt an urgent desire to call each other "husband" and "wife," sooner rather than later.

If you ask me, it's not necessary to be married to someone to love them wholeheartedly. Unconditionally. Or even to commit to them "forever." One need only say those words, and make those sacred promises, in quiet moments together, with nobody else around, to make them real and unbreakable. Certainly, based on what I saw of my mother and father's marriage, I'm not a believer that marriage turns a bad relationship into a good one. But, still, I must confess, the little girl in me has always wanted to marry my prince. And today, that's exactly what I've done.

As simple and small as our wedding has been, it's turned out to be as magical as I've ever dreamed it would be. Standing face to face with Savage, looking into his soulful, brown eyes, and hearing him say, "Laila, I promise to love and cherish you, forever, through sickness and health, and richer or poorer," felt every bit as soul-stirring and beautiful as I'd dreamed the words would sound. Even more so, actually, thanks to the look on Savage's face when he said them. He looked so beautiful in that moment. So overcome with love and happiness. I could barely hold it together to say my own vows.

I've decided to take Savage's name, though not professionally. My stage name will always be Laila Fitzgerald. But on all legal documents, I'm now, officially, Laila Savage. And it feels even more awesome than I could have predicted. Now, whenever Savage picks up his guitar and serenades me with his rendition of my song, "Savage Love," which he often does, it'll feel even more like he's singing a love song *he* wrote for *me*.

When Kendrick finishes his best-man speech, Kai and Titus get up to say a few words. And then, my bridesmaids: my sister, Aloha, Sasha, Alessandra, and Ruby. Savage made fun of me for having so many bridesmaids, especially for such a small wedding. But I told him, "It's like 'Birthday Truth or Dare.' As long as I don't maim, kill, or send anyone to prison, nothing is off-limits at my own wedding." And, of course, Savage replied to that, "Knock yourself out, Fitzy. It's your day." To that, I replied, "No, it's *our* day." And Savage replied, "Mostly yours, though." I didn't continue arguing the point, because I knew he was right. Savage would marry me on the beach in front of our house, if given the option, and then throw a party in our living room to celebrate. Anything more than that has pretty much been for me. The girl who grew up enchanted by *Beauty and the Beast*.

My mom takes the mic from Sasha and tearfully tries to tell Savage and me how happy she is, but she can't get more than five words out. Which, honestly, is even more meaningful to me than whatever words she's got written on that little scrap of paper in her hand.

I head over to my weeping mother and hug her as she cries. I understand her emotion completely. The magnitude of this occasion for her. She's not only weeping about my marriage to Savage, although she's obviously over the moon about it. Even more than that, though, I know my mother is crying because I didn't follow in her footsteps. Because I didn't wind up married to a man like my father, or to one of the many assholes I dated before my husband. My mom is crying because I've married a man who'll love me and treat me right, forever—which means all her dreams for me have now come true, every bit as much as Mimi's dreams for Savage have, as well.

As I'm comforting my mother, the familiar first notes of "Savage Love" begin blaring through the reception. I pull away from my mom, wiping my eyes, and instantly notice Savage standing on the edge of the dance floor, grinning at me. He gestures to the dance floor, clearly inviting me to dance with him. So, I take my husband's hand and let him guide me to the middle of the floor for our first dance as husband and wife.

As Savage holds me close, my own voice serenades Savage and me, and I'm struck by the unbridled truth of my words. I've got a savage love for this man, and I know he loves me the same way—because our love is, and always will be, infinite and everlasting.

Savage Love

One for the money
Two for the show
Three cuz you're so good givin' Os
Oooooooooh

Four for the cameras
Five for the fame
No catchin' feelings, only a game
Oooooooooooh

But then six came along when we had our first kiss
Six made me swoon, yell out "I call dibs!"
Six watched you sleep, whispered, "I want this."

Six held you tight in a white knuckled grip
Ooooooooooh

And now I've got a savage love for you
I've lost count of all the ways you've made me a slave to you
There's no doubt my love is here to stay, I'm addicted to you
I've got a savage love for you, infinite and everlasting

Six hit the road, now it's long gone
Seven came along, now you're second to none
Ooooooooooh

Cameras are off and our love remains
Eight, nine, and ten, our love never fades
Ooooooooooh

Fake became real and want became need
Can't live without you, I need you to breathe
You're swimming in my bloodstream, enmeshed in my heart
I dream about you, in pain when we part
Ooooooooooh

I've got a savage love for you
I've lost count of all the ways you've made me a slave to you
There's no doubt my love is here to stay, I'm addicted to you
I've got a savage love for you
Infinite and everlasting

Take my heart, take my soul,

Take my blood, bones, and flesh
Take the air from my lungs, every pound, every inch
Take it all, every ounce, I give everything
Savage love, my sweet addiction
Oooooooh

And now I've got a savage love for you
Infinite and everlasting

When the song ends, Savage kisses my cheek and whispers into my ear, "I've got a savage love for you, Mrs. Savage."

I kiss him, but I don't need to say a word in reply, since the song has already said it all for me. I've got a savage love for my husband, too. This beautiful, generous man. A love that's unbreakable and sacred. Unconditional and true. *Infinite and everlasting.*

Go to
http://www.laurenrowebooks.com/savage-love-wedding-dance
if you want to listen to "Savage Love".

THE END

If you want to hear Laila's acoustic version of "Savage Love," the one she played for Savage on her new baby grand during their first night together in their new house, go here: http://www. laurenrowebooks.com/laila-f-savage-love

To read a **bonus scene**, featuring Savage and Laila on their honeymoon, then go here: http://www.laurenrowebooks.com/hate-love-honeymoon

Check out all the music from *The Hate - Love Duet*, as well as tons of magazine articles, music, and extras from the world of River Records, here: http://www.laurenrowebooks.com/river-records

The original song "Hate Sex High" was written by Lauren Rowe and David The Optimist, produced by David The Optimist, and performed by Aiden Chance as Savage.

All songs performed by "Laila" in the duet were written and produced by Lauren Rowe and performed by Jessica Schneider as Laila.

"Fireflies" by 22 Goats was written by Lauren Rowe and Hunter Levy, original version performed by Hunter Levy as Dax Morgan.

Do you want to read about Fish and Ally? Their romance *Smitten* is available now.

If you want to find out how feisty Georgina Ricci brings stubborn Reed Rivers to his knees, start with *BAD LIAR*, the first book of The Reed Rivers Trilogy.

AFTERWORD

Music Playlist for the Hate-Love Duet

"Hate Sex High"—Fugitive Summer
  "Something I Can Never Have (Still)"—Nine Inch Nails
  "Grace"—Jeff Buckley
  "Fireflies"—22 Goats (as covered by Laila Fitzgerald)
  "True Love High"—Laila Fitzgerald
  "Savage Love"—Laila Fitzgerald

Acknowledgments

Special thanks to Sophie Broughton, my beta readers: Sarah Kirk, Lizette Baez, Selina Washington, and Madonna Blackburn.

Huge thanks to David The Optimist (Baby Cuz) and Matthew Embree (Cuz), for being my favorite rock stars, forever and always.

Thank you to Letitia Hasser for the kickass covers.

And thank you to Melissa Saneholtz for your unending help and support.

And most of all, thank you to my incredible, devoted readers! I love you all so much. I'm honored and grateful at the way you love my stories and spread the word about them. Thank you from the bottom of my heart.

BOOKS BY LAUREN ROWE

Standalone Novels

Smitten

When aspiring singer-songwriter, Alessandra, meets Fish, the funny, adorable bass player of 22 Goats, sparks fly between the awkward pair. Fish tells Alessandra he's a "Goat called Fish who's hung like a bull. But not really. I'm actually really average." And Alessandra tells Fish, "There's nothing like a girl's first love." Alessandra thinks she's talking about a song when she makes her comment to Fish—the first song she'd ever heard by 22 Goats, in fact. As she'll later find out, though, her "first love" was

actually Fish. The Goat called Fish who, after that night, vowed to do anything to win her heart.

SMITTEN is a **true standalone** romance.

Swoon

When Colin Beretta, the drummer of 22 Goats, is a groomsman at the wedding of his childhood best friend, Logan, he discovers Logan's kid sister, Amy, is all grown up. Colin tries to resist his attraction to Amy, but after a drunken kiss at the wedding reception, that's easier said than done.

Swoon is a **true standalone** romance.

Hate Love Duet

An addicting enemies to lovers romance with humor, heat, angst, and banter. Music artists Savage of Fugitive Summer and Laila Fitzgerald are stuck together on tour. And convinced they can't stand each other. What they don't know is that they're absolutely made for each other, whether they realize it or not. The books of this duet are to be read in order:

Falling Out Of Hate With You

Falling Into Love With You

The Reed Rivers Trilogy

Reed Rivers has met his match in the most unlikely of women—aspiring journalist and spitfire, Georgina Ricci. She's much younger than the women Reed normally pursues, but he can't resist her fiery personality and drop-dead gorgeous looks. But in this game of cat and mouse, who's chasing whom? With each passing day of this wild ride, Reed's not so sure. The books of this trilogy are to be read in order:

Bad Liar

Beautiful Liar

Beloved Liar

The Club Trilogy

Romantic. Scorching hot. Suspenseful. Witty. The Club is your new addiction—a sexy and suspenseful thriller about two wealthy brothers and the sassy women who bring them to their knees . . . all while the foursome bands together to protect one of their own. *The Club Trilogy* is to be read in order, as follows:

The Club: Obsession

The Club: Reclamation

The Club: Redemption

The Club: Culmination

The fourth book for Jonas and Sarah is a full-length epilogue with incredible heart-stopping twists and turns and feels. Read *The Club: Culmination (A Full-Length Epilogue Novel)* after finishing *The Club Trilogy* or, if you prefer, after reading *The Josh and Kat Trilogy*.

The Josh and Kat Trilogy

It's a war of wills between stubborn and sexy Josh Faraday and Kat Morgan. A fight to the bed. Arrogant, wealthy playboy Josh is used to getting what he wants. *And what he wants is Kat Morgan.* The books are to be read in order:

Infatuation

Revelation

Consummation

The Morgan Brothers

Read these **standalones** in any order about the brothers of Kat Morgan. Chronological reading order is below, but they are all complete stories. Note: you do *not* need to read any other books or series before jumping straight into reading about the Morgan boys.

Hero

The story of heroic firefighter, **Colby Morgan**. When catastrophe strikes Colby Morgan, will physical therapist Lydia save him . . . or will he save her?

Captain

The insta-love-to-enemies-to-lovers story of tattooed sex god, **Ryan Morgan**, and the woman he'd move heaven and earth to claim.

Ball Peen Hammer

A steamy, hilarious, friends-to-lovers romantic comedy about cocky-as-hell male stripper, **Keane Morgan**, and the sassy, smart young woman who brings him to his knees during a road trip.

Mister Bodyguard

The Morgans' beloved honorary brother, **Zander Shaw**, meets his match in the feisty pop star he's assigned to protect on tour.

ROCKSTAR

When the youngest Morgan brother, **Dax Morgan,** meets a mysterious woman who rocks his world, he must decide if pursuing her is worth risking it all. Be sure to check out four of Dax's original songs from *ROCKSTAR*, written and produced by Lauren, along with full music videos for the songs, on her website (www.laurenrowebooks.com) under the tab MUSIC FROM ROCKSTAR.

Misadventures

Lauren's *Misadventures* titles are page-turning, steamy, swoony standalones, to be read in any order.

- *Misadventures on the Night Shift* –A hotel night shift clerk encounters her teenage fantasy: rock star Lucas Ford. And combustion ensues.

- *Misadventures of a College Girl*—A spunky, virginal theater major meets a cocky football player at her first college party . . . and absolutely nothing goes according to plan for either of them.

- *Misadventures on the Rebound*—A spunky woman on the rebound meets a hot, mysterious stranger in a bar on her way to her five-year high school reunion in Las Vegas and what follows is a misadventure neither of them ever imagined.

Standalone Psychological Thriller/Dark Comedy

Countdown to Killing Kurtis

A young woman with big dreams and skeletons in her closet decides her porno-king husband must die in exactly a year. This is *not* a traditional romance, but it *will* most definitely keep you turning the pages and saying "WTF?"

Short Stories

The Secret Note

Looking for a quickie? Try this scorching-hot short story from Lauren Rowe in ebook FOR FREE or in audiobook: He's a hot Aussie. I'm a girl who isn't shy about getting what she wants. The problem? Ben is my little brother's best friend. An exchange student who's heading back Down Under any day now. But I can't help myself. He's too hot to resist.

All books by Lauren Rowe are available in ebook, paperback, and audiobook formats.

AUTHOR BIOGRAPHY

Lauren Rowe is the USA Today and international #1 best-selling author of newly released Reed Rivers Trilogy, as well as The Club Trilogy, The Josh & Kat Trilogy, The Morgan Brothers Series, Countdown to Killing Kurtis, and select standalone Misadventures.

Lauren's books are full of feels, humor, heat, and heart. Besides writing novels, Lauren is the singer in a party/wedding band in her hometown of San Diego, an audio book narrator, and award-winning songwriter. She is thrilled to connect with readers all over the world.
To find out about Lauren's upcoming releases and giveaways, sign up for Lauren's emails here!

Lauren loves to hear from readers! Send Lauren an email from her website, say hi on Twitter, Instagram, or Facebook.

Find out more and check out lots of free bonus material at www. LaurenRoweBooks.com.

www.ingramcontent.com/pod-product-compliance
Lightning Source LLC
Chambersburg PA
CBHW020605040726
47498CB00003B/638